Other books by Kirt Hickman

Worlds Asunder

Worlds Asunder
Venus Rain
Mercury Sun
Methane Moon

Age of Prophecy

Fabler's Legend
Assassins' Prey
Host of Evil

Nonfiction

Revising Fiction: Making Sense of the Madness

For Children

I Will Eat Anything
Purple

ASSASSINS' PREY

AGE OF PROPHECY: BOOK II

Into the Wild Lands
with anyone crazy enough to go

Kirt Hickman

Quillrunner
Publishing

Published in the U.S.A. by
Quillrunner Publishing LLC
Albuquerque, NM

Printed in the U.S.A.

Cover art by Elizabeth Leggett

Book design by Susan Schwartz-Christian
Typeset in: Iowan Old Style 11/14.5, American Frights, Valhalla

Cataloging-in-Publications Data is on file with the Library of Congress.
Library of Congress Control Number: 2020920788

ISBN 978-0-9851157-4-6

For Erle, Larry, Gerry, Rick, Ben, and Alex,
the real heroes of the story.

Acknowledgments

A book like this can't be created by one person alone. It took the tireless effort of many people to make *Assassins' Prey* a reality. My thanks go out to all of you.

To Erle Guillermo, Gerry Raban, Ben Valerine, Larry Koch, Rick McLaughlin, and Alex Raguini for your assistance in developing such a dynamic plot.

To my network of critiquers and test readers: Larry Koch, Alex Raguini, Ian Young, and others. Special thanks to David Corwell for catching the things the rest of us didn't.

To my editor, Susan M. Grossman, for ensuring that *Assassins' Prey* is the best that it can be.

To all my peers at SouthWest Writers, for your constant moral and technical support. I've learned so much.

To Elizabeth Leggett for the spectacular cover illustration.

To Susan Schwartz-Christian, for exceeding all my expectations for book and cover design.

To my wife, Terri, for giving me the time and encouragement to begin, to endure, and to finally complete *Assassins' Prey*. I couldn't have done it without you.

And most of all, to God for blessing me with the necessary time and talents.

CHAPTER 1

Nick Mirrin didn't know how long he'd been in the dungeon cell, a couple of weeks, maybe. It was hard to tell without any windows, or any light at all for that matter, save for the occasional torch when a pair of guards strode past his cell door. Every once in a while, someone tossed a lump of hard bread or dried meat through the bars for Nick to share with his cellmate, Xanth, an old man who, by his own account, had survived there for decades.

The two had talked seldom at first, the old man's voice halting after years of disuse. When they did speak, they discussed the history of the Civilized Lands. Xanth told Nick of things that had happened before Nick was born.

Nick brought Xanth up to date on recent events, finally coming to those that had ultimately landed him in Balor Culhaven's dungeon.

"Have you heard of the Prophecy of Mortaan?" Nick asked.

"I've heard many prophecies." Xanth's voice came from the darkness, still weak and hoarse. "I put little faith in them. That, perhaps more than anything, is why I'm here."

"Because you don't believe in prophecy? For that the monarchy would lock you down here?"

"Oh, yes. For much less than that, I'd imagine."

Nick sighed. "I suppose I'm here because I *do* believe the Prophecy."

"Now that does seem odd, doesn't it?" Xanth's tone turned shrewd. "There must be more to it."

Oh, there was. Nick and his friends had assassinated King Gremauld, who'd held the throne for only a few months. At the time, they'd thought he served the Master as one of the Chosen of the Dark Lord, helping to fulfill the cataclysmic Last Prophecy of Mortaan. In addition, Gremauld's death had put an end to the civil war that his illegal ascension had instigated. Nick and his friends had saved countless thousands of innocent lives.

But Nick's reasons no longer seemed important. He'd killed the king. He deserved to be in this dungeon. And as soon as the new king was crowned, he'd have the authority to execute Nick and his friends.

Nick fell silent for a long time. From the beginning, this had been his own fight, his own quest. It was *his* grandfather who'd spent a lifetime searching for a way to forestall the Prophecy. It was *his* home the Chosen had burned and *his* mother they'd killed in an attempt to destroy the journal his grandfather had left behind. None of it had anything to do with his friends. Yet Nick had pulled them into it. Because of him, they too would face the executioner. And it was all for nothing. The Prophecy would still come true. Darkness would reign. And as soon as the civil war had ended, Balor, now the heir to the throne of Trondor, had revealed himself as the Chosen Nick had assumed Gremauld to be.

Still, Nick wasn't ready to admit his crime to Xanth. "My friends and I came to the palace looking for the original Codex of Mortaan, the book in which Ageus Mortaan had written the prophecies in his own hand. The heir didn't want us to have it."

"The heir?"

"Balor Culhaven. He's made a bid for the throne."

"I didn't know it was vacant."

"Yes. Twice now in the past year."

Xanth shifted, with a rustling of rags, and padded on bare feet to the gate of their cell, his outline barely visible against the meager glow of torchlight from down the hall. "That's unusual. But it'll not change my plight, I'm afraid. It's not the throne I threaten."

Nick thought again to ask what the old man had done, but that would take the conversation into territory he wanted to avoid.

"What's in this Codex that threatens him so?" Xanth asked finally.

Nick took a deep breath. "Balor is part of the Prophecy. My friends and I were trying to stop it."

"I see."

After a few moments, Nick spoke, just to fill the silence. "He's one of the twelve Chosen of the Master—the High Priest of Vexetan. Together, it's foretold, they'll conquer the Civilized Lands and bring an end to the Age of Prophecy. The Master will rule in darkness."

"And you believe you can prevent this Prophecy?"

Nick scratched absently at the new hair sprouting from his head, which he'd shaved to avoid being recognized after Gremauld's murder. "I used to. According to the legends, the Master can't be defeated, but there're other versions of the Prophecy. Other endings. I'd hoped the common legends would prove false and that we could bring one of the more promising endings to pass. I was wrong. The original Codex says the Master can't be harmed by any weapon forged of this world."

"What weight can one give to the printed word? The stars control the fates of men."

Nick sighed. "Mortaan's prophecies were sent to him by one of the gods—either Aeron or Vexetan. He's never been wrong. The Master can't be defeated."

Xanth shuffled back into the shadows. "Yet you're willing to try." The old man's voice had an aspect Nick couldn't quite identify—an intensity of interest, perhaps—behind his casual façade.

"I was."

"It sounds to me as if you still are."

Nick sought him in the darkness but could see nothing. "If I had the means, I'd oppose him."

"Then what you need, my brave friend, is a metal from the stars from which to forge your weapon."

Nick nearly dismissed the comment based on its sheer absurdity, but the casual manner that had masked Xanth's intensity was gone.

The clang of the lock on the guardroom door echoed down the corridor, followed by the creak of heavy hinges. Nick's gut growled at the prospect of a few bites of food, though he'd have to choke it down past the smell emanating from the waste bucket in the corner. Within moments, flickering light sent the darkness, and a rat, skittering away.

Nick squinted at Xanth's scrawny silhouette as a pair of palace guards carried a torch past the cell and disappeared around a corner. Not mealtime, just a changing of the guard. In a few minutes, the two guards they were relieving would come back through in the opposite direction.

Nick dropped his voice to a whisper. "What are you saying?"

Xanth settled himself on the cot next to Nick. "When I was your age, the divine orders banded together and convinced the monarchy to abolish the Sorcerers of Tradestar. Apparently we threatened their beliefs. So the king's men stormed our guild house, rounded up as many of us as they could, and imprisoned us in here. The rest, they hunted down and killed. As far as I know, I'm the only one left."

"You know magic?" Nick asked, suddenly hopeful.

"Not as you understand it. But I know this: throughout the ages, objects have fallen from the sky—rocks containing metal ore." He held up a shadowy fist. "I've held small pieces in my own hand. Nothing larger than an elderberry, mind you, but enough to prove that a metal from the stars exists."

Nick stood and walked to the bars. The old man must have been daft. "What I need is a key to this cell."

Rancid Sevendeath checked the fit of his Trondorian army uniform one last time before pulling down the helmet's visor to hide the telltale scar that crossed his face from his left eyebrow to his right cheekbone. *This must be it.* He'd followed the whore's directions exactly—every corridor, every turn. He descended the stone steps and pulled open the heavy steel-banded door at the bottom. Two guards occupied the torchlit foyer beyond. If his luck held, they wouldn't notice he never used his left arm, which hung limp at his side—a man with such a disability would never be allowed to serve in the uniform Rancid wore.

"I need to see the prisoner." Rancid used his best authoritative voice.

The stout guard to his right grunted. "Which one?"

"The female."

"That one?" one of the men said. "I wouldn't exactly call it female. She's not even human." He hefted himself off the barrel he'd been using as a stool and wagged his matted black beard toward a passage on the right. "This way."

Rancid followed him through a second heavy door, down a damp corridor, and continued past several barred chambers. The smell was only marginally worse than that of the garbage tunnels in which he'd grown up.

As the guard's torch lit a cell on Rancid's left, Nick glanced up. He sat on a cot in the gloom, his cheeks sunken and his skin pale. Loose clothes hung on his frame. His blond hair was short, as if he'd shaved it recently. No recognition showed in his eyes. An old man with a wisp of gray hair and a matted beard, gaunt and dressed only in rags, sat on a second cot along the far wall.

Rancid didn't acknowledge either of them. He and the guard passed another man, a stranger, in a cage on their right.

The guard came to a halt just before a bend in the hallway and kicked the bars of yet another cell. Torchlight chased away the shadows to reveal Nick's friend Jasmine sitting cross-legged on a cot against the far wall. The young demon-kin monk opened her eyes. She unfolded her arms and legs in a single fluid motion.

"Visitor." The guard banged the bars three more times, but Jasmine made no effort to hurry. She stood and padded slowly across the floor. The claws of her taloned feet clicked on the smooth stone. As she approached, the torchlight cast her triangular face, with its well-defined eye ridges, smooth, flattened nose, and pointed chin, into sharp relief.

"Where is it, demon-spawn?" Rancid filled his voice with contempt. "Where's the copy of the Codex?"

Jasmine regarded him for a moment. "Right here." She tapped the side of her bald head with a clawed finger.

"You brought a copy into the library. Where'd you stash it?" Rancid took a step toward the bars.

The guard grabbed his arm and pulled him back. "Not too close. She's more dangerous than her size would suggest."

Jasmine answered carefully. "What do you want with a copy? You already have the original."

"Don't play games with me. The Council wants the copy too." He'd almost said, "Balor," but Balor wasn't yet king. "I don't question my orders."

"I told you. It's in my head. I have no other copy."

"You have until this time tomorrow to decide to tell me where you hid it. If you don't..." He motioned down the corridor. "I'll execute your friend. What's his name? Nick?"

Jasmine tilted her head slightly to one side, as if she might have recognized Rancid's voice.

He spun about and marched back to the guardroom. Though his

heart was pounding, he lingered for several seconds before stepping through the door. He could see into the king's wine cellar and store-room. The guards served a dual purpose here, it seemed.

Rancid hadn't seen Zen or Vinra, the two who'd left with Nick and Jasmine the day they'd departed Palidor, but there was one more passageway, opposite the first, that Rancid hadn't had an opportunity to check.

"If she doesn't talk," Rancid told the guard before he left, "I'll have to deliver her human friend upstairs for execution."

"We can't release him without a writ from the Council."

Ah, but you can release him. That was all Rancid needed to know.

R ancid returned to Jasmine's cell twenty-four hours later, with the bearded guard from the previous day practically breathing down his armor. "Where is it, demon-spawn?"

Jasmine met his gaze with calm resolve and said nothing.

"Fine." Rancid turned to the guard and motioned to Nick's cell. "Open the door."

The man extended a hand. "Your writ from the Council?"

Rancid pulled a strip of rolled parchment from a pouch on his belt. His heart raced at a full sprint. With just one good arm and a second guard in the guardroom, he'd have to do this quickly and quietly. Just as the man reached for the parchment, Rancid let it slip from his fingers.

The guard raised an eyebrow and placed his hand on the pommel of his sword. "Pick it up."

When Rancid bent to do so, he used the motion to hide his good arm as he reached across his body to draw his sword. In a flash, he ripped it from its sheath.

The man reeled back, a little too slowly. Rancid sliced a bloody rent in the man's gut.

The guard jabbed at him. "Intruder!"

Baron's blood!

The guard's torch dropped to the stone floor. Its burning tip scattered bits of hot ember at their feet. Running footsteps echoed down the passageway. The response was too quick. Rancid had no time to look. The first guard's sword flashed.

Rancid ducked and spun on the incoming sentry, a red-headed behemoth with broken teeth. He raised his sword too late. Red's blade slammed into Rancid's helmet. His head swam as he staggered back against Jasmine's cage. Sparks of pain shot from his forehead to the base of his skull. He staggered to one knee and fought to remain conscious.

Jasmine whispered from behind him, "Glad to see you." She grabbed the knife from his belt and launched it at Red, who dodged to the side.

Rancid blinked to clear his vision. Somehow, the first guard had remained on his feet. Rancid thrust his sword upward, through the soft tissue of the man's belly, into his chest. The pungent smell of bile filled the corridor. With a gurgling wheeze, the guard fell, lifeless at last, to the floor.

Red stared at his partner's body. His lapse lasted only a moment, but it was enough. Rancid pushed himself to his feet. He battered at Red's defenses for three swings. Four. Five. The sword flew from Red's hand, and Rancid plunged his blade through his chest.

He sheathed his sword and searched the guards until he found the keys to the cells. Within moments, Jasmine's cage door swung open with a loud creak.

"We have about four hours before the next change of guard." Rancid opened Nick's cell as well. "Where are the others?"

"I think Zen's down that way somewhere." Nick pointed past the torchlit entrance to another darkened hallway. "The rest are dead."

The prisoner across the hall from Nick rattled his cell door. "Take me with you. Please."

"You know this guy?" Rancid asked.

Nick shook his head. "He came in yesterday."

Rancid nodded once and sprinted away.

"Hey!" The prisoner yelled after him.

Rancid found Zen at the far end of the passageway in a cell that had a fine mesh screen filling the spaces between the bars, apparently to prevent Zen from escaping by morphing himself into some small animal. The lock on the door was dwarven-made, one Rancid couldn't have picked if he'd had an hour to do it. He jammed a key into the hole. The mage's beard had become ragged and his shimmering, blue-gray robes were worn and dirty.

As soon as the gate swung open, Zen gestured toward a metal-banded door across the hall from his cell. "Can you open this one?"

"Why?"

"Our weapons are in there. And my staff."

Rancid fumbled with the keys in his good hand.

"What happened to your arm?" Nick asked.

"That's a story we don't have time for right now."

"For that matter," Jasmine asked, "how did you find us?"

"And why are you in Trondor at all?" Zen said.

Rancid glanced from one to the other. "All part of the same story."

"Perhaps we'd better hear it," Jasmine said. "Especially after you tried to sidetrack us in Palidor."

"Is that why you're here?" Nick asked. "To get our help in pursuing your vendetta against the Black Hand bandits?"

"Later." Rancid pulled the heavy door open.

Zen rifled through the small storage space and emerged with his staff and several familiar backpacks. "Unless you've got a plan to get us out of here, there won't be a later. We'll never escape through the palace."

"There's supposed to be a hidden stairway into a labyrinth of catacombs under the city." Nobody ever returned from them alive, Rancid's sources had said, but rumors were rumors and always exaggerated.

"Guards walked past my cell periodically," Jasmine said. "I

glanced down the corridor a minute ago. It looks like a dead end, but there must be a hidden door there somewhere."

Zen arched an eyebrow at Rancid, who strode purposefully in the indicated direction.

"Wait." Nick rifled through his pack. "Our coin is gone."

Jasmine checked her supplies. "So is my copy of the Codex." She stared at the door to the guardroom for a long minute, as though contemplating an attempt to recover the book from the palace. It hadn't belonged to her but to the Order of the Sage, to the monks who'd raised and trained her. "I promised, on my honor, to safeguard it."

"Forget it," Zen told her.

"We also don't have any food or water," Nick said.

"There's food in there." Rancid pointed to a door adjacent to the guardroom and then disappeared into the liquor cellar. He returned with three rare-vintage bottles gripped by their slender necks in his good hand. "These ought to fetch a fair price."

The group padded those bottles and several more with emptied canvas bags from the storeroom and loaded up all the salt mutton and dried beans their packs could carry. Rancid broke down a flour cask and collected the slats to serve as spare torches.

"I can create ice for water," Zen said. "Let's go find the catacombs."

"The catacombs?" the prisoner in the cell across from Nick's said. "There're beasts down there to frighten an ogre."

"Who cares?" Zen strode by without so much as a glance at him.

"I swing a skilled ax, and I haven't been down here long enough to have lost my strength. I'll be of use to you."

Nick stopped at the bars and gave the man a hard look. He was human, or appeared to be, with thick black hair down to his shoulders, strong arms, and a barrel chest.

"What's your name?"

"Otto Lassel."

"What'd you do to wind up in here?"

Otto met his gaze. "I tried to hold back supplies from Balor's army during his rebellion."

"Leave him," Zen said from down near the end of the short corridor.

Nick hesitated. "We can't. He'll tell the guards where we've gone."

"We can't trust him," Zen insisted. "After what Vinra did, we can't trust anybody."

Rancid shot him a questioning look.

"Vinra turned out to be one of the Chosen," Nick told him, "a spy planted by the Master to make sure we never got the Codex. He killed Beltrann and Dara."

Rancid's stomach soured. He had known something wasn't right about that supposed priest of Robala.

Nick reached through the bars and pulled at Otto's collar. "No Medallion." At least this man wasn't a Chosen. "We'll help each other through the catacombs. Then you can go your own way." He motioned for Rancid to open the lock.

An hour had probably passed since Rancid had killed the guards. Time was ticking, and someone could happen by at any moment. It was quicker and quieter to free the man than it would be to argue about it. Within seconds, he snapped open the lock.

Otto hurried down the hall and returned with his own pack, a wicked-looking war ax, a crossbow, and a quiver of bolts.

Nick walked back to his own cell. "What do you say? Want to see the stars again?"

"I thought you'd never ask." The old man stepped from the darkness, looking like he hadn't bathed, shaved, or changed his clothes in decades. "I only hope I don't slow you down."

"Who's this?" Rancid asked.

"His name is Xanth."

Rancid took one look at the man's frail body. He would certainly slow them down. Again he chose not to argue.

Instead he joined Jasmine at the far end of the corridor. Hidden doors and secret passages riddled the hills beneath his father's keep back in Forlorn Valley, passages that Rancid had grown up in. He took Jasmine's torch and jammed it into the nearest sconce. The outline of the door, a seam in the mortared stone wall, was obvious, but the mechanism…

He tugged on the sconce. It didn't budge. He tried to twist its end. He pushed on the anchor bolts. Nothing. His companions crowded around him.

"Well?" Zen said.

Rancid pulled off the constraining Trondorian helmet, now dented from the sword hit it had taken, and shook loose his long black ponytail. His head still hurt, though his ears had finally quit ringing. He handed the helmet to Nick. "Move back. I need room."

As one, Nick and the others retreated several steps down the hall. While Rancid searched for the mechanism, Nick stripped Red of his uniform and donned it himself.

Rancid held the torch against the wall so the smallest bumps cast long shadows against the stone and darkened even the slightest depression. Still nothing.

Rancid repeated his search on the opposite wall. There, just below his knee and a little to the left, was a crack in the chipped mortar. Fresh scratches surrounded an opening just about the size of… He slid his military-issue Trondorian longsword into the slot all the way to the hilt.

A distinct snap emanated from behind the wall.

Rancid winced, expecting a poison dart or falling stone slab, but nothing happened. He applied his shoulder to the stone door and gave a long, steady push. The section of wall, three feet wide and six feet tall, slid inward eight inches or more with a soft grinding sound and then swung to the side. Beyond, his torch illuminated a stone staircase that descended through a rectangular hole in the floor.

"After you," he told Otto.

Nick took a deep breath and handed Otto a torch. The darkness in the stairwell was oppressive and the stone walls close. "Remember, there're guards down here somewhere."

After only a moment's hesitation, the man took the torch and led them down the stairway.

"At least two of them," Jasmine added. She and Rancid followed.

Nick stepped through the hidden door after Zen and Xanth, then pushed it shut behind them with a soft grating sound, followed by the click of the locking mechanism. "When we get to the guards," Nick asked Zen, "can you knock them out?"

"Sure." Zen wagged his fingers in the air in a mock magical weaving.

"Good. Rancid, give him your uniform." Red's uniform was much too large for Zen, but Rancid, also an elf-kin, was about Zen's size.

"What?"

Nick raised his eyebrows. "Give it."

"I paid good coin for this uniform."

"You've no need of it now."

Rancid stared at him for a long time before he finally humphed and unfastened the buckles. Within minutes, Zen had settled into the uniform and Rancid pulled on a dark green travelling cloak from his small pack.

"Thank you." Nick gestured to Rancid's travelling garb. "That seems more your style anyway."

Without a word, Rancid motioned to Otto and the group continued.

A hundred yards from the base of the stairs, the cut stone gave way to a dry natural tunnel that extended into the darkness. Generations of booted feet had worn a broad groove down its center. No one dared to speak until the flickering glow of torchlight appeared, illuminating the cave wall ahead from somewhere around the next bend. Otto stopped.

"Looks like we're up," Nick whispered to Zen. "The rest of you wait here."

Zen padded along the edge of the tunnel, stepping lightly in his soft boots. Just ahead, in an artificially widened chamber, rested a pair of sentries. One sat comfortably on the floor with his back against the wall and the other leaned nearby, sucking on a lit pipe. A pair of torches burned in sconces, with a pile of spares stacked beneath. Beyond, an iron gate barred the tunnel.

Nick put himself a step behind Zen and walked in his shadow to conceal, as well as possible, the blood that Red's chest wound had left on his uniform. Zen strolled into the torchlit chamber for all the lands as though he owned the place.

"Is it that time already?" the pipe smoker asked as he reached for the nearest torch.

The other man climbed to his feet.

"More so than you know." Zen planted his staff on the stone and, with a word, called forth a whirlwind of icy air.

"No!" Nick threw himself from the chamber and back into the darkened corridor as both sentries flung up their hands to ward off the blast. Frost coated Nick's uniform and his joints ached. He crawled stiffly away on cold, bleeding hands.

Within seconds, it was over. The others joined them, Otto's torch bringing welcome warmth, which seeped back into Nick's chilled limbs. He flexed his fingers, gritted his teeth against the pain, and returned to the chamber.

The guards lay on the floor, encrusted with ice, their blind eyes staring past frozen lashes at the smoke-stained ceiling.

"I said, 'knock them out,' not 'kill them.'"

Zen shrugged. "I thought you said, 'take them out.' Anyway, we don't want them to alert somebody before the next watch."

No tracks extended beyond the iron gate. From that point on, the stone of the floor was rough and natural, the dark and silence complete. "I don't think those guards were here to keep prisoners in," Otto said. "They were here to keep something else out."

CHAPTER 2

ithin minutes, Rancid found the proper key and opened the iron gate. It squealed, and flakes of rust trickled from the seldom-used hinges. The rest of the companions dragged the bodies of the guards through the opening and into a dead-end side passage. That done, and the gate relocked behind them, Jasmine led the way into the silent tunnel beyond. Shadows skittered along the walls, chased away by the flickering torchlight. The natural floor carried them ever downward.

Eventually, the passage opened into a cave so large that the torch illuminated only the nearest wall. Together, the party scouted the perimeter. The huge chamber seemed to be a hub of sorts. Natural tunnels emanated from it in several directions.

The tunnels Rancid had grown up in had been low and narrow. This place felt altogether different. The vastness and emptiness of the place proved disorienting, almost nauseating. It helped to keep his eyes on the cavern floor.

He pointed his sword at the ground. "Tracks."

"Guards?" Nick asked.

"An animal." Rancid examined the marks. "There's this too." Scratches marred the ground, as if by some sort of rodent or large insect.

Jasmine clawed the clay with her talon and compared her mark with the scratches.

Whatever had made them was bigger than any rodent or insect Rancid had ever seen. He frowned at her mark. "Now they'll know we came this way."

"Leave her alone," Nick said. "We've left too many boot prints to worry about a scratch in the clay."

"We'd better keep moving," Otto said. "If somebody sends a servant down to the storeroom before the next watch, we'll lose our four-hour head start."

Rancid picked the narrowest tunnel, which rose twice as high as necessary for even Nick to walk upright. "That one."

Jasmine led the way inside. Rancid followed, and then Otto and the others. The natural walls of the tunnel forced them into a single file for the first hundred yards, and then a scratching noise brought them up short.

The party fell silent. Jasmine listened.

Nothing. Not a sound.

She inched her way forward. The shuffling boots of the others clouded her hearing.

Beyond the light, a pair of pale eyes appeared, reflecting the torchlight. All at once, the creature burst into view. It stood four feet high in the center of its humped back, its body a mass of bristling brown fur and dark gray quills. A mouth full of teeth the size of daggers drooled and hissed. The creature closed the distance in an instant.

Its long tail, terminating in a vicious stinger, whipped forward. With reflexes born of a lifetime of training, Jasmine ducked the first strike. But the tail snapped back and whipped out again. The dancing torchlight made the movements difficult to see. It stuck her in the chest, yanked her from her feet, and slammed her to the cave floor behind itself.

The tail whipped up again and snapped forward. It hit something with a thud.

Jasmine struggled to her feet, now in the dark shadow of the creature. Searing pain radiated from the wound. A chill passed through her. She trembled as her body fought the rodent's venom.

Rancid muttered a curse and staggered back into Otto, clawing at a shallow puncture in his chest.

Behind them, Zen appeared lost in his magical weaving. Ice shards the size of horseshoe nails formed in his open palm.

Jasmine flung a throwing star into the rump of the creature.

As it swung its head toward her, razor-sharp ice shards sped past Otto and ripped into the rodent's exposed neck. A hiss filled the corridor. The creature spasmed once and collapsed to the floor.

Jasmine plucked a pinch of mungos root from her healer's kit with trembling fingers, ground it between her teeth, and sucked her saliva through it like tea in a strainer. It wasn't as bitter or effective as it would have been fresh, but even dry, it would help her body fight the venom.

That done, she squeezed carefully past the rodent's quill-covered body and rushed to Rancid's side. Lacking her demon-kin physiology, he lay in the corridor, his breathing shallow, his limbs twitching.

She administered a dose of the root. "Anybody else get hit?"

Silence.

Nick and Otto served as sentry at either end of the party as Jasmine gave Rancid an opiate to kill the pain.

After several minutes, his breathing slowed and his features relaxed.

"Can you stand?" Jasmine asked.

"I...I told you I should have kept the Trondorian armor." He slipped out of his backpack and climbed unsteadily to his feet. His face appeared ashen, even in the orange glow of the torchlight.

Jasmine rolled up her own meager bundle of belongings, tied it to Rancid's pack, and then settled the combined load onto her own shoulders. "Can you walk?"

Shivering, Rancid took a few tentative steps, one shaking hand braced against the cave wall. After a moment, he squared his shoulders. "I'm okay." His pallor belied the claim.

"There may be a nest of those things down here," Nick said. "We'd better backtrack."

Jasmine clambered her way over the rocks and boulders that made up the floor of a rough tunnel. She'd led the group down several passages that led away from the hub, but none had provided an outlet. The wound in her chest was shallow, but it burned with a venomous fire. So in tune was she with her physique, she could actually feel her body tapping its reserves to fight the poison.

She waited for the others to catch up with the torch before continuing. Nick and Otto practically carried Rancid. Zen kept his hands free to tap the weave again if necessary. Xanth struggled at the rear, his breathing raspy and labored.

After a brief rest, Jasmine approached a small chamber that had a couple of inches of standing water covering the floor. It had two exits: one to the right, the other, left.

Nick walked up beside her.

The passage to the right opened into a small dead-end chamber with a dry, sandy floor, where Nick and Otto sat Rancid against the cave wall. He curled his legs to his chest and shivered in silence.

Jasmine felt his forehead with the back of her hand. "He's feverish. He needs rest." She gestured toward the unexplored opening from the wet chamber. "I'll scout that tunnel and see where it leads. That will give Rancid and Xanth a few minutes before we continue."

Nick nodded. "Be careful."

Jasmine lit another torch from their limited supply and crossed the water quickly.

A short distance in, an additional side passage, one with more stagnant water, came into view and stretched away to the right. Not a breath of air stirred the torch flame as Jasmine walked past it—no likely exit that way. The main tunnel continued. The floor rose out of the water and became rocky, packed dirt.

Three steps past the first side passage, another wide room, rife with broad stalagmites, opened to Jasmine's left. If her senses spoke true, it led back toward the hub and therefore offered no escape.

The main passage continued straight, but before Jasmine went any farther, movements, furtive and restless, among the stalagmites brought her to a stop. She raised her torch to illuminate the space as an antlike insect skittered into view, and then two more, large as goats, each with a fire-red carapace. The ants paused when they saw her. One scrambled up the nearest stalagmite and its three-segmented body disappeared down a hole in the center. *Not stalagmites. Mounds! Dozens of them.* A fervent clicking filled the cave and a score of the ant things scrambled into view. They surged forward, walking erect with two of their six legs held before them like arms, mandibles clicking.

Jasmine sprinted back the way she'd come with a shout. When she reached the wet area, she motioned the others out of the dead-end chamber and back the way they'd come.

Rancid lumbered across, his movements stilted and slow. Otto followed. Nick scooped up the old man and ran. Zen remained in the opening as a rear guard for the others.

Jasmine caught up to him and spun to face the antlings. If she and Zen couldn't slow them, they'd overcome the others.

Zen chanted in the ancient elven tongue and thrust his staff past

Jasmine at the advancing hoard. A wave of cold swept the wet chamber. It left a layer of ice on the water and frost coating everything else, adding to the chill from the dank cave and the venom coursing through her. The antlings didn't slow. Apparently ice magic wouldn't harm these creatures. Two more of the things, twice the size of the others, probably warriors, each with a bulbous abdomen and a chest of spiny carapace, came into view.

"Go!" Jasmine shoved Zen toward the others.

In a flutter of robes, Zen fled down the corridor.

Jasmine eased back into the constricting mouth of the cave to try to limit the antlings' passage. She balled her fist, forced herself to focus, and lashed out. With a crack, she split the skull of the lead antling. The creature shrieked in a pitch nearly too high for human hearing, and then collapsed.

Jasmine kicked the next antling, with a similar result. The third and fourth skittered forward. Others climbed the walls with the ease of spiders. Jasmine swept two aside and four took their place. But Zen was still too close.

An antling dropped from the ceiling behind her and sank a mandible into her thigh. She gritted her teeth against the pain and fought on.

As one of the warriors emerged from the throng, Jasmine's foot swept up and slammed its head. It wailed its inhuman cry and trudged forward, trampling its smaller companions. Bites stung Jasmine's legs. She grabbed one of the smaller antlings with her clawed foot and threw it into the water.

The second warrior skittered up beside the first.

The antlings were too many now. Nausea rose in Jasmine's stomach, her heart began to palpitate, and her head swam.

Desperately, she spun, leapt over the antlings that had scaled the walls and gathered behind her. With a burst of speed, she put as much distance as possible between herself and the horde.

When she was about twenty feet down the corridor, a wall of ice sealed the watery cave and the antlings away behind her.

Slowing, she fumbled another pinch of mungos from her kit. The strength in her fingers failed and she dropped the bag into the stones. By then she already had the root she needed between her teeth. She chewed it quickly and sucked it down.

Immediately, her stomach settled.

Behind her, antlings scratched at the frozen barrier.

Jasmine labored to stay conscious. The antling venom sapped what was left of her strength. She scratched together the remains of her spilled healer's kit and withdrew with the others to the hub.

Of the four remaining passages, three proved to be dead ends. Nick returned from his brief exploration of the fourth. "Mounds."

Jasmine lifted the torch and tried to get a fix on her bearings. "Probably the opposite side of the same antling cave." Welts on her legs stung in painful memory.

Rancid touched her arm. "How long do you think we have?" All told, the party couldn't have travelled more than half a mile from the guard post.

"Any time now." Jasmine sighed. "We're running around from one hazard to the next without a plan and not so much as a breath in between. Soon the guards will come. I'm tired, Rancid is exhausted, and the old man's breathing pains even me. We must pause and assess our options."

With a chant and a weaving, Zen erected an ice wall between them and the opening into the antlings' cavern. The cold radiating from it seeped through to Jasmine's bones.

Nick nodded his thanks. "Perhaps we can buy ourselves some time. Zen and I can impersonate the guards at the checkpoint. When the search party comes down, we'll tell them nobody's come this way. They'll turn their search elsewhere."

"They'll recognize you," Zen said. "This uniform may work from a distance, and I can change my own appearance, but many of the guards know you from the dungeon. Perhaps Rancid—"

"I don't have the strength." Rancid slumped against the cavern wall. "Besides, what will we do when our relief guards arrive? Go back into the palace?"

Jasmine pointed a clawed finger at the ice wall. "Beyond the antling nest lay two unexplored passages. I suspect the smaller leads to a dead end. The other…" She shrugged.

"What about the passage beyond that spined rodent we killed?" Otto said. "We never explored that."

"No," Jasmine said. "The antling venom stings, and that of the warrior antlings will certainly make you sick, but the poison from that rodent's tail will kill any one of us in seconds." She produced her bag from beneath her robes. "My medicine bag is almost empty. I have no more of the root we'll need if we meet another one of those creatures."

"And rodents never live alone," Rancid added. "Where there's one, there're dozens." He glanced around as though he suddenly realized the threat the rodents might pose to their short respite.

"We could try to ambush the guards," Jasmine said, "possibly with Zen acting as an imposter, but that will only lead to more fighting. I, for one, have little fight left in me."

Nick remained standing, with his sword drawn. "I'll go back to the guard post. When the search patrol shows up, I'll run into the rodents' lair and force them to fight those things. With my uniform, I might be able to disengage in the confusion and work my way back. Either way, Zen can seal off the corridor and buy the rest of you some time."

Otto had been leaning on the handle of his battle ax. He swung it up to his shoulder. "You'll need help. I'll go with you."

"You don't have a uniform."

"It doesn't matter," Zen said. "The narrow corridor will be filled with guards. You'll never make it back out."

"Maybe," Nick said, "but I got you all into this."

Jasmine eased herself down beside Rancid. This debate, it seemed, would go on for a while. "I'm all for leading the guards into some of the residents down here, but the rodents' tunnel is too narrow. The far side of the antlings cave might work. A runner could lure the guards that way, throw a torch towards the antlings, and duck into a dead-end tunnel to hide."

"You're our fastest runner," Nick reminded her.

She nodded. "If I'm lucky, the guards will follow the torch, and I can sneak back. They'll stir up the antlings, and Zen can block their retreat."

Otto eyed the ice wall warily. It still sealed the antling cave, but a pool of melt had gathered at its base. "Don't underestimate the tenacity of the antlings. They've scented food and won't give it up easily. We'll not find rest until they're convinced we're gone, whether we feed them the guards or not."

"Whatever we do, we must do it quickly," Xanth said. His breathing had slowed.

"I agree. We can't wait for the guards to arrive." Zen gave Rancid and Jasmine an apologetic look. "We need to remember that Balor drives the guards, and that the Master drives Balor. Once we're spotted, they'll never relent. Our only hope for rest before we escape the catacombs is to avoid being seen or to allow no guard to escape."

"He's right," Nick said. "We have to get past the antlings."

"The first antlings will run into their hole to get help," Jasmine said. "That may buy us enough time to get past."

Otto shook his head. "They'll be ready this time. And if you try to hold them off for the rest of us, they'll swarm you."

Jasmine stood, resolute. "These things are too fast to outrun. We must rely on surprise and a head start."

"You won't have it." Otto held his torch near the ice barrier. Antlings moved on the other side.

Silence gathered around the companions like a cold fog. The ideas and debate seemed to have burned themselves out, along with the torch in Otto's hand. It sputtered and died, as if it had given up on any other fate.

CHAPTER 3

J asmine sat alone in the dark cavern, leaning against the wall and counting off the seconds. A new, unlit torch lay beside her knee and an open bottle of Balor's best whiskey rested in her hand. The smell of the alcohol soured her stomach, yet she was tempted to take a drink. Perhaps it would ease the pain.

Alcohol wasn't what she needed, however. She needed meditation, but she didn't have time.

Soon, the ice barrier would disappear and she would face her fate. Thankfully, the scratching of the antlings had stopped shortly after the torchlight had died away, and no sounds of an advancing search party yet reached her ears.

On count, she stood and placed her hand against the frozen barrier. A moment later, the ice vanished, signaling the readiness of Zen and the others.

Jasmine took a deep, settling breath. She struck a spark with her flint and the torch flared to life. With it, she lit the whiskey-soaked rag dangling from the bottle and tossed the flaming contraption into the antling cave. The bottle shattered as it hit the ground, and a bright wave of heat blew over her.

Antlings screeched and scattered. *I'll be damned. Rancid was right. It did work.* Jasmine didn't know if they could hear, but she yelled a challenge and waved her torch, trying to attract as many as possible. She must, if her friends were to have any chance of slipping past them on the far side of their cave.

Worker antlings scurried to escape the conflagration and more than a dozen disappeared into their mounds.

A couple of nearby workers ran headlong at Jasmine. With a sweep of her talon and a snap of her knee, she crushed the pesky things and waited for more to advance.

Within seconds, the flare of the explosion dwindled to the subdued light of a few burning pools of whiskey. The antlings re-grouped. Three of their warriors crawled from the nearest mounds and charged. More emerged behind them.

Her time up, Jasmine bolted toward the open expanse of the hub. The clicking and scratching of the warrior antlings drew nearer and she pushed herself to greater speed. She didn't dare look back.

Beyond the hub, the cave became treacherous with fallen boulders and moisture-bathed stone. Jasmine sprang to the top of the highest rock she could reach, already short of breath. The floor danced beneath her in the flickering light, yet she picked her steps quickly, leaping from stone to stone to maintain her lead.

When she was halfway to the water-floored chamber, her foot slipped. She crashed down onto a boulder with an impact that blew the breath from her lungs. The torch tumbled between the crags and plunged the cave into darkness.

The relentless warriors scrambled up the stones behind her, their chittering suddenly gleeful.

N ick and the rest of the party waited at the entrance to the small
water-floored chamber, a short distance from the backside of
the antling cave, beyond which lay their most likely route of escape
from the catacombs. The flare of the exploding whiskey lit the tunnel
wall ahead and Jasmine's shouts echoed down the passage.

Nick struck flint to steel and ignited a torch for himself, and then
one for Otto. With the antling cave full of fire, a couple of torches
around a bend shouldn't produce enough light to draw the antlings'
attention away from Jasmine and her efforts to draw them all out the
far side of the cave before she circled around to join the group.

As soon as Jasmine came into view down the long, rough corridor behind them with the antlings in pursuit, he urged the others
forward.

Rancid, the old man, and Otto had almost crossed the water when
Jasmine's torch went dark. Nick gasped and took a step toward her.

Zen stopped him with a hand on his shoulder. "Throw the torch."

Jasmine needed help, but Nick had no hope of outrunning the
antlings. He would only complicate matters if he went to her. So he
heaved the torch as far as he could down the tunnel to light her way.
It dropped short, failing to illuminate her or her attackers. Again,
Nick took a step down the corridor.

"No." Zen's grip became painful. He pointed. "There!"

At the edge of the light, Jasmine's lithe form sprang into view.
Antlings rose up behind her. She leaped from boulder to boulder
while the antlings scrambled down one rock and up the next. The
gap between her and her pursuers widened until she came within
range of Zen's staff.

Then a wall of ice closed the tunnel behind her, muffling the
sounds of the antlings' pursuit.

Nick released the breath he'd been holding.

He and Zen turned and raced across the water to catch up to the
others.

Beyond them, several large warriors came into view from the near
side of the antling cave. Otto handed his torch to Xanth and rushed

to engage the warriors before they could block the only remaining tunnel, the one Jasmine had suspected was a dead end.

By the time Nick and Zen caught up to the others, they faced a dozen or more warriors, some of them approaching past the nearest tunnel opening.

Zen threw up another ice wall, blocking both the antling cave and the sizable tunnel beyond, their originally planned escape route. Only the smaller tunnel remained open, with two antling warriors on the near side of the ice wall to oppose them.

Otto rushed the first warrior and shoved it back. "Go!" he yelled to Xanth and Rancid. When the second antling raised a claw to strike, Otto sheared off its arm with his ax. The antling screeched and fell back.

Xanth and Rancid leaned against each other. It was impossible to tell who supported whom as they stumbled into the narrow passage. Jasmine sprinted past, carrying the torch Nick had thrown, and followed them in.

When Nick reached the battle, he drove his sword through the armored chest of the closest warrior. If it had any vital organs, they'd likely be there. The antling fell to the floor. It lay on its back with its five remaining legs twitching in the damp cave air.

Shadows closed in as Jasmine and Xanth carried the torches away.

Otto severed two limbs from the remaining warrior. It turned to flee but found its way blocked by ice. One swipe of the ax separated the creature's bulbous abdomen from its armored torso, and it collapsed to the floor.

Otto chuckled shakily and shook his head. Nick let out a huge breath. Zen raced down the tunnel toward the others.

Nick and Otto caught up at the next junction.

"This looks promising," Nick said. Maybe it wasn't a dead end after all. The two tunnels appeared identical. "Which way?" he asked Rancid.

Rancid took the torch, looked into each opening, and then inspected the floor. "Left."

"I'll go first." Nick moved out in front.

Zen closed the passage behind them with a wall of ice. "That should slow the antlings, in case we need to backtrack."

The group spent the next several hours navigating the tunnels, which branched out in every conceivable direction. Dead ends appeared with maddening frequency. Nick lost track of where they'd been and had no idea which way might lead out. For this, he relied wholly on Rancid's judgment, as he'd done to their collective detriment in Palidor when Rancid had taken them off-course to try to find the hideout of the Black Hand bandits. It was unlikely, though, that Rancid had an ulterior motive here. He shared every reason the rest of them had for wanting to escape the catacombs, and as far as Nick knew, there weren't any Black Hand bandits to hunt in Trondor.

If Rancid's confidence wavered, he never showed it. He paused to inspect the floor at each fork and watched the torch smoke for signs of air movement. Once he made his choice, he proceeded with as much speed as his haggard body would allow. At each dead end, he returned without a word to the previous junction and chose the other branch.

Finally, exhausted beyond endurance, they came across a steep stone staircase rising from the cave floor.

Otto smiled. "Would you look at that?"

"Shhhh." Rancid passed his torch to Xanth and drew his sword. "There may be guards."

"In that case—" Nick mounted the stair— "I'll lead."

A hundred yards up, however, a cave-in had long ago closed the passage.

Nick slid his pack from his shoulders and let it settle onto the top step. "This seems as safe a place as any to rest. It's defensible and the antlings should slow Balor's pursuit."

Otto dropped his pack at the top of the stairs as well. "At this point, the antlings are the pursuit. But your friends are exhausted." He peered back down the steep incline. "At least the bends in the passage should keep our torchlight from reaching the bottom. I'll split the watch with you."

The watches were indeed a problem. Xanth had collapsed in a heap, like a scarecrow with a broken stand. His chest heaved with each breath. Jasmine rushed to him. She crushed some dried leaves from her pouch between her fingers and fed them to him.

When she finished, she stood tall and masked any discomfort she might have been feeling, but the flesh around her eyes appeared strained. The wound on her chest had sent angry purple and black streaks up her neck and past her shoulders. She needed rest or meditation, or whatever she did that induced her remarkable self-healing.

Rancid seemed to be asleep already. Zen, injured only by the knocks he'd taken while scrambling over treacherous footing for the past several hours, looked haggard behind his lengthening beard—as exhausted by his use of the weave as by his physical exertions.

And Nick didn't trust Otto, at least not enough to let the man sit alone over his sleeping friends. He might well earn his freedom by returning to the palace with all their heads in a sack.

Nick reluctantly put Xanth in the same category. The old man couldn't do much physically at the moment, though he might find a way to betray them at some point if he had a mind to.

"Suit yourself," Nick said finally, "but I'm too wound up to sleep. I'll take the first watch."

He grabbed his pack, drew out a bottle of wine, and descended a dozen feet down the staircase to where a hollow in the rocks formed a crude natural bowl. He filled the depression with wine and tested it. It burned slowly, producing less light than a torch, but enough to see by.

Grateful he wouldn't have to spend the rest of their torches just to get through the night, he settled in with no plans to wake Otto until it was time to leave.

Jasmine stayed up for an hour or so, deep in one of her healing trances. When she finally retired, some of the color had returned to her skin and her features appeared less strained. The purple on her neck and arms had faded.

After that, Nick had no idea how long he waited. He refilled his crude lamp twice before noises reached him from somewhere in the cavern below—not the scratching of antlings he'd expected, but the running of booted feet.

A voice spoke in the darkness, accompanied by the jingle of supplies. "Are they coming?"

"I don't know. Keep moving."

"Which way?"

"Who cares?"

There were at least three distinct voices.

"Wait. I can't see…" Most of the jingling quieted, as did the footsteps. The voices sounded closer. "Ow!"

"Hey guys, look at this!"

"Shhhh!"

Then a whispered, "What?"

"I don't know. It looks like stairs."

Nick came to his feet quietly, sword in hand.

"Hallelujah. Come on."

Nick popped the cork from a whiskey bottle, stuffed a rag in the top, and dipped it in his makeshift lamp. The cloth flared to life and he tossed it down the staircase.

"Whoa!" came a voice from below as a burst of flame lit the corridor. "Somebody's up there!"

"Good," said another. "Maybe it's a way out." Running footsteps echoed up the stairs.

With the approach now lit by a multitude of burning puddles, Nick stood his ground in the middle of the passage.

Moments later, a man rounded the bend. The guard's armor hung in pieces, half of it missing, his uniform shredded. His face showed no sign that he recognized Nick past the Trondorian uniform he still wore. Scratches and the familiar welts of antling bites dotted his exposed skin. "What's up here?"

"Dead end," Nick said as a second guard came into view. "Closed by a rockslide."

The man stopped short. "How'd you get here?"

"Come on." The second guard moved to pass. Though wounded, he appeared strong. A patch on his breast identified him as a lieutenant in the Home Guard. "We'll rest at the top."

But Nick stretched his sword across the lieutenant's path and gave him a hard look. "I said it's a dead end."

"So?"

Two more guards came around the corner, threading their way through the pools of flaming alcohol. One man, with a bow strung on his back, supported the other, who appeared to have been punctured by the tail of one of the spined rodents. He seemed near death.

"How badly do you want to get out of here alive?" Nick asked them.

The lieutenant took a step back and raised his sword. "What are you talking about?"

"We can join forces. Help each other." Nick kept his voice low.

"How many in your party?" the first guard asked.

A fifth ascended the stairs, dragging his feet and his sword. He looked up with glazed eyes filled with fatigue and despair.

"Who are you?" The lieutenant backed a few steps down the staircase. "Wait a second..."

Nick heard stirrings from above him. "You don't have to die down here. We can find an exit together. Then you can return to the palace and report whatever you want." These men weren't the enemy. They were just doing their jobs, trying to support their families or their vices. Like Nick and his friends, they'd become victims of the Master's Chosen.

"It's them!" The lieutenant lunged.

Nick parried. "We don't have to do this."

"Sir." The weakest of the guards, the one with the rodent sting, lifted his head and pleaded, "Think about this."

The man beside him propped him against the wall and readied his bow.

The first guard who had come up the stairs drew his sword and stood beside his lieutenant, who lunged a second time.

Nick parried again and backed a step up the stairs.

The weak man with the puncture wound continued to plead for wisdom from his lieutenant while the ragged guard in the back wheeled around to flee.

A wall of ice blocked the corridor beyond the fleeing man, who then drew his sword and turned back with an expression of hopeless defiance.

Forced now into combat he'd hoped to avoid, Nick battered at the swords of the front pair of guards, taking full advantage of his higher position, his strength, and the weight of his great sword. As one, the guards fell back.

Nick struck the lieutenant in the arm, and then in the gut. The man staggered and collapsed.

Ice shards whipped down the stairwell and struck the bowman, who tumbled backwards.

"We'll spare anyone who drops his sword now," Nick shouted over the din.

Shards flew past him again and the weak, punctured man fell. Only the first guard and the last remained.

The first guard attacked fiercely and forced Nick onto the defensive until the guard's balance wavered on a loose stone. Done taking chances, Nick bashed the man's sword aside and drove his own blade home.

The final guard stood with his back against the frozen barrier. His discarded sword lay at his feet, his hands raised in surrender.

Nick took several steps toward him. "Join us."

The guard nodded uncertainly, his eyes wide and his face ashen.

Nick slipped a dagger from the man's belt and relieved him of his pouches. "Did Balor Culhaven come into the catacombs with you?"

The guard shook his head.

"Dalen Frost?" Nick checked the guard's neck for a chain or medallion.

No, again.

"How many guards came into the catacombs?" Nick asked.

The man found his voice, which trembled as a spasm seemed to pass through him. "I... I don't know. Eleven, I think."

Zen stepped forward.

Nick stopped him with a raised hand and a shake of his head. "But more will follow?" he asked the guard.

"Captain Frost is gathering a more substantial force. Runners have been sent to all the villages. Search parties will scour the countryside."

"*Captain* Frost?" Nick said. "Dalen's been promoted?"

The man hesitated. "Yes."

"Where did your allegiance lie in the rebellion?" Though Zen's tone was casual, it carried a threat that few but Nick would have recognized.

The guard gave him a long look.

"Where?" Zen shouted. He no longer masked the threat.

"W— with my commander."

"His name?"

The guard answered as though he didn't think the question was important. "General Gundahar." One of the Master's Chosen!

Zen took the man by the neck and a sudden chill filled the tunnel.

Instead of reeling away from the cold, Nick shoved Zen aside to stop his attack. When he looked back, the guard's body was frozen to the ice behind him. His sightless eyes stared through a glaze of frost.

"I promised we wouldn't hurt him," Nick shouted.

Zen braced his staff on the steps and righted himself. Without a word, he dropped the ice wall. The frozen guard fell back onto the stairs with a crack, and his rigid body slid from view. "He was a liability we couldn't afford."

The man would have slowed them down, but a promise was a

promise. Nick glared at his best friend. "I don't know who you are anymore." He stormed off down the stairs.

At the bottom, he paused to collect his rage. Only a hint of light from the whiskey bomb reached him there. The darkness beyond seemed to amplify the sheer immensity of the cavern. Nick might have stared into the Abyss and not felt more unsettled.

Then, at the edge of his perception, he detected a quick, furtive scratching from somewhere in the distance. Antlings.

Without sheathing his sword, he bolted up the stairs.

Zen brushed at his shimmery robes and frowned at their state of filth and disrepair.

While Jasmine looted the bodies for torches, food, and water, he walked past her up the stairs. The guards would have nothing of interest to him. Thirsty, he produced a single sliver of ice from the weave and popped it into his mouth. In time, Nick would understand the necessity of what Zen had done.

Nick raced up the stairs. "Antlings!" He was out of breath from the climb.

Quickly, they all gathered their things, reached the bottom of the steps before the insects arrived, and slipped into some unknown passage. Zen sealed the tunnel behind them.

From there, the cave branched into a labyrinth of small tunnels, and somewhere in the midst of the maze, a voice touched Zen's mind.

Zenobrian Zersaash, this is Gwyndarren. I don't know how the others escaped, but I'm glad you're with them. Their escape serves both our purposes better than their execution does. Use the scroll to contact me when it's safe to do so. Let me know where you're going. I might be able to help you.

Gwyndarren, the elf who'd conspired with Zen in Palidor, who'd given Zen most of the enchantments he now carried, who'd talked him into betraying his friends... a knot formed at the back of Zen's throat. He'd betrayed even Dara. All because of Gwyndarren.

"Zen?" Nick said from beside him. "You all right?"

"Yeah. I..." He glanced down the tunnel behind them. "I thought I heard something, but I guess not." He placed his foot in Nick's cupped hands and Nick boosted him up the next boulder.

The tunnels wound their way through the Trondorian bedrock for many miles before the party rested again. Finally, Rancid found an alcove with a large enough stretch of flat earth to provide comfort for sleeping and room to fight. The mouth was narrow enough to seal with an ice wall should the need arise.

Though Jasmine and Rancid both seemed stronger than they had at their previous stop, Zen was exhausted. He hadn't tapped the weave since they'd left the antlings and the bodies of the guards behind, but he'd grown desperately short on sleep. Insomnia had troubled him since Balor had thrown them all into the palace dungeons weeks before. Every time Zen closed his eyes, Dara showed up in his dreams, smiling, laughing, and flirting with him—until a blade suddenly ripped through her chest. In the dreams, Zen always looked down to find himself holding the sword that had killed her. He might as well have. Her death was as much his fault as it was that of the man who'd murdered her. And both had acted at Gwyndarren's bidding.

That night, he didn't try to sleep. Instead, he pondered Gwyndarren's latest request. Before Vinra had revealed himself as the assassin Vinsous Drakemoor, a Chosen of the Master, Zen had had no reason to question his dealings with Gwyndarren. The information Zen had bartered had already been known to their enemies, so the risk of selling it to Gwyndarren seemed inconsequential.

But when Zen faked his own incapacitation to avoid attacking a Chosen, thereby keeping his agreement with Gwyndarren, Zen had crossed the line. He'd let his lust for power get in the way of... of what? Power was the reason he'd come on this dangerous quest in the first place. Still...

Gwyndarren was up to something. After he insisted that Zen refrain from attacking a Chosen, Zen had assumed the elf was working for the Master, or at least for one of the Chosen. But now the elf seemed to consider Nick's escape preferable to his execution. Nick, Zen, and their friends had already found the Codex of Mortaan. Maybe the Master needed them to find something else for him. The Guardian of the Abyss, perhaps.

No. Zen would do almost anything for power, but he wouldn't hand the Master the means to release the demons from their eternal prison.

Maybe Gwyndarren had been working for Drakemoor, or more likely with Drakemoor. That would explain how Gwyndarren knew that Zen would encounter Drakemoor. Yes. That made sense.

So who was Gwyndarren planning to work with now that Drakemoor was dead? Zen? Yes. That made sense too. This time Gwyndarren had asked for Zen's location, information he'd always seemed to know in the past. He must have been communicating with Drakemoor as he now was with Zen, through the use of enchanted scrolls.

But because Drakemoor was dead, Gwyndarren had no other contact within Zen's party. Therefore, Zen's value had greatly increased. He smiled. *All right, Gwyndarren. We'll see how your little game is played now.*

CHAPTER 4

With the exception of Nick and Otto, who also pled insomnia, everybody got a few more hours of sleep. But when Nick's eyelids became heavy, he decided it was time to leave. More guards would follow the first, and they would get past the antlings.

He roused the others, and they continued to climb their way through the caves until they stood at the opening to yet another chamber. Nick listened for sounds of pursuit or for occupants in the cave before them. They heard nothing except for the hollow dripping of water somewhere in the distance.

Rancid inspected the ground and studied the torch's flame. He glanced at Nick and back at the torch as if to say, "Did you see that?" Nick hadn't seen anything. Rancid strode purposefully across the chamber to another tunnel that extended into the darkness. There was no mistaking it now; the smoke drifted in the barest of currents.

And if Nick hoped hard enough, he could imagine that the passage sloped uphill. It took everything he had not to race ahead, but his armor would make more noise than was prudent, and Rancid had brought them this far. Nick motioned for him to proceed.

Rancid led them past a fork in the tunnel and through another chamber. As the breeze grew stronger, so did the smell of carrion and offal. Something else in the air stung Nick's nose. Nonetheless, Rancid pressed on.

A few minutes later, he paused. He handed the torch to Otto and padded silently forward. The hot breeze carried a soft bubbling sound, like a pot of boiling pitch.

When Rancid returned, sweat bathed his face and his exposed skin had reddened. "Hot," he breathed, his chest heaving for a breath of cool air. "There's something up there, sleeping in a chamber, between us and the exit."

It figured. Nick slid his great sword free from its scabbard. Nothing they'd fought in these catacombs had been easy. Never before, though, had they been so near an exit. Whatever it was, insect, rodent, or something new, he would get them all past it.

"You saw outside?" Jasmine whispered.

"No, but the air current is strong and the tunnel wide."

"What kind of thing?" Zen asked quietly.

Rancid shook his head. "Big. Armored, like an insect. It's curled up in a ball. I can't tell what it is."

Nick tugged at the collar of his chest plate. "Where's the heat coming from?"

"A pool of liquid rock. We'll have to pass between it and the creature."

Nick glanced at Zen uneasily.

The mage shrugged. "If it lives in this heat, it might be sensitive to cold."

"I'll scout the passage beyond." Jasmine took a step toward the chamber. "It may narrow to a hole smaller than we can squeeze through. I don't want to get caught between this thing and a dead end."

"I'll go," Rancid said. "I'm quieter."

Jasmine fixed her gaze on him. "If you wake it, you'll have no hope of outrunning it."

Nick put a hand on Rancid's shoulder. "She's right. Let her go."

But as soon as Jasmine rounded the bend, Rancid twisted away from Nick's grasp and followed.

"Orc's blood," Nick spat.

"I'll get him." Zen, too, moved out ahead.

Nick muttered another curse and followed. With half the party moving forward, the beast would surely wake. They'd need his sword.

When he caught up, Rancid and Zen were waiting in the chamber entrance, backlit by a glowing lava pool. Jasmine was picking her way across the cavern among myriad bones and carapace fragments.

The head of the beast snapped up and swiveled on a narrow neck until its multifaceted eyes fixed on Jasmine.

She glanced once at the exit, a smooth tunnel twenty feet in diameter, the lower half nearly blocked by a massive boulder. Then she sprinted back to the others.

A shriek split the air as the thing rose to full height. It looked like an antling standing on its four hind legs with two pincers snapping at the air. Erect, it stood twice Jasmine's height. Crawling, it wouldn't be slowed by the narrow tunnel that now forced the party to move in single file.

"The queen," Nick said.

Otto stepped up behind him. "No. She'd be surrounded by thousands of her brood."

"What, then?"

"A guardian, maybe. Some sort of warrior lord." Otto eased his way back the way they'd come, but stopped short.

Worker and warrior antlings filled the tunnel that led back into the catacombs.

Otto drew his sword. "Which way?"

"I'm tired of running." Nick pointed his own blade toward the warlord. "The exit's that way."

As one, they rushed in to face the monstrous creature in the cavern.

The heat hit Nick like a wall. Within seconds, sweat poured down his skin beneath his armor.

Once the whole party had entered the chamber, Zen sealed the entrance behind them with an ice wall, separating them from the lesser antlings in the tunnel for as long as the ice would last in the sweltering cave.

The warlord's head swiveled back and forth, eyeing the intruders. Its pincers and mandibles snapped at the air and it backed toward the cave wall. Six humanoids were too many, it seemed, for it to decide which to attack first.

Jasmine sped past without stopping to fight. She leapt to the top of the boulder.

Rancid gave the warlord a wide berth, skirting the edge of the lava pool as closely as he dared, his sword drawn but held low, as if to avoid any implied threat. He strode toward the boulder and the gap beside it, which looked just large enough for his elf-kin frame to squeeze through.

As soon as he placed a foot into the gap, the warlord sprang, a motion so quick that Nick barely saw it. A pincer snatched Rancid's trailing leg and swung him high into the air.

He'd have lost his head in that instant had Nick not batted the warlord's mandibles away. The warlord shrieked, dropped Rancid, and swatted Nick's blade aside. No wound marred its face where Nick's great sword had struck.

Otto ran up beside Nick, and the warlord knocked him away.

Without rising, Rancid scrambled through the cleft into the tunnel beyond.

The warlord snatched up Nick by the torso. His breastplate buckled until it pressed against his chest and he labored to breathe. He managed to get his legs up between himself and the warlord, and braced his feet against the monster's chest. With a shove and a twist, Nick wrenched himself free.

Otto swung his ax, two-handed, at the warlord's torso, but its carapace turned the blade aside. "We can't fight it!" he yelled. "It's too strong."

A scream echoed back from Rancid, fading as he rushed toward their only exit.

Nick didn't have time to ponder the implications of that scream. Otto's discarded torch lay in the center of the cavern. Jasmine was nowhere in sight. Zen remained in the middle of the chamber. Behind him, steam rose from a puddle of water at the base of the weakening ice barrier. Even now, a gap at the top had grown nearly large enough to admit the workers. And the antling warlord blocked their escape.

From a pocket of his robes, Zen produced his bottle of fairy mist and plucked out the stopper.

Nick skirted the warlord and reached the boulder just as a thick, disorienting fog filled the cave. He tried to climb, but the condensing mist made the surface slick. Clicking and scratching sounds betrayed the warlord's movements from... somewhere. In the mist, direction lost all meaning. Only the feel of the boulder anchored Nick's senses. It was the only thing he could be sure of.

Xanth brushed past his shoulder. Nick grabbed the old man's tattered robes and guided him to the cleft. A mere wisp of flesh, the old man slipped easily into the tunnel beyond. Nick crouched to the floor, where the opening was at its widest, and shimmied through, with Otto close behind.

Of Zen, he heard nothing, saw nothing, and knew nothing.

Nick, Otto, and Xanth groped their way out of the fog and ran. When they rounded the final bend, daylight shone through an opening large enough to have admitted his uncle Harimon's wagons. *Thank you, Aeron!*

But between Nick and salvation flew thousands of blood flies, the bane of every livestock rancher in the Civilized Lands during the summer months. This swarm hovered in the tepid pocket between the sweltering cave and the cool Trondorian air. With the warlord behind them, the companions could do nothing but run.

Nick slowed where the air cooled and the flies thinned. Rancid waited there. Like Nick's, Rancid's skin raged with welts the size and color of ripe raspberries.

Jasmine returned from scouting beyond the cave opening. "Mounds."

Nick's hopes sank. "Antling mounds?"

She nodded. "For a hundred yards or more in every direction. We're out of options. We have to sprint through."

While they were waiting for Zen, Nick stripped off his armor. His crushed chest plate constricted his lungs and the weight would slow him down. Otto helped him. When they got it off, Zen was still missing. The fog that had been creeping up the tunnel began to recede.

"Zen!" Nick shouted. Of all people, Zen should have been able to find, fight, or trick his way out of the warlord's burrow. "Zen!"

No answer.

Nick started to head back toward the burrow, but the antling warlord emerged from the mist. When it caught sight of the five, it launched into pursuit. Out of time now, they bolted into the mid-afternoon sunlight. Only Nick's need to run kept him from breaking down in exhaustion, sorrow, and regret. Zen!

He glanced back. At the opening, the warlord shrieked in protest and recoiled from the brightness of the day. Its bulk almost completely blocked the opening.

Antlings appeared at the tops of several mounds ahead. They too shied from the light.

With no other choice, the companions ran, even after they cleared the antling grounds. They slowed only when Xanth collapsed.

Zen started forward, and then stopped. Which way was the exit? The sounds of movement seemed to echo from all directions until, one by one, they died away, except for the faint scratching of the antlings on the far side of the ice wall.

The cool mist muted the heat of the lava pool, but one side did seem warmer than the other. That's it! The lava had been on his right when he'd entered. He would put the warmth to his right and walk. That should take him to the exit. The lava had been on the right. Hadn't it? He wasn't even sure which way was right. Short of stoppering the bottle—a warrant of death—all he could do was move and hope. He took a few slow steps forward.

A moment later, his hand touched the wall. He didn't know where he was in the cavern but at least he hadn't blundered into the molten pool. The enchantment of the mist clouded even his memory. He could no longer see the room in his mind, so he inched his way around with one hand on the wall and his staff tapping the floor in front of him until he touched the ice, slick with runoff. He'd guessed wrong. He'd reached the opening where they'd entered the chamber, clear across the cave from where he needed to be. With the intervening mist, he had no hope of reaching the other side.

Then the ice split under the force of untold numbers of antlings, who poured in with a collective shriek of glee.

Ryanna Pruitt strode into Addicus' study. "Nicklan Mirrin has escaped, and Gwyndarren has heard no word from the ice mage. Can you find them?"

Without looking up, Addicus waved a frail hand in her direction. "I know, I know." He shuffled from the bookshelf to a small cabinet in the corner, gathered a silver box from the top shelf, and a handful of vials from elsewhere within. His gray hair seemed to float around his head as though chasing him. "Our Master told me too."

He arranged the items on a small table beside a wide brazier carved from a single slab of marble, which he polished to a glossy sheen after each use.

"Can you find them?" Ryanna asked again.

The aging scholar glanced up. His green eye and his yellow eye never seemed to gaze in quite the same direction at the same time, which always sent chills crawling across the back of Ryanna's neck. "Of course I can find him." He pulled a charred book from the top drawer of his oak desk.

Only a portion of the binding remained, and the pages threatened to scatter. The stained edges made it look as though someone had thrown the journal into mud to extinguish the fire that had nearly consumed it.

Addicus set the book carefully on the table and then settled himself onto a stool beside the brazier. "Make yourself useful. Go and fetch my tea."

She stared at the agitated old man who dared to speak to her in such a tone, but this Seeking was more important than a battle of respect—at that moment. Fortunately, she didn't need to leave the room to get it. She did have her orders, after all.

Addicus poured a milky oil into the bowl, beginning in the center and working his way out in a slow spiral until the oil covered the entire interior surface. He assembled a pyre of carefully dried bogweed shoots in the center, sprinkled them with a black powder, and set a pot of water on a burner beside the desk. He snatched the bag of tea from Ryanna's hand. "You needn't stay for this."

Ryanna slid a chair from the corner, settled it in front of the brazier, and sat down. She idly spun the gold ring on her right hand with the fingers of her left. "On the contrary."

Addicus muttered to himself as he continued his preparations. When he was ready, he grasped the onyx medallion around his neck and asked the Master for permission to remove it, asserting that it would cloud his Vision.

The corners of Ryanna's mouth turned up. Vornax couldn't control Addicus once the old man removed the Medallion, which was why the Master had ordered Ryanna to remain present for the duration of the Seeking. She had to admire the old man's guile, though. Whether the Medallion's effect on his Vision was real or not, Addicus had found a means to interrupt the Master's control over him, if only for a few minutes.

He laid the Medallion reverently on the table and struck a spark to the pyre. Low, smokeless flame rose up uniformly across the bowl's surface. Addicus poured himself a cup of hot water and sprinkled in a pinch of tea leaves.

Even from several feet away, the fumes that rose from the cup distorted Ryanna's mind. She gripped the arms of the chair to keep her head from spinning and focused on the gold-embroidered hem of her clean white robe.

Addicus sucked in a long breath of those same noxious fumes, yet he seemed unaffected. For many minutes, he sat across from her, sipping his tea and staring into the flames. Finally Ryanna's head began to clear and she could face him once more.

He looked calm, as he always did before a Seeking—relaxed, she suspected, as much by the lifting of the Medallion's burden as by the hallucinogen in the tea. At first, she'd thought the man crazed, a babbling idiot who passed off his delusions as some mystical sight, but he'd been right too many times for her to doubt him now.

When the tea was gone, he tore a page out of the ruined journal.

With the deft movements of a practiced weaver, Ryanna's hand snapped out to grasp his wrist before he could toss the parchment into the brazier. "What're you doing? It took us years to acquire that."

Addicus gripped the torn page, which contained only a few short phrases regarding the Shield of Faith, which apparently resided in the temple of Aeron in Spitfire. It was one of several artifacts that Gaddy Mirrin's journal had helped them to locate, but that the other Chosen had yet to acquire and deliver to their sanctuary. "I must sacrifice an object to link my Vision to the object's owner."

"But that belonged to Nick's grandfather. Nick had it only for a few weeks before Whisper took it from him." She didn't dare accuse Addicus of trickery, not until she'd discerned his motives.

He nodded with a patience bordering on disdain. "Yes. Ordinarily that would be a problem. But this journal, more than any other object—perhaps more than all other objects combined—has defined the person Nicklan Mirrin is today."

Ryanna released his arm.

"We must catch him quickly, though. The journal has only so many pages." He tossed the parchment onto the flame and followed it with a pinch of white powder. Smoke rose, thick and black, from the bowl until the white dust hit the flame. The center cleared, and Addicus seemed to go into a trance. "I see him."

Ryanna focused on the waves of heat rising between the two columns of black smoke, but she saw nothing.

Flames devoured the parchment within seconds.

"Would that I had a more durable sacrifice." His eerie eyes seemed to focus once more.

"You saw him?"

"I said I did, didn't I?"

"I didn't see anything."

Addicus gave her a clenched half-smile, as if she was a prized pupil who'd failed at a difficult task he knew she wanted desperately to accomplish. "Divination is a dying art."

Ryanna snapped to her feet, her knees knocking her chair into the wall behind her. "I care nothing for your hallucinations. But since Vornax believes them, I'm required to ask what you saw."

"I saw Nick Mirrin running across a field."

"Who was with him?"

"I can't divine that from a single sacrifice."

Ryanna's lips curled into a frown. "And you don't know where he is?"

"No, but the sun has nearly set, and his shadow stretches long behind him. He makes his way west on foot. Given the time of his escape from the dungeon, and barring any enchanted means of transportation, that puts him within a day west of the capital, in Trondor."

"Put on your Medallion. I'll notify Balor."

CHAPTER 5

ick helped Xanth to his feet. "Over there." He pointed to a small grove of trees, the only one in sight on the flat expanse of the Trondorian plain. "We can hide out until nightfall."

"No," Rancid said. "We're too near the city, and every patrol that passes this way will search that wood. We're better off stopping here."

The party was standing among several varieties of waist-high tundra grasses. That particular spot seemed indistinguishable from any other for miles in any direction. Anyone searching would have to practically step on them to find them. "You're right," Nick said. "We'll rest here."

Without further comment, they all dropped their gear and sprawled in the grass.

Just one night, Nick promised himself as the sun sank toward the horizon, and then Jasmine will be strong enough to stand watch. Just one night. Then he could sleep.

He felt worn, and a pervasive numbness had settled into him, save for a tightness in his chest that had nothing to do with his physical exertion and everything to do with Zen's absence. He'd experienced the same ache when he'd found his mother's body in the burned-out remains of his father's farmhouse. His father's voice in his head, always the voice of right, now told him he had to go back for his best friend. But another voice, the voice of prudence and practicality, told him Zen had either made it out on his own or was dead. Either way, going back would accomplish nothing.

Zen had power, and he'd proven himself resourceful. Nevertheless, Nick couldn't bring himself to a point of optimism. The mage could do only so much weaving in a day. The haggard look around Zen's eyes during the last hours in the catacombs suggested he'd already been running beyond his endurance. And the antling warlord, that invincible antling warlord... He kept replaying the battle in his mind, trying to find something that he could have done differently, something that would have made a difference. No, the more Nick thought about it, the more certain he became that Zen had sacrificed his life to give Nick and the others a chance to fight the Prophecy.

Nothing would stop Nick from at least trying to make that sacrifice worthwhile.

Nick had intended to rouse the group when darkness came and then use the night to escape the plains, perhaps even reach the low mountain range he'd spotted to the west. But when the sun disappeared, the cool night air washed over him and promised to keep him awake for a little bit longer. He'd wait until midnight. They'd still have time to travel then.

ick's eyes snapped open. *Orc's blood!* He'd fallen asleep. They could've all been captured, or worse.

A shout drifted across the plain, from somewhere to the south. He held his breath and listened, but he couldn't make out the words.

The moon, always stationary in the sky, was less than half full and still waxing. He hadn't slept long.

Another shout, more distant, reached him. Then the sound of hooves, from maybe a dozen horses.

There seemed to be only one reason why horsemen would ride out in force at this hour.

Fortunately, Nick's friends still slept. He'd wake them if the need arose, but not before. Otherwise someone, Rancid in particular, might be stupid enough to stand and challenge, or to run off to investigate.

Nick listened for several minutes before the sounds faded. Too on-edge to fall back asleep, he waited for at least an hour to make sure the men wouldn't double back. In the morning, he'd have to thank Rancid for keeping them out of the grove.

When the moon had waned to a narrow crescent, Nick roused the company. Prudence and practicality demanded that distance take precedence over sleep this night.

Otto sat up and scrubbed the sleep from his eyes. "Which way?"

"Good question," Nick said. "Any ideas?"

Rancid scanned the horizon. "The border lies to the southeast."

Otto tied his sleeping roll to his backpack. "The border will be guarded."

Xanth had no supplies of his own. He was sitting on a blanket Nick had lent him. "I have no faith in the prophets, but the stars have foretold a great war within my lifetime. Perhaps what you believe is true. If so, I can help you obtain a weapon to fight this Master of yours."

That should have been good news, but Nick was far too exhausted to feel any elation. The statement itself had barely registered in his mind.

"He's no master of ours," Jasmine said flatly.

"I misspoke. I apologize." Xanth aimed his appeal at Nick. "This Master you oppose, no weapon of this world will harm him?"

"That's what the Prophecy says."

"And you believe it?"

"If not the Prophecy, then Alamain. She said the same thing."

"Alamain?" Xanth asked.

"The High Priestess of Aeron." Jasmine helped him to his feet and gave him an evaluating look. "How do you feel?"

Rancid glanced about nervously. "Dawn's growing nearer."

Xanth ignored him. "I have about as much use for Aeron as I do for the prophets, but I want to help you, if I can. I owe you that much just to have seen the stars again."

Nick hesitated. "What are you offering?"

"Look up. What do you see?"

Nick did. "The stars."

"The sun, if we don't hurry," Rancid grumbled.

Again Xanth ignored him. "Precisely. Do you know what they are?"

Nick shrugged. "Lights in the sky."

"They're whole worlds, like this one. Some are mere rocks. Others burn with fire, like the sun." The old man spread his arms and spoke with the reverence of a priest. "All are interconnected by a single force that pulls them together, each contributing to the fate of all the others. That's why we look to them to learn the future."

"We don't have time for this," Rancid muttered to Jasmine.

"Sometimes the worlds collide," Xanth continued. "They break into pieces, some of which have landed here."

Nick shook his head. "I'm sure that's interesting, but—"

"Don't you see? The Sorcerers' Guild has collected some of the pieces. They're made primarily of metal."

Nick glanced across the field, beginning to share Rancid's impatience.

Xanth grabbed Nick's shoulders and gripped them firmly. "Forge your weapon from the metal of another world."

Nick's jaw slackened. Was it possible?

"Let's go to Brinheim," Rancid said. "Demonbane is there. Forged in the Abyss, it meets your requirements. The border is too vast to guard effectively. We can slip past Balor's patrols."

"No," Nick said. "Xanth is right. Demonbane was listed in my grandfather's journal, so the Master knows about it. He may already have it."

"We don't know that," Jasmine said.

"Besides," Nick continued, "Alamain said it wouldn't help us. Demonbane may not have been forged in this world, but it was forged from materials of this world. It was forged for slaying demons. Against a human adversary, it's nothing more than an ordinary sword."

"Where are these rocks from the stars?" Otto asked the old man.

"We have a few at the guild house. Mere pebbles. But from these we've learned their nature. And several years before the monarchy raided the guild house, we tracked a rock from the sky all the way to the horizon. It was huge by comparison. Maybe tens of pounds. Large enough to provide metal for a weapon."

That certainly wasn't in his grandfather Gaddy's journal and might not have been foreseen by the prophets. "Where is it now?"

"In the Wild Lands. We didn't have time to recover it before the raid. But there was a map in the guild house that estimated its location, and there was the Seeking Stone."

Nick snatched up his blanket and handed it to Xanth to wrap around himself in the cool air. "Seeking Stone?"

"It's an earth magic, from the dwarves. When it comes within range of a metal from the stars, it lights up. And the closer it gets, the brighter it glows. It can lead you to the rock from another world."

Rancid pulled Nick aside. "How do we know he's telling the truth?"

"He's at least as trustworthy as you," Nick said, recalling the weeks that Rancid's diversion to locate the Black Hand hideout had cost them in Palidor.

"Xanth has no reason to lie," Jasmine said.

"He could lead us to one of Balor's patrols to buy his own freedom," Rancid said. "He admits he doesn't believe in your prophecy. He cares nothing for our quest."

"Neither do you," Jasmine said.

"We've been a friend to him." Even in the faint starlight, Nick could see Rancid roll his eyes. He turned back to the old man. "Where is this guild house?"

"Just south of Tradestar."

"West of here," Otto supplied. "On the coast."

"Then we could bypass the border," Jasmine observed.

"Of course," Rancid said sarcastically. "Balor would never expect us to head for the nearest town where we could book passage on a ship."

Otto put a hand on Nick's shoulder. "Before we go anywhere, do you want to try to go back for your friend?" Otto asked Nick. "He might still be alive."

A lump formed at the back of Nick's throat. He couldn't swallow. "The antling warlord wouldn't have come after us if Zen was still alive in its lair. If he somehow made it out on the weave, we won't find him by going back to the catacombs. If not..." The words caught in his throat. If not, then Zen was another of Nick's friends to die on account of his quest. How much more was this prophecy going to cost them? How much more would the Master cost the whole of the Civilized Lands?

"I'm afraid I have to agree," Jasmine said.

We've got to go somewhere," Otto insisted. "And all of our options will be watched."

"West," Nick said. "To the guild house."

Rancid threw up his hands. "This way, then." He marched into the darkness.

Nick followed, with Otto at his side. Jasmine and Xanth fell in a step behind.

"If I were you," Nick told Otto as they walked, "I'd go my own way. Balor is one of the Chosen, he has a personal grudge against us, and he'll be driven by the Master himself in the search. You're not so recognizable. You'll fare better on your own."

"Perhaps."

They walked in silence for a time.

"You've seen the original Prophecy?" Otto asked finally.

"Briefly."

"I've heard only stories. Versions vary, but most relate the same dark and scary tales that left me with nightmares as a child."

Nick chuckled. "I've seen you fight. I can't imagine you're afraid of much."

"I fear nothing I can fight. But inevitable doom, foretold by a prophet who was never wrong…that would frighten any sane man." Silence stretched for a long moment. "You say this Master exists? That he lives now?"

Nick stopped, drawing the others to a halt with him. "Alamain herself has confirmed the presence of the Master, though Vexetan hides his identity from her. We have personally met four of the Master's Chosen, and killed one. We've seen the slave riots of Palidor and put an end to Trondor's civil war—both of which are preconditions of the Prophecy's fulfillment."

Otto's lips emitted a long, low whistle. "Sounds like it doesn't matter where I go."

Nick resumed his westward trek, knowing Rancid wouldn't wait long, if at all, for them to catch up. "We've also seen copies of the Codex. The original is enchanted in a way that prevents it from being accurately reproduced. Yet the copies match the original for this prophecy, and this prophecy only. I don't know what that means, but it gives me hope."

"Sometimes hope is enough."

Nick glanced at him through the corner of his eye. "You're brave, stranger, if you intend to get mixed up in this. So far the Master has guessed our every move, planted spies among us, and even used us to do his bidding, though we didn't know it at the time."

"I've never been accused of cowardice, but I must admit to a personal agenda."

"Oh?"

Jasmine and Xanth walked closer to them now.

"I was the constable in Twin Peaks when the civil war started. When Balor's general, Pandalo Gundahar, and his vanguard force raided the town for flammable oils, his soldiers went door to door, breaking them down if necessary. They searched each house and took every drop. I implored him to leave some for us. The winds blow bitter east of the Sharktooth Mountains and many won't survive on what they can acquire between now and the winter. He didn't care."

The sky behind them began to lighten with dawn.

Otto didn't seem to notice. "I organized a volunteer guard to try to protect the minimum stores I thought we needed, not more than ten percent of everything we had. I wasn't trying to hamper Gundahar's war effort. I told him he could take the rest. Well, you can guess what happened next. He labeled me a Gremauld sympathizer, arrested the whole lot of us, and took the oil. But that wasn't the end of it. If it was, I'd have been inclined to forgive."

Rancid dropped back as they moved into rougher terrain.

"When the war ended," Otto continued, "we should have been released, and most of us were. But Balor declared me a political prisoner and detained me until he could decide what to do with me. I'm sure he considered killing me and dumping my body, but too many people knew I was there for me to simply disappear. The death of a prisoner of war, after the end of hostilities, wouldn't sit right with those whose support he needed to gain the throne."

"What did he do?" Nick asked.

"He lied to the Ruling Council. He told them he'd released me with the others but that I came back to murder him."

Rancid shot him a pointed glance. "Did you?"

"No. But I would now, given the chance. Anyway, the Council passed sentence and threw me into the dungeon. They scheduled my execution for seventy-two hours later—yesterday evening, if my count is correct. You at least had until Balor's confirmation, but I'd have been dead by now."

Otto glanced at Nick. "You saved my life. That's a debt I can never repay. You fight a man to whom I owe vengeance. You seek to save all of the civilized races from the worst fate I could imagine, and from the thing I've feared most since before I was old enough to understand it. You ask why I don't go my own way..." He let out a low chuckle and waved a hand toward Rancid. "I don't know. Maybe it's because your guide has our only bottle of the king's bitterroot wine and I can't bring myself to part with it."

The sun touched the mountain peaks that rose a couple thousand feet above the flatlands and it became clear they wouldn't reach the mountains before the sun shone on the plain. The terrain was flat enough for search parties to see for miles, and Nick's party had moved beyond the tall grasses that had concealed them the previous evening. Rancid chose their path carefully among the few contours sufficient to conceal them if they kept their heads down.

By mid-morning they reached the foothills, and Nick, bone-weary, called a halt for everyone to get some sleep.

"I'm sorry about Zen," Jasmine said as Nick finally spread his blanket. "He was a good friend."

Nick struggled to focus through the fog that filled his mind. "He may yet be alive down there. I only wish we had some way to help him."

CHAPTER 6

Zen corked the bottle and gathered the weave. Strand by strand, he remade himself. This was no mere disguise, but a complete alteration of his form and substance into an antling constructed entirely of ice. With his antling eyes, he could see in the dark. The image was distorted, but he could make out the details of the wall in front of him. The antlings streaming by were but shapes in the mist. Several bumped him as they passed. One touched him with its antennae, but the ice of Zen's form would give his body no scent by which the antling could identify him as prey.

Zen climbed, hesitantly at first, but the movements seemed natural in his antling form. His appendages gripped the rock easily. Within moments, he reached the apex of the tunnel through which he and his friends had entered the warlord's lair, and walked along its ceiling until the mist dissipated.

Just beyond the next intersection, he found a cubbyhole in the cave wall, about twenty feet off the floor. He crawled into it and dropped his antling form.

With his staff, he sealed the cubby's entrance with ice to mask his scent from the antlings for as long as possible, releasing the barrier only when his air grew stale.

Though he remained trapped in the catacombs, his friends had likely gotten free. And he now knew the way out.

If he was lucky, the antlings would return to their mounds and seek nourishment from Balor's guards. As for the warlord...

Zen crept back to the warlord's cavern after what must have been a whole day of waiting, during which Zen had slept—apparently too tired for even his nightmares to wake him—and regained a measure of his endurance with the weave. The giant antling was still there, curled up as it had been before.

Zen's heart pounded. He fought to keep his breathing slow and quiet. This time he was prepared. He was well rested, and he knew the warlord's tricks.

The warlord was probably no more asleep now than it had been the first time Zen and his friends tried to creep through its lair. It was likely just baiting its trap.

Zen took a deep breath. *So be it.*

With a brief, whispered chant and a thrust of his staff, he erected an ice dome around the creature. It rose instantly, a huge shape behind the ice, shrieked, and threw itself against the barrier. The ice cracked. Zen reinforced the wall with another wall, then another, as he eased past the lava to the boulder-jammed exit. He squeezed through the opening, scattered the blood flies with a blast of cold air, and sprinted into the sunlight.

Once he'd made it beyond the field of antling mounds, he stopped for several minutes, sucking in lungfuls of the arctic air with his hands on his knees.

Nick had never discussed any destination beyond the catacombs, maybe because it had seemed unlikely they'd ever make it out. Which direction, then, should Zen go?

With nothing to go on, he started south, away from the nearest port towns where Balor would likely concentrate his search.

At dusk, he contacted Gwyndarren.

R ancid pulled his cloak tightly around himself as he led the others up into the minor mountain range that lay between them and Tradestar. The peaks rose only a few thousand feet above the plains but sat far enough north to remain snow-capped. There appeared to be at least half a dozen passes, but Balor would have them all watched. Instead, Rancid left the trails and braved the rugged highlands, where the trees and contours would conceal their ascent from search parties on the plains below.

At noon, Nick stopped them in a small glade to rest.

Jasmine scoured the clearing and surrounding woods for medicinal herbs, from which she made both teas to flush the venom from their systems and salves to sooth the welts on their skin. "You haven't been using your left arm," she said to Rancid. "Is it injured?"

Rancid shrugged the cloak off his shoulder and exposed the scar from a crossbow bolt with which the Black Hand had shot him in Palidor. "It's an old wound now." He dug a loop of cloth from his backpack, settled it around his neck, and pulled his bad arm through it, fabricating a sling, and then pulled his shirt on over it to keep it out of the way.

"Wait." Jasmine scooped some bitter-smelling paste from a bowl. "Let me put this on your welts. It will ease the pain."

"Suit yourself," Rancid said. Her own skin wasn't enflamed at all, except where the antlings had bitten her legs. "How come the blood flies left you alone?"

She shrugged. "Maybe they don't care for demon blood."

Otto turned his head their way.

Rancid glanced at him, then back at Jasmine. "Best keep your voice down."

Jasmine didn't look up from her work. "You asked. And if we're to trust him, we shouldn't keep it from him. The many differences in my anatomy are obvious enough."

Rancid grumbled, snatched his arm from her grasp, and stepped away.

Nick approached them. "Speaking of trust, I think it's time you told us how you came to be in Trondor."

"Does it matter? I saved you from Balor's dungeon, and from execution. What more do you need to know?"

"Much." Jasmine squatted, elbows resting on her knees. "Are we to believe you've given up your vendetta against the Black Hand and have suddenly decided to believe the Prophecy?"

Rancid nodded but said nothing.

"Does it have anything to do with whatever happened to your arm?" Jasmine asked.

Rancid just glared at her.

"Look," Nick said, "if you expect us to follow you through these hills, you have to come clean. We can't afford another detour like the one you took us on in Palidor."

"Fine." Rancid's attempt to lead Nick and his friends, unaware, into a confrontation with the Black Hand had earned him this interrogation, he supposed. "You might want to sit down. It's a long story."

Nick waved Otto and Xanth to opposite corners of the clearing to keep watch. Then he and Jasmine settled in beside Rancid.

"Remember Sorowyn?" Rancid began.

"You've mentioned him," Nick said. "A lieutenant to the Black Hand leader. He gave you that scar on your face."

"He also gave me this." Rancid pointed to the wound that had cost him the use of his left arm. "Or rather, Jade did when she and Sorowyn ambushed me. Anyway, I later discovered a party of orcs that Sorowyn had smuggled into the kingdom and tracked them to the Black Hand hideout."

"The one in Forlorn Valley?" Jasmine asked.

Rancid nodded. "We weren't far from it when Zen pulled us off track."

"You mean, when Zen put us back on track," Jasmine said. "Your Black Hand vendetta is yours alone. We have no interest in it."

"Then what happened?" Nick asked.

Rancid described how he'd crept into the entrance of the hideout and peered through a crack in a door, into some sort of audience hall with walls and floor of cut stone. One bandit had stood in a relaxed posture near the back wall, while an orc shuffled nervously in the center of the room.

"...have found Book of Mortaan," a deep, gruff voice had said.

"The *original* Codex of Mortaan?" a human replied.

"Chosen think so, or he not take from farm boy and demon monk after they found it in library."

"Demon monk" could have referred only to Jasmine. Apparently his friends had located the book they'd been looking for. Rancid had nudged the door open a few more inches, far enough to see both speakers. The guttural voice emanated from an enormous green-gray mass of goblinoid flesh, larger than any being Rancid had ever seen— an ogre—with a Medallion of Vexetan around its neck.

"Good," said the human, whom Rancid had come to believe was the Black Hand leader—a bald man wearing a clean silk tunic over a fine linen shirt. "Perhaps now you'll release my brotherhood from your service."

"Soon," the ogre said. "When Chosen be king, he kill farm boy and demon monk, send book to Master. Then you done."

Rancid glanced around the clearing. The salve Jasmine had applied to his blood-fly bites had cut down on the itching, but he wasn't about to admit that to her. "The ogre described everything that had happened here in Trondor," Rancid told Nick, "including how long it would take Balor to assume the throne. I don't know how he knew, but the details were too specific, the evidence too clear, to ignore.

"When I realized I had time to reach Trondor before your anticipated execution, I decided to steal a horse and come for you. I stole several, in fact, and more along the way to keep from running them to death. But the road was good and the weather tolerable. I made it here in just over two weeks." He shrugged. "The bandits will still be there when I get back. I'll have opportunities later to put Sorowyn's head on a spike."

Late the next morning, Zen, in the form of an ice snake, watched Gwyndarren from beneath the leaves of a skunk cabbage for at least thirty minutes to make sure the elf had come alone. Gwyndarren, somewhat aged by elven norms but not yet old, appeared frail with his slight frame draped in a worn gray travelling cloak. Yet Gwyndarren was anything but powerless.

The formidable elf carried only a lightweight day pack. Apparently he planned to return to the city, only a couple hours' ride away.

Zen slithered from beneath the cabbage, behind a spruce tree, and returned to his elf-kin form. Finally, he stepped from his concealment.

Gwyndarren dismounted as Zen approached. "Well met, my friend."

"'Well met,' my backside. You knew about Vinra."

Gwyndarren held up both hands defensively. "True, his real name was Vinsous Drakemoor, and he was a first-rate assassin, but I assure you, I'd never heard of him before I arrived here in Trondor, which was just about the time you and your friends actually found the Codex."

Zen planted the butt of his staff on the ground, ready to speak the words that would send a blast of frozen air into the elf. "No. You set us up."

"Your own quest did that." Gwyndarren's manner softened. "I'm sorry some of your friends were killed, but I spare no grief for Drakemoor."

"And yet you paid me not to fight him. Why?"

"I paid you not to fight any of the Chosen. I couldn't have known he was one of them. I did know that either Gremauld or Balor was a Chosen, though I hadn't yet determined which. Either way, he'd have an army behind him." Gwyndarren opened his hands in a placating gesture. "The rest was simple economics. I knew that when you found the original Codex, the Chosen would take it. But you and me...our business relationship has been lucrative. I didn't want to lose it."

"As a dealer in magic, you've gained nothing from me. So how has our relationship benefited you?"

Gwyndarren's eyes widened. "I'm not a magic dealer. I peddle information. Your price is magic, so I acquire the enchantments I need in order to pay you."

"It got *me* a prison cell and a promise of execution." Zen had tried to open the lock on his cell the way he'd once opened his mentor's office back in Cedar Falls—by conjuring a key of ice—but the dwarven-made lock was too complex to be so easily picked. "If I'd have fought alongside my friends, we might have won free."

"Balor knew you were there, and he knew you'd find the Codex. You never would have made it out of the palace. As for your execution, I'd already arranged for your release. I told Balor that you had agreed to stay out of the fight. Witnesses in the library confirmed that you kept your word. He was going to pardon you as soon as he became king. If you had joined the fight, you'd still be slated for beheading."

Zen glared at him, processing this new information, trying to discern if it contained any truth at all.

"Furthermore," Gwyndarren continued, "Balor throws a pretty tight net. I can help you escape if I know where you're going."

Zen knew he ought to kill Gwyndarren now and take any enchanted items the elf had proven foolish enough to carry, but he couldn't. He needed Gwyndarren's help, though not to escape the kingdom. Zen could turn into an ice hawk and simply fly away, if he had a mind to. "I don't know where my friends are going. We hadn't discussed anything beyond the catacombs, and now we've become separated. I thought you might offer me some way to locate them."

"I have no enchantments that can help you, but as always, I have information to trade."

Zen eyed him warily. "Let's hear it."

"Your friends were scryed yesterday traveling west toward Tradestar. Dalen Frost, captain of the Home Guard, is on his way there to intercept them."

"And your price?"

Gwyndarren handed Zen a piece of parchment. "By my count, you've used all your scrolls. When you find out what Nicklan Mirrin is planning, contact me. In the meantime, I'll see what I can do to help you all escape the kingdom."

Zen stuffed the scroll into a pocket inside his threadbare robes. If he did find his friends, he would have to tell Gwyndarren something. He didn't want to get on the bad side of such a lucrative supplier or make an enemy of someone with the resources Gwyndarren seemed to have.

Zen could decide later how much to reveal. "I'll need a horse to catch up. And the only wealth I have is a bottle of the king's wine."

"Say no more. I'll give you my horse for it and walk back to the city. But be warned, Balor has circulated your descriptions throughout the kingdom. You'll need to change your cloak and conceal your staff and headband before you enter Tradestar."

It was impossible to tell where the city of Tradestar began. The farmhouses gradually thickened and the plots became smaller. Shops and houses sprouted among the farms and ranches, growing denser by strides as Zen continued west. The sounds of horse hooves and wagons, and the smell of garbage and excrement, increased with the density of the population. Before long, he found himself threading his way through the crowds, wrapped in a weaving of subterfuge: hair and a mustache woven of snow mixed with soot, a long ponytail, bushy brows, and Gwyndarren's old, gray travelling cloak. He had shaved his natural beard.

Parchment signs adorned the front of an increasing number of businesses. REWARD, they said. 10,000 GOLD COINS...

Zen rode his horse onto the boardwalk, keeping an eye out for any nearby guards, and ripped one of the posters from its anchor so he could read the smaller print.

...FOR THE CAPTURE OR DEATH OF THESE FUGITIVES.

Nicklan Mirrin topped the list, drawing half the total reward. A HUMAN MALE, STANDS 6 FEET TALL, MUSCULAR BUILD, BROAD SHOULDERS, 220 POUNDS, BLOND HAIR (SOMETIMES SHAVED TO THE SCALP)... Nick's description went on, even listing the great sword he favored.

The poster described the others too, including Jasmine's triangular face, pink eyes, hairless pate, and other demonic features, as well as her typical means of concealing them; Otto's muscular build, thick black gray-streaked hair, eyes as black as polished onyx, and three-clawed scar down the length of his right upper arm; Xanth's spare frame and wispy gray hair and the beard that hung to his waist.

Zen was there too. He swallowed hard. Though he didn't consider himself religious, he thanked the gods for small enchantments and huge favors. Ten thousand gold coins...could Balor offer that much for their capture after having funded a rebellion? He could if he expected to gain the king's coffers come coronation day.

"What's the date?" Zen asked a nearby man who wore a linen shirt, black wool jacket and scarf, and carried a fine rapier on his belt—likely a successful local merchant.

The man hurried by with a glance full of disdain.

Zen dismounted and, still holding the reins of his gelding, intercepted another passerby, this one an elf-kin by the look of him. "What's today's date?"

The elf-kin eyed him warily.

"I've been patrolling the mountain passes for at least a week and have lost track of the days." Zen pulled his cloak open to reveal a bit of Rancid's Trondorian guard uniform. "I haven't got all day."

"Th— the twenty-ninth." The elf-kin stepped past him and hurried away.

Zen counted on his fingers. Balor's confirmation by the Council was a foregone conclusion, and only nine days remained until the coronation.

After that, Balor would no longer need to request resources from the Council in order to pursue them—the resources would all become his.

Zen stuffed the parchment into a saddlebag, mounted, and returned to the street. At every corner, someone seemed to be searching the crowd. Many wore the uniform of the Tradestar city guard. Those who didn't were probably mercenaries hoping to get lucky.

Without horses, Zen's friends were probably still on their way. He'd have to find some way to warn them of the posters and the vigilant population. But right now, he had more pressing matters to which to attend.

Zen rode down the street, through the now-abandoned gate into the old city, which had outgrown its original wall centuries before. He made his way to the docks, where a brisk salt wind was blowing in off the sea. Trondorian soldiers were stationed at the head of every pier. No one was boarding even the smallest canoe without being thoroughly questioned. Crates of cargo were pried open and the contents searched. Signs posted next to the reward posters promised a swift execution to anyone caught smuggling the fugitives or helping them to gain passage. The palace scribes must have worked night and day to have penned so many posters.

One thing was clear. Zen's friends would never make it aboard a ship in Tradestar. And though Zen might accomplish it alone, he'd last only as long as he could maintain his disguise.

So, with a last look down the row of piers, he rode from the port.

He didn't leave town right away. Instead, he combed the streets, asking questions of the citizens and city guardsmen. Within an hour, he was sure Nick and the others hadn't yet arrived.

"You there." The voice carried the confidence of a man in charge. Zen turned.

Dalen Frost, now wearing the uniform of a captain in the Trondorian Home Guard, brought his thoroughbred up short, inches from Zen's mount. The man's light brown hair had grown nearly to his shoulders. "By the brand, that horse belongs to the king's guard. Where did you get it?"

Zen unhooked the clasp at his neck and shrugged his travelling cloak from his shoulders, thankful his disguise was more than one layer thick.

A look of disgust crossed Dalen's face. "You will show that uniform respect and display it properly."

"I— I'm sorry, sir." Zen's voice wavered of its own accord. "I just came in from patrolling the passes. The air's wet up there, and the temperature cold. I failed to pack suitably and feared I'd freeze to death."

"What's your name?"

"Um...Dukart, sir."

"When you return to the palace, Dukart, you'll report this transgression to your commanding offer and request to be demoted to hostler until that gelding of yours is retired."

Zen straightened in his saddle. "Yes, sir. Thank you, sir."

"In the meantime," Dalen continued, "I'll take your report."

"Very good, sir," Zen said. "All the passes are guarded as ordered." Surely such an order had been issued. "No sign of the fugitives. The temperature drops below freezing at night. If they attempt a crossing without proper gear—"

"You underestimate them."

"Forgive me, sir, for being bold." Zen took a deep breath. "Perhaps they turned south and headed for the border."

"No." Dalen clasped an object that hung beneath his tunic—his

Medallion of Vexetan, which the Master's Chosen used to communicate with each other and with the Master. He continued to address Zen. "The sighting showed them moving west. They're coming here, or to the guild house of the old stargazer. Either way, we're ready for them."

CHAPTER 7

As Ka-G'zzin crossed the sanctuary, his bony claws clicking on the stone floor, Ryanna gave the demon room. The quest for the Guardian of the Abyss had been successful. Ryanna knew that much from reports she'd received through her Medallion, but success had apparently come at a cost. The demon, the most fearsome of any she'd ever called through the veil, dangled a stump where one of its pincers had been. She didn't dare smile about that fact in the demon's presence. Nevertheless, she experienced a sense of poetic justice, given what the demon had done to her those many years before.

Ka-G'zzin's huge, crablike body seemed to collapse upon itself as it squeezed into the tight corridor that led to Addicus' study. The air apparition, Whisper, stirred up dust behind it.

Claustrophobia, and something worse, closed in on Ryanna. She clutched her robes tightly around her body, took a deep, settling breath, and forced herself to follow.

Inside, the giant demon unfolded itself and then slammed a ten-inch-tall statue onto the desk.

Addicus' eyes widened and his face broke into a broad grin. He picked up the statue, that of an elven warrior holding an intricately engraved shield, as though it was the tiniest of babies. "The Guardian." He breathed a sigh as he set it down. "Another piece on the game board. And when Vornax returns, we'll have yet another."

The statue was not of gold as Ryanna had expected, but of bronze. Dings and scratches marred its tarnished surface. "Wait a minute..." Her fingers flashed in the air, drawing the weave to her and then wrapping its strands around the statue as she sought to sense its energy. It had none, save a residual warmth from the sun.

"What?" Addicus asked.

She dismissed the object in disgust. "It's a fake."

Ka-G'zzin uttered a low sound—part growl, part wail.

Ryanna backed away with a defensive weaving ready. "I sense no aura of enchantment."

Addicus considered her for a moment. Finally a snicker, and then outright laughter, escaped his lips.

Ka-G'zzin's head snapped from one to the other and back. Its remaining pincer clicked rapidly.

Ryanna glared at Addicus. Blood warmed her face.

It took a long minute for the old man to regain control. "The Portal of the Damned has two locks: one physical, one magical."

Ryanna's jaw tightened.

"You of all people should know that enchantments will hold a demon, let alone the hordes of the Abyss, for only so long."

A chill crawled down Ryanna's spine. She glanced at Ka-G'zzin and her gut knotted further. "But—"

"I discovered how to dispel the enchanted barrier years ago, but the physical lock is the most sophisticated machine ever devised by the civilized races. And though the Portal is enhanced by the weave, the part of the lock on this side of the veil is mechanical. The demons have been pounding away at it for three thousand years—"

Ka-G'zzin pressed forward, toward the old scholar.

"—But no more. This key—" Addicus gestured toward the Guardian— "is all we need to open it. We'll soon set all the demons free."

No words formed in Ryanna's brain from the sounds emitted by the demon as it spoke to the old seer.

"I don't know," Addicus said finally. "Nicklan Mirrin still has a piece to set on the board in this complex game we're playing, but I can't divine its nature." He paused. "And we've yet to place all of ours. We must wait for Vornax to return."

"In the meantime," Ryanna said, "why don't we capture one of Nick's pieces? The Demonbane sword isn't far from here."

Addicus shook his head. "There's no time. Vornax will be here soon. We must prepare."

It took three days to reach the more fertile and populated western side of the mountain range. Once there, Rancid stuck to the foothills, which eventually led the party, late in the afternoon on their sixth day out of the catacombs, to the base of Sorcerers' Peak. Someone had set up a large camp there, possibly mercenaries, if they'd guessed the fugitives' destination.

"Wait here." Rancid crept close to survey the site.

The camp was large enough to accommodate at least ten families, and there seemed to be no shortage of camping supplies, cooking implements, picks, shovels, and wash barrels. Heavy carts with large draft horses abounded.

No, these weren't mercenaries. This camp was more permanent than a mercenary camp would be. It had been here for some time. And there were families. Women tended to cooking and sewing while several small children played nearby. One elderly man ducked out of a tent, but of able-bodied men, Rancid saw none. They must have been nearby...somewhere.

Rancid withdrew quickly, looking over his shoulder often and scanning the brush for sentries or patrols.

When he returned to the others, he described the place. "They won't leave a camp like this undefended for long."

"We'll give them a wide berth." Nick turned to Xanth. "Which way?"

The guild house is at the summit of Sorcerers' Peak. The only route to the top is a trail that zigzags up the northern face from Tradestar."

"The trail will be watched," Rancid insisted.

Nick scanned the rugged mountain. Any other route would present a treacherous climb up a steep slope. "Maybe not. Xanth was imprisoned three kings ago. It's doubtful anyone now will remember his association with the old guild."

Xanth shook his head. "We can't count on that."

"Either way," Otto said, "Balor will have posted somebody on the trail."

Rancid led them north nonetheless, hoping to find an alternate route the old man might be able to manage. By dusk, he'd seen only a cave about forty feet up the mountain's east side, perched at the top of a slope of loose shale. At least the cave would provide shelter for the night.

Rancid made the climb behind Jasmine, his feet and good hand digging into the fine, shifting rock. The hole, when they reached it, stretched less than a hundred feet into the mountainside. It would keep the party out of sight. They dropped a rope to help Xanth up to the opening. Nick and Otto followed.

"I'll scout the summit," Rancid told the others as they settled inside.

"Now?" Xanth asked. "You'll never make it before full dark."

"We need to know if the guild house is guarded before we go bumbling up to the front door in broad daylight." Without waiting for a response, he slipped from the cave and began to clamber up the hillside. The shale had stopped at the cave entrance, and the climbing, though strenuous, proved manageable. Further up, the slope tapered and he made good time to the summit.

The peak wasn't tall, as mountains went, but broad, and high enough to have provided a commanding view of the landscape for miles around during daylight hours. Scrub spruce and other arctic trees near the top grew no taller than a two-story inn. Smaller foliage grew densely enough for Rancid to approach.

A sliver of moon gave him scant light to see beyond a few feet, but he could discern the outline of the guild house. The vine-covered wall seemed intact and stood twenty feet high. Beyond, a dark silhouette revealed a broad, two-story structure with a dome-topped tower near its center. The keep loomed dark and silent.

Rancid worked his way around to the front gates, which were framed by a pair of small guard towers and revealed nothing of the grounds beyond.

Something moved on the wall.

Rancid froze.

The stars near the horizon winked out and back, one at a time, in sequence. He focused his sharp elf-kin eyes on the phenomenon and waited. As the night progressed, the moon became more full, and he could eventually make out a humanoid form pacing the battlement against the charcoal gray of the night sky.

He waited for another hour and then returned to the cave. "The keep is guarded."

"I'm not surprised," Xanth said. "The Council knows the guild had power in its day and that I escaped with you. They're expecting us." He laid a frail hand on Nick's shoulder. "I'm sorry."

Nick looked from Xanth to Rancid, then from the cave opening to Jasmine. "We have to get in there."

"I know," whispered the old man. "I'm sorry."

Otto, propped up on one elbow beside his gear, thrust his chin at Rancid. "We'll need details. Numbers of guards. Positions. Affiliations, whether Trondorian soldiers, Tradestar city guard, mercenaries, or otherwise. Patrol patterns, watch schedule, weapons and armor, whatever you can determine. If they have horses, we need to know that too."

Rancid nodded. "I can't get close enough to make them out in this darkness, but I can bury myself in the weeds and observe through the day."

Nick, who'd been on watch when Rancid had returned, walked back to the cave entrance. "You'd better hurry. It'll be light soon."

Rancid grabbed a fresh water skin and a small sack of raspberries Jasmine had collected along their path earlier that day. "Stay put. Don't get into trouble while I'm gone."

Jasmine smiled. "Look who's talking."

The next morning, eastern sunlight revealed tool marks along the interior walls of the cave. There were no obvious signs of recent occupancy, but the sounds of movement and whispered voices drifted in from outside.

Jasmine peered around the edge of the cave entrance without stepping from the shadows.

A dozen men had surrounded the base of the scree slope, all armored in leather. Most wielded rusty mining picks. The rest, shovels. "You there!" yelled a monster of a man.

"We've got company," Jasmine said in a low voice to the others. She pulled her hood over her features in a move she hoped would seem casual.

"You're trespassing on the property of the Minotaur Mining Company," the man continued.

Jasmine kept her face averted. "I am sorry, kind sir. We didn't know. We shall leave at once."

"Not so fast," the man yelled up. "You stayed in our mine. Seems like you owe us something for our...um, hospitality."

The other men murmured their general agreement. One, to Jasmine's right, failed to suppress a snicker.

"What do you consider fair?" Jasmine asked.

"That depends. How many of you are there?"

She glanced into the mine. Rancid hadn't returned. "Four."

"Twelve gold coins, then."

More than the whole party would have paid at a high-rent inn. More, in fact, than they had among them. Extortion, even. Jasmine would have been inclined to challenge them on the price, but they couldn't afford to be recognized. "Very well. Just a moment." She retrieved a bottle from her backpack.

Nick and Otto remained out of sight, weapons in hand and ready for trouble. Xanth waited behind them, near the packs and supplies.

"Careful," Otto mouthed to Jasmine. He handed Xanth a dagger. "Just in case."

She returned to the entrance with Nick at her side. "We can offer you this bottle of wine." She read the label. "It's a Nedermeyer, an expensive brand from the vineyards of Meuribar."

Some of the men grinned and nodded, but the leader scowled. "Let me see it."

Jasmine edged into the sunlight, keeping her head down to shade her features. But she couldn't conceal the hand that held the bottle. Maybe the men were too far away to notice the details of her clawed digits. She placed the wine on the edge of the slope and backed away.

Another man, with a trimmed beard and unwashed face, ran to the leader and spoke in low tones, pointing up at Jasmine and Nick.

The big man frowned. "Bring it down here. I want to see what you offer."

Nick stepped up beside Jasmine. "We'll leave it and be on our way. It's worth far more than the price you've asked."

At that, the leader thrust his chin toward Tradestar, only half a day's hike to the north. The man beside him dropped his pickax and took off running in the direction of town.

"Oh, bugger," Jasmine muttered.

"We've been made," Otto said from behind her.

Jasmine sprinted across the small plateau that topped the treacherous slope of mining waste, toward a narrow ledge on her left. A nearly vertical wall of solid rock separated the ledge from the ground forty feet below. As she rounded the lip of the cave entrance, two more miners, poised on the shelf, barred her way. One drew a small pick from a brace on his belt.

Undeterred, Jasmine leapt from the ledge. She landed, nimble as a tiger, and sprinted after the runner.

"Holy Vexetan!" The man launched the pick at her from the ledge, but she batted it aside.

A miner on the ground sprinted to intercept her.

Nick stepped to the lip of the slope, his stomach tightening. Simple miners—a dozen or more—hoping for bounty, no doubt.

As he drew his sword, the shale gave way beneath Nick's feet. He fought for balance, then for a handhold, but the rock was too loose. He tumbled down the hill, all the way to the bottom.

The miners cheered and rushed forward.

Bruised and battered, Nick struggled to stand until the back of a shovel clipped the side of his head. Then the ground seemed to slam up into him.

He rolled onto his back. The morning sun stung his eyes. His mind swam in a haze. The murky forms of four miners loomed over him. Others waited behind.

More ran past and scrambled up the slope toward Otto.

Nick lashed out at the closest miner, kicking him in the knee.

A heavy pickax swept his leg aside. Nick's sword remained in his hand, but these men were not his enemy. He had no quarrel with them.

He blocked a blurry shovel with his left arm and the limb went numb from the elbow down. His legs thrashed wildly to keep the miners at bay and the men battered at them mercilessly. A dull pick-ax ripped his pants and tore a chunk of skin from his thigh.

With a yell, he swept his sword in an arc above him, knocking the picks and shovels away. The men retreated a step, and Nick wrenched himself to his feet, his footing uncertain on the loose shale. He rushed two of the men before him, and they backed away.

Nick limped to firmer ground. His vision faded in and out to the rhythm of his pounding skull. His body ached, blood ran freely down his leg, which threatened to give out at any moment, and the men had him surrounded.

Desperate to finish the battle before his consciousness failed, he put all of his strength behind his sword. Too many people had died for Nick's quest—Beltrann, Dara, and probably Zen as well—for him to give it up now.

These were no legal miners. They were extortionists. At least one had sworn an oath to Vexetan. Nick's sword ripped through the bowels of one man and sank into the chest of another. Both men crumpled to the ground, the latter clutching at the rip as though his hands alone could somehow hold the blood that poured from him.

The rest took a step back but raised their weapons in challenge. Two more filled the gap left by the fallen men. *So be it.* Nick would do whatever he must to preserve himself and his quest for the sake of the Civilized Lands.

Otto walked out onto the plateau to challenge the men scrambling up the hill. When he spotted a pair approaching along the shelf to his left, he retreated into the mouth of the cave, where the walls would limit the number of men who could come at him at one time.

The picks the men wielded were designed to be tools, not weapons, but the miners swung them with strong and practiced arms. He battered the first swing aside, then lunged at the lead miner and buried his ax in the man's chest. Otto braced his foot on the man's leather breastplate, yanked his ax free, and shoved the body back down the slope. After taking a glancing blow from a pickax, he sliced the arm of its wielder clean off at the elbow.

The miner screamed and stumbled down behind his dead friend.

A fifth man topped the hill. Still another came at Otto from his right. There were too many now. One man slipped past into the cave and turned to strike him from behind. Otto could spare him little attention, but then the man simply sank, with a grunt, to the ground.

Xanth stood over him, gripping a bloody dagger. He stepped up beside Otto as if to stand with him against the attackers.

One of the miners sneered and struck at the old man. Otto deflected the blow slightly, but it still slammed Xanth into the wall. The old man crumpled, bleeding from the side of his face.

Otto shouted a battle cry and rushed forward. His ax swept wildly. Two of the miners died instantly. The remaining miner retreated down the rocky slope.

Jasmine had returned to join Nick against the men at the base of the hill. Within minutes, eight miners lay dead. The rest ran off in the direction of the camp Rancid had scouted the previous evening.

"Jasmine!" Otto beckoned to her and then rushed to Xanth's side.

Vornax strode across the floor of the huge underground cavern, his body fit—not large for a human, but toned enough to warrant the pride he took in it. The gold-stitched hem of his black robe brushed the ground at the edge of a lightless chasm that dropped away to his left. The place was a furnace, twice as hot as the mid-summer highs in the Great Sand. Sweat poured from him in rivulets, each drop hissing on the floor and evaporating instantly. But the heat didn't matter. His god protected him.

A heavy grating sound emanated from beyond a bend up ahead. The floor vibrated in cadence with the sound. Vornax shrugged out of his backpack, leaned it against the wall, and quickened his pace.

When he rounded the curve, he faced the great beast he had sought: a huge black dragon with red scales on its underside that spanned from the tip of its tail, across its belly, and up its long neck to the point of its horned chin. The dragon lay, feet in the air, wearing an oddly satisfied grin. It swung its shoulders and hips from side to side to rub its back on the stone of the floor. A rumble escaped its throat.

When the torchlight reached the dragon's face, a single lid slid back to reveal a yellow eye, the pupil a vertical black stripe through the iris. The dragon rolled to its feet, the movement of the ground almost toppling Vornax.

The natural aura of terror that the mere presence of any dragon created in the hearts of all creatures thrummed in waves and threatened to overwhelm Vornax. Even he, the legendary Master of the Prophecy, protected as he was by Vexetan himself, had to force his feet forward one step at a time.

Without the dragon uttering a sound, its thoughts boomed in Vornax's mind. *Who dares enter?*

Vornax stood fast. He had nothing to fear. "My name is not important. I am a mere mortal in the presence of one who has lived for three-and-a-half thousand years."

The dragon roared, and the cavern trembled. *Tell me, mere morsel, why have you come? I've not tasted the flesh of man in eons.*

"What is your name, dragon?"

The dragon breathed a fountain of flame that engulfed the length and breadth of the chamber. Vornax stood amidst the conflagration, his knees locked and his teeth gritted against the searing pain that ripped through him. His robe and torch burned to ash and his skin boiled off his body. A test from Vexetan of his faith and determination.

When the onslaught subsided, Vexetan began to restore Vornax's flesh. It oozed out of his exposed muscles and recoated his body. As it did, the hot, searing agony subsided. Within minutes, he was whole once more. His long black hair once again draped his shoulders. He shook off the queasy sensation that always accompanied Vexetan's healing touch and flexed his hands into fists to test the supple new skin. Only the red-hot glow from the rocks around him lit the cave. Wary now, the dragon drew back its head.

Vornax said again, "Tell me your name."

Why should I?

Vornax stood his ground. Naked now, but completely healed. The aura of terror that accompanied the dragon's presence had receded to nothing more than a dim thought at the back of his mind. "Because I wish it."

The dragon wagged its head, as through trying to shake off the grogginess of a centuries-long nap.

L'Nordian. The dragon's eyes widened. *My name is L'Nordian.*

Vornax smiled. He couldn't remember a day when he hadn't gotten whatever he wanted simply by asking—provided that his request furthered the will of his great god. "Well then, L'Nordian, I have come to offer you a gift." Vornax held in his palm an onyx medallion with a solid gold border, inscribed with the holy runes of Vexetan.

L'Nordian extended its neck. Its head, twice the size of a man's body, came within inches of Vornax's hand. The dragon sniffed the offering. *I have no need of your gift.*

"Yet, you will don it of your own free will." Vexetan would not have brought him here, to this particular dragon, if it wouldn't accept the Medallion.

L'Nordian roared again.

When the grating cry subsided, Vornax listened for the sounds of the dragon's brethren, but the cavern had gone silent. "The time has come for you and your kind to once again fly the skies of the Civilized Lands."

L'Nordian's head dropped to within inches of the floor, little more than an arm's length in front of Vornax. With a snort, it choked the air with hot, sulfurous smoke, but it withheld its fiery breath.

Vornax coughed. His eyes and nostrils burned.

I remember, L'Nordian said in Vornax's mind, *the treatment we received at the hands of men. It drove us into exile.*

"With your help, I'll subdue the civilized races. Then they'll bother you no more."

But only if I accept your "gift?" L'Nordian spat the last word as though it left a foul taste in its mind.

"My gift is your freedom, and freedom for all your kind, from the depths of Spitfire Mountain."

And what, mere morsel, of this bobble you carry?

Vornax again extended the Medallion. "This is the price of your freedom. It will place you under my complete control, but only for a short time."

That time L'Nordian's scream carried the pain of three millennia of hiding. Its nostrils flared and fire scorched the ceiling. It thrashed its head, hurling giant bits of broken stalactites from one end of the cavern to the other.

Vornax held his ground.

Very well, L'Nordian said, finally. *I accept your bargain for the sake of my kin.* With its head bent low, it allowed Vornax to slip the long gold chain around its neck.

Warmth emanated from the matching emblem on Vornax's headband as Vexetan forged the telepathic link between the Medallion and Vornax's newest Chosen.

Speak your will, my Master, L'Nordian intoned, *and I shall see it done.*

CHAPTER 8

ick and his friends gathered the miners' bodies and stowed them in the cave. His head still pounded from the hit he'd taken. "What a waste."

Otto stripped them of usable supplies and enough pieces of leather armor to assemble a set that would fit Nick, in order to replace the platemail he'd left behind at the exit from the catacombs. "It was necessary. They'd have killed us, or detained us until Balor's soldiers arrived. Either way, it came down to us or them."

Nick gave him a long, disgusted glare. "Violence begets violence. A year ago, I would never have done something like this, no matter who started it."

"We live in darker times than we did a year ago. We all do what we must."

Of the miners who hadn't fled, one remained alive. Jasmine had bound his hands behind his back and tied his ankles together.

"How did you know we were here?" Nick asked him.

The survivor glared at him, hatred burning in his eyes. A mean lump distorted his right temple where Jasmine had knocked him out during the fight.

"We wouldn't have killed anyone if you hadn't attacked us," Nick said. "We would even have paid your exorbitant fee. We defended ourselves. Nothing more."

"You're fugitives," the miner spat. "What right do you have to kill innocent people in your own defense?"

"You don't know anything about us."

"I know you're outlaws."

So were the miners, more than likely, though the man would probably never admit it. Nick offered him a dipper of water. "We didn't want trouble. We just needed a shelter for the night."

The man ignored the cup. "The mine wasn't yours to use."

Jasmine stood. "I'm going to check out that camp we saw last night."

"No." The miner said, a little too quickly.

"Is the camp yours?" Nick asked. "The women and children?"

The man didn't reply, but Nick saw the answer in his eyes.

"Then I will leave them be," Jasmine said.

"How did you know we were here?" Nick asked the man again.

Otto drew his dagger and began cleaning his fingernails with the tip. "Don't make him ask a third time."

The man glared at him for a long moment. "We spotted somebody poking around our camp last night and followed him."

"Who else knows we're here?" Nick asked.

"Nobody. At the time, we didn't know who you were. We just wanted to collect a few extra coins." He sat up straight. "It's our mine. We've the right."

Nick rose and paced the width of the cave. Already the coppery stench of the piled dead bodies pervaded the space. Jasmine hadn't caught the miner who'd run off to Tradestar. Somebody would know soon enough that they were there. "As soon as Rancid gets back, we'll have to leave. In the meantime, we'll move farther up the hill."

Nick and Otto dragged the prisoner a few hundred yards up the slope and behind a thicket of skunk cabbage that grew nearly four feet high. They intercepted Rancid on his way down and filled him in on the fight they'd had that morning.

"That's it then." Rancid drew his dagger. "Let's kill him and get out of here."

Nick stepped between Rancid and the miner. "We've done enough killing."

"We can't take him with us, and if we leave him, he'll alert the Tradestar city guard."

"One of the miners escaped," Otto said quietly. "He'll bring them soon enough, regardless. They'll find the bodies in the mine and Balor will add these murders to our list of crimes."

"How long do you think we have?" Nick asked.

Otto shrugged. "I'm surprised they're not here already."

"Forget about the Seeking Stone and grab your gear." Rancid stowed his blade and exhumed his pack from the mound of supplies. "We'll find some other way to kill the Master." He took four steps down the hill before Nick caught up and grabbed his arm.

"There is no other way. I need a weapon that can kill him." He stared fiercely into Rancid's eyes. "The Master and his Chosen have been a step ahead of us since this thing started. This is the only move we can make that they might not have guessed."

Xanth had remained quiet throughout the exchange, but he spoke now, softly. "The road to the guild house begins at least a mile from here. It's steep, with many switchbacks. Even if the guards find the bodies and surmise our destination. It'll take several hours for them to reach the summit on horseback."

Nick didn't reach for his gear, but asked Rancid, "If we make it to the guild house, can we get inside?"

Rancid checked the bonds on the prisoner and then led the others far enough away to prevent the prisoner from overhearing if they kept their voices low. "We'll have to do it tonight. Then, stone or no stone, we leave Trondor."

"Agreed," Nick said.

"Okay. Six men atop a wall that surrounds the guild house grounds. And at least two more in the guard towers at the gate. Some wear the uniform of the king's Home Guard, others have a gold and red emblem, a ship with a star on the mainsail."

"Tradestar city guard," Otto supplied.

"Others have no uniform at all," Rancid continued, "probably mercenaries, come out of the woodwork for the reward. We can slip past if we're quiet. Vines on the walls will make them easy to climb, but the keep itself is probably occupied."

Xanth sat forward. "I doubt it. Many feared the guild. Superstitions ran high that a bad fate awaited those who entered unwelcome." He gave them a sheepish grin. "We did what we could to promote that suspicion so people would leave us alone."

"Apparently it didn't work," Otto said. "And even if the guards have stayed outside, there are thieves brave enough to loot it."

"Where did you keep the Seeking Stone?" Jasmine asked.

"In a strongbox, on the fourth floor of the tower, behind a locked door."

Rancid grunted. "Locks can be picked."

"Not this one. It's a celestial lock."

"A celestial lock?" Nick asked.

Xanth waved a hand in an arc across the darkening sky. "Look at the stars."

Nick did.

"The vast majority move through the sky together, but eight of them, the wanderers, each travel the heavens on its own, independent journey."

Nick shook his head. "What are you talking about?"

"The celestial lock is enchanted," Xanth continued. "The only thing in the whole of the guild house that is. We used to reset the combination daily based on the position and movements of the eight wandering stars."

"But you've been absent for thirty harvests," Rancid said. "Plenty of time for a thief to guess the sequence."

"The lock will accept only six guesses a day. After the sixth incorrect guess, it can't be opened by any means for twenty-four hours."

Rancid frowned, but he said nothing.

Jasmine went to check on the prisoner.

"And the map you mentioned?" Nick asked.

"We had calculated the approximate location of the rock from the stars. I don't remember much, but I know it landed somewhere in the Wild Lands. The map we sketched should still be in my personal chambers."

"Then it's probably gone by now," Otto said.

"Maybe, but it had no monetary value. A thief would have no reason to steal it."

A dozen of the king's Home Guard rode into the clearing at the base of the cave, half of them carrying torches. Dalen was with them

"Time to go," Nick said.

It took Jasmine and the others a couple of hours to climb the hill in the waxing moonlight. At the top, Rancid led them across a forested plateau to the Sorcerers' guild house.

They waited a few minutes for the shadowy figure of the guard to pass. Then Jasmine and Rancid crept forward. If they could incapacitate the guard quietly, and if Xanth was right about people being too superstitious to enter the guild house building, the rest should be easy.

But as they approached the wall, one of the vines that covered it came to life. A branch whipped out. Jasmine threw herself to the ground and it passed just over her head.

Rancid grabbed her arm and yanked her back to the others.

"Strangle vines," Jasmine said.

"What do you know about them?" Nick whispered.

"Carnivorous plants. Not enchanted, but mean." Jasmine bit her lip and scanned the length of the wall. "They can't go all the way around. The guards climbed the battlement somewhere."

She led them back into the shadows, and they circled around to the front of the grounds, approaching the wall twice to examine the leaves. Both times, the vines quivered, forcing her back. Finally, she located a section covered only by arctic ivy. The branches were broken and worn at least halfway up the wall. "This is where the guards have been climbing up and down."

"It figures." Nick thrust his chin in the direction of the gate-house, where more guards waited. "We're too close."

"There's another gate in the back wall," Xanth offered. "It might be accessible."

"All right," Nick said. "We'll try that."

Jasmine continued to look, unsuccessfully, for a safe place to scale the wall as they circled around the grounds. The rear gate, too, was covered in the carnivorous vines. At least the guards were more scarce there, only one along the entire length of the wall.

Nick watched him pace for a time. "Nearly five minutes between passes. Maybe we can clear the vines from the gate and spare the life of the sentry."

Otto unhooked the crossbow from his belt. "We can't clear the vines without making enough noise to alert him. Wait here." He disappeared into the shadows of some tall shrubs between the party and the gate.

Jasmine turned to Rancid. "May I borrow your rope?" As soon as he handed it to her, she measured half its length and cut it with a small knife she usually used for cooking. Rancid opened his mouth to object, but the sentry on the wall was too near for him to do so audibly. Jasmine suppressed a smile at his discomfort.

On the sentry's next pass, his head snapped to the side, and he dropped to the floor of the battlement.

A moment later, Otto returned. "Ready?"

Jasmine tied one rope each around her own waist and Rancid's. She handed the loose end of one to Nick, and the other to Otto.

As they approached the gate, the vines went wild. Jasmine, a step ahead of Rancid, ducked the first branch. A second ensnared her waist. It snaked its way toward her neck. She grabbed it with both hands and pulled to keep it from tightening around her throat. It constricted her chest and she labored to breathe.

Rancid stopped just beyond the plant's reach. The vines whipped at him. He hacked at them with his sword, shortening them as he inched closer, until none remained along the left half of the gate.

He spun then to help Jasmine, but she'd become too entangled. One bad sword stroke could kill her.

She fought against the vine, twisting and writhing, as the vegetation gradually engulfed her.

Nick released Rancid's rope and grabbed Jasmine's. He helped Otto pull against the strength of the vine.

With the branches around her neck and chest tightening, Jasmine let her mind slip into the meditative state she used for self-healing. Her heart rate and breathing slowed. This cost her some of her strength but would keep her alive for several minutes, even if she couldn't get the air she needed.

Rancid sheathed his sword and added the strength of his good arm to that of the others. As they pulled, a shudder passed through the vine and its anchors that gripped the gate gave way. It continued to entangle Jasmine, but it no longer had the leverage it needed to pull her in. Finally, its roots came up as well.

The men pulled it to the side, pried the branches from Jasmine, and dragged her into the darkness.

Jasmine took a deep breath and released it slowly. The tingling numbness that had crept into her extremities subsided. "I'm okay." She stretched out her limbs and climbed gingerly to her feet.

The party waited for several minutes to make sure the noise hadn't drawn the attention of any additional sentries before they rushed to the gate. Xanth felt along the wall for a minute, then pressed a panel that folded back on a spring-and-hinge mechanism to reveal a hidden latch.

Otto cut away the remaining foliage until the gate swung open.

Nick and the others huddled under the overhang of the battle-ment.

A murky pond that lay no more than a few strides from the gate reflected the now-waning moon in its placid surface. Darkness cloaked everything else.

"Where to?" Nick whispered.

"There's a window into the guild house, about midway along the wall. Somewhere over there." Xanth pointed.

"Wait here." Rancid drew his sword and, without waiting for a reply, vanished into the grounds.

The silence grew eerie. Ripples formed on the pond where a frog, fish, or some other small creature surfaced for a meal of insects. Despite the cool air, a bead of sweat ran down Nick's neck. A low growl reached them from somewhere in the darkness of the grounds. The sound became a chorus, then the ruckus of some immense beast crashing through the foliage.

Nick gave the others a worried look. So much for the grounds being empty, or their being able to slip into the building silently once they'd gotten past the wall. Surely the guards had heard that.

The creature yelped, like some huge dog, or perhaps a wolf. But from the sound of it, the pain only infuriated the animal. The snarls became deeper, angrier, more frenzied.

"Orc's blood," Nick muttered.

"It's no good." Otto said. "We've got to go."

"I'll get him." With a glance at the battlement, Jasmine vanished into the brush.

Farther down the wall, a guard arrived. He peered into the blackness of the grounds as though trying to determine what had disturbed the animals.

Nick clenched and unclenched his fist. He'd come this far. He wasn't leaving without the stone.

Horses' hooves suddenly pounded the cobbles outside the wall, and a shrill whistle pulled the guard's attention away.

"They're coming!" a voice shouted.

"Who?" the guard yelled back.

Nick held his breath.

"The fugitives who murdered the king. They're down the path, but I can't take them alone. I'll split the reward with anyone who helps me capture them."

A horse brayed and hoofbeats faded into the distance.

The guard on the battlement glanced once into the grounds, muttered an oath, and then sprinted away.

Nick couldn't make out Otto's expression, or Xanth's. *Someone* was coming up the trail, probably Dalen and the riders they'd spotted below the mine. Either they'd been seen or the surviving miner had gotten free of his bonds and reported on where Nick and his friends had gone. Three more guards ran by, toward the break in the strangle vines where Jasmine had said the wall could be scaled.

Nick waited to see if any more would pass. Mistaken riders on the trail at this particular moment was no coincidence. Nevertheless, this was his chance.

The snarling of the beasts had lessened in ferocity. Now they sounded as if they were scrapping between themselves over a piece of meat.

"Whatever's out there," Nick whispered to Xanth, "Otto and I will hold it off. You run for the window."

The old man's eyes grew large enough to reflect the moonlight. He nodded.

"Ready?" Nick asked Otto.

"Now or never."

Together, they sprinted toward the building.

Once-ornamental vegetation had seeded itself throughout the property, and weeds had overgrown the grounds. When Nick reached the cover of the landscape, he slowed, picking his way through the tangled footing as quietly as possible. The beasts were out there. With luck, he'd take them by surprise.

A moment later, the building loomed before him. Its pale stone surface seemed to glow in the moonlight. The dark hole of a broken window gaped more than a hundred feet to the left.

The nearest dog—if it was a dog—stood just outside the window, large as a draft horse, bristling with fur, teeth, and spittle. It peered through the gloom at Nick, with two of its kin nearby. Rancid and Jasmine must have made it inside. Nick and Otto would have to force the beasts back to have any hope of gaining the building.

The nearest beast growled, low and menacing. It bled from its shoulder but seemed not to notice.

"Arctic wolves," Otto said in a low voice.

Nick took a deep breath and nodded. He'd heard of them. Together, he and Otto charged forward, sword and ax drawn. Each cut a new wound into the wolf's hide, but it didn't slow. Its teeth tore Otto's leather armor as though it was made of lace, and tossed the big man to the ground.

Another of the wolves rushed Nick.

On the battlement, a guard appeared from farther down the wall. He stood, backlit by the stars, and thrust his hand forward as if to throw something. The wolf standing over Otto gave a startled cry and collapsed.

Otto rolled from beneath it, gathered Xanth, and practically tossed the old man through the hole where the window used to be.

Nick forced his attention back to the wolf at hand. He couldn't worry about the guard now. The man had obviously seen them. The best he could hope for was to get inside, retrieve the Seeking Stone, and get away before Dalen and his patrol arrived. First, he had to get past this wolf.

It advanced, wary of the reach of Nick's great sword, snapping at the blade rather than at its wielder. Nick drew blood twice, but his blade fell a split second farther behind with each swing, until something struck the wolf. It yelped and fled into the dark.

The third wolf, trapped nearby beneath a dome of ice, snarled and clawed at the wall of its frozen prison.

Recognizing the ice dome, Nick spun back to the guard on the battlement and scrutinized the man, trying to make out details in the darkness. "Go," he hissed at Otto.

All at once, the guard's bushy white mustache melted away to reveal a familiar face. *Zen!* A weight fell away that had been heavy on him ever since they'd left the catacombs. The ice mage shook a long bundle loose from his pack and extracted his crystal-tipped staff. Somehow he'd made it from the catacombs after all. Smiling, Nick wanted to run to Zen, but he just stood, as frozen as the dome of ice that held the arctic wolf, wary, unable to imagine how his friend could have possibly found them there.

Zen pointed toward the broken window with his staff and waved a get-moving gesture with his other hand.

The mage was right. Nick didn't have much time. With a quick smile, Nick waved at his old friend and dove into the blackness of the guild house interior.

Otto was beside him in an instant. "Which way, old man?"

"Wait." Nick grabbed Otto's arm. "Zen's out there."

Otto clapped him on the shoulder. "I thought as much. The guard on the wall?"

"Yes."

"If he made it out of the catacombs and found us here, he'll have no problem catching up. The real guards, on the other hand, won't be distracted for long. We have to keep moving. Which way?" he whispered harshly to Xanth.

"Left." Xanth led them through a heavy wooden door into a windowless room.

Nick glanced back once before following. Otto was right; Zen could obviously take care of himself.

Once Nick stepped through the door and it closed behind him, Xanth lit a candle, one of four nearly-spent nubs in a candelabra he'd borrowed from the dining table that dominated the hall. The long wooden table, fourteen chairs, a pair of cabinets, and four large paintings of celestial scenes were all coated in a thick layer of dust.

Xanth waved them toward a double door at the far end of the hall. "This way."

He led them past a swinging door that led to a kitchen. Some of the tracks seemed to lead into there, but the room was dark and silent now. Xanth followed the more prominent trail into the next room.

There, just past the threshold, lay the tattered body of some grotesque creature. Its long, pointed face was split by a vertical mouth filled with countless fangs. A dozen sightless eyes covered its head from ears to snout. Claws the length of swords tipped its three-fingered hands. The dark green blood pooled beneath it marked it as a demon.

Red and brown blood splattered the floor as well. The tracks stopped there, but no other bodies lay nearby.

Nick's mind tried to make sense of the scene as Xanth and Otto climbed a stone staircase to their right. After a moment, Nick followed.

CHAPTER 9

Rancid held his good arm across the stinging, ragged rents that one of the wolves had torn across his chest with its claws. His right leg throbbed where the demon had bitten him. He sat, gritting his teeth and holding his breath as his own sticky blood pooled beneath him on the larder's stone floor.

A flickering light shined briefly through the crack at the bottom of the door.

Jasmine, barely visible in the dim, passing light, appeared to have fared little better than he had. The demon's jagged teeth had riddled her thigh and waist with punctures, its weird, vertical mouth too well suited for gripping legs and torsos. They were both lucky to be alive.

Jasmine too made no sound. With the wolves still roaming the grounds outside, the candle and the muted sounds that accompanied it were not likely from Nick, Otto, and Xanth. And Rancid and

Jasmine had no strength left to fight any guards, soldiers, or mercenaries who might have taken up a position inside the building.

So Rancid hid with her in the darkness, at home among the rotten remains of the guild's old food stores, and wished he'd thought to erase their tracks.

A door opened and closed. The candlelight disappeared.

Still they waited.

When no sound or light had reached them for several minutes, Jasmine pushed open the door.

Rancid cringed at the creak of the old hinges.

A moment later, she tugged on his sleeve and coaxed him out, fumbling in the darkness through the kitchen, into the dining hall, and into the room with the demon carcass.

That room was dark as well. The picture window along the north wall revealed the grounds and battlement outside. The moonlight seemed bright by contrast with the darkness of the larder. Rancid limped to the window and studied the scene, his eyes now completely adjusted to the darkness.

No guards. No wolves. Nothing.

Jasmine pulled him back into the dining hall. "We need light." She struck a spark to a candle she'd taken from the table. When the wick caught, it cast its light upon a man standing just a few feet from them.

Rancid and Jasmine both jumped back.

The man calmly pulled back the cowl of his worn robe to reveal Zen's face, with a few days of stubble where his beard used to be and eyes as blue as the Trondorian sky.

"How—" Rancid began in a harsh whisper.

Zen put a finger to his own lips.

Rancid drew his sword. Zen couldn't have escaped the catacombs beneath Balor's palace or found them here at the guild house unless he'd had help. And the only person who seemed to have known they would come in this direction was Dalen Frost, that Home Guard scout who worked for Balor.

Jasmine snatched Rancid's wrist.

He struggled to free it, but not in earnest. In his present condition, he was no match for Zen. Yet his suspicion demanded consideration.

It was too much of a coincidence that Zen would show up from nowhere when the party was weakened by their bouts with the miners, strangle vines, wolves, and a demon, when they were once again in a building surrounded by the forces of Balor and about to gain a prize at least as important as the Codex of Mortaan.

Zen backed away from Rancid's blade.

Finally, Rancid relaxed his posture, more because he didn't have the strength than because he lacked malice. He yanked his wrist from Jasmine's grasp and glared at Zen. "You walk in the darkness."

Zen remained calm. "I can see in the darkness."

That's not what Rancid had meant, but he accepted the answer for now. "How?"

Zen waggled his fingers in a mock weaving. "A little trick my mentor taught me once upon a time." He glanced down at their injuries. "You look terrible."

"We'll take care of these as soon as the others catch up," Jasmine said.

Zen nodded. "They came in through the broken window a few minutes ago."

In that case, the light that had passed by the kitchen must have been Nick, Otto, and Xanth. With their help Rancid might be able to get Zen to account for his last several days.

Jasmine pointed toward the room where they'd battled the demon. "That way, then."

Zen motioned to the doorway.

"Oh, no. You first." Rancid wasn't about to let Zen walk behind him.

With a nod, Zen led them through the door. He followed multiple sets of footprints up a flight of stairs to the second story, and from there, up another into the central tower of the guild house. The dust was thinner here, but the tracks remained visible. He followed them up a ladder and joined Nick, Otto, and Xanth in a torchlit room above.

Rancid gritted his teeth as he struggled to make the climb. His hastily bandaged leg gave out halfway up and pain threatened to overcome him. Only Jasmine's bracing hand from below kept him from falling.

When he climbed through the hole, Nick was shaking Zen's hand. "Thank Aeron you're alive. I thought we'd lost you in the catacombs."

"I'm not that easy to kill," Zen declared.

"You'll have to tell me about it later." Nick reached out to Rancid, clasped his good hand, and helped him the rest of the way up the ladder.

Then he saw Rancid's wounded leg. "Orc's blood. What happened to you?"

Jasmine emerged from the hole. "We ran into that demon downstairs." She dropped her bundle and produced her healer's pouch from somewhere within it. "Sit down," she told Rancid. "Your leg needs tending."

"Not now," Rancid growled, aware that the Seeking Stone, like the original Codex, was a prize the Master might want. And, as with the Codex, he might be waiting for Nick and his friends to obtain it, just to have a spy take it from them.

Rancid wheeled on Zen. "How did you know we were here?" With the group together, they might determine Zen's purpose before recovering the Seeking Stone.

"Suit yourself." Jasmine sat down, cross-legged on the floor, and slipped into one of her meditative trances.

"You'd better hurry," Zen told Nick. "The guards won't be distracted for long."

Nick motioned for Xanth to continue.

The old man turned his attention to a rather odd-looking iron door in a wall that bisected the tower.

Embedded in the center of the door was an opaque black disk that might have once been a window but had somehow grown as dark as the night sky. A narrow shelf with four small indentations was mounted below it. Intricate scrollwork that looked like writing adorned the border of the shelf.

Xanth collected eight polished stones, each about the size of an apricot, from a bowl on an ivory-topped table in the corner. The stones, though probably once round, had been worn by centuries of use. A mottled color pattern ran through each. "These represent the eight wandering stars, named for the deities of the mortal races. The black and white are, of course, Vexetan and Aeron. The gray represents Kraggan, god of the dwarves. Green is Skoedorn, the goblin god. Blue, Merrana, goddess of the sea. Yellow, Tartarren, warrior god of the barbarian tribes of Cormont. Brown, Robala, patron saint of the wayfarer. And the last, the orange stone, for whatever deity they worship in the Wild Lands."

Rancid seethed at the mention of Robala, a reminder of the assassin Drakemoor, who'd claimed to be one of Robala's priests.

Xanth examined the stones in his hand. "It's been thirty years. Even if I knew the day we last set the lock, it would take weeks to calculate the positions of the gods in the sky on that particular day."

"Do your best," Nick told him.

Without so much as a glance at Nick, Rancid raised his dagger at Zen. "I asked you a question."

Zen shrugged. "I'll reply when you're inclined to listen."

Looking for support among those he trusted, Rancid found none. Only Otto seemed to be waiting for Zen to answer, and Rancid wasn't yet ready to call him "friend." With a huff, he shoved his dagger into its scabbard and planted himself on a faded velvet chair. The brittle fabric split under his weight and he sank into the stuffing. "Baron's blood."

"Why are there eight stones and only four dimples in the tray?" Nick asked the old man.

"A peculiarity of the wandering stars is that there are always four visible in the night sky. Never fewer, never more. I must choose the correct four and place them in the proper sequence, east to west, for the date the lock was last set."

"Just try something," Otto suggested.

"There are 1680 possibilities."

Jasmine emerged from her trance, her eyes alert, her features relaxed and refreshed. Her wounds were red and raw, but they were no longer bleeding. When she stood, a measure of her grace and strength seemed to have returned.

She set her healer's pouch on a table beside Rancid's chair. "Sit still."

Rancid came to his feet and shoved her aside. With her support, he could face Zen once more.

"Not now," Nick said. "First the stone. Our time is limited." He returned his attention to Xanth and the celestial lock.

"Okay, Zen." Rancid rested his good hand on his hip. "I'm listening. We told no one our destination. How did you know to come here?"

Zen met his stare squarely. "It was obvious."

"You're lying."

"How did you escape the catacombs?" Otto asked.

Xanth muttered to himself as he placed four seemingly random stones in the tray. Stars lit the black window, three bright, one dim. He examined the display for a moment, then grabbed from the table an odd device that consisted of several parallel strings of beads stretched across an oak frame. He sat down in a chair with the device in his lap and manipulated the beads, muttering all the while.

Jasmine ripped away Rancid's pant leg and examined the puncture wounds from the demon's teeth. He kept his focus on Zen and let her work. The wounds did need tending.

"I got out the same way you did," Zen said, "only later."

"Why didn't you come out with us?" Otto asked.

"I underestimated the disorienting magic of the fairy mist." He looked suddenly sheepish. "I got lost."

Rancid huffed. "You were right behind me."

"I wish I was. I got caught in the center of the chamber. I had no walls to follow. No reference points."

Nick pulled the green stone from the tray and dropped in the white, replacing the goblin god with Aeron.

Xanth gasped.

Nick shrugged. "It seemed Aeron ought to be in the mix."

Xanth studied the image in the onyx pane. All four stars shone brightly. He glanced from the stones to Nick and back to the image. Then he laughed, a hoarse crackle barely louder than a whisper. "That's it, my boy. That's it. Now I need to put them in proper order."

Jasmine smeared a cool paste on each puncture in Rancid's leg and the pain seemed to evaporate. "I saw some charts downstairs."

Xanth's head snapped up. "Where?"

"In a small study off the common room."

The old man waved his hand. "No, no, those are just birth charts." He moved back to the chair and continued his calculations with the beads.

"How did you find us?" Rancid asked Zen again. "How did you know we'd come here?"

"I knew Xanth was with you and that the guild was powerful in its day, so I guessed you'd come to Tradestar, either because of the port or because of the guild."

"And so you happen to show up at the guild, just as we arrive?"

"Ha!" Zen threw back his head. "I've been here for days. I stole a horse and rode into Tradestar disguised as a Trondorian soldier. The place is practically afire with excitement over the reward Balor has offered for our death or capture."

Rancid pursed his lips. It was possible, perhaps. And it fit Zen's style to hide in plain sight. "Who's the reward for?"

"All of us, except you. Ten thousand gold coins, all told."

Rancid said nothing, trying to piece together the truth of Zen's story. It was too tidy.

"Figures," Otto muttered.

Xanth returned to the tray and rearranged the stones. He examined the star map on the door, scratched his head, and sat down with his beads.

"I snooped around long enough to convince myself you hadn't come into the city," Zen continued. "Then I came here."

"Otto and I would have been food for the wolves if Zen hadn't shown up when he did," Nick said.

"You got here just in time?" Rancid asked skeptically. "Too convenient."

"Convenient?" Zen leaned against the wall, near the ladder to the lower levels. "I've been hiding in the woods, waiting for you to show up. The guards didn't enter the grounds once, so when I heard the wolves making a ruckus, I assumed it was you."

Rancid grunted. He eyed the hole in the floor and considered shoving Zen down it before he could seal their exit with ice.

Xanth climbed to his feet again and tried another sequence. "Hmmmm." He scowled, flipped a few beads, and shuffled the stones again.

"Only one try left," Nick said.

Rancid watched Zen's features for any signs of anticipation or concern, but Zen just stared, cold as his frozen craft, into Rancid's eyes.

"Let me see your neck," Jasmine said. "Show us you're not wearing a Medallion."

With an exaggerated sigh, Zen pulled down the neck of his cloak and lifted the back of his hair, so she could see his entire neck and shoulders. Jasmine peered down the front of his shirt and Zen blushed.

"He's clean," she said.

Xanth wailed in frustration. "I don't have enough information." His hands formed bony claws as he fought to contain his temper. "If I only knew the date..."

"Guess," Otto suggested.

"Guess right," Nick added.

"If I'm wrong, we'll have to wait twenty-four hours before we can try again."

Rancid felt suddenly lightheaded. The rips in his thigh stung. He had to brace himself against a table to keep his feet. "Would that be such a bad thing?"

"Yes." Zen stepped away from the ladder. "It won't take the guards long to figure out that I sent them on a fairy chase, that there really isn't anybody coming up the path. Then they'll be back."

Finally too weak to protest, Rancid sank back into the chair and let Jasmine bandage his leg.

She handed him a fresh green leaf. "Chew on this."

"What is it?"

"Peppermint. It will help keep you alert."

Rancid took it between his teeth. Within minutes, his lightheadedness subsided. His shoulders, back, and fist relaxed.

Xanth gazed at the ceiling as though he could see the sky. Finally, he took a steadying breath and swapped the positions of two of the stones in the tray.

A loud pop, and then a series of clicks, emanated from the door.

Xanth's smile consumed his face. He tripped the latch and the door swung wide, revealing a semicircular study with a large cherrywood desk. A chair behind it and a couch along the wall both matched the chair with the brittle cushion that had enveloped Rancid a few minutes earlier. The marble floor and a wooden display case along the back wall were nearly free of dust.

Nick motioned to a ladder that led to a closed hatch in the study's ceiling. "Where does that go?"

"The observatory. That hatch is the only way in." Xanth pulled open the bottom desk drawer and drew out an iron strongbox. Struggling with its obvious weight, he laid it on the desk as reverently as he could manage. "The Seeking Stone." A large padlock dangled from the front.

"Do you have the key?" Nick asked.

"Not anymore."

Without hesitation, Rancid rummaged through his pack until he found his suede pouch of lock picks. He unrolled it on the desk, selected a pick, and tried for several minutes to open the lock. "Ahhhh!" Finally, he slammed the pick onto the desk. "I can't do this with one hand."

Otto pulled his ax from his belt. "Then step aside." He swung it back and forth, as if testing its weight or balance while Rancid collected his picks and backed away.

"Careful," Nick said. "Don't hit the Seeking Stone."

With one stroke, Otto sheered the lock and its hasp clean off, embedding the ax in the top of the desk with a solid thump. The box hopped once and landed with the lid open.

Inside lay an ivory-colored stone, the size and shape of a goose's egg, polished to a high sheen.

"Is it dangerous?" Nick asked.

Xanth shook his head.

"Fragile?"

"It's a rock." The smile hadn't left Xanth's face. "Though I suppose if you dropped it from the tower it might crack."

Zen eyed the stone with more than a bit of skepticism. "Is that what you came for?"

"Mostly." Nick left the iron box on the desk and tucked the stone into his backpack. He scanned the room for anything else they might use.

"You'll need the map as well," Xanth said.

Zen shook his head. "We already have a map."

"Not like this one." Xanth passed through the celestial lock to the ladder they'd all climbed from the lower level. "Mine shows the location of the rock from another world and the known entrances into the Wild Lands."

Zen's brow furrowed briefly, and then his features cleared as if he'd gained some vital comprehension.

Xanth mounted the ladder. "Coming?"

Rancid rummaged through the desk drawers—nothing but writing instruments, ledgers and charts—before joining the others.

The party moved through the second-story corridors into a gallery of fine celestial art. Sculptures, paintings, and tapestries decorated every wall and corner, except for an expansive window that looked down on the grounds below. The wealth in this hall alone must rival that of his father and the Black Hand bandits combined. From here, they could finance a journey across the length and breadth of the Civilized Lands—horses, weapons, equipment, and supplies. They could even hire decoy parties to confuse Balor's pursuit, if they could find enough people willing to help them.

Rancid drew his blade and limped up to an intricate painting. The frame was too large to carry, but the canvas could be rolled and managed.

Xanth watched him in the ghostly light streaming through the window. "That's not yours to take."

"What?" Rancid did his best to look indignant. "We need the coin."

Xanth marched toward him as if he meant to rip the dagger from his hand and disembowel him with it. He stopped just beyond the blade's reach and shook his bony fist like a cudgel. "I've given you the Stone, the single most valuable object in the guild besides the telescope itself. I'll not let you rob me blind as well."

Rancid swept the dagger to indicate the wealth of artwork around them. "This stuff is no longer yours. The guild was abolished decades ago, when you abandoned the building."

Xanth didn't waver. "And yet it remains here, the guild house never reoccupied. That alone is a tacit recognition of ownership."

"He's right," Nick told Rancid. "These things don't belong to us." He glanced meaningfully at the window and the darkness beyond. The guards would return soon.

"Fine." Rancid slammed his knife into its scabbard and motioned for Xanth to lead the way.

"The door at the far end of the gallery," Xanth told Nick. "Through the workroom and to the left." He made no move to leave the hall as

Otto, Jasmine, and Nick filed out.

Rancid met his gaze long enough to prove to himself that Xanth wouldn't back down. Then he followed the others.

Beyond the workroom, Xanth led them down the hall and into a lavish private chamber, where he searched through a stack of documents on the inclined surface of a cartographer's table. He lifted one page carefully to the top of the stack. Despite his care, pieces fell away at his touch and drifted to the floor like ashes from a cooking fire.

The parchment was too brittle to try to take with them, so Nick exhumed Jasmine's map of the Civilized Lands from his gear and transcribed the information he needed from Xanth's original.

"You get it?" the old man asked him.

"I think so."

"Be sure," Xanth said. "You'll not get another chance."

Nick examined the parchment again and double checked the markings on his own, then nodded.

With that, Xanth scooped up the pile, crumbling each document into feather-light scraps that drifted to the floor. He crushed the larger pieces, gritting his teeth as though the loss of the documents pained him. When there was nothing left larger than the head of a carpenter's nail, he looked up from his handiwork. "That should slow Balor down if he tries to follow you."

Then he hefted the lid on a chest that sat at the foot of his bed and drew out a small felt bag. He handed it to Nick, who unknotted the twine that held it closed.

Nick's eyes grew at the sight of its contents. He poured a dozen gold coins into his hand. That would certainly buy them supplies if they could find a safe place to procure them.

"You know I can't go with you," Xanth said.

Nick nodded, apparently speechless.

"I would only slow you down," Xanth continued. "My place is here."

"It's not safe," Jasmine said.

"I've been thinking." Xanth took a breath as though collecting his courage. "There's a well and some fruit trees in the courtyard. And if you carve the flank off that dead wolf outside, I can preserve enough meat to last a few weeks. Maybe a month. I'll hide out here until Balor discovers you've gone elsewhere."

Otto cocked an eyebrow. "That's not a bad idea. We can pitch the demon out the broken window, make it look like the wolves got into a scrap with it. It should look real enough to fool the guards from the wall."

"Yes, yes." Xanth waved his arms excitedly. "And the other wolves will keep them from coming in for a closer look. I'll lock myself in the observatory for the next few days. Even if somebody does come into the guild house, I'll be safe behind the celestial lock."

"Then what?" Nick asked. "You can't lock yourself in here forever."

"When the activity dies down outside, I'll go into town. I had friends there once upon a time. Some of them should still be alive. By then, the authorities will have heard that you, and presumably I, have moved on."

Nick nodded and hefted the sack of coins in his palm. "Thanks for everything."

Xanth smiled, but tears moistened his eyes. "I'll see you out. It's the least I can do."

Nick and Otto hauled the demon carcass to the window. The arctic wolf was there, waiting in the shadows, teeth bared, eyes boring a hole into the blackness of the guild house.

Nick took the carcass by one bony leg and heaved it through the opening. The wolf was on it in an instant. It ripped a chunk from the demon's body, spat the mouthful of meat aside, heaved once, and emptied its stomach onto the ground.

Then the wolf vanished beneath a dome of ice.

Wasting no time, Nick and Otto leapt outside, carved several roasts from the flanks of the dead wolf, and tossed them inside. It took both of them to turn the beast over to hide the rents beneath its body.

Meanwhile, Zen stood ready. The wounded wolf was still out there somewhere.

As they retreated to the back gate of the grounds, Rancid took a few extra minutes to wipe out the most obvious signs of human passage. There were too many tracks for him to find and erase them all, but he could clear the cluster around the window. He brushed them with a branch, careful to leave several of the wolves' prints undisturbed.

By the time they reached the gate, the guards had not yet returned. The companions slipped through the opening and arranged the tattered vines over the gate as best they could.

"They're dead," Jasmine said of the vines that they'd unearthed or hacked off. "They'll wither quickly."

"That'll take a day or two." Rancid kept working. "We'll be long gone by then."

"But they'll know we've been here," Nick said. "They'll search the guild house."

Rancid glanced at him. "You got a better idea?"

At that moment, the sound of hooves and the jingling of gear reached them—many horses, at some distance, but coming closer, and then a shout in the darkness.

"Dalen," Nick said.

"We're out of time. Head south. I'll catch up." Rancid placed the last few shoots of dead strangle vine and then backed away from the gate, erasing their tracks all the way back to the nearest thicket.

When he caught up, he led the party down the southern slope of Sorcerers' Peak, rigging ropes to descend the steepest portion. At the bottom, he headed for the foothills of the mountain range, back toward the capital city of Trondor. By morning, they were nearly ten miles from the guild.

Then he realized he'd forgotten to obliterate their tracks at the base of the peak.

CHAPTER 10

hen Gwyndarren rode into Tradestar, he made no attempt to find Zen. He trusted their deal. After all, the ice mage had never let him down. Yet Gwyndarren had sensed a change in Zen the last time they'd met. An intangible hesitance, perhaps. A wariness of motive, maybe. He couldn't quite put his finger on it, but it had something to do with the consequences of the last deal the two had made.

Nevertheless, Zen had kept that deal, even at the cost of two of his friends' lives.

Gwyndarren couldn't help smiling. Even while those deaths made his job more difficult in some ways, they made it easier in others. They gave Zen a reason to count the cost of his greed, but they didn't seem to stifle his hunger for power.

Gwyndarren navigated the streets of Tradestar as he did the conundrum of the ice mage, as territory new to him but familiar in character. He selected a mid-range inn, the kind Zen had said he favored. Maybe he'd get lucky and run into the mage there, but he doubted it. Zen wouldn't likely maintain any measure of predictability in the nest of the enemy.

But Zen was here somewhere. Presumably, so were the rest of the fugitives. And when Zen found them, he would report.

It didn't take long. Gwyndarren woke in the middle of the night to the sound of his own name spoken inside his head.

We're going into the Wild Lands, Zen told him. There's a material there that fell from another world, from one of the bright points in the night sky. I don't know much about its nature, but Nick plans to have it forged into a weapon he believes can kill the Master of the Prophecy.

For a moment, it seemed Zen had finished. Then he added, *He'll have to take the weapon to Alamain for her blessing before he can face your Master with it.*

Alamain. The High Priestess of Aeron, in Gwyndarren's hometown of Lorentil. That was convenient. Gwyndarren lay smiling for a long time as he considered the implications of the message.

"He's no master of mine," he muttered, just before he fell back asleep.

Talen bent to the ground and pinched a few threads of hemp from the cleft in a rock. Based on the freshness of the tracks that led from the guild house to the top of the cliff, he hadn't missed the fugitives by much.

He could have begun the pursuit when he'd discovered the tracks the previous night, but at the time, his men hadn't slept in more than eighteen hours, and today was shaping up to be a forced march. At least now they were somewhat rested.

"Shall we search the guild house, captain?" the first sergeant asked.

"No. The fugitives have left." Unwilling to communicate through his Medallion in the presence of his men, Dalen scrawled a note on a scrap of parchment and tucked it into a tube tied to the leg of his hawk. "Go to Balor," he told Harriet. "He needs to know we've picked up the trail."

After Harriet took off, Dalen strode back to the top of the hill. "Mount up!"

By the time he and his men had ridden down the path, circled around the base of Sorcerers' Peak, and resumed the trail, he was nearly a day behind and his hawk had returned.

But these tracks would be easy to follow, five sets of prints—the mage's stride punctuated by jabs of his staff into the permafrost; Nick's and Otto's heavy, sunken prints; and the booted feet of the disfigured monk, betrayed by the peculiar weighting on the heal and toe of her taloned feet. The last set of prints, however, hadn't been made by the feeble steps of the old stargazer. The stride was longer, and the man obviously limping. Based on the overlay of the others' tracks, this stranger was leading them. These must be from the one-armed imposter who'd freed the fugitives from the dungeons.

That meant Xanth had remained in the guild house, but Dalen spared neither thought nor resources to go after him. Though the old man was a fugitive, as far as Dalen knew, Xanth didn't oppose the Prophecy. Dalen had no quarrel with him.

No, his prey lay before him.

But who was this man who'd freed the others? The only reasonable possibility was the elf-kin they called Sevendeath, whom Nick had left in Palidor many months before. Based on an earlier report from Groot, the ogre and Chosen of the Master who had taken control of the Black Hand bandits in Palidor, a wound had cost Sevendeath the use of his left arm, and the Black Hand hadn't seen him in more than a month.

For the second time that day, Dalen sent Harriet with a message for Balor.

Zen and his friends camped shortly after sunrise, taking refuge in an alcove recessed into a cliff face and shaded by an elm tree.

After Zen's night vigil, his exertions with the weave, and the arduous climb down from Sorcerers' Peak, his body was exhausted. Yet he couldn't sleep.

The image of Dara haunted him. His report to Gwyndarren early that morning had brought her back into his dreams, always resplendent in her beauty before he ran her through with a sword.

Zen crawled from his blankets and paced their shelter. At intervals, he wove an enchantment to hide them all from the scrying of the Master's Chosen, as if doing so could somehow redeem him.

When dusk finally rolled over them like a bank of storm clouds, the rest of the camp came to life. Jasmine cleaned the wounds on Rancid's healing leg and changed his dressing. Then the two of them contrived to make a false trail for Dalen to pursue. The rest stuffed their gear into their packs and followed Otto's lead farther into the hills, where the rough terrain would hinder Balor's horses.

"I can't find him." Addicus waved a hand disgustedly at the brazier. When his vision returned to his study, he remembered that the Master was actually in the room. "I'll keep trying," he added quickly.

But Vornax seemed unperturbed. "Explain."

Addicus mopped his brow and tossed the rag onto his cluttered desk. "Everything's shrouded in a dense fog, like looking into the winter sky just before a blizzard."

"Same as yesterday." Ryanna seemed to delight in advertising his failings. "At this rate, Nick's journal will be gone in a week and you'll have outlived your usefulness."

"No." His hoarse voice cracked. "I'm the only one who can open the Portal of the Damned."

Vornax frowned for a moment before turning to Ryanna. "Dalen is tracking them south from the Sorcerers' guild house. Take L'Nordian. Seed southern Trondor with Hunter demons. I'll have Groot send the Black Hand. If Nicklan Mirrin makes it out of the kingdom, we'll need them."

After six days of navigating the rugged foothills of the mountain range, Rancid brought the party to a point where, if Jasmine's map proved correct, the northern tip of the Black Forest encroached on the foothills. If they were lucky, they could slip into the woods to hide their passage south.

More than likely, though, Balor would have someone watching the crossing. All the ports were well guarded, making ship passage impossible to obtain. The only other way out of the kingdom was to the east, and the landscape offered few routes that provided cover. This one was too obvious to leave unguarded.

Rancid veered slightly south when the trees began to thicken. The appearance of the scrub spruce and a dark canopy of basswood signaled their approach to the road that passed between the mountains and the forest.

"Wait here," he whispered, and then slipped into the darkness. He crept up to the road in the light of the waning moon, alert for trouble—the trees would make for an easy ambush, but he saw no one.

He inched closer, and then paused and listened to the darkness.

Absolute silence. Not even the chirping of crickets.

A little closer, he perched on a rock to get a view of the roadway. It looked deserted. Just beyond, however, he could make out a couple of dark forms amid the shadows: two men, or a man and a woman.

One appeared to be sleeping. He couldn't make out the details of that figure. The other, a large man in a dark cloak, crouched in a hollow and watched the road.

With no glint of armor in the moonlight, these were not Trondorian soldiers or city militia from some nearby town. Mercenaries, then. They must know the number of fugitives in Rancid's party and something of their reputation—it wasn't every day that someone escaped from the palace dungeons. Two men couldn't take down Nick and Zen, let alone the whole party. These mercenaries wouldn't be alone. Rancid had to locate the rest.

A shrill whistle split the air from somewhere across the road. Rancid froze, willing his hunched form to become one with the boulder. A moment later, an arrow shattered on the rock at his feet. Baron's blood! Someone could see in the dark.

He leapt down, behind the boulder. A night critter, spooked from a patch of nearby growth, scurried into the darkness. Cringing, Rancid inched forward until he could make out the men he'd seen earlier. The sleeper was alert now, and both scanned the terrain in his direction.

Careful to keep the rock between himself and the road, Rancid fled up the hillside, making enough noise to leave the mercenaries with no doubt that he was retreating. As soon as he'd moved beyond their immediate sight, he yelled, "Mercenaries!"

When Rancid's call reached Nick, a low growl escaped his throat. His tolerance for Rancid's antics had worn to the thinnest of threads. He'd hoped to avoid any further bloodshed.

Otto crouched near the base of a tree that sat at the edge of the small clearing through which the mercenaries would have to pass, if Rancid led them directly back. He armed his crossbow and set several spare bolts on the ground beside him.

Jasmine disappeared among some bushes on the right-hand side of the clearing.

Zen shrugged, then strode to the top of a small rise that commanded a view of most of the approaches...for one with his sight in the darkness.

Nick joined Otto and waited.

Running footsteps approached. After that, there was nothing but silence. No footfalls. No shouts. No sounds of battle.

And for several minutes, nothing happened.

Finally, Jasmine crept from her cover and crossed the clearing, crouched and running, her steps nearly silent, toward a natural pit-like depression near the far side. She dropped to one knee next to a bush and peered into the darkness beyond, as though she'd heard something there.

Then her shoulder jerked backward, struck by an arrow or crossbow bolt. She grunted, then slowly tumbled forward into the pit.

Nick drew his sword and sprinted into the clearing.

"Wait," Otto whispered sharply over the clatter of Nick's gear.

Nick ignored him. With luck, his armor would slow an arrow if he got himself hit.

As he neared the edge of the pit, an arrow whistled past his ear. He dropped into a crouch. The missile, it seemed, had come from a patch of rocky ground just past the pit that offered little cover, save that of the night. But no shape moved there. No shadow hunched in the moonlight.

Nick shrugged off his backpack, propped it on the ground as a shield before him, and glanced into the pit. It was too dark to even make out its depth until Jasmine struck a spark to a torch and illuminated the whole of the cavity, which ranged from ten to fifteen feet deep. Jasmine stood roughly in its center with a broken arrow at her feet. Blood stained her robes in the fleshy part of her chest, just below the left shoulder. She seemed okay—in pain and embarrassed, but alert and steady on her feet.

In the darkness beyond the rocky rise, hasty footsteps retreated.

Jasmine heaved the torch out of the pit and illuminated the rise, but by then, the attacker had gone.

"Scout," Otto explained a few minutes later as they helped Jasmine from the pit. "Sent to ferret out our position and determine our strength. These mercenaries know their craft." Concern stretched his features. "They'll not come upon us unprepared."

"You all right?" Nick asked Jasmine.

She nodded tightly and yanked out the rest of the arrow. The wound didn't appear any worse than some he'd seen her heal with a few minutes of focused meditation.

"I've hired mercenary bands like this any number of times," Otto continued. "Those still around are good. They'll return. And they won't be easy."

CHAPTER 11

Rancid sprinted most of the way back to where he'd left the others and then scrambled into the lee of a rock. He pulled his knees to his chest, flung a dozen handfuls of dirt, dried leaves, and dead pine needles over himself, and drew his dagger. Sucking in the cool Trondorian air, he stifled the urge to shiver as sweat trickled across the back of his neck. He slowed his breathing to a steady rhythm and tried to silence his heartbeat by sheer force of will.

For many minutes, no one came. A scuffle of movements betrayed the location of Nick and the others, the blundering sots. Then the flickering light of a torch—a torch, of all things!—flared to life. It shifted as though one of his friends was searching for something, tempting Rancid to leap from his concealment and shake some sense into whoever had lit it.

But he didn't. He sat in the darkness and tried to convince himself that the light would actually help, that it would distract the enemy away from himself. What did he care if the others fell victim to whatever plan the mercenaries were concocting? And planning they were, or else they'd have been right behind him. But no. The mercenaries bided their time and studied their prey. They peered into the light of that gods-forsaken torch, evaluating the position and strength of Rancid's friends, and planned their attack.

A footfall nearby halted Rancid's mental tirade and focused him on his own purpose. His breathing had settled into the slow cadence of a man asleep, still and silent.

A woman appeared with an odd hooked blade in her hand, the same woman he'd seen sleeping near the road. She passed so closely, he could have reached out and grabbed her ankle.

No glove, he noted, though he had no cause to suspect a Black Hand presence in Trondor.

The woman stalked deliberately, eyes forward.

Rancid tightened his grip on the hilt of his dagger.

Then a man emerged from the darkness, a mage by the look of his robes, not three feet to Rancid's left. The woman glanced at the mage and pointed to the torchlight filtering through the trees.

The mage nodded once and continued his advance.

Two more mercenaries passed by, farther away, but not so far that Rancid felt safe from a lucky glance thrown in his direction.

In an odd way, the familiarity of the situation comforted him. All at once he was back in Forlorn Valley, ancestral home of his father and the band of thieves that infested his homeland like a blight—back in the old days, when the Black Hand were careless; before they'd learned of Rancid Sevendeath.

He smiled as the woman with the hooked blade shuffled a dozen feet to the right, crouched on a rock, and studied the torchlit clearing.

Carefully, Rancid came to his feet. The woman stiffened when his blade pierced the base of her skull and slid into her brain.

With his good arm, he eased her body to the ground and moved on to the remaining mercenaries. Three-to-one odds now, if he counted the silhouettes correctly against the glow of the torchlight. Just the way he liked it.

Jasmine's ears caught the scrape of a boot and the click of a crossbow being set with a bolt. She squinted across the clearing into the shadows beyond. The blaze of the torch prevented her eyes from adjusting to the darkness.

"I need to see," she told Zen, who had come up beside her.

He gestured in the air and set his hand on her shoulder. The night brightened around her, like a moonlit snowscape, until she could discern shapes moving beyond the torchlight.

She stiffened when the whistle of an arrow from another direction split the air, followed by a sickening thud and a cry of pain. Zen crumpled beside her, an arrow stuck completely through his thigh. Its fletching matched the arrow she'd pulled from her own shoulder. The archer had returned, now somewhere behind them.

Bugger. She scrambled to Zen's side.

"I'm all right," he said through gritted teeth. "Get him."

She nodded once and sprinted away.

The odd perception of sight in the darkness distorted her senses. Her feet felt clumsy on the coarse ground. Nonetheless, she ran quickly, scanning the edges of her new perception for the mercenary who dared to treat her and her friends like wooden dummies at one of sister Lily's throwing-star exhibitions.

She stopped atop a small ridge, thirty yards out and thirty feet high, an excellent vantage point for an archer. But there was no one there, just half a dozen spruce, a stunted basswood, and insufficient ground cover to hide a person. Yet Jasmine was sure the arrow had come from there. She circled the area to make sure it was deserted.

In the torchlight below, Otto had traded his crossbow for his ax and was facing off against a pair of mercenaries. Nick sprinted into the light to engage. Zen had regained his feet, though he leaned heavily on his staff.

Just as Jasmine had given up on the archer, something hit the ground behind her with the muffled grace of a mountain cat.

She spun to face the threat, a woman by the looks of her face, but her humanity seemed vague. Though she stood just a few feet away, her form seemed indistinct—not misty or ethereal as Whisper was, just constantly out of focus—translucent perhaps, or intermittently so.

But the swords in the woman's hands, twin blades far longer than Jasmine's reach, were plain enough...until they moved. Then their speed became too quick for her eyes to track.

In that moment, her training overtook her. *Never watch an enemy's weapon,* brother Yucca had drilled into her, time and again. *As soon as you do, it will prove to be a decoy.* She focused instead on what she could see clearly, using the woman's eyes to gauge movements in her indistinct body.

Jasmine ducked, twisted, and sidestepped as her instincts demanded, and for a time, the mercenary's blades slipped passed without drawing blood. Then Jasmine pivoted too slowly and a gash opened several inches of her side. Her keen awareness of self told her the cut was too shallow to immediately threaten her life, but it stung and ran freely with her blood.

Using the momentum of her spin, she dropped to the ground with one leg out to topple the woman. It was a gamble, but the maneuver was instinctive. As her foot swept past the mercenary's indistinct body, it met only slight resistance, as though the woman had leapt Jasmine's leg and she'd caught only the hem of a cloak.

Before Jasmine could get back up, a sword punctured her calf and withdrew. She rolled to her feet, away from the mercenary.

Limping on the damaged muscle, Jasmine feigned weakness and staggered—something her elders had taught her never to do, but she needed an opening.

The mercenary's eyes turned gleeful, and she advanced with renewed vigor.

Jasmine stepped inside the sword's stroke, ignored the pain as she put her full weight on her injured leg, and thrust her palm at the bridge of the mercenary's nose.

The woman twisted, and the blow glanced off her cheekbone. With a shift of her weight, she slipped past and overbalanced Jasmine, who stumbled suicidally forward.

A sword ripped through Jasmine's back as deeply as her ribs and shoulder blades allowed. She fell, half conscious and wholly disoriented.

The next half-second would have been her last, but the thing that had thrown her into confusion—the slope and the thirty-foot tumble to the bottom—also saved her life.

She lay there for a moment, or an hour, and contemplated how she'd lost control so completely... how she'd survived... how long she might live.

Her body went cold and thunder rolled through her mind, a vaguely familiar sound not at all like the summer storms in Meuribar. She opened her eyes, trying to place the sound, and reality flooded back in.

The top of the rise from which she'd stumbled was awash in a deluge of hailstones the size of apricots. She turned her head in the direction of the torchlight. Nick and Otto stood near the bodies of two mercenaries, and Zen was lit up with a pale glow that seemed to have no source.

A crossbow bolt sank into his gut.

It seemed like a dream, with the weird, distorted view of night vision and the complete wash of any sound over that of the hailstorm.

Zen staggered back and caught himself against his staff in one hand and the slender trunk of a small tree in the other. His face contorted in rage.

Nick, Otto, and Rancid raced in the direction of the mercenary who'd shot him.

Zen dropped to his knees and, with a tortured gesture, brought down another hailstorm.

Jasmine struggled to roll herself off her back, so she might stand and fight. When she did, her vision blurred and her mind went black.

Rancid raced past the hailstorm. He'd killed three of the mercenaries before they became aware of his presence, and one after. With no intention of stopping now, he plunged into a thicket of scrub, a most likely hiding place. If the crossbowman hadn't been caught in the hail, he was probably there. Someone grunted as Rancid hit the thicket's center. He and the enemy tumbled, as one, to the ground.

The mercenary, a man of maybe fifty harvests, came to his feet, his crossbow leveled at Rancid's chest, a broken bolt dangling from its tip. As Rancid scrambled to his feet, the man tossed the crossbow aside and drew his sword.

Before Rancid could engage, however, a crossbow bolt plunged into the mercenary's head. His dead eyes stared for a full second before he toppled to the ground.

Silhouetted by the torchlight, Otto lowered his own crossbow and turned away.

Instinctively, Rancid checked the man's hand for a black glove before following.

Jasmine came awake, or thought she did. Her head felt as though it had been split by an ax, both halves dangling at odd angles to one another, distorting her perception. Somehow, she was seated. *Seated?* Her gaze drifted across her blood-streaked body. How had she become seated? The answer was beyond her, so she went on to another, more urgent concern, that of her wounds.

She could heal them. The thought was as indistinct as her vision. The Order had taught her how, if only she could remember. She could...what? What could she do?

Focus, she told herself as her elders had admonished throughout her years of training.

Yes. That was it. She could focus her thoughts on her inner being, raise her body temperature, increase her metabolic rate. It would take only a few minutes, if she could focus.

Her mind wallowed with the immensity of the task and she fought for control. Like her body, her mind was hers to wield. But the harder she tried, the more her thoughts flitted past like the sights before her, vague and illusive.

Someone was speaking—a man, his voice calm and reassuring. "...wounds aren't that bad. That melon on your forehead appears to be the worst of them."

"Where..." Her voice failed. Seemingly of its own volition, her hand fumbled to her head, and a new stab of pain lanced through her. The world spun as it had when she'd tumbled from the ridge. That must be how she'd hurt her head.

"Shhhh," the man said. "We'll clean your cuts, but that's all we can do until you're coherent enough to make a poultice to keep them from souring."

"In the meantime," another, more distant voice said from somewhere in the fog of her perception, "we've got to get them up and moving. You can bet good coin Dalen's not far behind us."

The speaker paused, or Jasmine's mind went momentarily blank, and then the voice continued. "He'll be mounted. And as soon as we trade this mountainous terrain for the Black Forest, he'll have the advantage of speed."

Slowly, as someone bathed her with water-soaked rags, Jasmine remembered what had happened, her battle with the mercenary and her own, pride-crushing defeat. Not since her sparring lessons with brother Thistle had she been so humbled.

"All right. Here we go." A man lifted her into his arms.

The sights began to make more sense as the man, Nick, carried her across the road and into the woods. When Otto stepped into view, carrying Zen, Jasmine croaked, "Ice."

"What?" Zen asked, roused by the word.

"Ice...cloth and ice."

He conjured a handful of frozen water into a rag and handed it to her. She'd have preferred cold water, like that which ran down from the heights to the monastery, but the temperature was more important than the means. Jasmine pressed the rag to her forehead. At first, pain sliced through her. Then numbness seeped into the bruised tissues. She closed her eyes and tried again, without success, to achieve the meditative state she needed to heal.

Zen, his wounds wrapped as tightly as hers, replenished Jasmine's frozen poultice as needed. By the time her night vision wore off, her natural senses had returned.

All at once, Rancid emerged from the darkness ahead. He made an agitated, slashing motion across his neck, and Nick and Otto crouched silently where they were.

Unmistakably, from the woods to their right, less than a quarter mile away, came the sound of perhaps a dozen horses loping through the undergrowth.

CHAPTER 12

Rancid raced south, crashing through the woods and brush, making enough noise for the five of them. When he was sure he'd drawn the riders at least half a mile away, he returned by a circuitous route as silently as he could.

From there, he led Nick and the others east, which brought them closer to the edge of the forest. He was running out of room to maneuver, and with the sun coming up, time had grown short as well.

Eventually the hoofbeats returned, behind them and closing at a gallop.

"It's no good," Rancid said, as embarrassed by the tone of defeat in his own voice as by the fact that he'd failed to elude the pursuers. "We have to stop and hide."

Jasmine nodded. Her face was flushed with fever and madness had begun to show in her eyes.

Otto set Zen down in a thicket and collapsed. The constable's armor was awash in blood, some of it his own.

Nick laid Jasmine down next to Zen. "Rancid and I will keep watch. The rest of you, sleep if you can."

With that, they settled into whatever cover they could find and waited for the riders to pass.

At first, they did. A dozen riders maybe, screened by the trees. Later, they seemed to have separated and begun a search pattern. Twice, a solitary rider approached closely enough for them to hear weapons and gear clattering beyond a screen of fir and skunk cabbage.

Finally, one of the pursuers came into view—a beast with the body of a horse and the torso and head of a man. The creature stood eight feet tall, with a bow in his hands and an arrow readied. He paused between Nick's hiding place and Rancid's, and sniffed the air.

Out of options, Rancid rose to his feet with a dagger blade pinched between his thumb and forefinger, his arm drawn back to throw. He stared down the shaft of the creature's arrow. "Why do you hunt us?"

The creature cocked its head to one side. "I don't hunt you."

"You've tracked us since we entered the woods. Why?"

The creature sniffed the air. "We question all who enter our woods."

Nick stood then.

The creature's head snapped around to face him, but the arrow remained pointed at Rancid's chest. "Why do you hide?"

Rancid lowered his arm, an act he hoped the creature would see as a gesture of goodwill rather than as an opening to exploit. "We were assaulted last night. Some of the attackers got away, and we're in no shape to fight." That admission, too, was a risk, but the horse-kin had too many allies nearby for Rancid to try to bluff his way out.

The creature's gaze returned to Rancid. It released a shrill whistle into the crisp air. "I thought I smelled blood, some of it foul. You'll need aid. How many are in your party?"

"Five," Nick said quickly, as though he feared Rancid might lie.

"Who speaks for you?" The creature asked as several others like it came into view.

Rancid pursed his lips and motioned at Nick.

The speaker deferred to one of the newcomers, who was a head taller than the others, had spotted hindquarters, and wore an ornately beaded belt around the waist of his human torso. He approached Nick and sniffed. "I smell no evil about you. I'm Chengan, chief of the Appaloosa tribe. You are welcome here."

"You're centaurs," Nick said. "I've never seen your kind, though I've heard of you."

Otto stepped out of hiding. Jasmine and Zen struggled to their feet as well. The latter looked pale and leaned heavily on his staff.

Chengan snapped his fingers at one of the others. "Bring Yushu. These men need healing." Then to Nick, he said, "Come, you may rest with us."

Nick and his party rode into camp on the backs of the centaurs. The place consisted of a few cooking instruments and tools, the females and their young—nothing more. No tents, no cots or bedding, no clotheslines, nothing to indicate any degree of permanence. "How long have you been here, in this camp?" Nick asked.

"A couple of days," Chengan replied. "There are dangers in the woods, and rival tribes. We try to stay aware of our surroundings, but we must keep moving to remain safe."

Nick dismounted and helped Jasmine to the ground. Her bandages were soaked with blood. Apparently, she hadn't yet achieved her healing meditative state, which would have done more for her wounds than a week's worth of clean dressings.

Listlessly, she spread her blanket on the ground and collapsed onto it.

Otto helped Zen down while Rancid watched with a sour expression. "I just saw him gesturing," Rancid said in a low voice to Nick. "Weaving or whatever. He's using magic."

Nick nodded but said nothing. Though he understood Rancid's concern, especially in light of Drakemoor's deception, Nick had known Zen for years. The mage could often be moody and at times let greed cloud his judgment, but he could be trusted to do the right thing when it mattered. Sooner or later, Rancid would see that.

"What are you gonna do about it?" Rancid asked him.

"Nothing. Maybe he's trying to heal himself. Get some sleep. I'll stay up for the rest of the morning. You can have the afternoon watch. I don't trust these centaurs any more than you trust Zen."

Slow hours came and went. The canopy of trees shaded them from the sun, so Nick couldn't be sure of the time, except that it was still before noon when an elven female, a guide by the looks of her garb, rode into the camp with a pair of centaur escorts. Most of her body was shrouded in a travelling cloak that seemed to shift and change shades constantly to match its surroundings. Only her face and hands were clearly visible until she pulled down the hood and the enchanted cloak settled into a solid forest-green. In addition to her having an ugly black eye, welts and bruises covered her skin and she wore them like rage. But the look she shot at Nick as she entered the camp was one of pure, arrogant victory. "Chief Chengan, we meet again."

"Sierra Glenwood." Chengan gave the elf a dry look, excused himself from helping another centaur scrape clean a deer hide, and plodded across the clearing towards her. The two spoke in low tones that Nick couldn't quite make out.

She dismounted, handed Chengan a sheaf of parchment, and pointed toward Nick and his sleeping companions. The centaur leafed through the documents. He shook his head and also gestured to Nick.

At this, the elf raised her voice. "... murdered my team last night."

Nick approached. "What's going on?"

Chengan handed Nick a stack of Wanted papers.

He glanced at them. His own was on top. "What are you going to do?"

When Chengan hesitated, Sierra handed him another document. "This is a writ from the Ruling Council of Trondor. By treaty, you're obligated to relinquish any outlaws who take refuge in the Black Forest."

Nick's heart rate increased. With nearly two dozen armed centaurs nearby, Chengan could enforce the writ if he chose to do so.

Otto, awake now, leaned on his elbow and watched the conversation.

Nick motioned him to stay put. He thanked Aeron that Rancid, with his foul mouth and uncompromising temperament, hadn't awakened at Sierra's outburst.

Chengan locked his gaze on Nick's. "Are you an outlaw?"

"We're fugitives from the Council, but we fight an evil that threatens all the Civilized Lands, including your forest. The Council has been deceived by that evil."

Sadness entered Chengan's eyes. "If I don't honor the writ, the Council will have cause to invade the Black Forest and revoke our sovereignty."

A leer broke Sierra's features. "Disarm and bind them. I'll return with enough horses to convey them to the capital."

"I'm obligated to let you take them," Chengan said as she turned. "But not to wrap them for you like a gift."

Sierra spun on him, her long platinum hair whipping around her face. "You'll do as I ask, in accordance with the treaty." Her hands flexed over the pommels of twin sabers hanging at her sides.

Chengan said nothing.

"You have my word," Nick said. "We'll accompany this mercenary without resistance until we reach the edge of your forest."

"If you don't disarm them before you hand them over, you'll have done nothing more than let them go." The welts on Sierra's face darkened with her glare. "I'll inform the Council." Again she turned to go.

All of the adult male centaurs had gathered around. Otto ambled over to join the discussion, his ax on his belt. His relaxed posture reassured Nick that he wouldn't provoke the centaurs, or Sierra, unnecessarily.

Frantic, Nick searched for options. Losing their supplies now would cost them the Seeking Stone. Unless... "Does the writ cover everyone in my party?"

"Yes," Sierra answered.

Refusing to address Sierra directly, Nick waited for Chengan to reply; accepting Sierra's response would only reinforce her authority.

Chengan counted the posters—five in all—and nodded.

"Read the descriptions. You won't find our guide. We met him just before entering the woods and offered him coin to guide us through."

Chengan perused the papers and then handed the stack to Sierra with Xanth's description on top. "He's right. The old man isn't here."

"He's dead," Otto added, almost too quickly. "An accident in the mountains. You'll have to find his grave to collect the reward."

Nick faced Chengan squarely. "The four of us will surrender our weapons to you—" It felt as if he was announcing his own execution— "If you'll accompany us to the edge of the Black Forest. I don't want to become supper for some denizen of the woods. You've no need to bind us. I've given my word that we won't resist, and you have sufficient numbers to overwhelm us if my word proves false." He took a deep breath and continued. "You must, however, let our guide go. Rancid wasn't aware that we're fugitives, only that we required haste. The rest of our belongings, we'll give to him as payment for guiding us this far."

Otto raised an eyebrow. "You'll need to convince the others."

"That will satisfy your writ," Chengan announced formally.

Sierra treated it like a question. "More than adequate. Assemble them quickly. I can still make the capital before dark."

The centaurs relieved Jasmine and Zen of their gear before nudging them awake.

Rancid came up spitting ire. When he heard the news, he yanked his sword from its sheath. "How dare you give my charges to this wench."

Sierra made no move toward her weapons. "*Your* charges?"

"If you want to take them from me, you'll have to pay me the reward." Rancid advanced on her. "I captured them first. I'll not turn them over to you or anyone else but the Council."

"Rancid..." Nick laid a restraining hand on his shoulder. If Rancid gave Chengan reason to distrust them, they could all end up trussed over the backs of Sierra's spare mounts.

Sierra stood her ground, daring Rancid to swing his sword.

"She is a representative of the Ruling Council, with a writ of authority for our arrest," Otto warned. "If you take up arms against her, now that she's identified herself as such, you'll be outlawed as well."

"Speaking of writs," Sierra said calmly, "where's yours?" She cocked her eyebrow, shifting the bruises Zen's hailstorm had left on her forehead. "What do you think, chief? Did they behave as though they were this man's prisoners when they came into your camp?"

Chengan shook his head. "My duties are clear," he told Rancid. "But they don't include you." He glanced meaningfully at the numerous centaurs nearby. "I suggest you accept what I must do."

"May we rest for a day?" Jasmine asked Chengan. "We're in no shape to travel."

"No," Sierra replied to Nick. "You've insisted that the centaurs accompany us. Fine. You can ride them. It doesn't matter to me if any of you survive the trip. I'll get paid the same either way."

"I'm sorry," Chengan told Jasmine.

"May I at least have some clean bandages to redress my wounds?"

Chengan motioned for his shaman to comply.

Sierra glared at her. "Mount up or I'll drag you behind. We're leaving."

Nick and Otto helped the wounded onto the backs of centaurs before mounting. Within minutes, the lot of them launched out of the campground at a gallop. If Nick had any hope that Rancid would follow behind and rescue them, it died in that moment. Without a horse, he'd never keep pace, and the centaurs wouldn't likely carry him without Chengan's consent.

On the way, Nick's mind remained fixed on what he might do once they got to Sierra's horses. With Chengan and his centaurs among them, Nick and his friends couldn't hope to escape before they left the forest. Once Chengan no longer had any obligation, though, he wouldn't likely interfere. Could Nick and Otto defeat Sierra? If they had their weapons, he'd have no doubt. But unarmed, against Sierra's swords? Probably not. Jasmine excelled in unarmed combat, but she was in no shape to fight. Zen, if he could weave his magic in his current state, might sway the outcome in their favor. Rancid still had his weapons. Maybe the four of them could survive long enough for him to catch up.

They ran for nearly an hour, and the longer Sierra maintained her galloping pace, the less hope Nick had that Rancid would arrive in time to make a difference. That left Nick and Otto. Maybe he could pick up a stout branch to use as a club or find a suitable rock and take Sierra out with a lucky throw. Maybe...

Sierra brought the procession to a stop within a hundred yards of the forest's edge. There, tethered among the trees, waited half a dozen horses. She shuffled through her saddlebags and produced a length of rope.

She approached Zen. "Give me your hands."

"Not on your life."

Without the slightest change of expression, Sierra struck like a whip. She snatched the folds of Zen's robe and yanked him from his centaur's back.

In a heartbeat, Otto sprang from his mount.

Nick was torn. He'd promised not to resist before reaching the forest's edge, but he couldn't let Sierra bind them. And he didn't have to guess where Chengan's loyalties would fall.

Otto charged Sierra. His guttural yell split the forest air like a beast in agony, forcing her attention away from Zen.

Nick jumped from his own centaur and began walking toward the edge of the woods, as though he wasn't trying to escape. If he could reach it, it would fulfill his oath to not fight Sierra until he was out of the forest. He'd be free to act.

Aside from being a man of his word, if he broke his promise, Chengan might be forced to take up arms on Sierra's side. Then none of them would have any hope.

Sierra drew her sabers. She held them forth and let Otto finish his charge.

He skidded to a halt, teetering over the tips of her blades.

"Well then," she said, "it looks like you get to go first."

Chengan launched an arrow between the two. It struck a tree just beyond them and hung there, thrumming a discordant tone. "Hold! Everyone!"

When Nick turned back, half of the centaurs held loaded bows. The rest, swords.

"Chief," Nick said, "if she'll take us beyond the edge of the woods, we'll go willingly. But we won't let her manhandle us here. You agreed to accompany us for our protection. Not for hers."

Chengan replied to Sierra, "I made it clear that I wouldn't help you bind them."

Her eyes never wavered from Otto. "Yet your obligation to the Council requires you to release them into my custody."

"I will. At the forest's edge. That's what we agreed. If they are too many for you, we'll be glad to detain them until a suitable escort arrives from the palace."

That would cost Sierra the bulk of the reward.

Sierra pointed. "That one's a mage. At least let me bind his hands."

Chengan shifted his aim, placing it squarely on Sierra. "My pledge to protect them includes protecting them from you. I'll honor my obligation to the Council, but I'll also keep my agreement with these travelers. You may bind them, or do whatever else you must.

But do it outside our forest."

Sierra glared at each of them in turn. "You think the four of you can take me? On your honor, follow me past the tree line and let's find out." She wheeled away and marched toward the forest's boundary.

Otto squared his shoulders and fell into step behind her. Jasmine slid, almost listless, from her mount. Zen, sweating but back on his feet, revealed several ice shards in his hand, a frosty mist enveloping them, keeping them frozen.

Nick took heart from that, waved farewell to the centaurs, and strode alongside his friends.

Thunder rumbled through the air despite the cloudless sky. Moments later, a company of galloping centaurs emerged from the trees. One separated himself from the others and approached Chengan. "A company of the king's guard has requested entry from the north."

"The king's guard?" Chengan said. "They have no authority without a king on the throne."

The centaur's chest heaved with each breath. "According to the man who speaks for them, Balor Culhaven was crowned yesterday."

Nick, who'd stopped with the others, groaned at the news.

"He won't need the dungeons this time," Otto said from beside him. "Now he can execute us all straight away."

"He won't have to." Sierra's voice sounded strained for the first time since she'd entered the centaur camp.

"Nevertheless," the reporting centaur continued, "we turned them away."

Chengan's face darkened. "Why?"

"The man who speaks for them reeks of Vexetan."

Chengan spun toward Sierra, but Nick spoke first.

"Did he have a hawk on his arm?"

"He did," the centaur said.

"That's Dalen Frost, a captain in the Home Guard. He's one of the twelve Chosen of the High Priest of Vexetan, as are the new king and the general of the Trondorian army."

"What are you talking about?" Sierra demanded.

Though it wouldn't have occurred to him to try it before, Nick now aimed his appeal at her. "You ever hear of the Prophecy of Mortaan?"

"Of course."

"You?" he asked Chengan.

Though the centaur seemed unwilling to admit it, his expression suggested he hadn't. "We work hard to separate ourselves from the affairs of the humanoid races."

"It says the High Priest of Vexetan will select twelve Chosen to lead the world into darkness. You and your forest would not escape such a fate."

"He's bluffing," Sierra spat.

Chengan cocked his brow at the reporting centaur. "'Reeks of Vexetan?'"

The centaur nodded.

"You'll find he wears a medallion with an onyx center," Nick said. "The gold border carries the markings of the dark god."

"He's bluffing," Sierra said again.

Chengan ignored the comment. "Looks like you just lost your prisoners. I'll not deal with such a man. And I'll not keep treaty with such a king."

Sierra met his glare for some seconds before turning to Nick. "You think this is over? It's never over." She gathered her horses by the reins and stormed from the woods.

CHAPTER 13

The violence of the recent civil war had drawn the stray Devourers to the Trondorian countryside like carrion birds to gorge on the souls of the dead. Ellessar Miriel wiped the putrid blood of one of the demons, his fourth since entering the kingdom, from the blade of his rune-inscribed longsword.

The acrid smell, which soured the stomach of most elves, only invigorated Ellessar as he breathed in the brisk morning air. A tinker's wagon clattered by, ambling north on the frost-covered road from the ruins of Tawneydale. The sun shone brightly in the cloudless sky. It was a good day to hunt.

Though the war had made hunting demons easier these past weeks, it served as an omen he cared not to consider. It was but one of several that must take place before the Last Prophecy of Mortaan could be fulfilled, but given the infallibility that the legends ascribed to the foresight of Mortaan, one omen was too many.

A whinny from Spirit brought Ellessar around like a whip. Never one to shy, the horse now skittered in place, her head tossing and her eyes wide. Only her loyalty and training seemed to keep her from bolting.

Ellessar scanned the edges of the nearby woods with his keen elven eyes and placed a calming hand on Spirit's neck. "What is it, girl?" Even the presence of demons had never unsettled Spirit before. "What do you sense?" Without sheathing his sword, he whispered a humble prayer to Aeron. "Grant me the sight to behold your enemies, so I might vanquish them." He examined the deep recesses among the trees once more.

Before he finished, a shadow, large as a cloud and swift as an arrow, passed over them. Spirit jerked the reins from his hand. Her eyes locked onto something in the sky, her body quaking.

Ellessar flipped up the brim of his demon-skin hat and squinted into the morning sky. What he saw turned his blood as cold as the Trondorian night. His body froze as if it was permafrost.

He just stared, unable to even pray for salvation.

Once the dragon had passed, Ellessar sank to his knees, cradled his holy symbol in his hands, and asked Aeron to forgive his inadequacies and to grant him the strength to fight what was coming.

When he rose again, the dragon had become but a point in the distant sky, gliding toward a peak jutting eastward from a curve of the Sharktooth Mountains.

No one had seen a dragon in the Civilized Lands since the end of the Age of Dragons, nearly five-thousand years before. *This* omen could not be mistaken.

Ryanna climbed from L'Nordian's neck. She could never have even approached the dragon through the aura of terror that it cast like shadows, but Vornax's order and the Medallion around her neck compelled her to do so. Once she and L'Nordian took to the air, however, with the kingdoms of Brinheim, Meuribar, Faldor, and finally Trondor sweeping by beneath them, she had felt free for the first time since she'd abandoned her keep to escape the demon Ka-G'zzin fifteen years earlier.

She'd sworn then never to call another demon. And for many years, she hadn't. Then she met Vornax. She didn't know him as "The Master" then, only as a young, charismatic man with a striking lock of white hair and a flare for the macabre. She was so drawn to him, to his vision and passion, that she had foolishly accepted the Medallion she now wore—the Medallion she couldn't remove without his permission, which he never gave; the Medallion by which he now ruled her utterly; the Medallion she loathed.

At his bidding, she began calling again—minor demons at first, until she regained her confidence—but never something so powerful and violent as a Hunter.

Her feet touched the rocky ground on a promontory of the Shark-tooth range. Icy wind whipped her hair—and nerves—into a frenzy. This was no place to do a calling, without a summoning chamber or even a circle of protection, but it was secluded. And with the population of Trondor soaring higher than that of any other kingdom, privacy was at a premium.

She surveyed the landscape to make sure she was alone with the dragon, drew in a breath of cold, hard courage, and found a place that at least provided firm footing.

Though Vornax had told her to call a Hunter—no, several Hunters—the task was beyond her in more ways than she dared to consider. Fortunately, this particular command was not yet a compulsion.

Only once before had he commanded that she call a Hunter. When she refused, he drove her to do it through the power of the Medallion. The calling required the name of the demon, and she'd pleaded for the time to seek the name of another. Again Vornax refused. He forced her, in a violation of her will as heinous and debasing as rape, to call the only Hunter whose name she already knew: Ka-G'zzin, the only demon who'd ever broken free of her control.

As one, demons hated slavery even more than they did the Abyss. And the weaving in which Ryanna had ensnared Ka-G'zzin was nothing short of that—involuntary servitude to the solitary will of a *human* master. He broke free and took his revenge in ways as humiliating and more horrifying than merciful death.

And Vornax, her own Master, had *made* her work alongside that very demon.

No, she would not call a Hunter today. Even if she could control one without a circle of protection, Ryanna couldn't bring herself to face it. Even if she knew the name of one she could call, even if the pit of loathing in her gut didn't sap her courage at the very thought, she would never call another Hunter.

Not unless *he* compelled her.

Satisfied that she and the dragon were alone on the promontory, Ryanna began to chant. She picked at the weave of the veil, the barrier between the Abyss and the world of men, seeking a weakness. She plucked and stretched the threads until she created an opening large enough to admit the demon she sought. Waves of corruption, the essence of the evil beyond, wafted through the rift as she called the demon's name.

Instantly, it slipped through, and the opening vanished.

It appeared before her, skin glowing with the deep red of a cooling ember, momentarily disoriented by its sudden displacement. The demon stood erect, no larger than Ryanna herself. The claws on its hands and the horns on its head reached over two feet in length. Foul pus seeped from the pores of its tanned hide and dripped from the corners of its fang-filled mouth.

This was an Assassin, less powerful than a Hunter but more cunning. She'd chosen it because she could control several of these before she exceeded the limits of her strength and will.

The Assassin's eyes flared with vengeance when it saw Ryanna, but before it could strike, L'Nordian rose up behind her. The demon's mouth gaped and it staggered back toward the cliff behind it, never taking its eyes off the dragon.

In that moment, Ryanna thrust her will into the Assassin with a force almost physical enough to knock it over the edge. When it brought its eyes back to Ryanna's, it was hers to command.

"Nicklan Mirrin," she said simply. "He's out there somewhere." The broad sweep of her arm took in the whole of Trondor. "Find him and kill him. Then you may return to the Abyss."

With the speaking of Nick's name, an invisible thread of the weave spanned the gap between him and the Assassin, a thread that could be broken only by the death of one or the other.

Sneering, the Assassin bowed once, a mockery of the human gesture. Then it scrambled down the cliff to obey.

Ryanna sighed. She'd never have attempted that without L'Nordian, but the depth of the demon's fear had encouraged her. She needed to call four more Assassins, but to do so here would pose too great a risk that the demons would find one another and come after her. Yet she smiled at the opportunity to do what Addicus had failed to do: Find the fugitives.

Nick, his friends, and their centaur hosts returned to the camp the way they had come.

On the way back, they ran into Rancid. He was out of breath and sprinting toward the forest's edge. He'd made it farther than Nick would have expected in the time since they'd all left him. He had with him only his own sword and Nick's backpack, which had enough supplies for a sustained pursuit and the group's two most important possessions: Nick's map, with the notations he'd made at the Sorcerers' guild house, and the Seeking Stone.

Chengan picked him up, and Nick filled him in on the events that had taken place with Sierra and the centaur patrol.

"You know Balor will invade the Black Forest to catch us," Nick told Chengan.

"Perhaps. But he'll need time to organize his armies and evaluate his soldier's loyalties following the war that won him the crown. He won't come for some time. Weeks, I'd guess. Maybe a month."

"He has the Home Guard," Otto pointed out. "They don't care who's king. They're loyal only to the throne. He can send *them* right away."

"They're only a few hundred strong. We have sufficient numbers and knowledge of the forest to repel them. In the meantime, I can leverage any early attacks to rally the tribes. Most will set aside their squabbles to unite against invaders."

"You have risked much." Jasmine's voice was weak. "We are grateful."

"You're still welcome to spend the night. I doubt anything will happen before morning. Tomorrow we'll carry you as far as Brendan Falls if you wish."

Nick dismounted. "Thank you. But by now, Dalen knows we're headed south and east. He'll try to cut us off. We have to keep moving."

Jasmine's dressings were again soaked with her own blood, but she was sitting up straight on the centaur's back.

"Change your dressings and prepare yourself for travel," Nick told her. "I'll bring your supplies."

"Can you make it?" he asked Zen.

"I'll do what I must," the mage replied through his teeth, shifting his leg in obvious pain.

The whole situation stank. Every day, it seemed, his quest pulled more people into conflict. More and more people suffered because they decided to help him. He wasn't even sure that Zen would survive his wounds this time.

"Stay mounted. I'll be right back." Nick recovered his pack from Rancid and gathered the group's supplies. He even checked the Seeking Stone to make sure it was present and undamaged. Everything appeared to be in order.

Seven centaur warriors, five to carry the companions and two to scout the trail ahead for rival tribes and other dangers, bid farewell to Chengan and the rest of the tribe, who stayed behind to organize the defense of the forest.

They travelled until dark before setting up camp in hopes of a good night's sleep. When Jasmine changed her dressings that evening, her wounds appeared as though they'd been healing for a week.

"I envy you your demon blood," Zen told her as he hobbled by, his face looking pale and haggard.

"My blood has nothing to do with it. It's a matter of self-discipline. The body can do amazing things if you teach it how." She opened her healer's bag and sifted through her meager supplies, apparently without finding what she needed. "Lie down. I'll clean and dress your wounds. I don't have any opiates or hemp to ease the pain, but I have birch leaf. That will help some."

Zen removed his robe and settled himself on his bedding. He gestured, as though weaving, and then rolled up his shirt and the leg of his undergarments.

Nick brought a torch to light Jasmine's work while Rancid started dinner and Otto organized the defense of the camp.

Zen winced when Jasmine scrubbed away the crust over the punctures in his leg and abdomen.

"Sorry," she said softly. "The wounds are too deep for me to allow them to close. They must heal from the inside out or they'll turn sour. I fear the one in your gut may already be doing so. Try to get some rest."

When she was done, she followed Nick to the campfire. "I'll try to find some thyme tomorrow to disinfect his wounds."

Nick sucked his lower lip. They'd been travelling too fast for her to try to identify plants along the way. The thought of Dalen beating them to the southern tip of the forest had consumed him. If the Home Guard cut off their path to Faldor... "Keep an eye on him. Let me know if he worsens."

Nick gathered Otto, Rancid, and several of the centaurs around the fire. "What can you tell us about southeastern Trondor? You too, Otto. We need to know where we're going."

One of the scouts, a centaur named Glazzer with a full beard and a blocky torso, emerged from the shadows with a long stick in his hand.

Nick cleared a patch of ground for the centaur to draw on.

"Here's the Black Forest." Glazzer drew a large oval on the ground. "The capital city of Trondor lies about five miles from the middle of the northern edge. Directly across from it to the south sits the township of Pinewood."

"Which is the longest way around for Dalen and his men?" Nick asked.

"A road encircles the forest from Trondor to Tawneydale, at the eastern edge." Glazzer added cities to the map as he spoke. "The road continues through Pinewood, northwest to Raven's Beak, and back to the capital. From the point where we met Dalen Frost, it's about the same distance to Pinewood whichever way he goes.

"Southeast of the Black Forest," Glazzer continued, "just across the road, lies an expansive cluster of thickets called the Ponderosa Groves. The tribes who live there aren't centaurs. They're a form of lion-kin, aggressive and mean, but the groves extend southeast as far as Brendan Falls." The centaur drew the groves and a road leading from Tawneydale to Brendan Falls.

"How far from there to the border?" Rancid asked.

"I'm sorry. I've never been out of the Black Forest."

"About forty miles," Otto supplied. "Two days' hard ride across the populated southern plains."

Rancid shook his head. "We'll never make it."

"Ten miles south of Brendan Falls lies a small stretch of hill country that'll take us to the coast," Otto continued. "There's a fishing village there named Lanlibar. We may have better luck booking passage there than in Tradestar. We won't find an ocean vessel, but we might catch something down the coast to Redstar, in Faldor."

Nick consulted his own map of the Civilized Lands as they talked. "If we can't, we'll be stuck. It's a dead end."

"The hill country can get us within twenty miles of the border," Otto noted.

"Too predictable." Rancid leaned over to see Nick's map. "Any other options?"

"Some stretches of the Ponderosa Groves approach the main road, which is fewer than twenty miles from the Sharktooth foothills," Otto said. "The population is more dense near the road than out on the plains, but we can cross it at night and follow the Sharktooth range all the way to Faldor. That whole stretch of the border is rugged mountain country. We should be able to slip past Balor's patrols."

"We'll need horses to cross to the mountains in a single night," Rancid observed.

"We have the king's wine," Nick said. "Can you trade it for what we need without being recognized?"

"I'm not buying—" Rancid began, but a sharp look from Nick stopped him.

"We'll cross dangerously close to Tawneydale," Otto warned. "It was the seat of Balor's power before the war, and because Gremauld razed it to the ground, the populace will be fiercely loyal to Balor."

Rancid's wicked grin flashed in the torchlight. "Then that's the last place he'll expect us to be."

"We must first cross the road into the Ponderosa Groves." Glazzer pointed to a spot on the map, about ten miles west of Tawneydale. "This is the only place where the two forests touch."

"No," Nick said. "We tried something like that when we crossed from the mountains into the Black Forest. Sierra had an ambush waiting for us. I wouldn't put it past her to try that again. How far southwest can we go and still cross in one night?"

"All the way to the southern edge of the Black Forest. Twenty miles across, but it'll cost you two additional days to get there and two to get back to where you propose to cross into the Sharktooth."

"Then we go all the way east and cross just outside Tawneydale,"

Otto suggested. "The following night, we—"

Glazzer's head snapped up. He held it poised as if testing the air. "Something foul has entered the woods."

"Can you tell what it is?" Nick asked.

"No. But it poisons the very ground it walks on."

Nick glanced into the shadows around him. "Is it close?"

"Dalen?" Otto guessed.

The centaur hesitated. "No. And no. This is no human. This is evil incarnate."

Nick stood. "Let's double the watches and ride at dawn."

For two days the centaur scouts kept them from encountering any of the rival centaur tribes. No news came from the north because the centaurs travelled as fast as any messenger from Chengan could.

Jasmine's condition improved.

Zen's worsened. The wound in his belly stank. Fever overcame him and he eventually fell into bouts of delirium from which he muttered the word "no" over and over. He used his moments of lucidity to tap the weave. What enchantment he wove, Nick didn't know, but it clearly wasn't one of healing.

Late on the third day, the scouts returned with an elf they'd discovered in the woods. The broad brim of a leather hat shrouded the newcomer's face. Curly black hair hung in tangles about his shoulders. His coat, tailored from some exotic leather in a two-tone design of putrid green and rust brown, brushed the ground as he walked. A holy symbol, with an emblem that Nick recognized from the Temple of Alamain, hung from a silver chain around his neck. It wasn't identical to the symbols he'd seen at the temple, but the similarities were obvious enough to reassure him.

Leading an immaculately groomed horse with a gleaming white coat, the elf scanned the company as though looking for someone in particular.

Jasmine pulled her clawed feet and hands into the confines of her cloak and turned her head away.

Zen seemed suddenly lucid, though pale as a frozen lake. Sweat poured from him as though he was melting.

Rancid's good hand gripped a dagger by the blade, drawn back to throw. "Who are you? And why are you here?"

The elf eyed him shrewdly. "My name is Ellessar Miriel." He spoke the words calmly as though not to provoke, but his voice, harsh and grating, sent a shiver up Nick's spine. "I'm a demon hunter from the Order of the Shining Star. My prey has brought me into these woods."

"You hunt demons?" Jasmine spoke from within the folds of her cloak. "What do you do when you find them?"

Ellessar tilted his head as though trying to gain a vantage from which to observe her features. He spread the edges of his leather coat to display the garment. "Skin them, of course."

"That's, um, a good thing to do with demons." She spoke the last phrase a little too quickly.

Ellessar's eyes narrowed before he turned his attention to Zen. "You're not well. You should be resting. What urges you that's worth dying for?"

"We're driven by the Prophecy," Nick said. "And flee the Chosen of Vexetan."

"Then we share an enemy. Rest a few moments, and I'll help your friend if I can."

Zen started to protest, but his strength was already failing. The exertion of the past few minutes seemed to have halved his distance from death.

The centaur scouts had returned to the forest. The others began to prance in place.

"What is it?" Nick asked their leader. He, too, felt the press of even a few wasted moments, but he couldn't ignore Zen's obvious need.

"We sense no evil in the elf," Glazzer assured him. "We can rest here if he can help. But we must be brief."

Otto dismounted and helped Zen from his centaur's back while Nick spread a blanket for the mage to lay on.

The demon hunter knelt beside him, cupped the holy symbol in his hand, and murmured a prayer to Aeron. He cut away Zen's robes and placed a hand upon the wound in the mage's gut. Ellessar's hand glowed with a golden aura for several seconds. When he lifted it, the wound was gone. The pus that had oozed from the rotted opening had disappeared, leaving clean, raw skin behind. A faint pink print of Ellessar's hand remained on the skin as though the sun had burned it there.

"He has a wound on his leg as well," Jasmine said, "though I don't think it has soured."

Ellessar worked Zen's clothing away from that wound and repeated the healing ritual. "The wounds may still pain you for a few days. Treat them with care."

"Thank you," Zen said. Some measure of strength had returned to his voice.

"You say your quest takes you north?" Nick asked when Ellessar had finished. He breathed easier, as well, seeing his friend finally on the mend.

"My prey lurks there."

"Then I must warn you. The new king of Trondor and two of his most powerful men are Chosen of Vexetan. We expect—"

"Then my path is true," Ellessar said.

"Cocky bastard," Rancid muttered, just loudly enough for Nick and Ellessar to hear.

"We expect," Nick continued, "they'll invade the Black Forest with the full force of the Trondorian army behind them. If you go that way alone, you go to your death."

"If that is Aeron's wish." Ellessar paused. "If you oppose the Prophecy as you say, why do you not face the minions of the Master and defeat them?"

Because they're too strong. We can't defeat them by blind faith and brute force. Ellessar didn't seem the type to respect the prudence and practicality of such reasoning, so Nick said, "Aeron guides us along another path."

Ellessar nodded. "Then I bid you his blessings, and farewell."

Zen rose uneasily to his feet, his face flushed with color it hadn't shown in days. His features appeared less strained as he climbed onto his centaur.

Nick took Ellessar's hand. "Thank you, again."

"My pleasure." Ellessar tipped his worn hat to Glazzer. He mounted and rode north.

The next morning Ellessar knelt before Aeron. "Show me the way, so I may do your will."

His god never spoke to him in words—the glory of Aeron's message could never be conveyed in such mortal terms. Nevertheless, he granted Ellessar's request. As though it was instinctive, like the sense that guides birds to warmer climates in the cold months, Ellessar knew where his prey lurked: a half day's ride to the south. Apparently he'd passed the demon during the previous twenty-four hours.

Because Aeron granted this gift of guidance only once each day, Ellessar frequently passed his demon prey, often several times, before he came close enough to identify it.

Yesterday, the demon had been a day and a half to the north. Now a half day to the south. That meant he'd passed it just about the time he'd met the travelers.

The monk pulled her feet and hands into the confines of her cloak and turned her head away.

The demon must be moving south quickly to be half a day ahead already.

"You hunt demons? What do you do when you find them?"

Did the travelers know they were in danger—

"That's, um, a good thing to do with demons." The monk spoke the last phrase a little too quickly.

—from within their own ranks?

"Blessed Aeron, forgive me." It had disguised itself as a human among them. How did they not know? How could Ellessar have missed it?

Without breakfast, he leapt upon Spirit and sped south as fast as the growth of the forest allowed.

CHAPTER 14

As Nick and the others approached the southeastern boundary of the Black Forest, the centaur scouts returned.

"A contingent of the Home Guard just passed on the road," Glazzer said, "at a full gallop toward Pinewood. The man you called Dalen Frost is among them."

This far east, the Ponderosa Groves lay ten miles distant, across populated farmland. Nick had planned to wait until dark to make the crossing, but the sun would be up for at least six more hours. Dalen could double back by then. "We'd better cross now. Cloaks and hoods for everyone. Let's do this quickly. Make no contact with the farmers."

They reached the Ponderosa Groves by dusk and located a suitable point to cross the plains to the Sharktooth range by midafternoon the next day.

"You'd better get back to your tribe," Nick told the centaurs.

"We'll send Rancid out to a few of the farms to buy us some horses. Thanks for everything."

"Do you have enough coin?" Glazzer asked.

"We have several bottles of wine from the king's cellar. That should be sufficient."

"Farewell, then. Good luck."

"We don't need to buy horses—" Rancid began as soon as their centaur escort had left.

"I know," Nick said. "But the centaurs might not approve of stealing. We'll wait until dark. Then you and Otto can go."

"Otto may be recognized," Zen said. "I'll go."

"No way." Rancid made his appeal to Nick and Jasmine as though Zen wasn't standing there. "I'm not going out there with him. I still don't trust him. I'd rather risk being recognized than go out alone with Zen."

"We're talking about Tawneydale," Otto put in. "If we're recognized, we're finished."

"He's right," Nick said.

"You know—" Zen had a wicked gleam in his eyes— "we left Sierra with a bunch of extra horses. I could—"

"What do you want to do?" Rancid spat. "Go back for them?"

Zen sighed. "I could disguise myself to look like Sierra. Give myself long white hair—it'll look enough like her platinum blond, I think—and frost burn some spots on my skin to mimic her welts." His eyes brightened. It was nice to see some life back in them, now that his wounds had just about healed. "I'll steal some horses, make sure I'm seen doing it, and then escape. When she shows up with all her extra mounts..."

Nick studied him. "You'll have to shave your new growth of beard, but you just might pull it off."

Otto nodded. "That would certainly slow her down. You could borrow Rancid's cloak. The green is a close enough match for Sierra's—"

Rancid's head snapped up. "What?"

"Yes," Nick said.

"No."

"We've got to slow her down, and this might work if nobody sees Zen too closely."

"They won't." Zen was already rummaging through his pack, from which he produced a blade to shave with.

Rancid stood with his good hand on his hip, glaring at the lot of them. "I'd rather go by myself."

"Then we'll separate," Zen said. "I need to be seen alone anyway if this is going to work."

"Sure you're up to it?" Nick asked.

Zen nodded.

"All right." Nick glanced at each of them in turn. "It's decided."

Rancid huffed, but he made no further protest.

Nick continued, "The rest of us will wait here until you get back. We'll cross the plains tonight."

Seven centaurs racing through the woods had left a swath of snapped branches, broken twigs, and beaten ground cover that Ellessar couldn't miss. At intervals, a clump of rotted brush or a sickened branch showed where the demon monk had apparently touched the vegetation.

When the sun set, darkness forced him to slow, but with his elven eyesight, he refused to stop until exhaustion overcame him. The humans were apparently unaware of the true nature of their cloaked companion. Ellessar might already be too late.

When he caught up at dusk the following night, the shadowy bulk of one of the large men stood guard near a mass of brush. One of the others—smaller, probably one of the elf-kin—patrolled the shadows at the far side of the camp. The rest must have been sleeping in the bushes. One thing was sure: the centaurs had left.

Ellessar prayed in his native elven tongue, "Aeron, grant me your sight, so I might see our enemy." He scanned the woods until he found the demon. Up in a tree, a human-like shape the size of the monk glowed red as rage in Ellessar's divine vision. It leapt to the ground with a muffled thump and charged the camp.

The large man on guard duty intercepted it and swung his ax. The demon ducked beneath the blade and continued its charge.

"Nick!" the man yelled. "Wake up!"

Nick snapped awake at Otto's call. Before he could grab his sword and scramble from his blankets, a creature rushed him from the shadows, its skin glistening in the moonlight. It crashed through the brush like a charging bull, leading with long horns and claws. Venom or saliva dripped from three-inch fangs.

Jasmine dove at it with her *sai*. The weapon's pointed shaft, as long as her forearm, pierced the creature like a skewer, and the thing tumbled to the ground. As Jasmine rolled to her feet, the shaft of her *sai* disintegrated into dark flakes and fell to the ground. Only the hilt remained.

"Don't touch it," she yelled.

Nick grabbed his sword, forced his way out of the growth, and swung at the prone creature. In that instant, it vanished. Not into the woods, for it hadn't moved at all. It had simply disappeared.

The three scanned the shadows and listened for movement. At first there was only silence. Then a voice called out in an ancient tongue, and a figure advanced into the clearing with his bow raised at the lot of them.

Jasmine produced a throwing star from her belt, and Nick moved to intercept the newcomer. Otto strode toward the thicket where he and Nick had stashed their belongings.

Nick closed on the shadowed figure—Ellessar the demon hunter, by the cut of his hat and coat.

Otto shouted a warning as Ellessar released his arrow. It whipped past Nick's ear and into the creature that had disappeared, knocking it aside as it leapt at Nick from behind. The arrow disintegrated, as Jasmine's *sai* had done.

The creature hissed and scrambled single-mindedly after Nick.

Jasmine buried a throwing star into its back, but it kept coming. Sword-like claws ripped into Nick's arm.

Otto smashed it with the butt of his ax, and the weapon's wooden handle began to dissolve. With the remaining end, he sliced a gash across the creature's belly.

It shrieked and writhed, spilling dark green blood that pooled on the ground. The head of Otto's ax crumbled to dust, and the creature vanished once again.

"Back to back," Ellessar ordered. "Eyes open."

Otto pulled his crossbow from his belt, and Jasmine held her remaining *sai* ready. The four remained in a tight knot, facing outward for several minutes.

The rents in Nick's arm stung and bled, but he kept his grip tight on his sword.

"I cut it pretty bad," Otto said finally. "Maybe it's gone off in search of easier prey."

Ellessar shook his head. "Not this thing. It may not come back tonight, but it will return."

The others turned to face him.

"It has but one prey, which it must kill to free itself from servitude."

"You know what it is?" Nick asked the elf.

"It's the demon that drew me into the forest. I've never seen one of its kind, but I recognize it from the texts." He took Nick's wrist gently and examined the lacerations on his arm. "You're lucky it touched you only with its claws and not its skin."

"What do you know about it?" Otto asked.

"It's an Assassin, called from the Abyss for a single purpose and given a specific target, which it hones in on by instinct."

"Nick," Jasmine guessed.

"Apparently. Assassins are cunning and patient. It'll track its target for as long as it must to find a moment of weakness." Ellessar retrieved the *sai* handle from the ground and displayed it to the others. "The demon's skin secretes a corrosive compound that makes it difficult to fight and leaves its prey defenseless. It heals quickly. And it can translocate at will."

He passed the *sai* handle to Nick. "You're in great danger."

CHAPTER 15

As soon as Jasmine had cleaned and dressed Nick's wounds, and Zen and Rancid returned with the horses, Nick and the others mounted.

"I'll accompany you?" Ellessar said. "The demon will continue to come for you. Staying by your side is the surest way for me to find it again."

Nick gave Ellessar and his horse a quick appraisal. The horse was lathered with sweat that glistened even in the dim light of the torch Jasmine had lit so she could bandage Nick's arm. "We can use the extra sword, and you've proven your skill as a healer, but your horse looks exhausted. We can't wait for you."

Ellessar nodded. "Spirit is the best of a sturdy breed. She'll make it."

"Suit yourself."

Jasmine, who'd hung back in the shadows, motioned Nick to her side. "Have you forgotten Vinra? What if this so-called demon hunter is a spy or assassin for Balor?"

"I thought about that, but Ellessar wears a holy symbol of Aeron. He couldn't wear that with a Medallion of Vexetan."

"And if he is who he claims to be, what of my demon blood?"

"We'll cross that valley when we come to it." He placed a reassuring hand on her shoulder. "You have too many friends here for him to harm you. In the meantime, we need all the help we can get."

"We might have said the same about Vinra."

"I know." Nick flexed his arm. He winced at the sting of the wounds the Assassin had given him. "But I don't think we can afford to turn down his help right now."

He returned to the others. "Farmers wake early. Let's get this done."

At that, Jasmine set down her torch and doused the flame with dirt. She mounted her own horse and took her place at the rear of the party.

Otto nudged his horse forward to the edge of the trees, glanced back once, and bolted into the night with Nick and the others quick on his heels.

They crossed the main road just southeast of Tawneydale by the time the moon became full and then cut across harvested fields. When the light waned, they slowed to let the horses pick their way more carefully until Otto located a wagon trail, which they followed nearly all the way to the foothills.

Near dawn, as they passed the last of the farmhouses, an elderly man emerged from his front door, bundled against the late fall air. Halfway to the chicken coup, he must have heard the horses' hooves. He looked up and watched Nick's procession pass. The man was close enough to make out their numbers, but it was doubtful he could discern their features.

Nick followed Otto's lead and waved to the farmer as they passed.

The group was climbing into the foothills before the sun came over the peaks. Exhausted from twenty-four hours of flight—among them, only Nick had gotten any sleep at all—they sheltered inside a small canyon. Ellessar groomed Spirit and inspected her legs and hooves, then walked her until she was cool. Nick did the same for the other horses. In the meantime, Otto prepared a quick meal over a small fire.

Zen tapped the weave briefly.

Rancid scowled at him, then patrolled the perimeter of the camp. Jasmine inspected Nick's and Zen's wounds before moving off to the far side of the camp and rolling herself into her blankets. Then, with Nick at watch, the rest of the party bedded down for the better part of the day.

Anxious to keep moving, however, Nick woke the group early that afternoon and they made a few more miles before dark. The six continued east, deeper into the hills until the moonlight failed them as well. There, they camped on a riverbank until mid-morning.

When Ellessar awoke, he folded and packed his blankets, sank to his knees in supplication before Aeron, and prayed for what must have been thirty minutes.

Rancid rolled his eyes and went about preparing breakfast, a few bits of smoked fowl and some pasty meal the centaurs had provided, boiled in water until it was reduced to a flavorless mush.

Jasmine made herself scarce, searching beyond the camp for herbs she could use for either cooking or healing. Nick broke out his fishing tackle, which he hadn't used since before they'd left Meuribar, and fished with Otto. The two caught enough brook trout to feed the party for the rest of the day.

"Aeron's guidance is imprecise this morning," Ellessar said once everyone had returned to the group. He didn't seem overly concerned about the fact. "The Assassin is somewhere south of here. I don't know how far. The impression is vague."

"What does that mean?" Nick asked.

Ellessar shrugged. "Maybe I'm not meant to pursue it, since it's pursuing us."

"Maybe we outran it," Otto offered.

"Perhaps. But it's guided by Vexetan. It will follow. And it will find us."

Nick had been thinking less about the Assassin this morning and more about Dalen. As an elite of the king's guard, Dalen was an accomplished tracker. He was mounted, and he could requisition fresh horses at need. "We'll make better time if we travel during the day. In these mountains, I'm more concerned about our speed than about whether we're seen. But before we go—" He turned to Ellessar— "you should know with whom you travel. Balor has reason to hunt us beyond our opposition of the Prophecy."

Ellessar raised a forestalling hand. "Aeron has led me to you. For the moment, we share one path. I'll hear your confession if you wish, but not now. If you still wish to tell me tonight, I'll listen then." He rose and scraped his bowl clean.

The weather remained cold but clear. They made good time and camped at another river overnight. Rancid prepared the fish from that morning while Otto and Nick caught more for the following days. Jasmine searched the riverbank for anything that might help replenish her empty healer's bag. When the fire died down to embers, Nick asked Ellessar, "Will you hear my confession now?"

"If you wish."

Nick settled in beside him. "We came into the civil war late." He took a deep, calming breath.

"Go on," Ellessar said after a moment.

"When we did enter the conflict, we joined the rebels and put an end to the war."

"Indeed? That's quite a claim."

"Dalen Frost was a double agent. He got us an audience with the late King Gremauld. By all accounts, Gremauld was a savage. People called him, 'the butcher of Tawneydale and Twin Peaks.' Once we got inside his tent, we killed him." Nick had no reason to honey-coat the truth. Whatever justification he thought he had at the time, it didn't excuse the fact that they'd committed murder.

"I care not about your crimes nor the events that surround them.

They're for Aeron alone to judge. As for me, I must remain until I've destroyed the Assassin. Then I'll go wherever Aeron bids me." For a moment, he seemed deep in thought. "Why does Balor hunt you? If you won the war for him, you handed him the throne of Trondor."

"He used us. Now he hunts us because we oppose the Prophecy, which we believe will soon come to pass. But all those who now search the hills, forests, and fields of Trondor on his behalf do so because we killed their king."

"After more than fifteen-hundred years, what makes you think the Prophecy's fulfillment is imminent now?"

"The civil war, for one thing," Nick said.

Rancid joined them, clutching a large, dead rabbit by its ears. "Many of the goblin slaves in Palidor have escaped their masters and are massing, with the help of orcs, under an ogre named Groot, a Chosen of the Master."

"And finally," Nick continued, "we believe one of the Chosen knows the location of the key to the Portal of the Damned. It's only a matter of time before he recovers it and releases the demons."

"That leaves only one portent," Zen added. "The return of the dragons."

Ellessar's nod was somber, his focus distant. "I saw one in the sky less than a week ago."

Nick should have been surprised, but he wasn't. "Then time is shorter than we thought."

"If it's Aeron's will," Ellessar said, "I'll kill the demon that hunts you, and you'll see your way clear of the kingdom."

Jasmine approached from behind Ellessar, keeping her hood up and her head turned. "Forgive me. I could not help overhearing. You know our history?"

Ellessar turned toward her. "Yes."

"And you still plan to keep our company?"

"I must."

"Then you should know something else as well." She lowered her cowl and faced him squarely. "I carry demon blood."

"I thought you a full demon until the Assassin invaded your camp." Ellessar scowled, pensive for a moment. "Yet Aeron doesn't bid me to kill you." He rose to his feet, his hands free to draw his sword. "How do you justify yourself?"

Jasmine straightened. "I do not. I need only justify what I do, not what I am."

"By your own words, you're a demon."

"I believe I'm the product of some foul experiment perpetrated by my father. I need not justify my demon blood any more than you must justify your elven heritage."

"She's right," Rancid said. "We all have pasts we'd just as soon forget."

"Will you submit to a Zone of Truth?" Ellessar asked Jasmine.

She backed a step away from him. "What is it?"

"An enchantment used for interrogation. Anyone who speaks falsely within it will die."

Nick held up his hand. "You don't have to do that, Jasmine." To Ellessar he said, "If you need justification, look to her actions. She fought with you *against* the Assassin."

"Be that as it may..." Ellessar's lips pressed into a tight smile. "The moment Aeron bids me to do so, I *will* kill you."

Zen stood. "It'll be the last thing you ever do."

"If that is Aeron's will. Excuse me. I must pray." He turned his back on the lot of them and strode into the mounting darkness.

Zen wove a night-vision enchantment so he could see beyond the faint glow of the dying fire. "I'm going to go practice my weaving."

"Wait." Nick rose when Zen was several strides from the others and caught up to him. "I've seen you weaving nearly every night since we left the guild house." He kept his voice at a whisper.

"Every night, actually, and every morning. It's a veil to prevent scrying."

"Scrying?"

"To keep the enemy from using enchantments to observe us from afar. It's taxing—"

"But prudent."

"I think so."

"And your nightly practice?"

"That's taxing too, but it keeps my skills honed. I'm always working on something new."

Nick nodded. "Also prudent."

"Yes."

Both remained silent for a moment.

Zen could still see Ellessar. The demon hunter had perched himself on a small rise about a hundred yards out. "Anything else?" he asked finally.

Nick hesitated. "You sleeping okay?" He already knew the answer or he wouldn't have asked.

"Sure," Zen lied. "Why?" Nightmares of Dara's death had continued to plague him.

"Several times a night, I hear you muttering and tossing in your sleep. Sometimes you cry out."

Zen's heart raced. "What have I said?"

"The only word I can make out is 'no,' over and over again, like someone was torturing you."

Zen shrugged, breathing easier. "If I'm dreaming, I don't remember anything about it in the morning."

"Maybe Jasmine can give you something to make your sleep more restful."

"Thanks. I'll ask her. But really, I feel fine." He patted his friend on the shoulder and moved off into the darkness to keep an eye on Ellessar.

That evening, he practiced his hand movements only—gestures with no power in them. He was unwilling to tap the weave and tax his strength until Ellessar finished his prayers. When he did, Zen intercepted him on his way back toward the camp. "I wanted to ask you about the Assassin's translocation ability."

Ellessar eyed him warily.

"I assume it's magical. Do you know how it works?"

Still no answer.

"I want to be ready when that thing returns. Maybe there's a way I can counter the ability, a way to keep the demon from escaping so you can kill it."

Nick and his friends travelled throughout the next day, and by evening, they gazed down on the broad valley where the foothills receded and the southern Trondorian plains stretched all the way to the mouth of Stunted Spruce Pass, the valley where Nick had first met Balor Culhaven. At the time, Balor was the hero of the southlands, fighting a valiant and righteous battle against the atrocities of the pretender, Gremauld.

Otto came up beside him. "The pass will surely be watched, and probably this valley as well."

Nick gauged the height of the sun near the western horizon. "Then we'll cross in the darkness."

They waited for the moon to brighten just enough to see by, crossed quickly, and reached the hills on the far side before sunup.

The companions had seen no sign of pursuit since they'd left the Ponderosa Groves, and their spirits were higher than they'd been since they'd found the original Codex. Nick began to hope, dared to hope, that they would actually reach Faldor.

Ellessar, however, kept that hope in check. Each morning, he reported the presence of the Assassin somewhere to the south. It remained there for the next two days, paralleling their path, waiting for a chance to strike.

Otto led them eastward until the mountain range swung north and a broad stretch of hill country marked the border of Trondor. Expecting patrols, they crossed in the dark hours of the morning and rode onto the plains of Faldor with a full day before them.

Balor's army had no jurisdiction there, so Nick felt free to travel the plains without concealment. But the party rode quickly, to put as much distance behind them as possible. The Assassin demon, Sierra Glenwood, other mercenaries, Dalen, and the rest of the Chosen would ignore political boundaries.

"Go, all you," Groot had told Halidreth. "Meet Chosen in Brinheim. Find Sevendeath."

As leader of the Black Hand, Halidreth had thought to refuse, but with the goblin riots reaching a climax in Palidor, and with orcs—and now, reportedly, trolls—wandering the countryside, regular caravan traffic had all but come to an end. So, too, had the profitability of banditry. The only thing left for the Black Hand to do was to leave the kingdom.

Brinheim seemed as good a place as any to ride out the storm. And if this Chosen could help them reap revenge from Rancid Sevendeath in the meantime, so much the better.

The only problem now was identifying the Chosen they were supposed to meet. Groot had said nothing about what this person would look like. "Put your gloves on," Halidreth told his remaining twenty-three bandits as they rode into Brinheim's capital. The symbol of the bandit gang wouldn't likely be recognized beyond Palidor's border, and it would give the Chosen some means to identify them.

Before they arrived at the center of town, a dust devil, the worst he'd ever seen, whipped up a cloud that clogged the air. The townspeople scattered for the cover of the buildings, and the bandits' horses pranced backward. When the whirlwind subsided, a cloud of dust hung in the air behind it, drifting ever closer.

Halidreth grabbed a rag from his saddlebag, soaked it with drinking water, and held it over his mouth and nose. A shining ring materialized in the air before him, spinning as though flipped like a coin from some unseen hand. Halidreth squinted toward the point at which it had appeared. A form blocked part of the cloud as the dust overtook them. Halidreth could discern the rough shape of some invisible humanoid, or perhaps goblinoid, who stood motionless until the cloud became so thick that everything beyond a few feet disappeared from view.

The simple gold ring lay at his horse's feet. Halidreth climbed down and retrieved it with one hand on the hilt of his sword. As he did, a whistling sound filled the air, like a blast of wind past a leaky doorframe. He lowered the dust-clotted rag and slid the ring onto his hand.

"—am Whisper, Chosen of the Master Vornax." The words whipped past his ears like a cold wind, born from the whistling in the air. "I'll be your tracker and guide as we seek out Sevendeath and his friends."

A bag of coins materialized in the air and fell where the ring had. "Rest and resupply," the wind said. "We leave for Loran at dawn tomorrow."

Four days Sierra Glenwood had waited in a cell in the Tawneydale lockup, one of the few buildings strong enough to have withstood Gremauld's razing during the war. When she'd come into town, a hostler had claimed to recognize her as the woman who'd stolen one of his horses the previous night—the same night four other horses had also gone missing. But Sierra had come into town with six spare horses, not five, and all of the victims eventually admitted that none of Sierra's horses were any of those that had been stolen.

The delay had cost her time, but this coin had two sides. She didn't believe the event was coincidental, and when the Council had given her the writ for these particular fugitives, they'd warned her that the ice mage, Zen, could alter his appearance. The theft of these horses had put her back on the scent.

The roads of the area, however, were too well-traveled to track a specific trail, especially one made by horses' hooves. So she'd gone from house to house, searching for anyone who might have seen them. It had taken three additional days to find one.

"How many were there?" she asked the agitated old farmer.

"How should I know? It was dark. Maybe half a dozen."

"Early morning?"

"Yes, yes. That's what I said. Weren't you listening?"

"Could you see their faces?" Sierra sat astride her mount, six horses still in tow behind her.

The old man squinted at her as if he was looking into the sun. "Are you daft, woman? I said it was dark."

Sierra whipped both swords from their sheaths and crossed them at the farmer's neck. Her face tightened and her jaw clenched with a week of suppressed frustration. "I am no woman. Do not insult an elf."

The old man staggered back, bringing his hands up to fend her off. "I, I meant no offense. I didn't see any faces. They wore cloaks."

"All of them?"

He nodded and pointed toward the east. "They rode that way, into the hills. Several days ago," he repeated. "Just before sunup."

There was nothing between Sierra and the foothills. This man's farm was the last before the land became too rugged for crops. No roads. No trails. She could think of no reason anyone would be going that way in the darkest part of the night.

Unless they were on the run.

She yanked the reins and pulled her horses into line, then galloped ahead until only a few tracks remained. If these were her prey, they'd made no attempt to hide their trail. That alone was worrisome. Surely the fugitives would have attempted to do so. Nevertheless, she followed. The tracks were the only lead she had.

Before long, however, she came to a camp where several people had lit only a small fire. Tracks showed where someone had walked a number of horses in circles to cool them down. Then she found the three-pronged tracks of the demon-kin's deformed feet. With no doubt left in her mind, she followed them at speed. The hills were rugged, but the fugitives had left many signs of their passage. Each day, the tracks became more and more fresh.

CHAPTER 16

As Nick and the others readied their mounts the morning after their first night in Faldor, the ground began to rumble and the horses to prance.

Nick's gaze sought Spitfire Mountain, a solitary peak on the southern horizon. It was always smoking, and it even shook the ground every now and then, but not at this distance. As the rumbling continued, it grew louder, became more immediate. The source of the tremor seemed to move closer. Within minutes, it threatened to knock them from their feet.

"That's not a volcanic tremor," Ellessar said.

"No." Nick motioned for the others to gather closer. "It's a ground shark."

"Ground shark?" Rancid said. "What in the baron's bloody bath is a ground shark?"

Nick drew his sword. "Bad news."

The prairie erupted in a shower of grasses, dirt, and gravel. A huge armored beast, standing eight feet at the shoulder and fifteen feet long, burst through the surface, its maw snapping at the air.

Nick wheeled back, sword flailing to keep the beast at bay.

The shark lumbered forward on short, powerful legs. During Nick's years with his uncle Harimon's caravan, he'd passed through Faldor many times, but he'd never seen a ground shark firsthand. It moved more quickly than he'd have thought possible.

Rancid, Jasmine, and Zen gave the shark some room. The horses reared and whinnied until Ellessar swatted Spirit's rump, and then they all sprinted away.

The shark's toothless jaw, more beak than mouth, snatched up Ellessar. The demon hunter gritted his teeth and growled in obvious pain, but the shark seemed unable to penetrate his armor. Finally it tossed him aside.

Rancid and Jasmine bounced daggers and throwing stars harmlessly off the shark's armored side, trying to draw its attention as Ellessar scrambled to his feet, one of his arms bleeding. Nick drove his sword into the shark's face, but the beast merely snapped at the irritation as it advanced.

"Back away!" Nick shouted over the thunder of the shark's movements. "Everybody back away!" He faced it squarely and the beast chomped at him again.

Finally, one of Rancid's daggers sank into the shark's left eye. The orb popped, gore splattered Nick's armor, and the beast thrashed wildly. Its armored head smashed into Ellessar with a sickening crack and he flopped, broken, to the ground.

Nick swung again, a glancing blow against its armor.

The shark continued to thrash, lifting its enormous bulk onto its hind legs and then coming down with a force that rocked the earth.

Nick staggered before recovering his balance. "Get back! All of you!" Without armor, the others could be crushed by the shark's massive jaws. His friends seemed unwilling to let him perish alone while they escaped to safety, but Nick had no intention of dying.

He battered at the shark's face and it came for him. As he lured it forward, Jasmine raced behind it to get to Ellessar, working at the strings of her medicine bag as she ran.

Finally he lured the shark far enough from the others to give Zen a clear angle. A blast of frigid air slammed into it. Nick screamed against the biting cold and staggered away on nearly frostbitten legs.

Used to the moderated underground temperatures, the shark stumbled to the left, shaking.

Another blast of arctic air made it reel. A thick crust of ice formed on its side. By then, Nick had also backed beyond the range of Zen's staff.

A third blast dropped the shark to the ground. The tremor of its impact knocked them all from their feet.

Nick picked himself up, weakened more from relief than from fatigue. He turned in a full, slow circle to make sure the Assassin hadn't translocated among them during their brief distraction. Seeing no sign of the demon, Nick ran to Ellessar.

Jasmine knelt by the elf's side. Blood pooled beneath his head.

"He's alive. Barely." She grabbed a handful of powdered yarrow and a glob of tree sap from her healing kit and mashed them together into a clean rag. She'd used the same salve on his arm after the demon attack. Gently, she placed it over the split in Ellessar's scalp and bound it with a strip of cloth.

"Get him up," Rancid said. "Nick, catch the horses. A dead carcass this size will attract things we don't want to fight."

"Like the dragon," Zen said.

Jasmine shook her head. "If we move him, we might kill him. His breathing is too shallow. I can barely hear his heart."

Rancid scanned the sky as though he expected to see the dragon above them already.

Zen stood over them now. "As much as I hate to agree with Rancid..."

Jasmine pursed her lips, assessed the monster, and then glanced at the sky. "Do you really think it will draw the dragon?"

Nick had made no move to recapture the horses. They were too skittish. They'd need time to settle down before anyone could approach them. "If it's connected with the Prophecy, we can count on running into it sooner or later. I have no desire to rush the meeting. Rancid's right. We have to move."

Concern creased Jasmine's forehead. "We'll need a litter."

Rancid drew his sword and slid it between two plates of the carapace that protected the monster's back. The tissue seemed to cut easily. Blood poured onto the ground as he sliced around the plate. Nick and Otto helped him pull it free. It came loose with a wet sucking sound and the sweet smell of blood. Within an hour, they had the inside scraped clean and two holes bored by daggers to harness it behind one of the horses.

By then, Rancid had separated three more of the plates and lashed them in a blanket to be tied to one of the horses.

"There." Rancid nudged Nick and pointed at Zen. "He's doing magic."

By the time Nick turned, Zen had finished weaving.

"I don't think that's Zen." Rancid spoke so only Nick and Otto could hear.

"What do you mean?" Nick asked.

"He never used to do that. Zen only uses magic with flashy effects, and only during battle." Rancid glanced over his shoulder at the mage. "He never used to 'tap the weave,' or whatever, for no apparent reason. Ever since he showed up at the guild house, he's done it several times a day. What's more, he hasn't been sleeping well. If I didn't know better, I'd say he was having nightmares. Zen never used to do that either."

"We're all under a lot of stress."

Nick waved for Zen to join them. "Rancid's concerned about you."

Zen put his hand over his heart. "I'm touched."

"I think it would ease his mind if you told us what enchantment you were just weaving."

"Not that I feel any obligation to ease Rancid's mind, given the trouble he caused us in Palidor." Zen's eyes had a playful gleam that seemed to annoy Rancid as much as his words did. "I was looking for the magic aura of Ellessar's swords, to see what kind of enchantment they carry."

Rancid planted his hand on his hip. "And?"

"There isn't one. The runes are fake. I'm not sure why he carries fake magic, as Vinra did, but it's probably better if he doesn't realize we know."

Nick cocked a patient eyebrow at Rancid. "Satisfied?"

Rancid huffed once and stomped back to Jasmine.

Zen waited for Rancid to get beyond earshot. "And Ellessar, too, is posing as a priest. Sound familiar?"

"Indeed it does." It was the same ploy Vinsous Drakemoor had used to infiltrate the party. "We'll have to keep an eye on him."

Rancid set about catching the mounts. Spirit was much too nimble and agitated to approach. The others, however, with their reins still tied to one another from the night before, were hindered enough for Rancid to capture them.

He and Jasmine tied the litter behind one of the horses, and then the group began a slow trek to the hills, no more than five miles to the south. Jasmine walked behind the litter, holding the back end off the ground and watching Ellessar closely. She insisted Rancid keep the pace at a crawl.

Nick watched the landscape behind them constantly, always expecting to see the Assassin or a Trondorian patrol. He kept one eye on the skies for the dragon or Dalen's hawk.

If the Assassin demon showed up, however, it probably wouldn't come from behind. More likely, it would materialize in front of him while he was looking back. He'd find a fistful of two-foot-long claws in his chest or a mouthful of teeth in his neck before he could draw his blade. So in a rare gesture of unease, he held his sword in his hand as he walked.

Porting Ellessar, it took a full day to cover the five miles to the hills. Spirit followed, always keeping her master in sight but never venturing close enough to be captured.

Jasmine stayed up with the demon hunter throughout the night. In the early morning hours, during Nick's watch, he began to stir and moan. At one point, he regained consciousness. He squinted his eyes as if trying to figure out who it was sitting beside him.

"It's Nick and Jasmine." She touched his arm gently.

Without responding, Ellessar closed his eyes again. Barely, his lips moved.

For an instant, the sun seemed to crest the horizon. A blaze from the sky struck them. Then it became dark once more.

Jasmine leapt to her feet.

Nick scanned the camp, expecting some attack or enchantment. But there was none. The camp remained quiet, his friends asleep.

When Ellessar opened his eyes a few minutes later, he seemed lucid. "Aeron's blessing to you." His voice was quiet but clear, and he tried to sit up.

"Wait." Jasmine placed a hand on his chest until he lay back down. "Let me change your bandage."

She prepared another dressing and carefully unwrapped his head. After scrubbing the dried blood away, using a towel moistened with drinking water, she parted his hair and inspected the wound. "I'll be an Elder of the Sage. Your head is almost healed. Scar tissue has already formed over much of the wound."

"I've been touched by the hand of Aeron," Ellessar said. "He protects those who serve him."

"Be that as it may..." Jasmine dressed the wound before allowing him to stand.

When he did, he staggered. "I'm still weak, however." He righted himself and faced Jasmine squarely. He looked her in the eye. "I'm grateful for your care."

"We'll rest here for the day," Nick assured him. "We can afford that much time, I think."

"Don't be hasty. I'll seek the Assassin. Then you may decide."

He walked as if he were drunk to the top of the nearest rise and then knelt in supplication.

Nick let him be. The sun would be up in earnest soon and the camp awake. "What do you make of it?" he asked Jasmine.

She seemed to consider her words before answering. "There is much of the gods that I don't understand. I've read some of the texts, but..." She shrugged. "I've never seen anything like that before."

"But it's not *fake* magic?"

"No. The healing is definitely real."

"Look at that." Nick gestured at Spirit, standing vigil over Ellessar during his prayers. When the demon hunter returned, his horse walked by his side.

"We have some time." The demon hunter's skin was pale, even for an elf's. His eyes appeared sunken and he wavered on his feet. "The Assassin is more than two days west of here."

"We're outrunning it?" Nick asked.

"It may not be able to keep pace with a horse, but demons never sleep." He paused. "It will catch up."

Sierra Glenwood came down out of the last hills along the border and into the wind-swept plains of Faldor. Here, the trail vanished into a sea of grass. And she was still a day behind.

The fugitives would need supplies. They could acquire them in either of two cities: the capital to the east, or Spitfire to the south. The capital was by far the larger of the two. The fugitives could probably lose themselves among the populace, but Sierra didn't think they'd go there. The capital was the first place an emissary of Trondor would go to bring news of the fugitives and of the offered rewards.

No. Spitfire was the better choice. If she hurried, she could probably make it in a day and a half. So she pointed her mount toward the solitary peak smoking in the distance and spurred it to a full run.

CHAPTER 17

By the time Rancid led them out of camp toward Spitfire, El-lessar seemed as strong as he had the day they'd met him.

After the sun had set that evening and the cold of night had settled in, the companions came across a road that led into the foothills around the solitary smoking peak. Merchants, farmers, and ranchers packed the road despite the late hour. Families, some with children, traveled among them. Lanterns dangled from wagons, hands, and horses. All were heading for the city.

Rancid breathed easier. Whatever the reason for such heavy traffic at this hour, a greater stroke of good fortune couldn't have befallen them. He pulled up the hood of his cloak to hide his features and waited for the others to catch up. When he was satisfied that all were properly bundled, they stepped onto the road and lost themselves in the throng.

The road approached Spitfire, a walled village nestled against the southern slopes of Spitfire Mountain, after three or four miles of winding ascent through the surrounding hill country. The guards appeared alert, watching the crowd for signs of trouble, but the gate remained open, and the sentries molested no one.

Even now, nearing midnight, the streets remained packed with late arrivals. Raucous shouts and music drifted out of a tavern as they passed. A gentleman stormed out the front door of the Lazy Horse Inn, shoved a pedestrian aside, and signaled for his carriage. "Try the next one," he told the driver. "This one's full."

Rancid turned to Nick with a cocked eyebrow. This quaint village was large enough to house maybe a thousand residents. There must have been several times that many people just in the streets at that moment. Finding accommodations seemed unlikely.

Nick shrugged, apparently not knowing what had brought all the people in.

"Come on." Ellessar pushed his way past the others and took the lead. "Aeron has a temple here. We'll stay there." Six blocks farther down the main street, he entered the crowded square, maneuvered right, toward the volcanic peak, and took the main cross street to the temple. The emblem of Ellessar's order got them past the guards without questions.

"Have you been here before?" Nick asked him.

"No."

"How did you know where to find the temple?" Rancid asked as they passed through the gates into the courtyard.

The demon hunter didn't take his eyes off the main building. "The volcano itself is the only suitable backdrop in this town for a temple of Aeron."

Rancid bit his tongue on the retort that came to his lips. Though Zen had tried to divert suspicion from himself by reporting Ellessar's magic as fake, the demon hunter's arrogance couldn't be mistaken. He was a genuine priest of Aeron, all right. One that Rancid would just as soon be rid of.

Ellessar marched to the front doors, giant wooden portals banded in steel. The temple, constructed entirely of granite, reminded Rancid of the library in Eckland, but the architecture here was more stylized. Spires reminiscent of a castle, but too narrow to serve as guard towers, rose at each corner. The stonework around the doors and windows contained intricate carvings.

"We've come for refuge and repast," Ellessar told the sentry.

Though not armored like the guards at the village gate, the guard did carry a sword. Otherwise, he wore only the white robes of service to the church. "Of course, brother. Enter and be welcome."

The hall within was dimly lit by burning oil lamps perched on stone pedestals. The air was cool and dry. An elderly man in white robes approached from an antechamber to greet them. Fine wisps of hair that matched his clothing clung tenuously to his scalp.

"Welcome, brother." He held out both hands to Ellessar, who took them as if the two were old friends. Yet something about the ritual greeting, a subtle formality perhaps, gave Rancid the impression that the men had never met before.

The priest, if priest he was, addressed the others. "Welcome. I offer you the humble hospitality of the church."

Rancid rolled his eyes. He'd never known an order, religious or otherwise, to be nearly as humble as it claimed to be. Instinctively, he took stock of the furnishing in the entrance hall. The fabrics were of good quality but woven of common threads. The stone statues, all an image of the same elf in some impractical fighting posture, portrayed exaggerated grace and beauty. They'd be more valuable for their subject and craftsmanship than for the stone from which they'd been carved. Clearly, this temple didn't have the resources of Alamain's in Lorentil. Rancid forced his attention back to Ellessar.

"...must warn you of why we've come here. The Order of the Shining Star—" Ellessar lifted his pendant and drew the priest's attention to the star toward the upper left— "is the brotherhood of demon hunters."

"Your order is known to us," the priest said without the slightest change in his tranquil tone.

"I travel with these people because a demon hunts one of them."

"Indeed?" The priest glanced at the others.

"It's an Assassin demon. Fast, cunning, and powerful. We managed to run it off, but it trails us and will strike again if we allow it the opportunity."

"I see."

"I don't believe it will enter the village, especially with the population swollen as it is tonight, but someone should warn the city guard in any case."

"I'll send one of the acolytes immediately." The priest plucked a bell from a small table that also held a silver pitcher of water and several goblets, and rang it.

"One more thing," Ellessar said. "The Assassin can translocate across short distances. It need not pass through the gates to enter the city, nor pass through the door to enter this temple."

A boy of maybe fourteen harvests, wearing a white robe and slippers, ran into the room. "I'm sorry, father." He skidded to a halt and approached the priest at a more respectful pace.

The old man scribbled a message on a piece of parchment, gave it to the boy, and sent him away with instructions to wake the captain of the guard if necessary.

That done, the priest returned his attention to Ellessar. "You'll need rooms for the night."

Ellessar bowed in acknowledgement.

"They're not much." The priest turned to the others. "But they're warm and quiet, suitable for reflection upon your life and your manner of living."

The next morning, the entire party gathered in Nick's tiny stone bedchamber to inventory their supplies. They each tossed their coins into a pile on the cot—a hundred gold or so, maybe a little less, most of it given to them by Xanth. "What do we have to sell?" Nick asked.

"Spirits from Balor's cellar." Rancid rummaged through his pack.

The others produced bottles as well, eight in all.

"Keep the bitterroot wine." Otto gestured to the gilt-labeled bottle as Rancid set it on the cot.

"Why?" Rancid sounded annoyed.

"It's our most valuable bottle. And you can only get it in Trondor. The farther south we go, the more valuable it'll become."

Rancid scowled as though he didn't quite believe the constable, but he stuffed the bottle back into his pack anyway. "We also have several armor plates from the ground shark, probably enough to fashion a few shields. The armor smith might pay something for them."

"Isn't steel stronger?" Jasmine asked.

"Maybe not," Rancid said.

"Then why does everyone use steel?"

"Would you go hunting ground sharks just for the carapace?"

"Rancid's got a point," Nick interjected. "My sword can penetrate platemail five times in ten, but it only cracked the ground shark's face once, and the plates from its back are much thicker. Its rarity might drive the price up even if it's only marginally stronger than steel."

"Okay. What else?" Jasmine asked.

"The ring." Zen gestured to the gold band on Rancid's left hand, which Rancid had looted from one of the Black Hand bandits the day the air apparition, Whisper, had stolen Gaddy's journal from Nick.

Rancid covered it with his right hand. "It's proven useful. We may need it again."

"Useful?" Zen asked. "What do you mean?"

"It lets me understand languages I can't speak. Once we get past the Great Divide and into the Wild Lands, we'll probably need it."

"Let's see what we can afford," Nick said. "Then we can decide whether the coin is more important." He thought for a moment. "First, we need swords. When that Assassin comes at us again, we'll want spares."

Ellessar gestured toward Nick's weapon, which was leaning against the wall. Though its blade had corroded nearly halfway through from their first encounter with the demon, it had survived. "A sword like yours is going to cost some coin. My armor needs repair too. And we're running low on food."

"Throwing stars," Jasmine added. "And I want to replenish my healer's bag."

"You can do that here at the temple," Ellessar said, "for a suitable donation."

"Okay, okay." Rancid threw his arm in the air as if this were all a conspiracy against him personally. "I'm willing to sell the ring if it gets me an exceptional sword in return. I mean a really good, dwarven-made sword. The best."

"You don't want much, do you?" Zen said.

"It's all right." Nick held up a placating hand. "Dwarven-made weapons are expensive, but they're around. It's his ring. He can spend it however he wants. Besides, maybe a better sword will actually stand up against the secretions of the demon's skin."

"Unless the sword is enchanted, don't count on it," Ellessar said.

A bell rang out from the temple's tower.

Ellessar rose and stretched his back. "Somebody make a list of what we need. I'm going to the morning service." He squeezed past the others and left the cramped room.

Nick and the others followed a few minutes later, looking for the temple's mess hall.

As soon as they entered the main foyer, the elder from the previous night intercepted them. "Excuse me, young souls, might I speak with you?" He appeared agitated despite the politeness of his words.

Nick scanned the foyer for Ellessar before returning his attention to the priest. "Of course."

The old man led them into a private office and closed the door before continuing. "I sent an acolyte to the gate last night to warn the guards of your demon."

Nick nodded. "I remember."

"After he delivered the message, he saw an elven guide speaking to another of the sentries. As he passed, he overheard the guide give a description that he recognized. Yours." He indicated Jasmine. "The acolyte lingered close enough to hear the rest of the conversation."

"What did this guide look like?" Otto asked.

"An elven female with platinum hair, wearing a solid forest-green cloak. She's a mercenary with an official writ from the Ruling Council of Trondor."

Rancid spat into the corner. "Sierra Glenwood."

"Young man." The priest thrust his chin at Rancid. "You may not have learned civility or manners wherever you grew up, and I'm not acquainted with your beliefs, but you will show respect in the Temple of Aeron."

Rancid bowed his head. He had no respect for authority and even less for any father figure, but he seemed to understand that with Sierra in town, their lives might depend on what this priest decided to do about them. He nodded weakly without taking his eyes from the floor.

"What did the mercenary say about me?" Jasmine asked, drawing the old man's attention from Rancid.

"Not just you. She gave descriptions of all of you—except brother Ellessar, which doesn't speak well for his choice of company." The priest's pause grew long, but no one spoke to fill it. "She asked the guards if they'd seen anyone matching your descriptions, though she didn't say why you're wanted."

"What are you going to do?" Rancid's hand gripped the hilt of his dagger.

"Nothing." The priest seemed surprised by the question. "I'm not going to ask what you're accused of, or if you're guilty. This temple is a sanctuary to all who seek the justice of Aeron."

"I don't—" Rancid began.

"Why do you tell us this?" Nick shot Rancid a harsh look.

The priest seemed not to have heard Rancid. "So you'll be warned. Even with the streets crowded by the festivities, you may be recognized if you leave the temple."

"Festivities?" Rancid asked.

"It's Harvest Festival!" Nick slapped his palm on the table, his face must have beamed. "Orc's blood, I'd lost track of the days."

"Yes." The priest laid a hand on Nick's shoulder. "Still, you shouldn't go into the streets. The temple can't protect you if you leave its walls."

The need for weapons and supplies prevented the companions from holing up indoors. Zen could change his appearance and Ellessar wasn't on the wanted list, so they alone ventured out into the hordes of people that had inundated the city for Harvest Festival.

"I can only maintain my disguise for about an hour," Zen admitted as soon as the temple was out of site. He'd mimicked, as well as he could, the form of an elderly priest he'd seen in a hallway of the temple and borrowed an acolytes' robe to bolster his disguise, but he also hoped to get a better deal from the vendors if he claimed to be on church business. "We can finish more quickly if we split up."

Ellessar scanned the mass of people that clogged the street. "Fine."

"I'll sell the ring and the wine and try to find a suitable sword for Rancid. If I'm lucky, I'll find one that's enchanted. You sell the ground-shark scales and price the weapons and other supplies we need."

"Are we selling? Nick asked us only to solicit offers so we'll know what our items are worth."

Zen had to talk over the commotion of a farmer hawking live chickens nearby. "I've been to bazaars like these. Prices change by the minute. If you get a decent offer, take it."

As they walked, Ellessar shouldered his way past a pair of men haggling over the value of a lantern. "All right, mage. Have it your way."

Zen smiled. "Meet me back here in forty-five minutes." He waited until Ellessar was out of sight before reaching into his robes for his private purse, which held 381 gold coins he'd counted the night before. He hid the ring in a secret pocket sewn into the hem of one of his sleeves. It was worth far more than he'd get in a town like this, even if the ring wasn't enchanted. Besides, he ought to be able to find a dwarven sword for less coin than he already had. Rancid would be satisfied with that.

Now. Where to sell the king's wine?

When Dalen rode into Pinewood, he had only a few men with him. He'd scattered the rest along the road that surrounded the Black Forest to search for signs of the fugitives' passing.

Unfortunately, his soldiers had few trackers among them, other than Dalen himself, and he was just one man. It would take weeks, or months, to complete a detailed search of the forest's perimeter.

As soon as he entered his room at the local inn, he pulled the Medallion from beneath his shirt and used it to contact Balor. "I believe the fugitives have fled into Faldor, your majesty. I'll need your permission to take troops across the border."

"No," Balor replied. "Vornax has flung his own net across Faldor. If the fugitives are there, it's unlikely they'll make it out of that kingdom alive. Return to the palace. We must prepare for the next phase of our Master's plans."

CHAPTER 18

Later that day, Rancid prowled the halls of the temple. Zen had sold his ring for 350 gold coins and bought him the best sword the mage could find, for 285, so Rancid had some coin left over. Still, the enchanted ring should have fetched a better price.

If Rancid had gone out himself, he probably could have picked up the sword for free, or at least cut enough purse strings to buy it without having to sell anything. By the baron, he never should have given it to them. He never should have let Zen go with Ellessar. He never should have let either of them out of his sight.

He should have gone with them. He could have hidden his ponytail and his otherwise-bald head beneath the hood of his travelling cloak. And even if Sierra had seen him and recognized his scar, he could have lost himself in the crowd. It was the Harvest Festival, for baron's sake.

Rancid passed one closed door after another, too close together to lead anywhere but to more sleeping chambers. He'd wandered well beyond the foyer, the mess room, the worship hall, the guest chambers, and the offices of the abbot and his clerks. Rancid wasn't sure what he was looking for, but he knew he wouldn't find it in the public areas.

Zen and Ellessar had come back with enough coin to pay for everything the group needed, with a little left over. There was even enough to buy Nick another suit of plate armor. Still, the ring should have fetched more.

In compensation, Rancid wanted to steal something. His palms itched for it. It was the only way he could sooth the frustration that burned inside him. How had Zen and Ellessar let his ring go for so little coin? They were only supposed to determine its value, not sell it. Now Rancid had to make up the difference.

As soon as the two had returned, Zen had left again, out into the throng to learn what he could of Sierra. It was obvious why she'd come to Spitfire. But did she know the companions were there, or was she guessing?

Zen was supposed to get the answers. Bah. He'd gone out alone. Out of sight. Out of anyone's control. He was going to make up the answers. He might even sell them all out in exchange for some of the reward, then use the coin to purchase power.

As soon as Zen left, Nick and the others had gone searching for the abbot to find out if the Shield of Faith was really in Spitfire, as Nick's grandfather had recorded in his journal. And if so, to try to talk him out of the Shield, which had been crafted of dragon scales and was supposedly proof against the breath of any dragon. According to sources the group had found at the Order of the Rose and in the library of Eckland, it was to be released from the church when the dragons returned to the world of men and there was a need for it to be wielded.

At least one dragon had returned, if you believed Ellessar. Rancid didn't. Nevertheless, the need for the Shield was as real as it would ever be. But why in all the Civilized Lands would the abbot give it to the likes of them, a rag-tag band of outlaws who could barely get along with one another, let alone fight the Master?

Rancid continued to case the corridors. The art was too big to steal. And though the carvings and tapestries carried value in their intricate detail and the obvious skill of the artist, the only market for such items outside the church would prove too rare and difficult to find in the time Rancid would have to sell it.

No. He wasn't looking for that kind of wealth.

He rounded the corner into another dead end and then searched the hall for a false door or trip mechanism. This temple obviously had wealth. Some of it must be in the form of coin, gemstones, or some other small, salable commodity.

Nothing. No secret doors or latches. He retraced his steps.

Nick and Jasmine hadn't even let him go into the streets to buy supplies while they groveled before the abbot. Just one night in this place and Rancid was already going stir crazy.

As he returned to the foyer, Nick emerged from the abbot's office. "Good news. They'll let us borrow the Shield of Faith."

Jasmine emerged as well. "There's a catch. We have to pledge an oath to the abbot to abide by the teachings of Aeron."

Rancid's jaw dropped and his head rolled back. "You've got to be kidding."

"Afraid not," Ellessar said as he too came into the foyer.

Rancid planted his hand on his hip. "I won't pledge an oath to some imaginary god."

Jasmine took him by the shoulders. "Listen. This is important. It's not an oath to Aeron. I've already taken an oath to the Order of the Sage; I cannot take an oath to any god."

The girl had lost her mind. "Look around. We're in *his* temple."

"The *church* owns the Shield of Faith," she said. "The abbot just wants to make sure we don't use it to achieve a purpose contrary to their teachings. This is a promise to the abbot, not a pledge to Aeron or an acceptance of Aeron as our god."

"That's right," Nick said.

"I questioned the abbot carefully on this point," Jasmine continued, "before I agreed to take the pledge. We are not being asked to promote or spread Aeron's word or his teachings, only to employ methods that are not contrary to them."

Otto closed the distance to Rancid's side, opposite Nick. "The vow's only binding for as long as we carry the Shield."

Rancid felt like he was being surrounded. His hand had drifted to the hilt of his dagger. He pulled it away. These people were his friends, the only people he'd ever considered to be friends. Emphatically, he shook his head at the lot of them.

Ellessar squeezed between Jasmine and Nick. "Brother—"

"I'm not your brother."

"—you follow the path of Aeron more closely than you realize. By all accounts, you fight evil with a zeal beyond even my own. You need only recognize—"

Nick stopped Ellessar's sermon with a brusque gesture of his hand.

This was wrong. To take a vow to some fabrication of the church seemed absurd. Rancid believed what he saw, and he'd never seen any god. His feelings must have shown in his eyes.

Jasmine pulled him aside. *Where there's conflict, seek resolution;* wasn't that one of her creeds? She was going to try to talk him into something.

He walked with her to get away from the press of the others. "Jasmine, I can't."

"Do you seek justice against evil?" she asked softly.

"I seek *vengeance* against evil."

"Is there a difference?"

Not to Rancid. But there was a trick here somewhere. He could feel it.

"That's what we're being asked to do. That is what Aeron teaches."

Rancid remained silent. He ground his teeth on words that wouldn't quite come to him. The oath was simple on the surface, but the subtleties of trickery ate at him. What justice? Whose justice?

"What else?" he asked finally. What other bonds of deception did the abbot seek to put on him?

"To defend the weak. You do that already. You fight the Black Hand because they prey on the weak."

"I fight the Black Hand because they're evil."

"They're evil because they prey on the weak."

"If the weak stand between me and evil, I'll go through the weak to get to the evil."

Jasmine's demon-kin features softened. "You say that. But you never have, not since I've known you."

"I'll fight evil in any manner, at any cost." Rancid was defiant now; his hand had returned to his dagger. He didn't remove it.

"You'll do anything to gain the means to fight evil?" Jasmine asked.

"Anything."

"Steal?"

"Yes."

"Kill?"

"Yes."

"Lie?"

"Anything!"

"Then what is an oath to you? Take it. We will use the Shield to fight the root of evil."

Rancid faced Jasmine squarely. He couldn't argue with his own logic. She'd trapped him with it. He looked beyond her to the others, who waited across the foyer.

Would Zen take this oath? He wasn't there. He didn't yet know of the oath. But he'd take it if it meant moving one step closer to the power he sought. He'd take it and never mean to keep it.

Could Rancid do any less? He released the air that had grown stale in his lungs. Without a word, he walked away.

The Black Hand rode up to the township of South Bend. They'd found no sign of the fugitives in Loran, which is about what Halidreth had expected. They were still a long way from Trondor, but every town brought them closer to their prey.

His gang no longer wore their black gloves. Somehow the symbol seemed inappropriate here, so far from their old life that they might never make it back. They might return to Palidor, but back to banditry? With so many of his gang gone, Halidreth would have much to rebuild. And with Groot's plans to let orcs overrun the kingdom, the political landscape would likely be very different.

The baron of Forlorn Valley, for example. Would he still be there? Would the new ruler of the region let the Black Hand hide out there? Would he even be human?

And what of the orcs? Would their goods be worth stealing?

Halidreth set the thoughts aside as he approached the gates. Whisper had gone to do a sweep of the countryside for evidence of Sevendeath and his party. Halidreth queried the guards to see if they'd seen anyone matching their descriptions. It seemed a long shot. None of them knew where the fugitives were headed. And South Bend sat two kingdoms away from Trondor, just about as far south as one could get without crossing the Great Divide. Still, Whisper seemed determined to be thorough.

If they found no sign of their prey by the following evening, they'd move on toward Silversmith.

Rancid stood in the temple's worship hall, following the morning service. The abbot was there with Jasmine, Nick, and Otto, all of whom had already taken the oath, which required more than Jasmine had promised. Much more. *Seek justice and defend the weak.* Bah. That wasn't the half of it. Seek justice, he could do. It was all he did. And he could defend the weak if they didn't get in his way, but the rest he could never do. He couldn't even pledge to do it.

Zen approached the altar. Bloody baron! The abbot had the audacity to claim that the pledge was to him alone and not to his god. Yet he expected them to speak the oath at the altar of Aeron.

It was all nonsense.

Rancid measured the distance to the door, but he had nowhere to run. He wasn't trapped by the temple, the abbot, or even by Jasmine and the others. He was trapped by himself and his upbringing, by his own internal code of justice: fight evil by any means. That was his mantra, but it wasn't that simple.

"Do you pledge to act with honor?" the abbot asked Zen. A giant bronze likeness of Aeron loomed over the mage, wielding a sword, shield, and elven chainmail, looking down upon him as if in judgment of his words.

At least the abbot had declined Ellessar's offer to invoke a Zone of Truth during the oath-taking ceremony. Zen met the abbot's gaze and nodded.

"You must speak your answer. Will you act with honor?"

"Yes." Zen's voice contained no hesitation or hint of falseness. He remained calm and composed.

Yet this was no simple pledge. *Act with honor.* It was a simple phrase, but honor was no simple thing. Rancid could work with that, perhaps. It was both the chain that would bind him and the lock that he might pick.

"Do you pledge to defend the weak?" the abbot continued, as if reciting scripture.

This was too ceremonial. It smacked of a religious rite. Rancid had no use for religion. Or for the gods.

"Yes," Zen said.

"Do you pledge to seek justice?"

"Yes."

What was justice? Justice was death to all things evil. This church, this temple, the altar, the abbot—they all felt wrong. They itched under Rancid's skin like a rash on his soul. Anything that felt like this must be tainted. The world teemed with evil men who hid behind a mask of virtue.

He measured again the distance to the door.

"Your turn." Ellessar wore a smug smile.

No one responded.

"Rancid?" Nick touched his arm gently. "Your turn."

Panic welled in Rancid as he climbed the stairs to the altar. Only he stood between his friends and the Shield of Faith. "Why do we need the Shield?" He tried to suppress the pleading in his tone.

"You want to fight a dragon without it?" Jasmine asked.

"Why do we have to fight a dragon?"

"Do you honestly think," Nick said, "that if the dragons have returned, the Master will fail to send them against us?"

Rancid shrugged. He believed only what he saw, and he'd seen no dragons. Ellessar claimed to have seen one, but he was a part of the church, and the church couldn't be trusted.

From this vantage, his friends appeared small. The dais rose only a few feet, but his friends were cast against the backdrop of the congregation hall. Hundreds of seats, monstrous stone pillars, and ornate glasswork windows set his friends adrift in a sea of hypocrisy.

The statue, when Rancid deigned to look upon it, reminded him of the waste cellars of Forlorn Keep. His father, the baron, had looked down at him like that. "Go back to the garbage heap and beg for the charity of the scullery maids, boy. That's the only life you'll ever deserve." Rancid had been seven then, maybe eight, and it was the last time he'd seen his father. The next time he escaped the garbage pits, he'd left the keep altogether.

"Do you pledge to act with honor?" The abbot's voice brought him back to the present. His father would've never asked him that question. His father didn't know the meaning of the word.

Rancid didn't respond, still searching his mind for a way out.

"Do you pledge to act with honor?" the abbot asked again.

Who could know the meaning of such a word? Every sect, every order, and every kingdom—indeed every man, elf, and dwarf—lived by his own code of honor. "I pledge to act with honor, as I understand the meaning of honor."

The abbot didn't flinch. "Do you pledge to act with honor, as Aeron understands its meaning?"

"How am I to know what Aeron understands?"

"His word fills the Book with all we know of his will."

The Book of Aeron. Rancid had thrown a copy out of his chamber every time he'd stepped into it. Then every time he left, he found another copy sitting by the lamp when he returned. "I'm not going to read a thousand pages of scripture and try to decipher the gibberish of the church. I'll abide by my own honor. That's my pledge."

"Those who wield the Shield of Faith must uphold the teachings of Aeron. His teachings must guide you and your actions. Brother Ellessar may serve as your guide in such matters if you don't comprehend the texts."

"Our foes are many. They're powerful and come against us at every turn." Rancid waved a dismissive hand at Ellessar. "I don't have time to consult brother Ellessar in the heat of battle. Suppose I make a mistake."

"You're human—"

"Elf-kin." Though Rancid had never known his elven mother—she'd died in the baron's dungeons shortly after his birth—he wasn't proud of his human ancestry.

"My point is, you're not perfect. No one can fault you for being mistaken. It's what's in your heart that concerns me."

There, a chink in the chain. Rancid lived by his own honor, different from that taught by Aeron—of that he was sure—but honor nonetheless. And since he'd met Nick and the others in Traveler's Roost those many months ago, he'd found a place for friendship among his many definitions of honor.

Until then, his only friends had been the kitchen hands at the baron's keep. Having been thrown into the garbage pits on the day he was born, he'd lived on the pity of slaves. Goat's milk at first, and then the leavings of the baron's noble guests. Scraps from their discarded plates had been his fare until he was old enough to help in the kitchens. After that, he stole what he needed to survive, before it passed through the hands of some corrupt aristocrat.

That's where his honor had begun. Live. Survive by any means. Then his thoughts turned to escape, first from the garbage pits, then from the kitchens, and finally from the keep itself. He stowed away beneath a pile of refuse, taken by wagon to a nearby ravine where it was dumped into the river. The fall had nearly killed him, but a woman had pulled him to shore and nursed him to health. A ranger, she called herself. At the time, she'd seemed to be an angel within a halo of sunlight. But she was no friend. As soon as he was well enough to stand, she left him.

As he explored Forlorn Valley, he learned how the system worked. The Black Hand owned the wilds. They preyed on the innocent and paid fealty to the baron in exchange for allowing them to hide out in the region. That was where Rancid's father got his wealth and power. That was the support upon which his high and mighty father stood.

That was the evil.

Once Rancid was old enough, he tore down that evil, one bandit at a time, until the Black Hand drove him into Meuribar, where he'd met these people he now called friends. Since then, he'd redefined evil to encompass a greater scope. With it, he began to redefine honor.

His friends had saved his life more than once. Now they needed the Shield of Faith. How could he deny them?

"If I make a mistake?" Rancid repeated to the abbot.

"The pledge is to act with honor. I expect you to keep it as best as you can."

Rancid released a breath through his clenched teeth. The kids who played with him in the tunnels beneath the kitchen—when their parents, the slaves, allowed it—had a saying: A promise is only binding if it's made with both feet planted firmly on the floor. It was nonsense, of course, but it gave their conscience succor when the need arose.

Rancid lifted the heel of his left foot. "All right."

The abbot didn't seem to notice. "Do you pledge to act with honor as Aeron understands its meaning?"

"Yes." Rancid waved his hand in dismissal. "Fine. Whatever."

"Do you pledge to defend the weak?"

"Sure." If they didn't get in his way.

"Do you pledge to seek justice?"

Whose justice? Rancid pressed his heel back onto the floor. "Yes." He sought to destroy all things evil. Let that be their justice.

The abbot reached up to the statue of Aeron and removed the Shield. It looked small on the statue's arm, but it had size enough for a large man to hide behind it. The red dragon scales from which it was made had browned with age to the color of bronze. He handed it to Ellessar. "The Shield is blessed, not enchanted. Its divine properties will only work in the hands of a true believer."

Ellessar bowed reverently to the statue beside the altar before returning his attention to the abbot. "Thank you, father. We shall use it well and return it when our need has passed."

As the others filed out of the sanctuary, Ellessar paused beside the abbot.

"What troubles you, brother?" the abbot asked.

"Rancid. I don't believe he took the oath honestly."

The abbot nodded.

"Then why did you give us the Shield?"

"Because he took the oath. Whether he keeps it or not is between him and Aeron."

CHAPTER 19

The company gathered again in Nick's cramped sleeping chamber.

Nick sat on the cot next to Otto. "According to the priests, the town of Dragon Tears lies two days down the southern road. And we should reach South Bend in a week. Xanth's map showed a pass from there over the Great Divide into the Wild Lands." He patted the side of his pack. "Then we have the Seeking Stone."

"First we need to get out of town without being seen," Rancid said.

Zen leaned on his staff in the corner of the room. "I spoke to Sierra yesterday."

All eyes snapped to him.

Most of the others' mouths hung open.

Rancid's jaw tightened. "You *talked* to her?"

The edges of Zen's mouth turned up as he nodded. "I was scouting for information about what she knows. What better way than to talk to her?"

"What did she say?" Nick asked, before Rancid could start an argument. Zen had always displayed a tendency to take the most direct path to whatever he wanted, despite the risk.

"She doesn't know we're here," Zen said. "She's given our descriptions to the guards at all three gates, but nobody's recognized us. In the meantime, she's recruiting another team of mercenaries."

"Anything else?" Nick asked.

"Rancid's been added to the official list of fugitives since the Black Forest." Zen indicated Jasmine. "She describes you as a deformed human, perhaps a cross with one of the goblinoid races. Apparently she's not aware of your demon, um, blood."

"Good," Ellessar said. "She won't try to use demon-seeking enchantments to track us."

"Sierra's descriptions of the rest of us," Zen continued, "though fairly accurate, are unremarkable. If Otto hides that scar on his arm and you, Nick, keep your sword out of sight, your descriptions could apply to dozens of men in a town this size. As for me, her description relies largely on my staff, robe, and headband."

"They do make you stand out," Otto observed. "Together we're about as recognizable as a mule in a goat herd. And now that the guards at the gate know what to watch for, leaving in the dark of night will just make us appear suspicious." He paused. "The festival's over. Most of the out-of-towners will be leaving today. I suggest we split up, blend into the crowd, and leave one or two at a time. We can rendezvous a few miles past the gate."

"Not too far out," Ellessar said. "The Assassin is still out there, and not far from town. If it catches Nick alone..."

"Are the horses ready?" Nick asked.

Ellessar nodded. "The hostler at the temple stables can't rightly be called a blacksmith, but he can shoe a horse. The new shoes should confuse any tracker who might have found a distinguishing mark in any of the horses' tracks."

"So where does that leave us?" Otto asked.

"I'll go first," Zen offered, "disguised as a merchant. I'll scout the gate for anyone besides the guards who might be looking for us. I can wait just outside until you're all through and watch for anyone following."

"I'll go next," Rancid said, "and keep my cowl pulled close against the wind. That should hide my face and hair. If there's an ambush on the road, I'll try to spot it."

"Then me," Jasmine said. "Sierra probably knows that if we're here, we must be mounted. It's the only way we could have arrived from the Black Forest by now. I'll leave on foot. If I'm spotted, I can outrun even a horse over a short distance. Zen can take my horse on a tether, laden with our food and cooking supplies to boost his disguise."

Then she turned to Ellessar. "You said you skin the demons you slay?"

"The ones that have hide worth keeping."

"Do you have any extra pieces? I fight best with my bare hands. Maybe some strips of demon skin will help me protect them from the Assassin's secretions."

"They might at that." The elf dug into his pack and produced a small bundle of leather scraps.

"Good." Nick stood. "That leaves me, Otto, and Ellessar. If the demon attacks, the three of us should be able to fight it off."

"One more thing," Ellessar said. "The Shield of Faith. It's too conspicuous for me to carry out the gate. I'll wrap it in a blanket and strap it to Zen's spare horse."

Rancid scowled, but he said nothing.

"It's settled then." Nick opened the door to let the others out. It all sounded too easy.

A few miles down the road, Nick and the others regrouped.
"I've been thinking," Jasmine said. "This demon is going to track us until it finds us vulnerable. By then, we may be somewhere in the Wild Lands. With its translocation ability, it can come at us, take a couple of hits, and retreat. The demon can heal, but in the Wild Lands, we might not be able to replace our swords." She glanced from Nick to Ellessar. "We should bait it now, bring it out into the open, and kill it. If it escapes, we can replenish our sword supply in Dragon Tears and try again."

"Seeking resolution?" Zen asked with a smirk.

"Something like that."

Nick didn't miss the fact that *he* was the bait in Jasmine's plan. "What do you propose?"

She got a mischievous gleam in her demon-kin eyes. "We just came from the Harvest Festival, a gutter of filth and disease. Maybe we ate some bad food. You don't look well, Nick. Neither do Otto and the others."

Rancid surveyed the road ahead. "The hills are thinning. It may be hard to find a good ambush spot up ahead."

"But Nick looks terrible." She winked at him. "I think we better head back toward Spitfire. It's not far. Maybe we can make it. If not, we'll just have to turn off the road and make camp."

Nick smiled in spite of himself. The plan was practical, if not altogether prudent. "I like it." But the demon wasn't human. It might miss the point entirely. "It'll have to be totally debilitating, and I'm no tavern player. The physical symptoms of severe illness may be difficult to fake."

"I can help there." Jasmine patted her healer's kit. "I'll make you a tea typically used for purging ingested poison. It'll make you vomit, add some authenticity to your performance. You'll feel sick for a few minutes before it happens, but once you empty your stomach, you'll feel well enough to fight."

"I'm sure the Assassin can see us," Ellessar said in a low voice, "though it's probably not close enough to hear. We should keep moving down the road. We'll get sick gradually. Double back in about an hour."

By midafternoon, the group had turned around. Nick and Otto were leaning over the necks of their horses and Ellessar lolled weakly in his saddle. Zen slowed his horse as if he couldn't keep up or didn't want to catch whatever the others had.

"Rancid," Jasmine yelled. "We need to stop. These men need medicine, or they'll never make it back to Spitfire."

"Then get them off the road," a stranger grumbled as he passed in the opposite direction. "You want to start a plague?"

The comment was so perfect that Nick had to cough to keep from laughing out loud. To him, the hack sounded dry and fake. He no longer guided his horse. If it wandered off the road, so much the better. But it didn't. It followed the others until Jasmine grabbed the reins and pulled it to a stop.

She led them a dozen yards from the road, unpacked her healer's bag, and started a small cooking fire to heat water for the tea. Nick, Ellessar, and Otto stumbled from their horses and lay down nearby.

Rancid gathered the mounts. He started coughing as well. "We'll have to move farther from the road," he said, more loudly than necessary. "We'll be prey for bandits here."

Jasmine shook her head. "No. They need a healer and Ellessar is in no shape to help. We have to make it back to town if we can."

Rancid indicated the distant peak of the volcano. "It's hours to Spitfire. I don't think they'll make it."

Jasmine mixed several ingredients into the boiling water. It smelled brackish. "For their sake, we have to try. But perhaps you better scout out a campsite, just in case. Somewhere out of sight." She lowered her voice. "Someplace that gives the demon an advantage. A ravine, maybe."

Rancid scowled, but he returned to the road and headed toward town, scanning the hills. Surely he knew better than to leave the protection of the road. Though he wasn't the Assassin's target, it might attack him if it found him alone. Doing so would reduce the protection around Nick.

Jasmine finished brewing her tea and administered some to Nick, Otto, and Ellessar. "Are you sure you don't want some?" she whispered to Zen as the two of them helped Nick mount his horse.

"Quite sure."

At that point, Nick's stomach kicked at his sides, and he felt as though Jasmine's concoction would drag out his stomach if he let it come back up. If the Assassin struck now, they really would be too weak to fight. He took comfort from the nearness of the road and density of the traffic.

"Travel ahead of us," Jasmine told Zen. "Warn everyone that sick men are coming though. Move them to the west side of the road. We'll stay to the east."

He did and, not ten minutes later, Ellessar hurled the smoked fish he'd eaten for lunch onto the ground. The sick smell of it made Nick do the same. Somehow, Otto managed to hold onto his, for the time being. Nick's stomach settled after that. He wanted to rinse the taste from his mouth with water, but he didn't dare reveal that he had the strength to do so.

Jasmine rode up beside him with a flask of leftover tea. "Have some more."

Nick just hung there on his horses neck, hoping she would go away. The last thing he wanted was more of her foul medicine, but Jasmine seemed determined to play it up. She pulled the horse to a stop, lifted Nick's head, and held the flask to his mouth. Because he wanted the demon, he pretended he was too weak to resist. Immediately, his stomach twisted.

"Hold it down," Jasmine whispered. "Just for a few minutes."

Nick rolled his eyes back into his head and lay back down on his horse.

Minutes later, Rancid returned. "How are they?"

"They need rest. I'll treat them tonight and we'll try for town again tomorrow."

The party followed Rancid to a gully, far enough from the road that any cries for help wouldn't be heard. Nick threw up along the way and began to doubt the wisdom of Jasmine's tea. She didn't administer any more, and by the time they got to the gully, his stomach had settled.

As soon as they came to a stop, Nick let himself tumble to the ground. Bruises would heal. He wanted that demon.

The late afternoon sun rested low on the horizon. Jasmine built up the fire to make sure the demon would have no trouble finding them, then she brewed another tea. "This one will help to settle your stomach." She dipped a clean cloth into the brew and trickled some down the throats of the sick.

Rancid climbed into a tree to keep watch.

Zen pointed to a copse of waist-high shrubs. "I'm going to sleep over there. I wasn't present during the previous attack. If the Assassin hasn't come close enough to the road to see me with you today, my hiding will make the group look weaker. If it does know I'm with you, then it'll look like I'm sleeping separately to avoid the illness." He tucked his pack into the bushes and settled in.

Jasmine continued to care for the ill.

"Take my armor off," Nick whispered. It'd make him look more vulnerable and would protect the armor from the demon's corrosive secretions.

She did, then helped Otto and Ellessar out of theirs as well. After that, Ellessar and Nick lay still, as though asleep or too weak to move. Otto, shivering violently, wrapped himself in a blanket and hunched near the fire for warmth.

Though he hadn't meant to, Nick eventually dozed off.

He woke to a shout from Rancid and looked up to see a rust-colored shadow standing over him in the moonlight. Claws pierced Nick's chest before he could react.

He rolled away and tried to stand, but another set of claws found purchase and threw him to the ground.

One of Rancid's daggers sank into the Assassin. The blade deteriorated and the hilt fell away, but it slowed the demon enough for

Ellessar to step between it and Nick.

Jasmine jumped up, her hands wrapped in the strips of demon skin Ellessar had given her. Otto sprang upright as well.

Nick staggered to his feet, his chest burning. His breath came only in ragged gasps. He couldn't get any air.

The demon's claws hovered in the air to keep them all at bay, but its eyes never left its target. Nick was unarmed, his shirt hung in tatters, his ripped skin stung like venom, and his own blood soaked him from the chest down. He managed to remain upright only to convince the Assassin that its job wasn't yet done, to keep it from translocating away.

Finally, the demon lunged for him. Jasmine's fist collided with its head. Ellessar's sword and Otto's ax slashed its sides. A wave of ice shards struck it as well. In an instant, it lay dead.

Nick slumped.

Ellessar caught him, a prayer on his lips. Nick had almost blacked out when the fire of Aeron's healing coursed through him. It felt like burning ice for a moment, and then he sucked in a deep breath that sustained him. Gradually, the sharpness of the pain receded and warmth returned to his body.

When Nick went back to bed to sleep in earnest, his wounds still hurt, but Ellessar and Jasmine agreed that they no longer threatened his life.

In the morning, Ellessar removed the deadly corrosive from the demon's flesh with a cleansing prayer, then skinned the thing.

He went through his daily seeking ritual. "It appears we have another demon. No more than an hour from here, north or northwest."

Nick's head snapped in Ellessar's direction. "So soon?" One of Ellessar's swords and Otto's new ax had already been ruined.

Ellessar nodded.

"In that case," Rancid said, "we'll need swords that can stand up to the oils on its skin." With a dagger, he severed all six fingertips from the demon's corpse and cleaned the two-foot claws.

"Is that unusual?" Zen asked Ellessar. "To find two Assassins so near one another?"

"It's unprecedented, even inside the Abyss, let alone out here."

CHAPTER 20

Ryanna couldn't track her Assassins directly. Her only hold over them was their compulsion to follow her commands, which she'd created when she called them into this world. She held that compulsion by a tenuous thread of her consciousness.

When one of the threads broke, Ryanna knew the Assassin was gone. She didn't know whether it had died or had completed its mission and returned to the Abyss, but she had a vague sense of where the event had happened: somewhere to the south, in the heart of Faldor. Ryanna turned L'Nordian in that direction.

Dragon Tears wasn't so much a single township as it was three separate and distinct fishing communities, one gathered around a harbor on the seacoast, one a crescent that wrapped around the western shore of the southernmost lake in the Dragon Tears chain, and the third threaded along the bank of a river that the locals called Old Skip. Each sat a few miles from the others.

Nick led his party straight for a cluster of buildings that sat in the middle of the three and that bound the communities together. This merchant district also sported the only two-story structure within at least a day's travel in any direction: the Fairweather Inn.

The group couldn't afford to stay at the inn, but the merchant district offered the only place they might find a blacksmith. The trap they'd laid for the Assassin demon had been a success, but it had severely damaged one of Ellessar's swords and Otto's axe. Nick was eager to see if the twenty-inch demon claws could be fashioned into short, serviceable rapiers that would resist the corrosive secretions of an Assassin's skin.

They arrived just after dark and found everything except the inn closed. "The people need to rise early for the fish," Nick said. "We'll backtrack about a half mile and set up camp. We can try again in the morning."

"Keep a tight watch," Ellessar added. "Sleep with your weapons nearby. The last demon didn't attack until it thought we were unprepared. A simple show of diligence could keep us safe through the night."

The next morning, Zen went off on his own, counting on sunlight and population to keep the demon at bay. If it was another Assassin, it was probably after Nick. Even if it did come for Zen, it wouldn't likely see past his disguise: a tangled, frost-colored beard and Rancid's travelling cloak. He sought a magic shop, but the closest he could find was an apothecary that sold alchemy supplies, healing herbs, and a few phony charms. Unfortunately, the owner, a slender woman with long, graying hair and a simple hemp dress, seemed the only person in town who might pay good coin for the claws of a demon, and Nick and the others needed money to pay for the services of a blacksmith.

Zen presented them.

"How do I know they came from a demon?" she asked.

"Look at them." Zen held them before the woman's face. In spite of his need to disguise himself, he'd retained his expensive staff and headband to lend credibility to his negotiations. "Have you ever seen an animal with claws like these? Not even the elven forests can boast such a beast."

The woman reached toward the claws tentatively. "Are they poisonous?"

"They're safe enough to touch, but if you scrape filings off and brew them like tea, they might be."

The woman squinted at the claws and then at Zen for several seconds before responding. "Nine gold coins."

"Nine?" Zen said, aghast.

"I don't even know if I can sell the things. I've got to convince somebody they're worth something."

"Each," Zen insisted. "Nine gold each."

"How many you selling?"

"Two."

"All right." The woman pulled a bag from beneath the counter and extracted the coins. She scowled at the claws she'd just purchased as though her stomach had soured.

After the sale, Zen dropped the coin off at the campsite, left his staff and headband with Nick, and went to scour the town for news of Sierra or any of the Chosen.

Late that evening, he trolled the dirt streets near the Old Skip dockyard. He observed a man who appeared wiry and thin but not weak. From the quickness and grace of his movements, he seemed spry as an elf and energetic as a child. Something about the man's eyes suggested both wisdom and cunning, despite the rags he wore.

Finally, Zen gathered his worn travelling cloak about him and approached. "Good evening, friend."

The man scrutinized Zen's face, seeing the gray sideburns, pasty complexion, and days of white stubble that Zen had woven to disguise himself. "Friend I might be, if it seems worth my while." He scanned the length of Zen's body as though looking for something in particular among his meager belongings.

Zen brushed his cloak aside, revealing a coin pouch. "I seek information."

"Everybody does." The man's eyes narrowed. They seemed drawn to Zen's own, as though he sensed that something wasn't right about the mage. "I've been here a long time. I know many things. What sort of information you looking for?"

Zen settled in beside him on the boardwalk with his back against the wall and stared out into the darkened street. "We've recently arrived and need to get the lay of the land."

The man offered Zen a drink from a bottle sitting beside him. Zen shook his head. If he muddled his mind, the weave might waver and betray him.

"Bah, it's mostly water anyway. Just for show, ya know." The man set down the bottle. "My minimum price is five gold coins, but for that you'll learn much."

Zen winced. He had barely five gold coins left. He counted them out and passed them to the stranger, who bit each in turn to make sure they were genuine. The man's gaze returned to the street and he sat in silence.

The quiet lasted for so long that Zen feared the man had fallen asleep.

"I have a client." Zen's bowels felt like they were twisting in his gut. This was a bad idea, but he'd already paid the man, so he might as well ask what he came here to ask. He scanned the length of the street in both directions before continuing. "A man of some means, looking for items of magical enchantment. Do you know where I might find some in town?"

The stranger gave him a shrewd look. "You wanting to buy? Or steal?"

"Either." Zen's throat became suddenly dry. "As long as I don't get caught."

"Now there's a promise I can't make."

"Maybe you could steal something for me." He almost doubled over, his gut seized in a cramp.

The man shot to his feet, bottle in hand. "What do you take me for? A thief?"

Zen remained calm. "I meant no offense. I just—"

"Come back in the morning. I'll see what I can find." He spun away and disappeared into the darkness.

When Nick and the others arrived at the blacksmith's shop with the coin from Zen's sale, Ellessar was already there.

Rancid set the remaining claws on the table, except for one, which he handed to the blacksmith. "Can you fix a pommel to this?"

The rotund man turned the oddity over in his hands for a few seconds. "Sure. Why would you want me to?"

"Never mind why," Rancid said. "How much?"

A line creased the man's brow for a moment. "For you, twelve gold coins." He laid the claw on the table as though to give it back to Rancid.

"Twelve gold? I can buy a good sword for less than that. With these, we're providing half the materials."

"That's true," the man said. "But it'll take time and experimentation to fashion an appropriate pommel. You don't want the handle coming off during combat, do you?"

There were no other smiths in this community—Nick had already checked. If they wanted the swords, they'd have to pay this man's price. "How long?"

"Three days," the smith declared.

"No way." Rancid's good fist was anchored to his belt.

The smith gestured to the claws with open hands, again as though to return them.

"Why three days?" Nick asked.

"This is a new material for me. I don't know how hard it'll be to work with. Besides, I have a priority order ahead of yours."

Nick saw Ellessar's sword propped against the wall behind the smith. Its bone pommel and engravings were unmistakable. "You?"

Ellessar nodded.

"He just needs to buy a sword," Rancid said.

"No, I don't," Ellessar replied calmly.

Rancid spun on the demon hunter, but Nick cut him off. "What are you buying?"

"I'm having a new blade attached to the pommel, and the blade engraved."

"The runes are fake," Rancid blurted. "We're in a hurry."

Ellessar didn't seem surprised by the accusation. "The engravings aren't enchanted. They're prayers."

"Do you need them?" Nick asked.

"Of course he doesn't need them," Rancid spat.

"I fight a divine foe. I do so with a prayer on my lips, a prayer in my heart, and a prayer on my sword. It's the way of my order."

"Let's move this outside." Nick pushed the demon claws back to the blacksmith's side of the table and dropped forty-eight coins beside them. "We'll take the swords. If you can finish a day early, we'll pay an extra ten percent on delivery." He grabbed Rancid by the shoulder and shoved him toward the door. "This is no place to talk."

Nick motioned to Otto and Jasmine as they emerged from the shop next door, that of the cobbler, who also served as the town's only tanner and leather smith. Jasmine had gone in to order a special set of boots to fit her taloned feet, in case she ruined the pair she had in a battle with an Assassin.

The group walked back to the campsite together and found Zen there.

Rancid spun on the others. "We have a demon hunting us, along with at least one mercenary and her gang, Dalen, the entire Trondorian army for all we know—" He counted their enemies on his fingers— "the Master and the rest of his Chosen, the Black Hand."

Zen rolled his eyes at the mention of the bandit gang.

"We haven't seen the last of them," Rancid insisted.

"Would they come all the way to western Faldor?" Nick asked. "Do they hate you that much?"

"Do you remember how we met? And where?" Nick remained silent, so Rancid went on, speaking to Otto and Ellessar, who hadn't been with them at the time. "The bandits chased me across two kingdoms into Meuribar—where I met Nick and Zen—and from there to the Order of the Sage.

"Remember the air apparition?" he asked Jasmine.

"Master of air and darkness," Nick quoted from the Prophecy.

"It killed Nick's mother and burned his home to get his grandfather's journal, which contained his speculations on ways to stop the Prophecy. And then the apparition showed up at the monastery with the Black Hand. So we know the Black Hand work for the Master, and that at least one among them is a Chosen." He paused. "They *are* coming. It's just a matter of time. How long are we going to wait for our enemies to catch up?"

"And if there's another Assassin out there," Nick said, "we can assume it'll keep coming until I'm dead. We haven't enough coin to keep replacing our swords."

"It *is* an Assassin," Ellessar added. "Or it wouldn't be following us. We need weapons that'll stand up to its defenses."

"He's right." Jasmine produced jerky and hard bread from the group supplies. "We need to wait for the new demon-claw rapiers."

Ellessar accepted some of the food. Zen declined with a grimace.

"You okay?" Jasmine asked.

"Upset stomach."

She handed the provisions to Otto to distribute. "I'll make a tea."

Nobody even mentioned the dragon. It was out there too. Somewhere. Its presence was a condition of the Prophecy. Involuntarily, Nick scanned the sky. Somehow it would intersect their quest.

Zen lay in camp all morning, lacking the strength to climb from his blankets. He hadn't even been able to weave his protective shroud over the party for the past two nights, let alone work on widening his portal to the plane of ice.

"You're dehydrated," Jasmine said. "You need to drink."

Just the thought of it twisted Zen's stomach. He tried to push her water flask away.

"Drink it." She shoved his hand aside and touched the mouth of the flask to Zen's lips. "I added peppermint. It'll settle your stomach."

No it won't. Zen couldn't speak. Ever since his conversation with the vagabond by the docks of the Old Skip, nothing would settle his stomach. He'd even tried sucking on small slivers of ice before he lost the strength to produce them from the weave. Ultimately, he'd been forced to spit them all onto the ground. Maybe the man had been so offended by Zen's request for him to steal that he'd placed a curse on him.

Zen sipped the water, and as it had before, it initiated a long, painful series of dry heaves.

When the others returned, Ellessar tried a healing prayer. "This is no disease. It's a divine ailment. One of Aeron's making."

"But we're doing the work of Aeron," Nick said.

"Unless he violated the oath." Rancid spat onto the ground near Zen's feet. "I knew that oath was a bad idea."

Ellessar eyed Zen carefully. "Did you break the oath, brother?"

Oh, spit. The oath! Zen nodded weakly.

"That's good," Ellessar said.

"Good?" Rancid said. "We're lucky he didn't curse us all."

"How is it good?" Nick asked.

"It's easily remedied the first time it happens. But if he does it again..."

Easily remedied? How? Zen couldn't force the questions past his swollen throat, so he just stared pleadingly at Ellessar. What must he do?

"Renounce your crime. Vow within the core of your being that you'll not break the oath again. But—this is important—you must mean it, for Aeron knows what's in your heart. If your crime against the oath is what ails you, you'll then be able to drink. Your body can begin to heal."

Zen lay back and closed his eyes. He'd thought stealing power to fight Aeron's enemies was just. But, he supposed, that failed to deal honorably with the people who owned the enchantments he sought to steal. The owners deserved fair compensation.

A smile cracked Zen's parched lips despite his pain and nausea. This trap would catch Rancid more than once, he'd wager. But not Zen. Not again. Not now that he understood the oath and what it really meant.

Immediately his stomach settled. He pushed himself up onto one elbow, more relaxed than he'd felt in a day and a half, and then nodded at Jasmine.

She touched the mouth of the water flask to Zen's lips. "Just a sip."

At that moment, the cool water felt more comforting than the power of the weave and more refreshing than a dip in the frozen lakes near Icecap.

Never again would he break the oath, he promised Aeron silently as he drifted into sleep. Not as long as he accompanied the Shield of Faith, anyway. After that...

The companions left Dragon Tears late the next day, after picking up the demon-claw rapiers and Ellessar's sword from the backwater smith. By then the sun had set, but the need for haste drove the party down the road in the darkness. Midnight had passed before they finally made camp.

They hit the road again at sunup, traveling south, a few miles inland from the sea, toward Silversmith. Fog misted the morning air. They rode single-file.

Jasmine had positioned herself at the tail end of the procession, behind Ellessar, as they approached at least a dozen oncoming riders. The elf seemed unconcerned that the men and women of the passing party were obviously not merchants. They had no wares. Armed to the man, they didn't seem to be escorting some nobleman or messenger either. Mercenaries then, perhaps between jobs, looking for a caravan to protect. By the look of them, these riders could have escorted a king's ransom through Palidor and not have worried about goblin raiders or the Black Hand bandits.

Jasmine tucked her legs under her cloak and folded her hands into her sleeves as the riders approached. She dipped her head and willed them to look away from her. The leader, a bald man in a clean silk shirt, merely glanced in her direction. But the second rider, a large, slovenly man with a huge war hammer, leaned over in his saddle, scrutinizing her.

Mercenaries. The companions may have outpaced Sierra, but there were others. These riders were looking for someone.

Despite her need to turn away, the man's unclean stare, rank smell, and focused attention drew her to look at him. It was a sidelong glance past the hem of her cowl and couldn't have exposed much of herself. As the man's eyes widened, she recognized him from the prairies of Faldor. The man, whom Nick had called Sledge, was a survivor of the Black Hand party that had pursued them from the Order of the Sage monastery.

A guttural sound poured from Sledge's throat as he raised the war hammer. His roar filled the morning air. "It's them!"

"Black Hand!" Jasmine flattened herself onto her horse's neck just beneath the sweep of Sledge's hammer. Her horse shied and skittered off the road.

The ring of weapons sliding from their sheaths set all the horses on edge. Only Spirit, immediately in front of Jasmine, held firm in the wave of panic that swept the line of mounts from Jasmine, past Ellessar, Zen, Otto, Nick, and Rancid, all the way to the far end of the Black Hand riders.

The man behind Jasmine, the lead rider in the Black Hand group, wheeled his mount to face her as his sword cleared its sheath.

Jasmine wasted no time trying to control her mount. Instead, she braced her feet on the seat of her saddle and leapt onto Sledge's horse, catching the bandit around the middle and pinning his arms to his sides.

Sledge broke her hold and swung his elbow back into her jaw.

Gritting her aching teeth, she balled one taloned hand into a fist and smashed it into the pressure point at the base of his skull. The hammer dropped from his hand as he slid, limp, from the saddle.

At that moment, an immense shadow passed over her. She raised her head to the sky and her heart froze. There, not two hundred feet above them, a black dragon with a belly as red as blood swooped toward the road.

CHAPTER 21

As quickly as Nick's sword cleared leather, something slammed into him from his right—from off the road. The force knocked him from his saddle, headlong toward the row of bandits on his left. He managed to hold onto his reins and sword as he landed, disoriented but with his feet beneath him. The sudden movement spooked the nearest horse and it shied away, its bandit rider fighting for control.

Nick made out a vague, transparent shape, clear in the middle, blurry around the edges. It was the apparition, air incarnate, that had tracked him across Faldor and stolen his grandfather's journal. The apparition slammed Nick's horse, forcing the breath from the animal in a loud huff.

Then a large shadow swept the battlefield. Instinct told Nick to look up, to confirm his fears, but he fought the urge. If he took his eyes off the apparition, he might not find it again.

Everything went suddenly still. All eyes, man and horse's, stared into the sky. The prancing of the nervous horses, the ring of swords, the chanted incantations of Zen's weaving, all fell silent.

All but Nick and the apparition.

The creature continued to batter Nick's mount, which had become a barrier between them.

Nick skirted behind the horse and struck at the air. He felt no resistance as his sword passed through the apparition. It came at him, and he swung again. This time the creature had begun to gather substance, and it writhed at the sword stroke.

It slammed Nick, nearly knocking him from his feet.

Nick shoved his blade at it again.

Otto appeared and swept through it with his ax.

With a screech like a barn's tin roof being ripped away by a spring twister, the apparition retreated. Nick lost the creature in the morning mist.

Sound returned as some of the combatants recovered their wits. Several of the horses at the rear of the bandit party fled, with their riders' eyes still fixed on the dragon.

One bandit, a young girl with flowing locks woven with lilacs, leapt from her petrified mount with a serrated blade in her hand. She rushed Rancid, who hadn't yet recovered from the dragon-induced terror.

Nick and Otto sprinted to intercept.

Nick struck first. The girl parried. She was just a kid—maybe fourteen harvests—yet somehow she'd fallen in with this lot. There were too many Black Hand for Nick to spare any time to try to talk her down, to try to save her life. She would kill him if he gave her the chance.

His second swing bit into her side, sinking into flesh until it snapped her spine. He felt sick. What a waste.

here. Ryanna pointed to the road below, where two groups of travelers fought. She'd learned not to shout to L'Nordian. The strong wind produced by the dragon's flight swept her words away before they reached his ears. Instead, she let the dragon read her thoughts.

I see them. L'Nordian descended for a closer look.

That's low enough, Ryanna imparted, before the dragon could bring them within effective arrow range of the combatants.

The riders below—six in one group, twelve in the other—all wore travelling cloaks against the cold. She could make out none of their features, but one of the riders near the middle of the southbound group carried a staff with a crystal tip.

As chaos broke loose below her, Ryanna ignored everyone but the man with the staff, who raised a hand in the air and waved it toward a woman in the northbound group. The woman stiffened, shuddered, and tumbled from her saddle.

There was no doubt now. The man was a mage.

As one, the riders froze with dragon fear, staring at L'Nordian, until he passed the battlefield and gained some altitude. Ryanna craned her neck to keep the road in sight past the dragon's bulk.

When a deluge of hail enveloped several of the northbound riders, she grabbed her Medallion and reported to the Master that she'd found the ice mage and the rest of Trondor's fugitives.

"Don't engage them," Vornax warned her. "Don't risk yourself or L'Nordian. I'll need you both later. But keep an eye on them."

Though Ryanna had shuddered at the Master's vile presence, even through the Medallion, she felt no comfort when he left her. He'd shared none of his plans for her, but she could count on one thing: They involved demons. Nobody in the whole of the Civilized Lands or anywhere else could call demons as powerful as those Ryanna had already brought forth from the Abyss. She had no desire to call more.

Something else bothered her too. If these were the fugitives from Trondor, the bane of the Master's plans, then where were the Assassins she'd sent against them? She wheeled L'Nordian north in search of them. If the riders stayed on the road, she'd find them again easily enough.

As Jasmine leapt to the ground at the Black Hand leader's flank, the bandit had sprung from his petrified mount and traded sword strokes with Ellessar. He seemed to realize, though, that much of his gang had fled, either voluntarily or on the backs of panicking horses.

"Disengage! Withdraw!" He retreated to the edge of the road.

Jasmine spared a glance toward the sky. The dragon had made its pass but was circling back. The Black Hand were clearing the road at an alarming rate, leaving Jasmine and her friends wide open for the dragon. What she'd heard of dragons was mostly rumor, but all the stories agreed on one point: A dragon's breath was hot enough to burn brick.

Nearby, a large bandit in a blue tunic jumped from his mount. He grabbed the reins of a second horse and dragged both of them away from the road.

The bandit leader worked his way around the mounts to join Blue Tunic.

Ellessar urged Spirit after the leader, battering his sword against the bandit's upraised shield.

If the dragon's rider cared at all about the Black Hand, it would be safest near the bandit leader. Jasmine rushed to engage him and Blue Tunic.

Suddenly, a pattern of swirling, sparkling lights engulfed her, Ellessar, and the two bandits. The effect startled her for a moment before she recognized it: a weaving she and her friends had used against the guards in King Gremauld's tent the day they'd murdered him. The display was dazzling. Mesmerizing. Had she not seen it before, she might have become entranced. As it was, only Spirit seemed to succumb. This was no effect of Zen's, however. The bandits had a mage.

Blue Tunic swung himself onto his horse and wheeled away.

Overhead, the dragon passed without attacking and winged away toward the north.

Ellessar swung his blade at the Black Hand leader, who parried and countered.

Leave the sword fighting to men with swords, Jasmine thought. Brother Thistle would have called her a coward, but with the beating she'd taken from Sierra still fresh in her memory, Jasmine considered it prudence.

She leapt after Blue Tunic, but was too late. The bandit kicked his horse's flanks and fled.

A moment later, the Black Hand leader sprinted from the sparkling lights, swung his leg over the remaining horse—he was covered with blood now, much of it his own—and spurred the horse toward safety.

Nick spun away from the young bandit as she crumpled to the road. The remainder of the Black Hand had fled. Of his friends, only Zen remained on his horse. He hadn't moved since the start of the battle, but neither was he idle.

As he waved his arms, a small piece of ice appeared in his hand. It grew to an undulating ball of slush and ice, which he hurled at the fleeing bandit in the blue tunic. The ball gained power and girth as it flew. When it engulfed the horse and rider, it imploded, leaving both dead.

An arrow thumped into Zen's back. He cried out and swayed in his saddle.

Nick spun toward the brush and prairie grasses from which the arrow had come, but saw no one. Beyond, though—farther south—a woman on a horse waved her hands in a manner that Nick had learned to associate with weaving. A shape coalesced in the air between Nick and the bandit mage. It took the form of a large, feral dog, appearing in mid-leap. The animal, if it was an animal, stood at least four feet high at the shoulder. The color of ochre smudged with soot, its eyes glowing like burning embers, the dog barreled straight for Zen.

Nick sprinted to intercept the foul creature, which breathed smoke and stank of burnt flesh. As it tried to leap over him to get to Zen, Nick impaled it. By the time it slid, lifeless, from his blade, the Black Hand mage had fled.

Four bandits lay dead or unconscious in the stillness that followed. The dragon was nowhere in sight.

Ellessar strode up beside Nick.

"Demon?" Nick pointed his sword at the doglike creature the bandit mage had conjured.

"No. Demons bleed." Only smoke poured from the wounds of the fiery canine. Ellessar helped Zen from the saddle and laid him, face-down, on the road.

Jasmine knelt beside him. She tore open the fabric of his robe and inspected the wound. "It's lodged in your shoulder blade. Hold still." She gripped the shaft and yanked the arrow free.

Zen bellowed. Blood spurted from the hole.

Ellessar took his symbol of Aeron in one hand and placed the other over the wound. Words of prayer flowed from his lips. When he finished, Zen's face relaxed. The wound remained red and swollen, but the bleeding had stopped. "That'll probably pain you for a few weeks, but your life's not in danger."

"Yes it is." Rancid inclined his head toward a hill half a mile to the south. The surviving Black Hand, who still outnumbered Nick's company, had gathered there, watching. Once they regrouped, they made no further move toward leaving.

CHAPTER 22

halidreth joined his gathering band of survivors and dismounted the horse. He snatched up the reins of his own mount, who'd followed the others away from the battle.

"W— was that a dragon?" asked a young, disheveled-looking elf, a recent recruit whose name Halidreth couldn't bring to mind.

"Who cares?" Halidreth snapped, his voice hoarse.

"What do you mean, 'who cares'?" said a second, older, elf.

Halidreth waved a dismissive hand at the sky. "It's gone now, and we have other worries." He found a rag in his saddlebags, tore a strip from it, and tied it around the worst of his wounds, a gash on his right forearm, and pulled the knot snug with his teeth and his left hand.

Minshara, his mage, cantered up the rise and glared down at him. "Disengage?" Incredulity rang in the woman's voice. "Withdraw?"

Halidreth mounted so he wouldn't have to look up at her. "You question my authority?" He put as much menace into his glare as he could, despite the power Minshara wielded.

"Of course not."

"My wisdom then?"

Frustration crossed the woman's brow. "No. I merely—"

"We just lost four men." He ignored the pain in his arm as he thrust a finger toward the battlefield. "Maybe you didn't notice."

Minshara no longer met his glare. She studied her saddle horn as if seeking runes in the leather tooling.

"Where's Dorlan?" Halidreth's eyes swept the gathering bandits.

"Here." The dwarf, whose face and clothing had been painted in camouflage colors, rose from where he'd been crouching in the grass. He'd unstrung his stout bow but kept the weapon in his hand.

"Mount up," Halidreth said. "Several of us are wounded. Or green," he added with a pointed look at the recent recruit. "I don't like the odds." The rest of the Black Hand were to meet Halidreth in Dragon Tears that very day. They hadn't likely passed by yet or they'd have already engaged Sevendeath and his friends, who hadn't appeared to have fresh battle wounds. Behind, then, but probably not far. "We'll lead or drive Sevendeath south until we meet our brethren." He glanced at Minshara. "Then we'll fight."

"I approve." Whisper's voice was no more than a breath on the wind, but the enchanted ring on Halidreth's hand translated the words.

Halidreth cringed inwardly but keep his features neutral. The Chosen of the Master had been the downfall of his once-mighty Black Hand. He yearned to be rid of their meddling. If he could, he'd put this one in the path of the ice mage.

Without a word or gesture of acknowledgement, he turned his gaze toward the battlefield, where Sevendeath was methodically killing any wounded bandits.

When the fugitives from Trondor had finished looting the dead, they mounted and continued south, staying on the road until they came to the point nearest to where the Black Hand watched. There, the six of them conversed for a moment. Then, with Sevendeath in the lead, the group charged toward the bandits.

"That's our cue." Halidreth wheeled his horse south and spurred it to a gallop, his bandit gang close behind.

When he looked back, most of Sevendeath's friends had slowed, as though they'd meant only to flush the bandits, but Sevendeath himself and one of the others, the big man Whisper called Nicklan Mirrin, kept coming. Reluctantly, the others followed.

Halidreth smiled to himself. Organized, his bandits were formidable. If the dragon hadn't appeared, the outcome of the battle would have been different.

Significantly, Zen had been the first to falter from pursuit and the most reluctant to resume it when Nick and Sevendeath ran on. The ice mage was wounded, spent, or both. Minshara remained strong.

Still, Halidreth had no intention of fighting now if he could improve the odds by waiting. He had thirteen more bandits who'd split off in South Bend to make sure the Black Hand didn't miss Sevendeath in the city of Meuribar before continuing north. Those bandits could be an hour behind, or a day, but if Halidreth could stay ahead of Sevendeath long enough to reach them, he'd have no doubt of the battle's outcome.

He made a gradual arc back toward the road and ran on for an hour or more, with their pursuers trailing a thousand yards behind. Then the horses began to tire. The three that had been caught in Zen's hailstorm fell behind. Halidreth slowed to preserve his own horse and to keep his men together. Within minutes though, Sevendeath's band had closed half the distance.

At that point, Halidreth veered off the road into the grassy countryside, found a defensible position, and stopped. "Hold here," he told his men.

A hailstorm appeared in the gap between him and the three lagging bandits.

"Ride!" Halidreth yelled to the young elf recruit over the pounding of the hail. "Find the rest of the Black Hand and bring them here!"

The recruit nodded once, his eyes wide, and then spurred his horse.

Several other bandits dismounted and sought cover. Minshara galloped ahead.

As the recruit pulled away, he went down under a second hail-storm. When the pounding ceased, the bloodied young elf crawled away from his dead horse into a patch of brush.

"You'll have to go for help yourself," Whisper breathed from somewhere near Halidreth.

"I can't leave my men to fight without me."

"I can't afford to let your ring fall into an enemy's hand. I must communicate with whoever may lead among you."

Halidreth wheeled toward the sound, but couldn't make out the apparition against the landscape. Without a target, his retort died on his lips.

"The Master has resources beyond your band of thieves. Don't prove that you've reached the end of your usefulness."

Halidreth didn't reply.

"The dragon rider is still near. I can call for her."

Halidreth's jaw clenched as he spoke. "Then you stay here and fight with my men. They'll be of no use to you if they're dead."

"I will stay," Whisper said evenly.

That, at least, was something. Halidreth's mouth stretched into a fierce grimace. He spurred his horse into a gallop and caught up to Minshara, who waited a thousand yards ahead, out of range of the hailstorms. As he approached, she conjured a beast that looked something like a hippogriff—half horse, half eagle. With a flash, it appeared from the ether, smoky gray and smelling of rotten meat, and winged toward the fray.

Halidreth brought his horse to a stop beside hers. "I'm going for the others."

Minshara's eyes clouded with contempt.

Running was the Black Hand's nature. They never fought a fair fight if they could avoid it. They'd even left men behind to die so the others might escape, if the occasion required it—it was how they'd gotten this far. But to leave his entire gang to fight while he fled alone, like a coward in the night…that would cost him the respect he needed to lead the Black Hand.

"Conjure what you can to help them," he said. "But don't kill the ice mage. We need him. Then follow me." Without waiting for an answer, he galloped away, angling his path to intersect the road, where he'd make better time.

When the Black Hand had fled, Nick's friends slowed. All, that is, except Rancid, who continued to charge the bandits. Nick hesitated a moment as well. His farming days at home and three years with his uncle Harimon's caravan had taught him prudence.

Despite their losses on the road, the bandits still had them out numbered eight to six. Several were wounded, but so were Nick and some of his friends. Zen wouldn't be able to stay on his horse if it hadn't been for Ellessar's hasty prayer. Nick had so many hurts he could no longer tell which were recent. The pain he felt most in the presence of the Black Hand was the death of his mother.

That loss, and the taste of revenge so close at hand, drove him to follow Rancid. To the Abyss with prudence. To the Abyss with his friends if they chose to stay behind.

They didn't. The six of them drove the bandits before them for a hard hour before the Black Hand horses faltered. After Zen wove a hailstorm in their midst, most of the bandits finally dismounted and took up defensive positions. Their horses scattered. One bandit tried to escape, then the leader himself turned tail and ran. Some of the others drew bows or crossbows and shot a hasty volley while distance remained between the two parties. None hit. By the time Nick veered his horse off the road, some of the bandits had disappeared, hidden somewhere in the landscape.

Nick approached the nearest bandit, a seven-foot giant of a man with broad shoulders, stout leather armor, a fistful of spears, and a shield nearly as large as himself. Otto and Jasmine followed.

Zen slowed and dropped behind.

Nick reined in his horse and dismounted as Otto, battle ax held high in his right hand, charged the standing giant.

The bandit waved his shield, and Otto's horse shied sideways. He hit the ground with a grunt and a rush of air from his lungs.

Ellessar veered right, launching arrows toward some nearby brush.

Alone, Nick charged the giant, who dropped his spears and drew a sword from a sheath at his belt. The blade, nearly as long as Nick's but less broad, might as well have been a short sword to this man. Quick as a banshee, the man hacked with his blade as if it was a hatchet.

Nick lugged his sword from one parry to the next with weary arms. Finally, Otto regained his feet and came at the giant from behind.

The man spun toward Otto, but at the last second, he reversed his thrust and jabbed Nick's forehead with the butt of his pommel.

Nick's vision split, then went red and fuzzy. Blood poured down his face as he staggered back, no longer sure he was still on his feet.

One bandit, still mounted, charged though the gap with a spear held out as if to impale Zen on its shaft.

Jasmine leapt from her horse and raced to intercede, but Zen was already chanting. Ten yards from his target, the bandit dropped his spear and grabbed his skull with a cry of pain. His horse skirted wide as it ran past. The bandit never returned.

Zen spurred his horse, intent on helping Nick and Otto. His staff's magic could reach the huge bandit from where he sat, but it was imprecise and Zen was nearly too exhausted to tap the weave without it. Anything he did was likely to kill Nick and wound Otto. If he got close enough, though, he might manage a few ice shards.

A screech in the sky pulled his attention away. Flying over the battle from the south was the most hideous hippogriff he'd ever seen. No, not a hippogriff—this was something else. The back half of the beast was similar to that of a horse, but the front was no eagle. It more resembled some kind of dragon-kin with its lizard-like mouth, sharp teeth, leathery wings, and spiked tail.

It ignored the battle beneath it and flew straight at Zen. A hundred yards behind it, another followed. Beyond, a third winked into being. On the fringes of Zen's sight, the Black Hand mage sat astride her horse, the same mage who'd called the fiery dog to attack him on the road.

Zen raised his staff and sent a blast of frozen air into the leading creature. Without so much as blinking, the beast swooped down at him with a screech that made his spine shiver. Whatever this thing was, it was apparently immune to extreme cold. Zen's horse fidgeted, but he held it fast, his mind racing for options. Could it be an illusion? Did he dare to stand against it to find out?

At the last moment, he dove from his saddle. The beast's claws sank into his horse's flesh. It rose, but the horse proved too heavy. The fiend dropped it to the ground, where its neck snapped with a crack.

This was no illusion, and because cold didn't even slow it down, Zen had no means to combat it. For a moment, he considered erecting a dome of ice around himself and hiding beneath it until the danger passed. But that would leave his friends at the beasts' mercy when they already had their hands full with the bandits.

He sprinted to Jasmine's horse, snatched the reins, and pulled himself into the saddle. "Fly!" He spurred the animal. "For your life and mine." He couldn't fight these things, but he might be able to draw them away from his friends. Calling an animal, from this world or any other, caused a stretching of the weave that could be maintained for only a short period of time. Then the weave would snap back, returning the creature to wherever it had come from. Zen could outrun it, outlast it, if Jasmine's horse was fast enough.

R ancid charged the Black Hand before him, a low-ranking bandit by the look of him. His clothes and weapons were battle scarred, travel worn, and in need of repair. A ranking bandit would have had his pick of gear.

The bandit swung his blade wildly above him and Rancid's horse shied.

Rancid swung his leg over the saddle and let the horse slip from beneath him. He landed in a crouch and slid his blade underneath the man's sternum.

The man's eyes widened. He staggered back and his sword dropped from his grasp.

Nearby, Nick's face poured blood down the front of his armor. His pallor was ashen and he kept blinking as though his eyes wouldn't focus.

The huge bandit beat Otto's ax out of the way, then spun to finish Nick.

Rancid broke into a sprint.

As the giant turned, Otto raised his ax, but the bandit reversed his stroke and smashed the pommel of his sword into Otto's cheekbone. Otto spun with the impact. Blood gushed from a split in his face, but his stance remained strong.

When Rancid arrived, the bandit put his back to the bushes and faced the three men grimly, determined to take their lives in exchange for his.

Excellent swordsman that the man was, Otto and Rancid proved too much for him. Rancid ripped through the man's defenses, punctured his lung, and brought him to his knees. He grinned, fierce and jubilant. He was back in his element, fighting the bandits of his homeland once again—once and for all.

He left the giant for dead. Otto had enough strength to finish the job if the bandit found the will to continue breathing. Sevendeath had more killing to do.

Ellessar and Jasmine engaged a pair of bandits beyond a patch of small pinion trees. The bandits were faltering. Jasmine and Ellessar didn't seem to need his help. Seeing no other targets, however, Rancid ran to them.

As he approached, movement caught his eye. Another bandit, a dwarf by his size, faded into and out of sight among the trees, never clearly visible. As well camouflaged as the dwarf was, if he remained still, Rancid might lose him.

Rancid angled in behind the dwarf, picked his way through the foliage, careful not to make any sound the dwarf might hear over the din of combat, and then he buried his sword into the dwarf's back. *Everything's legal in the fight against evil.* Then he and his friends—the word no longer sounded foreign to him—finished off the remaining bandits.

Rancid scanned the battlefield for signs of hidden Black Hand, the merest breath, the rustle of a bush, the slightest trace of dust stirred by an errant movement. He couldn't tell if any of the footprints lead to an unseen bandit. That would take time to discern. But a simple body count revealed that only one bandit had slipped away. One, and the air apparition.

Rancid collected the leather gauntlets from the pockets and pouches of those he'd killed. The others gathered the coin, food, and weapons from the bodies of the dead.

When Zen returned, he reported that the horse-dragon hybrids were gone.

"Gone?" Rancid asked. "Dead? Vanished? Or still out there somewhere to attack again?"

The shifty mage didn't elaborate.

Ellessar placed a hand on Nick's forehead and spoke a prayer of healing.

Maybe if the priest pressed his luck, he would run out of prayers, overstay his divine welcome, so to speak. Rancid chuckled at the thought.

After a few minutes, Nick thanked the demon hunter and then handed the reins of a leftover Black Hand horse to Zen. "There are more enemies behind us than in front, and we still have an errand to complete."

As a group, they mounted up and slogged southward. With the exception of Rancid, the life seemed to have drained from the entire party. They'd become overconfident. The Black Hand had caught them unaware, and they all bled as a result. Some—Zen probably, and Nick—would be dead if it hadn't been for Ellessar's healing prayers.

Rancid had to hide his own elation. Halidreth had come out of his hole in Forlorn Valley. He'd come all the way to Faldor to find Sevendeath. That meant *all* of the Black Hand were in Faldor. He need only find them, or let them find him. Then he could finish the job he'd started so long ago.

His friends didn't seem to notice that he'd set a pace much slower than that required to rest their mounts.

halidreth and his mage galloped down the road toward Silversmith for three hours before reaching the turnoff toward Meuribar. His remaining Black Hand would be down this road. He'd hoped to find them before now, but Meuribar was a big city to search. Sorowyn, Jade, and the others must have been held up. Groaning through gritted teeth, Halidreth turned his horse down the Meuribar road and spurred it on.

He didn't have to go far, however. An hour later, he met the remainder of his gang. Now fifteen strong, he led them back the way he'd come, to catch Sevendeath.

CHAPTER 23

Just before dusk, a cloud of dust appeared on the road, nearly a mile ahead, and approaching too fast to be a merchant caravan or band of casual wayfarers. Rancid clenched his teeth into a grim smile and quickened his pace.

Jasmine walked her horse beside him. Until now Rancid had set a pace that allowed her to do so without falling behind. She gripped his leg. "That may well be the Black Hand leader and mage, but they're coming this way, which means they've found help."

Rancid scowled at her, but he said nothing.

"Or it could be Sierra," Jasmine continued, "with a fresh band of mercenaries. Or yet another of the Chosen travelling with some new threat. Let us see who they are before we commit ourselves to battle."

Rancid looked from her to the dust cloud, closer now and too large to have been stirred by a single pair of horses.

"Where we have ignorance, we must seek knowledge," she said gently.

He growled between his teeth and pulled his horse off the road.

"There." Ellessar pointed to a low rise, about thirty feet away, high enough to hide the horses and topped with grasses and sage. "Quickly." He spurred his horse.

The thunder of hooves reached them as they dismounted behind the rise. While Otto gathered up the reins of the horses, Rancid, Nick, Ellessar, and Jasmine crawled to the top and pressed the tall grass aside to watch the riders pass.

Rancid pulled a dagger from its sheath and settled the blade between his thumb and forefinger.

Fifteen riders appeared on the road—the Black Hand, with Halidreth at the front. Sorowyn, Jade, and several others whom Rancid recognized from Forlorn Valley, but whose names he didn't know, rode with him. Their mage brought up the rear of the bandit party. They'd picked up a spare horse somewhere along the way, likely a stray from the previous battle.

Rancid tucked his feet under him and drew back his good arm. The throw would be long, but if he hit, he might kill the mage before the battle began.

"If you do this," Ellessar said softly, "you do it alone."

Nick and Jasmine nodded their agreement.

Jaw clenched, Rancid kept his arm poised until the bandits passed well out of range and the sound of their hooves receded.

Rancid pointed across the road to the southeast, roughly the direction of South Bend. "Take the others that way until full dark and find a safe place to camp. We can save time if we cut the corner off our journey and skip the town of Silversmith. I'll catch up."

Ellessar stood and walked back to his horse as though it wouldn't bother him at all if Rancid pursued the bandits to his death.

"What are you planning to do?" Nick asked.

Rancid waved toward the road as if the answer was obvious. "Hide our tracks where we leave the road. The Black Hand horses are tired. If my guess is right, they've been running like that for hours and won't stop until they find the rest of their gang, dead where we left them." He met Nick's gaze squarely, hoping he'd mistake determination for sincerity. "Our horses are rested. The bandits won't catch us tonight. With luck, we can lose them here and now."

After the others had gone, Rancid erased the tracks as well as he could in the dying light. He'd thought to deliberately leave some signs of their passing, but that seemed unnecessary. The Black Hand had tracked them this far. They wouldn't lose the trail now.

Rancid slept little in the three days it took to reach South Bend. The Black Hand were out there and in pursuit. They hadn't come this far just to give up. And they wouldn't have found him in Faldor if they didn't have sufficient skills to follow the simple tracks of six galloping horses. Still, he kept up his role by backtracking to conceal what he could of their trail every night.

His friends' wounds were healing, thanks to Jasmine's herbs—as much as Rancid hated to admit it—and Ellessar's prayers. Together, the six should be more than a match for the Black Hand, especially since the bandits would have traveled quickly to catch up, with little time for rest and healing. A river crossing two nights before would have been a perfect place for an ambush, and of all the threats that pursued, the Black Hand would've been one less to manage. But there was more at stake than just the Black Hand.

The horses were tired and the whole party sleep-deprived. Jasmine hadn't meditated for more than a few minutes at a time since they'd left Dragon Tears, and her disposition was gradually tending toward her demon half.

Other than for healing, Ellessar prayed only long enough to cast his divine sense about for the Assassin, which had apparently fallen nearly a day behind. Just a few good nights of rest for the party, though, and the demon would be on them again.

Zen spent more time on the outskirts of camp practicing his magic than he did sleeping. Every chance he got, Rancid had ventured close enough to observe, trying to determine if Zen was contacting the Master, any of the Chosen, or possibly even directing the dragon rider, who'd passed overhead more than once since they'd fought the Black Hand. All Rancid could visually discern in the darkness was that at least once, Zen had opened a portal of some kind, probably to the plane of ice. A vapor, like breath on a cold morning, had wafted from the opening.

"If the dragon rider is an agent of the Master," Jasmine asked as the party looked down on the ferry that crossed the river between them and South Bend, "why hasn't she attacked? According to the legends, the dragon could burn us all to a toasty crisp with a single breath. Isn't that what the Master wants?"

"The legends are probably exaggerated." Ellessar finished his inventory of coin and food supplies and began to repack his things. "That's the way it is with demons. My brotherhood has spent generations sorting out truth from myth about the denizens of the Abyss."

A screen of trees hid them from the guardsmen and ferry operators at the base of the hill. The Great Divide, the barrier that separated the civilized races from the horrors of the Wild Lands, loomed now at their backs.

"Or she's waiting for us to find what we're looking for before she kills us," Zen said. "Like Vinsous Drakemoor did. Only this time, I figure a dragon ought to be able to get the job done."

Rancid nodded. He'd fought the Black Hand often enough to know how their evil minds thought. They'd let men who were good and right and just toil for riches and power. Then they'd seize a moment of weakness and take it all away.

But that problem lay in their future. Right now, the party had to decide how to get the supplies they needed from South Bend without their presence there becoming known. They couldn't even cross the river without the ferry, which meant somehow hiding their many recognizable features and belongings from the guards, or anyone following would know they'd come this way.

"I still say Ellessar and I should go alone," Zen said. "I'll disguise myself as a merchant and take Jasmine's horse to carry the supplies, and we'll meet the rest of you at the fork down river."

Zen shed his cloak, staff, and headband, then donned one of Nick's travelling tunics. He borrowed Jasmine's horse to carry his wares and adopted the same disguise he'd used to escape from Spitfire as a merchant.

He and Ellessar descended the slope to the ferry, where four guards and a pair of workmen manned the crossing.

As a merchant, Zen was charged three gold coins to cross, one for himself and one for each horse. The men charged Ellessar, dressed in the vestments of his order, only two silver. Three gold coins was enough for a week at any reasonable inn. Apparently they understood the profitability of a merchant in a town that practically straddled the gateway between the Civilized Lands and the Wild Lands.

Once they crossed the river, Zen and Ellessar traveled another three miles to reach the city. A twenty-foot-high, ten-foot-wide wall wrapped the town in a façade of security. Though the wall might have been adequate to repel the denizens of the Wild Lands, it'd do little good if the dragon and its rider decided to raze the city.

The gate lay open, however, and the guards manned their posts with a relaxed posture.

"Apparently it's been a long time since anything worrisome has crossed the Great Divide," Ellessar said, once they were safely out of earshot. "Where to first?"

Zen gestured toward the armory. He patted the sacks hanging on Jasmine's horse, which carried the multitude of weapons they'd salvaged from the Black Hand bodies. "These ought to buy us everything we need to survive for weeks, if necessary, in the Wild Lands."

Even as he said it, he laughed awkwardly at the notion. He'd traveled many places, but always in the Civilized Lands. He'd heard stories of the Wild Lands, mostly speculation about what lived there and why people rarely returned. Nobody seemed to know what it actually took to survive there. Sure, they'd buy the basics, and they'd bring shovels, in case they had to dig for the rock they sought. Food and water, they had. Weapons too, but if the Assassin followed them—and it certainly would—a few steel blades wouldn't last long against it. Should they keep their excess weapons or trade them for better weapons or armor? Did the inhabitants of the Wild Lands value some particular commodity? Dyes, beads, or ale, maybe? Would Jasmine need a specific medicine to fend off some new disease? And, most importantly, what enchantments would best serve Zen there?

When they walked into the armory to sell their weapons, Zen's heart sank. The walls, racks, and cases were stocked to the hilt. The armorer certainly wasn't hurting for inventory.

Ellessar examined one of the swords. "Dwarven-make."

"Only the best," said the stout dwarf from behind the counter. "At a good price, too."

After a lengthy negotiation, the dwarf talked them into unloading their entire Black Hand take for a pittance, just enough to buy a pair of dwarven-made swords. They stopped at the provisioner's for picks, shovels, and a couple of strong leather sacks.

Afterwards, Zen renewed his disguise enchantment, lengthening the beard a bit, and Ellessar exchanged his vestments for his typical demon-hunter's garb.

"Don't you think bringing a pickax into a bar is going a bit too far?" Ellessar asked as he and Zen approached the nearest tavern.

"No disguise is complete without props, and what prospector worth his gold doesn't have a pickax?" Having left his staff with Jasmine and the others, it was comforting to have something with a long handle to hold in his hand.

With a shrug, Ellessar followed him inside.

After about twenty minutes of cheap ale and discrete inquiries, a customer directed them to a one-armed old man who looked like he'd been settled into his corner booth for weeks.

"Is there really gold there?" Zen asked the man after buying him a pint of mead.

The old-timer grunted. "If there is, I ain't never seen no one who's found it."

"Well, I heard it's there."

The man shrugged, apparently willing to humor him as long as Zen was buying the drinks. "You know where you're going once you get there?"

"Nope. Figured I'd follow my nose."

"He's got a sense for it." Ellessar sipped his ale. "It's uncanny. Eerie, really."

The old man grunted again, but said nothing.

"We heard you might be able to tell us what to expect on the other side of the Divide," Zen said.

"I been there a time or two. Used to scout for anyone crazy enough to go." The old man took a long pull and wiped his mouth with the stump of his left arm, which ended just past the elbow. "At least a half a dozen times I crossed the Great Divide and made it back to tell the tale. Half a dozen times I convinced myself I'd taken enough coin to make the trip worth the risk. Last time out, some coot wanted to go into the swamp. Had an in with the lizardfolk, he said. Turns out he was just after their hides to make fancy boots—thought he could make a killing at it. Ha!" Another pull on the mead and a swipe of his stump. "Lost my arm on that trip. Never went back to find it."

Zen and Ellessar exchanged a nervous look while the old man flagged down the barmaid.

"Can you tell us about it?" Zen prompted.

"Course I can. I'm not senile, just hungry."

The barmaid arrived with another round of drinks. Zen gestured to the old man. "Whatever he wants."

"Whatever's on the menu." The man waved his stump in dismissal.

"Make it three," Ellessar said.

When the barmaid turned back toward the kitchen, the old man began, "Nothing there is anything like what we got here. The natives of the plains are some sort of wolf-kin. Or coyote, maybe, I never did know for sure. They're savage most of the time, but not stupid. They run in packs, use tools and weapons. Even speak a language of sorts, but savages just the same. It's them that comes over the pass mostly."

"They come over the pass?" Zen asked.

"Never get past Roybal Keep at the northern end. Other things come too."

"Demons?" Ellessar asked.

The old man pursed his lips and thought for a moment. "Some folks say they are. I say they're just beasts. Growed up different than beasts here, but beasts just the same. Now demons, they're something else entirely."

Ellessar nodded. "That they are."

The barmaid showed up with three bowls of mutton stew and a loaf of cornbread, hot from the oven.

The old man tore off a piece with his good hand, seemingly unbothered by the heat through the layers of old calluses. "Best bread in town."

Zen gave the man time to chew a mouthful and chase it with some of the steaming broth. "What kind of beasts?"

The old man waved his spoon. "All kinds."

"What about magic?" Zen asked.

"What about it?" The man spoke around a mouthful of stew.

"Any kind of magic in the Wild Lands?"

"There's magic in some of the beasts."

Not the kind Zen was looking for, not the kind he could steal—that's to say, not the kind he could acquire at a fair price, he amended quickly, recalling the oath. He liked this errand less and less the more he learned about it.

"Just stay out of the swamp," the old man warned.

"Why?" Ellessar asked. "What's in the swamp?"

"Things big enough to eat a horse whole." He paused. "Ain't never seen no lizard-skin boots. That's all I'm saying."

"Thanks for the help." Ellessar tossed a gold coin onto the table, enough to pay for all of their food and drinks, plus a healthy tip that the barmaid would probably never see.

CHAPTER 24

The last of Sierra Glenwood's agents arrived in Faldor City late that evening. He was a young man who'd played a lyre on a street corner for coins during the Harvest Festival in Spitfire but had had no place to go afterwards. He claimed to be practiced with a sword and quick on a horse, so she'd hired him to ride to Redstar to seek news of the fugitives there while Sierra went to the capital. It had been weeks since she'd lost the fugitives' trail at the Trondor-Faldor border, but she'd lost prey for longer than that and had always managed to track them down.

The young man approached Sierra's table, his boots clomping on the loose boards of the taproom floor. "No news, milady. The fugitives haven't been through Redstar. Or Spitfire since you left."

Sierra clenched her jaw at this last statement.

"I didn't dally," the young man said in a rush. "I stopped for only a few minutes to question the guards as I came back through. I thought the information would be worth the brief delay. Any news from the others?"

"No. Sit." Sierra motioned to the chair across from her. The night was late. She sat, half slumped, in her chair and massaged her forehead, unable to gather enough coherent thoughts. She'd sent her recruits in an arc that swept Faldor from North Reach to Redstar in an effort to pick up the fugitives' trail. All had returned with nothing. The fugitives must have slipped past by avoiding the towns, cities, farms, and ranches, of which there were frustratingly few. How they'd gotten supplies after escaping the king's dungeons, she couldn't imagine, but that mattered little now. "Everyone else has returned. You're the last."

"I'm sorry, milady, I—"

She waved his apology aside. "You had the farthest to travel. I hadn't expected you sooner."

He bowed his head. "Thank you, milady."

Despite the foul mood she'd nursed throughout the day, the young man made her smile. Nobody had ever called her 'milady.' She was so far from nobility, the word rang like blasphemy. Maybe that's why she enjoyed it so much. "The men are supplied. Tomorrow morning, we ride south."

"South?"

"According to King Culhaven, the fugitives originally came from Palidor. If they'd had any business between there and Trondor, they'd have settled it on the way. That suggests they're heading south."

"Of course, milady." Oh, his voice was melodic.

She looked up. "Are you thirsty?"

He nodded.

"Good." She tossed a gold coin onto the marred tabletop. "Buy a bottle of their elven best and meet me in my room." He wasn't a bad-looking young man. A bit naive perhaps, but that would only add to the fun.

ick and his companions made it halfway to the Great Divide by nightfall and started out early the next morning. The dragon and its rider flew overhead a couple of hours later, the first time it had done so during the day since they'd battled the Black Hand.

Nick traded uneasy glances with Jasmine and Ellessar, Rancid glared at Zen, and Otto just shook his head, but nobody commented on its passing. It always came at them from behind, high enough to prevent Zen from striking at it with the weave. This time it headed toward Roybal Keep and the pass.

Nobody suggested that they detour or abort their errand.

By noon, they reached the gates of the garrison. A guard on the battlement yelled down from the wall. "State your business!"

Rancid spoke before anyone else could answer. "Prospecting. This crazy coot—" He stabbed an accusing finger at Zen— "thinks he'll find gold in the Wild Lands. Everywhere else but Gildstone is mined out, and the dwarves aren't sharing."

Zen hadn't adopted his prospectors disguise. "Ha ha! Don't need no dwarven gold. The lines of the weave clearly point that way." He thrust his staff at the gate with such an emphatic gesture that the guard flinched. Zen gave Rancid a look past the edge of his cowl that could have frozen an arctic wolf.

Nick jumped in before Rancid could concoct a façade none of them could hope to maintain. "Word has it this is the only way across the Great Divide for a hundred leagues in either direction. We're prepared to pay for passage."

"You don't need payment going in," the guard hollered. Several more had gathered on the stone battlement to gaze at these fools who dared to travel south. "We're here only to keep undesirables from coming north."

"Then hoist this annoying barrier from our path," Zen said, "so we might be rich by nightfall."

"Oh, I doubt you'll be that." The guard motioned to someone in the courtyard below and the iron portcullis rose. "The pass takes a full day to traverse, and it's not an easy hike."

As soon as the gate was high enough, Zen spurred his horse, waved his staff around his head like a madman, and galloped into the keep. Nick raised an eyebrow at Rancid, who just shrugged and followed Zen in. Jasmine kept her hood up, head down, and her taloned hands tucked into the voluminous sleeves of her robe.

"You're welcome to sup here and spend the night," a sentry on the ground told Nick as he passed. "The food ain't much, but it'll do you well enough. Got a pub too, with the staunchest of dwarven spirits, if you're brave enough to drink it and strong enough to keep it down."

The keep was little more than a bunkhouse, mess hall, tavern, and a few basic shops: a blacksmith—who served as an armorer—a leatherworker, provisioner, and stable master, all of which catered to the keep's military residents. The entire fort was constructed of stone block, the southern battlement twice as high and much thicker than the one on the north side. It stretched across the pass to cliffs on either side that would challenge a mountain goat. An eagle soared overhead, the first bird Nick had seen since the passing of the dragon. Pens of sheep, goats, and chickens provided live stores for the soldiers, and the nearby river was easily accessible from the northern gate.

"Let's take some time," Nick suggested. "This is our last chance to gather information and supplies before we cut ourselves off from civilization."

"I'll try to stay out of sight," Jasmine said softly. "And do my best to keep Zen out of trouble." She quickened her pace toward the mage, where he'd stopped a dozen yards ahead. The two soon disappeared into the bunkhouse.

Nick went straight to the provisioner.

"Afternoon," the man said.

Nick approached the counter. "I'm looking for a map with information about the Wild Lands."

"Aren't we all?"

"That mean you don't have one?" Nick set his meager bag of coins on the counter with a clink and scanned the shelves.

"Son, let me be clear. Nobody has a map of the Wild Lands, 'cause that would require someone to go in, map it, and come back out alive."

"Nobody's ever come back alive?"

"Oh, it happens. Don't get me wrong. Just not that often. And nobody goes in just to map the place."

Rancid stepped up beside Nick. "Who was the last person to enter the pass?"

"A group of missionaries came through here about a month ago. Never came back."

"Thanks." Nick collected his coins. "If we decide we need anything, we'll be back."

"I'm sure you will."

Rancid and Nick crossed the courtyard, maybe an acre in size, to the armory. There, Nick gazed at swords of every shape and size, axes, war hammers, crossbows, daggers, halberds, and glaives, all of dwarven make. The ordinary swords sat almost unnoticed, hilts sticking from a wooden cask like so many pokers for the fire.

Ellessar, who had already been in the shop, lifted a sword from the rack and tested its balance.

"We're your last chance," the blacksmith said smoothly. "End of civilization."

"Even so, your prices are quite competitive. I'd expect to pay twice as much for such a weapon in Trondor or Palidor. Nevertheless..." Nick started to put a great sword back on the rack, the price a little too high for his purse. Then he noticed something on the hilt.

"South Bend keeps us well supplied," the blacksmith explained, "seeing as how they'll be the first town hit if the denizens of the Wild ever make it past us."

"What kinds of things come over?" Rancid asked.

"Some kind of wolf-kin beasts mostly. We get an errant pack every now and again. Eager to expand their territory, I expect."

Nick was only half listening. He scurried from rack to rack, rifling through the wares, examining the mark stamped in ink on the leather wrap of nearly every handle, the mark of ownership stamped by the merchant who'd purchased them from the dwarves.

Nick rushed the counter with an armload of weapons. "Where did you get these?" He dumped them onto the counter with a clatter, spilling several on the blacksmith's side, forcing the man to jump back. He then snatched one up and brandished the ink marking. "This is my uncle's mark. He'd have never sold these for less than the price you're asking."

Nick's face flushed with heat. "*All* of these were his." There was probably half a wagonload just in this little shop. "Where did you *get* them?" It took every bit of his self-restraint to refrain from using the word *steal*.

The blacksmith dropped his gaze to the dirt floor. He bent to pick up the fallen swords and set them onto the counter. Something in his demeanor stilled Nick's tongue when he wanted to shout, "Where?"

When the blacksmith's eyes met Nick's, they were moist. "This merchant was your uncle?"

Nick nodded. *Was?*

"A caravan got hit along the southern road about six months ago. These weapons were scattered for a mile along the roadside."

Nick shook his head. It didn't make any sense.

"It was during the height of the goblin riots. We think the caravan was making for Palidor. These weapons would have fetched fine coin there. That's for sure."

"Why... Who..." Nick couldn't form the proper question.

But the blacksmith went on. "The caravan was ravaged by a monster of some kind, some say from the far side of the Great Divide. If so, it didn't come through the pass, or we'd have at least tried to stop it."

"Of course." Ellessar put together Nick's thought for him. "If it were bandits, they'd have taken the load. Especially one this rich."

"There's more." The blacksmith reached out, but Nick backed away. "We found several bodies among the wreckage. Some whole. Some in pieces. Some burned to a crisp as if roasted on a spit. I didn't see it myself, but the stories are gruesome. It's said they found the severed leg of some crablike beast. The leg to the second joint stood as tall as a man, black as night, with a shell as hard as plate steel."

"Any survivors?" Ellessar asked.

The smith met Nick's black stare. "I never heard anything about survivors. South Bend was the closest town. They'd have probably showed up there." He walked over to the rack and took down the dwarven-made sword Nick had first admired. "This one's on the house. I hate to be the bearer of bad news. I'm sorry."

That offer, more than anything else, told Nick that the man was telling the truth.

An hour later, Nick and his friends walked their horses through the southern gates of Roybal Keep onto the narrow, rugged path. Cliffs rose skyward to pinnacles lost in the glare of the early afternoon sun.

"Watch the weather in the pass," the sentry at the gate said.

Nick nodded. The sky was a spotless blue and had been for the past three days.

The sentry grabbed his arm. No levity showed in the man's eyes as they met Nick's. "I mean it. It can get tricky near the summit."

Nick couldn't see the summit beyond the high walls that shouldered the trail. He couldn't even be sure of which direction the trail went beyond the next bend. The peaks of the Great Divide didn't seem high enough to attract severe winds, dense clouds, or snow.

A fairy perched on a ridge, in a patch of scrub juniper, high above the summit of the pass, having guarded it since she'd been left behind by her kin when they'd fled to the Mist Isles eons before. She'd had a name once, but she could no longer remember what it was. In truth, the fairy had been in the pass for so long she couldn't even distinguish between herself and the land she called home. She'd grown dependent upon it, and it upon her.

The fairy stiffened on her perch. Once again, creatures intruded upon her solitude. Usually the intrusions came from the south, from the Wild Lands. Today the intruders approached from the north, and she could sense the presence of a demon among them.

A demon. The evil the fairies were created to destroy.

She'd sensed demons before, of course, but this one felt different somehow. The aura of its being seemed indistinct, less focused or less intense than those of its kin. Maybe the fairy was losing touch with the senses that guided her. It had been centuries since a demon had come through the pass.

Until now...

Glee stretched the fairy's features, a faint hiss of laughter escaped her clenched teeth, and she made her preparations.

She didn't need to ask any god to grant her prayers. As a fairy, she tapped Aeron's power directly. She erected defenses about her being; enhanced her ageless body for greater speed; sharpened her senses, thoughts, and reflexes; called for the rocks to hide her and the vegetation to aid her; and charged the air with energy. Then she waited.

The first intruder to come into view was an elf-kin cloaked in dark green, his face scarred by time and circumstance, but familiar with the ways of nature. The fairy had no quarrel with him.

Soon, others rounded the bend: an elven warrior—a favorite of Aeron—and an elf-kin mage. The rest were human. Why they befriended a demon, the fairy neither knew nor cared. Maybe they didn't know the true nature of the female among them. The fairy would spare them if she could, but one way or another, she *would* kill the demon.

CHAPTER 25

As the afternoon wore on, the high cliffs darkened the trail prematurely, and the temperature dropped as the companions climbed higher. A pit formed deep in Jasmine's stomach, a primal sense of foreboding as the party neared the summit of the pass. She scanned the sliver of clear sky that was visible between the cliffs. Not a cloud in sight. No dragon. No hawk. She glanced back at the short stretch of trail she could see behind them. No demons. No bandits. No mercenaries. Yet her sense of dread persisted.

"I'll see if I can find a suitable campsite." Rancid eyed the rugged cliffs with skepticism as he moved out ahead of the group.

"Be careful," Jasmine said, just before he rounded a bend and disappeared from sight.

Minutes later, a breath of sharp air whipped Jasmine's cloak. A bolt of lightning cracked the clear sky and struck her saddle, between her legs. Thunder reverberated down the canyon as she dove from her stunned horse. Her skin tingled with the residual charge. A thin wisp of smoke trailed upward from a charred circle in the saddle's leather. Her horse tried to bolt, yanking Jasmine off her feet, onto one hand and knee.

The vegetation in the pass, the scant bushes and scrub grasses, and the few hardy trees struggling for purchase in the crevices of the rock, came to life. Tendrils snaked from the brush or pushed their way up through the packed dirt of the trail and wrapped around Jasmine's ankles and waist, and around the legs of her frenzied horse.

A second stroke of lightning hit her squarely in the back. Her teeth clamped shut, every muscle in her body spasmed, and she lost all sensation for a moment.

When she regained consciousness, she lay on the ground, tendrils of vegetation strengthening their hold around her torso and moving toward her neck. These were not strangle vines. Some enchantment had been placed upon several varieties of native plants. She ripped at the knotted branches around her, rent them with her claws and pulled herself free. Her horse was stuck fast, thrashing and likely to break a leg in his panic.

The new overgrowth ended just before the summit of the pass, no more than fifty yards ahead. Jasmine leapt to her feet and launched herself toward it. A flash of lightning came down behind her as she scrambled to stay on top of the malevolently writhing flora.

Before she got there, lightning struck her again.

Zen recognized the lightening immediately. Not in any specific sense, but the power to pull adverse weather from a clear sky was one he'd wielded ever since he'd acquired his staff. The weaving of the fabric of nature was the same in either case; only the source of the energy was different. This was no natural lightning. This was the work of a powerful mage.

When the shoots and tendrils gripped the legs of his horse, he welcomed them. If they held, he wouldn't have to chase down the animal later. For now, his fingers danced in the air as he wove himself into the form of an ice hawk.

His sharp eyes made out details of the rocks that he couldn't have seen as a man, and from a hawk's soaring vantage, he should be able to find the enemy mage. He launched himself from the back of his horse and flew up the cleft of the pass.

Rancid must have heard the thunder, since he sprinted back. He rounded the bend, his dagger already in his hand, just as Zen reached the summit. When Rancid threw the blade, Zen realized his mistake. The form he'd taken out of convenience was the form for which they'd watched the sky ever since they'd left Trondor. Thoughts of the dragon and its rider had pushed Dalen's hawk out of his mind.

The dagger clipped Zen's wing. Pain seared him, and he faltered. With the wing no longer able to hold his weight, he glided toward a shelf high on the left wall of the canyon, beyond a protrusion that would shield him from Rancid's sight.

Zen refused to give up the hawk's form, however. He still needed its acute vision, so he ignored the pain as he scanned the cliffs. Because the lightning bolts came from the sky and therefore revealed nothing of the whereabouts of the mage who wove them, the only hints Zen had were Jasmine's location and what Zen knew of his own magic. These strikes were precise, and they followed Jasmine's movements as she tried to dodge them. The enemy, probably Sierra, the dragon's rider, or the Black Hand mage, could see Jasmine. But from where?

The hiking path below was narrow, the walls to either side steep but climbable, with numerous ledges and cracks that might hide an adversary. Then he spotted her, a small woman crouched in a clump of brush below him and to his left.

Now Zen needed his hands. With his mind, he plucked at the arcane threads that sustained his hawk's body. He released the animal's form to the wind and resumed his own, the rent tissues of his wing reforming. His arm ached, but he could now use it.

The enemy seemed to be keeping an eye on Zen, dividing her attention between him and his friends on the trail.

Below, Nick leapt from his horse, grabbed it by the reins, and yanked it toward Rancid.

Zen wove a ball of ice and slush in his hand. "I found her!" He launched the frozen sphere at the mage. "She's there!" It engulfed the brush and rocks in which she hid and exploded in a fury of ice and wind.

The small mage reeled for a moment, her limbs encrusted with frost, her frozen, brittle hair breaking where it scraped the brush. Then the frost on her skin melted away. Her raw, frostbitten flesh returned to a fair hue.

Zen didn't give her time to heal herself. He wove a handful of ice shards and launched them into her. If they pierced her skin, however, she didn't bleed.

Despite Zen's best efforts to distract her, she continued to rain down lightning bolts on Jasmine. Her monk's robe lay charred and tattered on the trail. Several burn marks splotched her thick demon skin as she scaled the cliff toward the mage. Another bolt struck her. Her body stiffened on the rock, her talons ripping at the stone.

Though the fairy wielded significant power, the demon below her proved both quick and agile. An astounding half of the fairy's lightning strikes missed their mark. But she kept at it.

The fairy, a creature of the gods, lived among the peaks of the Great Divide, where winter temperatures dropped low enough to freeze blood. Her metabolism protected her from the extremes of the climate, but nothing had prepared her for the blast of cold the mage had delivered. Her breath froze in her chest and her limbs went numb. Her fingers were so cold she feared they'd break when she forced them into motion. Another ball of frost like that, if it came too soon, would do her in.

Quickly, she wove a thread of heat through her bones, and feeling returned to her limbs. The mage's splinters of ice, when they struck, melted before they could pierce her skin. But every attack he made weakened her defenses and drained her strength.

Regretfully, she turned her lightning upon him.

Z en wove another sphere of frost. As it took form, lightning struck. His fingers spasmed. The magic escaped into the ether and vanished, the threads of energy ripped from him like a handful of hair, painful and maddening.

When Jasmine reached the ledge, the enemy emerged from hiding, and Zen got his first good look at her. She wasn't a woman at all, but a girl of maybe six or eight harvests. Then she disappeared in a wink.

Zen gathered up the weave, transformed into an eagle of ice, and took flight once more. From there, he could see the whole of the canyon. Ellessar, Otto, and Rancid crouched near their mounts searching the cliffs for the girl. Nick hid behind his horse and clawed at his armor with a dagger. The buckles and fittings glowed red hot and smoke wafted up from the singed padding beneath. Piece by smoldering piece, he dropped it, ruined, to the ground. Blackened rents in his clothing exposed blistered skin beneath.

Never had Zen seen a mage who could weave so many enchantments so quickly without tiring. He would have already depleted his own energies by now if they hadn't been bolstered by the focusing powers of his headband and the catalyst in the staff. Even with those, his strength would soon be gone.

The fairy didn't go far. Her duty was clear. The demon must die. She had traveled the weave only to the far wall of the canyon, to another of her favorite hiding places. From there, she rained another lightning bolt onto the demon. How many times had she struck it? She'd lost count even of how many times she'd tried. But the demon didn't slow. That was what made them so hard to kill. When a fairy expended herself in battle, she gradually weakened until she had nothing left to fight with. But demons fought on, strong as the moment they were pulled from the Abyss, full of rage and vengeance. It was impossible to tell how much they'd been hurt. Sometimes it wasn't even clear when they died.

When Zen spotted the mage in a brush-filled crevice, he screeched and dove at her.

"There!" Ellessar loosed an arrow.

"I see her," Jasmine called.

Zen veered to the side, toward a shelf, no more than twenty feet from the girl.

Jasmine leapt from the heights of her perch. She landed with a somersault, came to her feet, and raced up the steep, opposite slope toward the girl. Lightning bolts chased her all the way.

As soon as Zen's feet touched the ledge, he released the weave and resumed his elf-kin form.

The girl straightened, bringing herself into full view. She was a beauty, and no child—that was certain—only small in stature. Her body, built like that of a goddess, was covered only in patches of woven fern. He almost couldn't look at her. Her beauty was so great, it made his eyes well up with tears.

She struck Zen with her glare. The force of anger in her eyes hit him physically, breaking his heart. His mind reeled, and his grip on his staff went limp. It hit the rock at his feet and tumbled down the cleft.

The mage was an elf-kin, so instead of striking him physically, the fairy directed every emotion she could muster into his mortal mind and prayed he'd retain enough of his faculties to keep from falling to his death.

The demon, excellent climber that it was, would reach her soon enough, so the fairy called again to the plants around her, coaxing growth from dormant seeds. A writhing mass of foliage slowed the demon's ascent.

The fairy's resources were nearing an end, however. With no energy left to continue the fight, she had but one trick left.

Jasmine reached the lip, where the wall tapered to a more gentle slope, now choked with writhing brush. Above her, the fleeing enemy scrabbled up the cliff face. Jasmine could see her beauty clearly, like a spiritual aura around her. She was no woman, but a god, or like a god. Jasmine had no right to look upon such a creature with her vile, mortal eyes. The radiance seared itself onto Jasmine's mind and struck her blind.

After a sudden moment of vertigo, Jasmine felt her way up until her feet gained the shelf, halfway to the top of the cliff. Branches wrapped around one ankle. Loose shale slipped from beneath her other foot. She grabbed blindly at the vegetation to keep from falling.

Vines ensnared her arms. She used them for leverage to pull her legs free. Her demon muscles and her training from the Order gave her strength beyond that of any human. The vegetation couldn't hold her.

She crawled on all fours, out of the gripping vines, into a more benign clump of brush. There she took refuge to consider her options.

Pebbles pattered on the shelf around her as the enemy continued to climb above her.

The child of the gods shouted, "Take your blind demon and go."

To the Abyss with that. Jasmine wanted the girl dead, but the teachings of the Order imposed themselves upon her emotions. To fight here, now, in this way, would only weaken her friends and their cause further.

"Dispel these weeds and we'll be on our way," Ellessar shouted up from the trail.

When the vines seemed to settle, Jasmine crawled from the brush, groping her way on her hands and knees. She'd never been so helpless. Here, halfway up a cliff, she couldn't even stand safely.

"It's all right," Zen said from beside her. "I'm with you. The plants are gone. I'll help you down."

It was all Jasmine could do to nod her thanks. She'd always been self-sufficient. Despite the outward humility taught by her elders, she'd prided herself on the things she could do that others couldn't. Now she could do nothing without help.

By the time she and Zen made it down, Nick had retrieved her horse. He tried to boost her into the saddle, but she shoved him away and climbed up. This, at least, she could do for herself.

After Zen had retrieved his staff, Jasmine's horse finally lurched into motion as the party moved out.

"You should look into your heart before you attack those you don't know," Ellessar shouted back into the pass, "or you'll find your efforts misplaced as they were today."

"It's no use," Nick told him. "She's set in her ways."

"I hope so," Ellessar replied, "If demons draw her wrath, then perhaps she'll be useful when our Assassin friend follows us through this pass."

CHAPTER 26

"Nobody draws a weapon unless I draw first," Halidreth shouted to his men. He wheeled his horse around and galloped to the gate of Roybal Keep.

"State your business," the sentry yelled from atop the battlement.

"We seek fugitives wanted by King Balor Culhaven of Trondor. We have reason to believe they passed this way."

"The king of Trondor holds no sway here," the insolent sentry pronounced.

"Sergeant!" another man snapped from within the tower.

"I'm sorry, sir. It's just that—"

"You will treat our visitors with respect." The superior, nothing more than a shadow against the darker skyline, approached the sentry. "This keep is here for the benefit of all the Civilized Lands."

Though darkness shrouded the battlement, a pair of lanterns bracketing the gate illuminated the Black Hand. Halidreth waved back to the stragglers, urging them into the light. All except Whisper. He didn't care what the air apparition did. Nobody more than a few feet away would be able to make it out anyway.

"Welcome, emissaries of King Culhaven of Trondor," the superior called down.

"My apologies," Halidreth returned. "You misunderstand me. We're not emissaries of the king. Nor are we from Trondor. We're mercenaries, seeking fugitives for the sake of coin." There seemed no reason to honey-coat that particular point. They had no honor guard or uniforms, and no writ of authority from any kingdom, so claiming to come on behalf of the king just didn't seem credible. "We've tracked them to your doorstep."

"What do these fugitives look like?"

"A mage who wears a shimmering blue-gray robe. An elf-kin with a scar on his face, bald save for a long black ponytail. Two large men. An elf with a fancy hat and leather coat. And a female who looks like she just stepped off a ship from the Goblin Isle."

"Fugitives, you say?"

"Yes, sir."

The superior grunted and gestured to the sentry. "I knew they were hiding something. Open the gate."

Halidreth could just make out the words on the wind. "They're here then?"

The portcullis rose. "They were. Only stayed for a couple hours. Headed into the pass late this afternoon. I told them they wouldn't make it over before dark, but they seemed in a hurry. Now I know why."

Halidreth passed through the gate into the courtyard. The entire garrison was dark and quiet. Only the guards on the outer wall stirred.

"We must keep going," Whisper breathed from somewhere nearby. "The fugitives lingered too long. We can catch them in the pass before morning."

Halidreth didn't reply. It would only cause suspicion and delay if he had to explain Whisper's invisible presence to the soldiers. Then again, this would be a good place to discuss his plans with the Black Hand without having to worry about Whisper overhearing.

"Can we navigate the pass at night?" he yelled up to the sentry.

"No," the guard replied. "It's too treacherous, even with lanterns."

Halidreth nodded, satisfied. "May we quarter here?"

"Of course. The fee is nominal."

"We leave at dawn," Halidreth told his men, as Whisper brushed by him and moved away. He gave a knowing look to Jade, Sorowyn, and Minshara, the mainstay of his remaining force. Each nodded, in turn, but they didn't arrive in his room until well past midnight.

The group was nearly an hour past the summit, no more than a couple of miles of winding canyon trail, by the time the failing light forced them to stop for the night. Nick dismounted and unrolled his blanket right on the path, there being nowhere else to camp.

Ellessar dismounted and helped Jasmine from her horse. "How are your eyes?"

"The same. Black as night."

Ellessar grunted. "Right now, that's all any of us can see. I'll pray for you tonight and examine your eyes in the morning."

Nick had to turn away. Jasmine had been the most-skilled warrior he'd ever known. Even now, she showed much more stoicism—

"That's okay," Jasmine replied to Ellessar. "I'll meditate. Maybe I'll regain my sight by then."

No, not stoicism. Jasmine showed more *optimism* than Nick could have managed himself under far less-dire circumstances.

Shamed by his pity for Jasmine, whom he respected as much as he had his late mother, Nick focused on his own preparations for the night. He laid both of his great swords next to his blankets. Unsheathed.

Zen spread his own bed next to Nick's. His face seemed haggard, exhausted by the day's efforts. He seemed to have aged at least ten years since that morning.

Ellessar gestured toward Nick's swords. "The fairy won't come after us. By the word of Aeron, she's not evil. She merely mistook Jasmine's nature, as I once did."

"Is that what she is? A fairy?"

Ellessar's nod was barely visible against the deep gray of the night.

"I'm not worried about her," Nick said, "just about the demon that tracks us. You said yourself it was closer this morning. This pass has slowed us down. And right now we're weak, even vulnerable."

"That's true, and the trail won't hinder it. Neither will the keep. The demon can translocate past it. Nevertheless, the fairy may solve that particular problem for us."

A soft snore escaped Zen's throat.

"Not if she's as spent as our own mage."

At dawn, the fairy sensed the demons' approach, several of them this time, each with a more visceral presence than she'd sensed from the female the previous evening. After such a long absence of demons, several in less than a day could only mean that Vexetan was making a move. What it was, the fairy could only imagine, but the consequences would surely be dire.

Four, she counted as the demons passed beneath her. Exhausted from the previous battle, she could do nothing against so many. She hadn't the strength to build the layers of defenses that had kept her alive against the lesser-demon's mage. She could bring down the lightning as she'd done earlier—she had enough strength for that—but it would only alert the demons to her presence. To attack them in her current condition would be suicide. At least the demons were headed south, away from the Civilized Lands. If they tried to return later, she would deal with them then.

These were Assassins, demons that always hunted a specific prey. What prey did these four seek? Four of the humanoids who traveled with the lesser-demon female? That would make sense if she had been a captive, but she'd clearly been fighting alongside the humanoids, defending them. They were her allies.

The fairy's gut felt as if the bottom had just dropped out of it. Her senses hadn't diminished—she could feel the Assassins as keenly as she'd always sensed demons. Therefore, the female wasn't a lesser-demon at all, but only part demon. A demon-kin—if such a thing could exist.

The admonition of the elf came back to her. *Look into your heart before you attack.* Could the female be an enemy of demons? Could she be the prey the Assassins hunted? With that, the fairy did something she hadn't felt the need to do in ages. She closed her eyes and sought the will of Aeron.

After Ellessar's morning prayers, Aeron revealed to him the proximity of the Assassin that hunted their party.

"It's close," he told the others, "but before we can leave, I have a promise to keep."

He sat before Jasmine, each with their legs crossed in front of them. "Can you see any light at all?"

"No."

He checked first for any physical damage—a wound to the eye's surface or surrounding tissue—and found none. Jasmine's eyes remained clear, not cloudy like many of the blind who came to the Order of the Shining Star to seek the divine healing of Aeron. When Ellessar shaded her eyes, her pupils dilated. When he told her to look right, left, up, and down, she did so, and her eyes moved normally.

He spoke a prayer of healing, but to no avail.

"As far as I can tell, there's nothing wrong with you physically," he told her.

"Except that I can't see." Jasmine's voice held no hint of criticism or disappointment. "Thank you for trying."

"Is there anything you can do for her?" Nick asked Zen.

"Like what?"

"I don't know. Maybe her blindness is from some enchantment."

"If I knew the right weavings, maybe." He sighed as if he was disappointed with Jasmine for losing her sight when they had all manner of foes converging on them, or with himself for not having enough skill to help her.

Jasmine rose and felt her way to her horse. "It's okay, gentlemen." She mounted. "I will meditate and heal, or I will adapt. The world has greater hardships than this, I'm sure."

"I fear those hardships are coming," Otto interjected from the rear of the party as they moved out.

Ellessar nodded quietly. He rode Spirit alongside Rancid's horse, at the fore of the procession, and urged them all to a pace as brisk as the horses could manage on the rocky trail.

The walls through which their path had threaded fell away just after noon, and the trail zigzagged down a steep hillside to a lush valley below, which stretched to the horizon in every direction. The tranquility of the scene belied the name the civilized races had given the land. It seemed like a paradise.

Nick rode up beside him. "Why did you stop?"

"We should scout the path and the valley before we proceed," Ellessar replied.

Nick gestured at the vegetation-filled landscape. "Seems safe enough."

"That's what worries me," Zen said. "Give me ten minutes." He waved his hands in the air, wove patterns with threads only he could see, and morphed into a bald eagle of pure ice, perched on his own saddle. His horse fidgeted with the sudden change of weight. With a single bound, Zen leapt into the air and soared out over the valley.

Ellessar dismounted and dropped Spirit's reins. "I'll scout the trail below. We've no reason to expect an ambush, but there may be other dangers."

Not to be outdone, Rancid turned his horse back to the canyon. "I'll see to our back trail, make sure nobody's following too closely."

Otto and Nick stayed beside Jasmine at the mouth of the pass.

Ellessar descended the first few hundred yards of the trail. Though the hillside descended steeply, the trail, with its many switchbacks, seemed manageable, if somewhat overgrown from disuse. About the time he reached the second turn, the wind shifted. For a moment, it blew up from the valley, carrying the stench of rot and decay. It smelled much like Dreadwood Swamp in southern Brinheim. At that moment, he realized that the vegetation and greenery for as far as he could see—a deeper, darker green than that of grass or fern—was that of a fetid swamp. So much for paradise.

Before he could turn back, six horses thundered down the trail with Rancid in the lead. Otto, Jasmine, and Nick followed. Spirit and Zen's horse brought up the rear.

Ellessar stepped off the trail, in case they intended to run past, but Rancid skidded to a halt just before him, stirring up clods of dirt choked with scrub grass.

"What is it?" Ellessar asked him.

"Demons." Rancid pointed. "Assassins. Not more than five minutes behind us."

"Assassins?" *Plural?* The Order of the Shining Star had no record of multiple Assassins ever being called at one time.

The fairy in the pass would have been no match for them. She'd let them pass, or they had destroyed her.

"Quickly!" Ellessar hurried up the trail. "We mustn't let them out of the pass. They'll have to fight single-file."

Nick dismounted and drew his great sword.

Otto remained mounted in their path. "Hold on, demon hunter. We, too, must fight single-file. The demons can translocate from one end of our party to the other. If we get the best of them, they can vanish altogether. But if we come up hurting, we'll have no escape. I like the idea of facing them in the open."

Given the steep slope of the hillside, Ellessar and the others could climb straight down if necessary, but it'd be reckless. In its own way, the hillside was as restrictive a place as the pass to fight the demons, who were probably more agile in this kind of terrain than either humans or elves were. "Those demons are the reason Aeron bade me to join your party," Ellessar said. "Never before have I been so certain of their location."

Support showed in Rancid's eyes, and Nick's. Jasmine's held only doubt.

"With unknown dangers down there—" Nick jabbed a finger at the swamp— "and dangers we can't count behind us, I'd like to eliminate this one. The odds are better now than they'll be if we let the demons choose their timing."

The eagle returned, alighted on a jutting rock nearby, and morphed back into Zen. He seemed to recognize the tension in the group. "What's going on?"

"Multiple Assassins in the pass," Nick told him.

Zen raised an eyebrow at him. "More than one? Guess the Master's got it in for you worse than we thought."

"We were waiting for you," Otto added. "And trying to decide whether to face them here or in the canyon."

"That choice will be taken from us if we don't decide quickly," Ellessar said.

Zen gripped his staff as though for confidence. "How many?"

With one fierce movement, Rancid drew his demon-claw sword. "Four."

"Four!" Ellessar said. "That's unheard of."

Rancid glared at him. "I know what I saw."

Zen walked up the trail to a point where he could see the opening of the canyon and the trail that disappeared into it. His friends gathered close around him but left him a path to view the opening.

Shapes milled at the edges of the cleft, took refuge in the cover provided by the canyon.

Zen wove a small chunk of ice into his hand, expanded it into a ball of ice and slush, and then hurled it at the canyon entrance. The shapes retreated into the confines of the rock as it approached. When it exploded, ice, rock, and a wave of cold air sprayed from the opening. It left a fine layer of dusty frost over everything in the vicinity.

Carefully, the six of them approached the opening.

Jasmine sat astride her horse, holding the reins of the other mounts. Nick, leading her horse, kept his eyes fixed on the canyon's mouth.

When they arrived, the place was empty. Only tracks remained.

Ellessar stooped to examine them. These were Assassins, all right. And there were indeed four of them. They had approached as far as the mouth of the canyon and then waited, apparently observing the party, probably measuring its strength.

Assassin demons were among the higher order of their kind, and among the most intelligent. The compulsion imposed by the mage who'd called them didn't drive them to stupidity. It allowed as much time as the demons needed to kill the prey they'd been called to kill. These four wouldn't attack until they were ready, until they were sure.

The tracks retreated into the canyon. Several prints near the mouth had been damaged or destroyed by Zen's weaving. One demon appeared to have been swept from its feet. A larger disturbance in the dirt betrayed where it had landed. But from there, it scrambled to its feet, retreated a few yards, and vanished. All four trails ended abruptly, between one clawed footprint and the next. "They're not ready for us yet. They've translocated away."

"What about blood?" Zen asked. "Did I hurt them?"

"You hit one, but there's no blood."

"How could that be?"

"The Abyss is a realm of extremes. Many of the demons who live there are accustomed to a wide range of temperatures."

"Are you saying they're immune to cold?" Zen's eyes showed fear for the first time since Ellessar had met him."

"Possibly immune. Maybe just less sensitive."

Rancid spat onto the ground. "Well, that's just great."

CHAPTER 27

halidreth and his ragged remnant of the Black Hand broke free of the confines of the pass just as the sun set. The smell of decay blowing up from the valley saturated the air.

Whisper spoke from the wind. "There was a struggle here, no more than a few hours ago." The creature's voice completely lacked emotion. "We'll camp in the clearing below. Tomorrow we'll ride hard and catch them."

Halidreth turned toward the empty voice, surprised he could make out the apparition. The setting sun rippled through its vague shape and cast streaks of color upon the air. "Fine." He didn't bother to disguise the loathing in his voice. "But this time we do it my way. We've done it yours for too long, and its resulted in nothing but the death of my people." He plunged on before Whisper could object. "We'll wait until nightfall, Jade will reconnoiter the enemy camp, and then I will choose the right moment to strike. And *I* will determine the battle plan."

"We'll strike as soon as we catch them," Whisper declared. The apparition was a consummate tracker, but as a tactician, its mind was as insubstantial as its being.

"They're too strong. We haven't enough men to take them without an advantage. Give me time and I'll find that advantage. Otherwise—"

"The Master is running out of time."

"Otherwise—" Halidreth's voice sharpened to a sword's edge— "we will fail. And so will you. You might as well kill us all now, before we enter this accursed country."

Whisper grew as still as the deepest chambers of the Black Hand caves. The last of the sun passed over the horizon, and it seemed the apparition ceased to exist.

"Besides," Halidreth added, at the risk of undermining what he'd started, "don't you want to find out what they've come here for?"

The pause seemed eternal. Whisper might have left him, perhaps to search for more signs of their prey's passing. When its voice came back, it struck harsh as a winter wind. "Very well. But if Nicklan Mirrin leaves the Wild Lands alive, the Black Hand will not."

That night, their first in the Wild Lands, the companions set up camp on the hillside overlooking the swamp. Only the biting flies were worse than the smell of rot wafting up from the bog.

Nick took the Seeking Stone from his pack and unrolled the bundle of clothes in which he'd wrapped it for safekeeping. The night was as black as any he'd seen, overcast and starless. He couldn't help wondering if it was normal for this side of the Great Divide.

He wasn't sure what to expect from the stone. *When it comes within range of a metal from the stars,* Xanth had said, *it lights up.* But how brightly? Would Nick even recognize the glow?

The polished stone felt heavy in his hand. At first, he saw nothing. It was pale, the color of an egg in the moonlight. Yet no moon shone. His eyes widened and he glanced up at the others. All but Jasmine stared at the stone.

"What do you see?" she asked.

"It's glowing," Rancid said.

"Faintly," Nick amended. He didn't want anyone to get their hopes up. The Wild Lands were larger than any single civilized kingdom, and Xanth hadn't elaborated on what he meant by "within range." Was it miles away, or days? It could be anywhere in the Wild Lands. "What do you think?" he asked Zen. "You're our expert in magic."

Zen thrust out both hands as if to fend off the question. "That stone doesn't radiate any kind of magic I've ever heard of."

"Ellessar?"

The priest shrugged. "The old man who gave it to you said it's supposed to glow?"

Nick nodded.

"I'd say it's glowing. What else did he tell you?"

"He said the closer it gets to the rock from the stars, the brighter it will glow. Guess we'll look at it again tomorrow night." He wrapped the stone carefully and put it away, then settled in for the night, heartened for the first time since they'd left Sorcerers' Keep.

They skirted the mountains for another day, moving east, but until they made some sense of the signals from the stone, they had no clear direction to follow. East was their only choice in any case, unless they wanted to go into the swamp, which the old man in South Bend had pointedly warned them not to do.

The next night, the stone glowed again, faint and colorless. If there was any change in its illumination, Nick couldn't discern it. "We're either a long way from the rock we're looking for, or it's directly south of us."

"Through the bog," Otto observed.

"Or in it," Ellessar added.

The companions spent a day and a half walking as far away from the swamp as the cliffs of the Great Divide would allow, at times no more than a few hundred yards. Inhuman wails, guttural croaks, and the burp and gurgle of large creatures moving through the muck penetrated the outer barrier of the swamp's fetid vegetation with alarming frequency. And as they'd seen from the mouth of Roybal Pass, the bog extended to the horizon in every direction.

Otto spat on the ground as if to rid his mouth of the taste of swamp air. "I'm in no hurry to go in there. I say we continue east until we're sure we're headed in the wrong direction."

A mumbled consensus rippled through the group like a wave. The issue decided, if only for the night, they organized watches and slept.

Jasmine took the first watch that night, along with Zen. He tried the weaving that enhanced vision in the darkness, but her vision didn't improve. Nonetheless, she insisted on sitting up for one of the shifts, a ploy to hide her weakness from the demons. And, as she pointed out, her ears worked fine.

Jasmine had meditated for hours at a time, trying to sense some internal damage to her brain or to its connection to her eyes. But she'd discerned nothing. Something about the fairy's magic worked on her mind rather than on her body. It was mere deception. That much she'd known by the end of her first full day in darkness. But how it worked, and how she could reverse it, eluded her.

The thoughts that the fairy had thrust upon her at the exact moment she'd lost her vision replayed themselves over and over again. Her recollection remained as clear and sharp as any sight she'd ever seen. *The fairy was no woman, but a god, or like a god. Jasmine had no right to look upon such a creature with her vile, mortal eyes.* The fairy's radiant, godlike beauty was the keystone of her deception. Jasmine could feel it. She'd meditated on that fact during her last days in the saddle. Yet the blindness persisted.

But the fairy was no god. Though her beauty might be godlike, the fairy herself wasn't. Her beauty was real, the blindness wasn't.

But the fairy's beauty was not real. It was an enchantment, an illusion. As a god, the fairy was a fraud.

Fine. It was all a deception. Jasmine had put the fairy on a pedestal she didn't deserve. So what? Her realization of that did nothing to restore her sight.

With the night black again, overcast with a blanket of obsidian, the group decided to forego a fire and dine on the cold, salted fish they had purchased at Roybal Keep. They'd each taken a piece of trail bread as well, but Zen discarded his in a nearby bush. It had already begun to mildew, as if the swamp was spreading its disease through the air they breathed.

Their cold camp wasn't a precaution against the Assassins, the dragon, the Black Hand, or even Sierra Glenwood. The demons would track them in any case. The dragon, too, seemed to find them preternaturally, so much so that Rancid had begun to accuse Zen of weaving enchantments to lead their enemies to them, rather than to *evade* scrying.

The Black Hand, if they'd gotten as far as Roybal Keep, would have no difficulty tracking them from there. Since they'd left the keep, they'd had no choice of paths. And, as far as they knew, they'd left Sierra behind long ago.

Despite the dangers behind them, however, they most feared the unknown threat to the south. A fire could, and likely would, attract any number of hungry or curious creatures from the swamp.

Each morning, following his prayers, Ellessar reported that the Assassins remained nearby—probably just inside the border of the marsh, where they couldn't be seen. Their presence lurked at the fringes of everyone's mind, fraying nerves and shortening tempers. Two days brought the party to a broad plateau between the swamp and the mountains, a vast prairie.

"I'll scout ahead." As Zen assumed an eagle's form, he tried to ignore the Assassins, who would probably attack as soon as the party found itself in battle with some new enemy. But the demons were too nimble and elusive for the group to try to launch an offensive against them.

Ellessar dismounted from Spirit. "I'll hike up the hill a ways and look for a place to camp."

"Be careful," Nick said.

"I won't go far."

"I'll go with you," Rancid offered.

Zen soared first along the slopes of the Great Divide, which receded northward as he flew east. He cut across the plains, a prairie full of game and grasses. A small herd of deer passed beneath him, bounding north as though fleeing a predator, followed a few minutes later by a half-dozen furry creatures that walked erect like ill-proportioned men.

Zen swooped down for a closer look. The creatures had the snouts and ears of wolves, meaty thighs, and odd legs that bent forward where their knees should have been. They carried spears and pouches. A sash of hide draped from one of the creature's shoulders. They sniffed the air frequently. *Primitive hunters.*

Zen soared higher, finished his sweep of the prairie, and then ventured over the swamp, cloaked as it was by a canopy of cypress.

He stretched his concentration as his enchantment began to run out and then headed back toward his friends. Once there, he alighted on his mount's back and resumed his own form.

"—suitable camp up the hill, about a hundred yards or so," Ellessar was saying. "The horses will make it if we walk them."

Zen urged his horse into the midst of the conversation. "I saw six of the wolf-kin that the old tracker in South Bend described." He gestured back toward the prairie. "They look pretty primitive. Hides and spears. Probably hunting."

"Headed our way?" Otto asked.

"No." Zen dismounted. "Headed north, three or four miles from here."

"All right." Nick sounded satisfied. "We'll camp up the hill tonight and cross the valley in the morning."

Ellessar led them in a procession to the campsite, which proved to be sheltered enough to afford a small fire. He spoke a prayer of purification over their food to banish the growing mold.

There was no change in the illumination of the Seeking Stone that night. "Maybe your stone is broken," Rancid said.

"I'm pretty sure our objective is to the south," Nick reminded him. "We've been moving crosswise to where we need to go."

Zen glanced down at the dark sea of shadow that even his night vision couldn't penetrate. He had no more desire to enter the swamp than any of the others did, but he had no particular fear of it either, despite what the old tracker had said. If he must, he could always take wing and fly out of it, or try the translocation weaving he'd been working on. What he feared was that all of this side-tracking to the east would cost them time and gain them nothing.

Nevertheless, Nick remained insistent, and he was backed by most of the others. So, when morning came, they headed east again, across the plains.

Zen scouted from the sky, watched for any reappearance of the dragon, and steered the party around the nomadic wolf-kin that populated the prairie.

But by the end of the next night, it became clear that they would have to enter the swamp. The mountains had closed up against it, its cliffs diving into the cypress from hundreds of feet above the valley floor, leaving no gap to pass through. Other than backtracking, the swamp was their only option.

halidreth rode hard to catch the fugitives. Not out of obedience to Whisper, though the air apparition had ordered him to do so. No, he drove his people to near exhaustion because he wanted to rid himself of Whisper. And now that he had a plan, he was eager to see it done.

Nonetheless, by the morning of the third day, when the valley opened into a broad plateau of wild grass, Whisper estimated that the Black Hand were still a few hours behind.

At that point, Whisper moved out ahead to track. Any grasses that had been flattened by the passage of the horses' hooves had sprung back into their original shape by the time the bandits arrived, doing much to hide the fugitives' passage.

Halidreth, a competent tracker in his own right, was no match for Whisper's skill. Once he betrayed the apparition, he'd have to make sure he killed it, or he'd have that thing tracking him. More fervently than ever, he vowed to make sure the conditions were perfect before he made his move.

But when the time came…

He was committed now. His hatred of Whisper had grown greater than even his hatred of Sevendeath. That wasn't true for most of his men, so he'd had to purchase their cooperation with a promise to finish Sevendeath as part of the bargain, which suited Halidreth just fine.

Whisper returned from its scouting. "We must detour."

"Why?" Halidreth asked the disembodied voice.

"There's a large tribe of indigenous humanoids ahead. Dozens of them. Turn north."

"Are they coming for us?"

"No. They appear to be following the trail of our prey, but they move slowly. We'll go around."

Halidreth turned his men north. It would cost them time, but not nearly as much time as a pitched battle with the locals would, a battle that might cost more Black Hand lives. He'd lost too many men in the name of the Master already.

CHAPTER 28

Before the party entered the swamp, Zen flew over the canopy of trees as far south as he could and still return before he had to refresh the weave that held his eagle's form together. The canopy was dense, broken only in splotches. The ground below, swallowed by shadow, appeared as a mottled patchwork of gray-green groundcover and oily pools of filth.

Sidetracked by an effort to estimate the proportion of land to water and determine if the swamp was even passable, Zen ran out of time. His eagle's form began to fray to the point where flight became impossible.

Quickly, he selected a tall, dense cypress, with branches that looked thick enough to support his full body weight, and landed. He stretched his wing to the trunk and let his weaving evaporate into the stagnant swamp air.

As his weight shifted, so did the slimy branch on which he stood.

Sixty feet above the jungle floor, he snatched at a clump of leaves. They ripped loose and left him to tumble. In desperation, he dropped his staff to grab the branch on which he'd meant to stand. The wood was slick with moisture and green slime, so he uttered a phrase that encased his hand and part of the branch in a solid chunk of ice.

On its way to the ground, his staff knocked several branches and stirred up a large-beaked bird with a rainbow of feathers.

A low rumble, a kind of growl, reverberated through the swamp. Ripples vibrated across the surface of a gooey pond at the base of the tree, in which his staff lay upside-down and half-submerged.

From somewhere nearby, something large crashed through the brush, moving closer. Zen held his breath, afraid to move. His encased hand ached from the cold.

Then a beast appeared. A huge lizard, fully twelve feet in length, ran with its belly nearly brushing the ground. Its snout was broad and round. Sharp teeth the size of dirks gnashed down on a bit that cut across the corners of its mouth. It came to a stop and bellowed again. A lizard of an entirely different sort sat on its back as a man would ride a horse. The rider's tongue flicked, tasting the air. Its yellow eyes darted back and forth as if seeking danger. A short-hafted tool in its hand and a quiver of arrow-like projectiles on its back served as a warning.

Slowly, Zen reached up and grasped the branch with his free hand. The slight rustling was drowned out by another bellow from the lizard mount.

After a moment, the rider urged his mount forward. The beast lumbered, as though its bulk was nearly too much for its wide-splayed legs to hold. It swung its head slowly from side to side and snorted.

The rider passed by the butt of Zen's staff but apparently failed to recognize the wooden stump as foreign. It searched the area for several minutes, then moved from sight.

Zen breathed a prayer to Aeron, realizing only afterward that he'd done so. He released his hand from the ice and clambered onto the branch. After flexing his aching fingers for several minutes, he resumed his eagle's form. He swooped down to recover his staff, careful not to let even the claw of his talon penetrate the oily surface of the pond, rose through the canopy before the rider could circle back, and returned to his friends.

"The old tracker was right," he told Ellessar while he cleaned his staff with a spare cloth. "There're lizards in the swamp. At least two different kinds." He tucked the rag away until it could be thoroughly laundered.

Ellessar shrugged. "Not a surprise."

"I don't think it saw me," Zen added. "Its weapons didn't seem very advanced."

"They don't have to be." Rancid eyed the edge of the marsh. "If they're tipped with poison."

"Or if the swamp carries disease that will infect a wound," Jasmine said.

Otto tightened the cinch on his saddle and checked the buckles on his bags. "What are the odds that they'll let us pass in peace if we leave them alone?"

Rancid snorted. "Who knows?"

"It's not the lizard-kin I'm worried about." Ellessar spread the ashes of the previous night's fire as well as he could to hide the campsite. "It's the larger beasts the old man warned us about. The ones that are big enough to swallow a horse whole."

Throughout the exchange, Nick listened to the others as he prepared his horse and gear for travel in the swamp. He took the reins and walked to the south end of the campsite. They'd already decided to walk the horses rather than risk losing one to quicksand or a submerged tangle of roots.

All this talk of wariness and danger only served to weaken the party's collective nerve. They must traverse the swamp. There was no way around it. Best to do it and be done with it. He just hoped this metal rock they sought proved to be worth the disease, rot, and ruin that the bog promised.

Ellessar joined him and waited for the others to catch up. Then, without a word, Nick began the slow trek, his pace allowing Rancid time to conceal their tracks from the campsite to the swamp without falling behind.

Once inside, the smell overtook his senses, stinging his nose and making his eyes water. For a time, he covered his nose and mouth with a clean rag dampened with drinking water, but the towel only made the air more humid, nearly too wet to breath. So he cursed the swamp, stuffed the rag in a pocket of his travelling cloak, now weighted with mud and slime up to his knees, and trudged onward.

The ground varied from hard earth, to a spongy, fern-covered loam, to dense, cloying mud. Ellessar tied a rope to Spirit's saddle and the other end to Nick's waist as a precaution against quicksand or a vegetation-covered sinkhole. Stagnant pools of slime, which varied in size from puddles to lakes, bubbled around them. Nick skirted them as well as he could, working his way deeper into the swamp. A mist that clung to the ground grew thicker as they went.

Animals scurried through the groundcover, heard but unseen. Occasionally a ripple in a pond betrayed some creature beneath its opaque surface.

Ellessar constantly scanned the trees for dangers lurking overhead.

Zen searched the deepening shadows with his staff clutched in his hand.

The sounds of animals scurrying beneath the ferns reached them, as did the bellow of a lizard mount, so distant that it sounded more like an exhalation of the swamp than the utterance of any living thing.

"I hear them," Jasmine said softly.

The whole party paused to listen.

A splash, somewhere to the right, and a series of rapid, muffled footsteps.

A movement in the shadows, furtive and silent, caught Nick's attention, and then disappeared behind the trunk of a broad tree. Without taking his eyes from the spot, he held up his hand to signal the others. With his other hand, he pointed to the tree, and waited.

A head, green and scaly, with a pointed snout, lipless mouth, darting tongue, and yellow eyes eased from behind it and emitted a sharp clicking sound, like that of a distant woodpecker.

"Hear that?" Jasmine whispered.

The sound was echoed by another, then a third and fourth, from points all around them, yet the creatures made no threatening moves.

After several minutes of silent standoff, Nick led his horse forward.

The others followed.

So did the lizards. The splashes and clicks of their presence neither receded nor drew closer for what must have been half a day of slogging through the terrain, until Nick led the group into a dead end, a peninsula of land blocked on three sides by a horseshoe-shaped lake of slime. The lizard-kin congregated behind them. Now the companions would find out what the lizard-kin intended.

Nick couldn't help wondering how far back the Assassins were. If a battle broke out here, the demons would likely enter the fray. And if they were resistant to cold, the only magic the company had with which to fight them would be useless.

Zen eased his hand into his pocket and thumbed the enchanted ring he'd purchased from Rancid onto his forefinger. He heard voices speaking from the mist, hissed whispers that came at him from all around.

"They are many."

"They are too many."

"What are they?"

"Ssseen their kind before."

"Kill them."

"No. Wait."

"The lizards are talking," Zen said. "I can hear them. They're trying to discern our intent." He didn't say how he understood them. Let his friends assume what they would. The ring allowed him only to understand their language, however, not speak it.

Rancid eased his pack off his shoulder, plucked a chunk of lye soap from one of its pockets, and offered it carefully to a nearby bush.

The voices continued.

"What isss it?" A lizard-kin stepped from the bush with a sword in his hand that appeared to have been carved from the bone of some much larger animal.

"It'sss a rock," another voice said.

The lizard pointed its primitive sword toward the ground and approached Rancid, eyes on the soap. "Not a rock. Sssomething elssse."

"It isss a rock."

The lizard sniffed the air. "No."

"It isss a rock."

"He deceivesss usss."

The lizard reached for the soap.

"Kill them!" another said.

"Careful," Zen warned.

The lizard focused its eyes on the soap and jabbed its sword at Rancid's belly.

Rancid sidestepped the blade, dropped the soap, and drew his own sword. "Sneaky bastards."

Trees and bushes rustled all around them. From above, a lizard twice the size of the others, wearing bracelets and a breastplate made of small bones woven with vine or sinew, glided from the canopy on stretched folds of skin, like a flying squirrel, and landed gracefully before Nick, near Otto and Jasmine.

Jasmine, who'd been walking with one hand on Otto's shoulder, took a few steps back from him and crouched.

Two more lizard-kin, small like the first, rushed Rancid.

The oily water of the lake erupted. A pair of mounted lizards and two more on foot charged at the group.

With the exception of Spirit, the horses scattered. One of the lizard mounts snapped up Otto's fleeing horse by the abdomen and ripped out half its entrails. It swallowed the chunk of meat, nearly the size of a man's torso, in a single gulp.

Jasmine's head pivoted left and right, her fists poised to strike if the sounds came too near.

Rancid ran his sword through the lizard nearest him. As suddenly as the creature had attacked, it fell dead. The point of no return.

With a ring of warriors surrounding them, Zen began to chant.

The lizard chieftain, for that's what it must have been, struck Nick on the shoulder with a club the size of a tree trunk before Nick had freed his sword fully from its sheath.

Nick staggered toward the edge of the lake. The two lizard-kin who'd emerged from the water on foot closed on him. Otto and Ellessar intercepted them.

Zen completed his weave and froze the brain of the chieftain from the inside out. The creature emitted a primal scream, choked off almost as soon as it started. With a gasp, it toppled to the damp ground.

"Where are they?" Jasmine hissed. "Point me at one."

Zen hesitated only a moment. "Mounted lizard with an ax. Ten steps in front of you."

CHAPTER 29

Jasmine forced herself cautiously forward. Nick's footsteps moved alongside her, his breathing heavy. She stopped when she heard the sweep of his great sword. Her hands came up to ward off incoming blows. Ridiculous. How could she block a blow she couldn't see?

The head of the beast loomed somewhere in front of her. She could hear it snorting. She struck out with her foot, but her kick connected with nothing.

Beside her, something heavy struck Nick. He grunted and stumbled backwards but recovered quickly. The sounds of battle continued.

Jasmine kicked again and hopped back a step. Huge teeth gnashed together in front of her. Sounds from Nick's opponent came more from above her than from beside her, so she had a sense of the lizard mount's size. The beast's teeth snapped like the jaws of a steel trap.

Her mind was completely focused now. Her life depended on her defeating an enemy she could only hear. She lunged forward and struck with her fist. The scaled ridge of the mount's nose, hard as the bone beneath it, met her at her own chest height. And the movement of it... That maw came for her, its breath warm against her chest and legs. The outline of its teeth, some figment of her mind's eye, filled the space before her.

She'd have died then, if not for that image. The beast's mouth seemed large enough to swallow her whole. And because she saw it, in some faint, imagined form, she sidestepped.

Zen didn't wait to see how Jasmine fared. Instead, he rounded on the other lizard mount, the one that had felled Otto's horse. It was closing fast.

Zen wove an explosive concoction of ice, slush, and power from the weave and heaved it at the advancing beast. The blast ripped through it and its rider, taking them and another nearby lizard. The wave of cold air washed the trees in a fine dusting of frost.

By the time Zen turned back to the others, three more lizard-kin lay dead, one at each of Ellessar's, Otto's, and Rancid's feet. Several survivors sank into the murky lake, along with the remaining lizard rider, its mount limping. Another lizard retreated into the mist.

The voices continued. "They are too many."

"We are not enough."

"Watch them."

"Wait for the others."

Others? Assassin demons? More lizards? Something else? Zen didn't take time to ponder the meaning. "You all right?" he asked Nick.

"Yeah. I'll be ready for them next time."

"We all will," Zen replied. "They'll be back in greater numbers."

Rancid marched up to him, suspicion in his eyes. "How can you understand them?"

"Not now," Ellessar said. "We have to move. Jasmine?"

"I'm okay." She stared ahead with no focus to her eyes.

Ellessar touched her arm. "You sure?"

"Yes. It's just that I…" She shook her head.

"You're a brave one. One of those mounts disemboweled Otto's horse in a single bite. I'm not sure I would have faced one blind."

Jasmine swallowed hard. "I didn't know about the horse."

As soon as Nick, Zen, Sevendeath, and the others turned south and disappeared beneath the canopy of the swamp, Ryanna banked L'Nordian northward toward the Great Divide. She'd done as much here as she could. The Assassins had been within the fringes of the wetlands for days—she could feel the subtle tug of their presence—and with her help, Whisper and the Black Hand had caught up to within a half-day behind.

"I can no longer see Nick Mirrin's party," she told the Master through her Medallion. "And based on the sheer size of the swamp, I have no reason to believe they'll come out of it any time soon. Whisper, the Black Hand, and the Assassins will do what needs to be done."

"Return," the Master ordered her. "It's time."

The noises around Jasmine were constant: the chirping of insects and croaking of frogs, the calls of the jungle birds, the rustle of small animals buried somewhere within the undergrowth or in the canopy overhead. She heard the lizard-kin too, their woodpecker call and the bass bellow of their mounts.

These creatures kept their distance, though. The battle, and the speed with which her friends had won it, must have made the lizards more cautious.

For Jasmine, the lizard-kin attack had come out of nowhere and out of everywhere, all at once. Both lizard-kin and their beastly mounts had charged her friends, but the lizards had left her alone as if they didn't consider her a threat. Her friends had probably formed a protective ring around her, but that particular point was irrelevant.

In her present condition, Jasmine was no threat. Nevertheless, she couldn't stand by and let her friends fight her battles for her. She had to learn to cope.

She felt her way, holding a short rope dangling from her horse's saddle as though it was her leash, and considered what she'd seen.

The more she thought about it, the more convinced she became that she really had seen something besides darkness. She could have put the image together from her knowledge of the facts—the size and position of the head she'd felt with her fist, its movement from the feel of its breath, its shape from Zen's description of the mount he'd seen during his recon flight—but she hadn't. She'd actually *seen* something. Something dark against the blackness of her mind, vague and momentary, yet something. While she slogged through ankle-deep water as warm as that in any bathhouse but more putrid than a taproom full of unwashed bodies, Jasmine tried to pinpoint why.

Fear, maybe—for the first time since she'd lost her sight, Jasmine had been afraid. But that fear had been tempered by discipline.

Peril, then. Though her fear was buried so deep within her that she barely felt it anymore, the peril had been at the forefront of her mind. Her training had taught her to be aware of it, to assess the threat of any situation, to seek out and acknowledge its dangers. But how could risk to herself free her mind of blindness?

Today, she had cared not for gods or deceptions, for beauty or blindness. Today, she had pondered peril. Somehow the battle had forced her mind into a state that allowed her to see something. If she could determine how, she might be able to repeat it.

For hours she plunged through the darkness of her thoughts and the dampness of the swamp. Never did the question leave her mind.

During her watch that night, she sat with her face toward the warmth of their small, sputtering fire and replayed the battle in her mind, putting herself back into it over and over again.

When she crawled into her blanket, she didn't even try to sleep. Instead, she fought the lizard mount. She kicked, she punched, she felt its breath, its size, its movement. And when the teeth came at her, and she understood her peril, the discipline of her training shoved everything else from her mind. For the first time since the battle in the pass, Jasmine had ceased to think about the fairy, the beauty, and the blindness.

And some small piece of her vision had returned. Just for that instant.

Jasmine sat up. For days she'd chipped away at the deception, the keystone of her blindness, the root of the fairy's magic. Tonight, she forgot that deception. For the first time, she considered that the beauty and godliness might be real. Jasmine had been trying to see through that beauty. She'd stared at it for days to convince herself it was false. Tonight, she simply turned away from it. She no longer cared whether it was real or not. She focused her thoughts on recognizing that it was no longer before her.

Jasmine had no right to look upon such a creature with her vile, mortal eyes.

Fine. She wouldn't.

She acknowledged that the fairy was superior—supreme, perhaps even divine—that Jasmine may have had no earthly right to look upon her. Then she acknowledged, so deliberately and with such determination that she didn't realize until later that she'd slipped into a deep state of meditation, that the creature of beauty was no longer before her, that if she opened her eyes and was able to see, she wouldn't see the fairy.

Then she did open her eyes. The blaze of the meager fire stung them like the sun. She thrust out her hands to ward off the light, but she refused to close her eyes. For the first time in days, she could actually see. At that moment, no amount of pain could have made her close them.

"Follow the interlopers," the lizard-kin, Saassh, told his warriors. The death of their chieftain, which had happened more quickly than Saassh cared to consider, had left him in charge of those who remained. But what could he do against such powerful beings? "Go for the tribe," he told another. "Bring them all."

His warrior and the wounded croc on which he rode slipped beneath the surface of the bayou.

It would take days for the tribe to arrive. In the meantime, Saassh followed Otto as they slogged aimlessly through the bog, towing their ill-adapted mounts with them. At night, they communed with a glowing white rock. And in the morning, they slogged on again, apparently looking for something.

By the second day, Saassh's problem grew worse. A group of four creatures arrived, with wicked claws on their hands and horns on their heads, alien to Saassh's eye and almost as numerous as the soft-skinned strangers from beyond the great mountains. Everything the creatures touched seemed to wither and die.

Beyond them, another group of soft-skinned strangers followed the first, much as Saassh and his warriors did. The leader of this new group conversed with himself in words of gibberish, sometimes angry, sometimes pleading, but always the second group remained hours behind the first.

Another thing bothered Saassh: sounds he couldn't define, movements he couldn't see. Something else had come into the swamp with the new group. Something hidden and dangerous.

Saassh had to follow behind the second group to keep from being seen himself. He maintained a greater distance than he would have liked and waited for his tribe to arrive.

At that point, there were more interlopers than even his whole tribe could hope to drive out.

When Nick woke the next morning, Jasmine was cooking breakfast, a foot-long reptile that she was holding over the fire on a skewer. From the hole in its side, it looked like Otto or Ellessar had killed it with an arrow or crossbow bolt.

"Can you see?" Nick asked her.

She looked up at him, beaming.

"Aeron has blessed her." Ellessar was checking the horses' hooves for signs of rot.

"Wasn't that fairy supposed to be a servant of Aeron?" Rancid asked.

"That fairy lost her way a long time ago," Ellessar said.

"Regardless—" Jasmine sprinkled some herbs on the roasting meat— "I have found my way through her deception."

"Thank Aeron for that. Good to have you back." Nick squeezed her shoulder as he walked past her to Ellessar. "Any word on the Assassins?"

"They're close. We should keep moving."

With that, the party packed up quickly, split the hot meal Jasmine had prepared, and set out.

By mid-morning, it became clear that Nick and his party were going to have to cross the water. He stared out over the sickening, oily, green film that coated the surface of a lake, maybe fifty yards across. In some places, streamers of bubbles sizzled on the surface and hinted at submerged predators or some unknown phenomenon within the bog.

"This place looks worse than it smells," Jasmine remarked.

"Smells like home," Rancid said.

Nick nearly laughed out loud at the look that drew from Ellessar, who hadn't yet heard about Rancid's filthy childhood in the waste tunnels of Forlorn Keep.

Otto stared out over the lake with a look of disgust. "How do you want to do this?"

"Very carefully." Nick gestured to a wild, riderless lizard mount that watched them from the far side of the lake. "There may be more."

"I'll take a look." Zen waded a few feet into the water and transformed himself into a lizard mount made of polished ice, nearly invisible even before he dropped beneath the surface.

"Everybody else mount up." Nick climbed onto his horse. "Perhaps the lizard will keep its distance if we appear large and stay together."

With the Assassins behind them, they couldn't wait for Zen to report back. They had to count on him to intervene if the lizard mount decided to attack.

So, in a tight group, the five of them goaded their horses into the lake. By the time they reached the middle, the water became deep enough for the horses to swim. Ultimately, they made it across unmolested by any creature larger than a leech. On the other side, it took nearly an hour to rid themselves and their horses of the bloodsuckers and their gear of the wet residue left by the lake.

"Look at this." Rancid pointed out a track in the loam that looked as if it might have been made by a lizard mount, but it was larger. Much larger. The foot that had made it was at least two feet long and a foot and a half wide.

By then, Zen had joined them on the bank. "That must be the beast the old coot in South Bend told us about."

"It's days old," Rancid assured them. He searched for more tracks, but found only the one, the rest apparently obliterated by the constant suck and ooze of the mud. "Let's hope it doesn't come back."

With the return of Jasmine's eyesight and spirits, Nick felt a sense of optimism for the first time since they'd crossed the Great Divide. "At this point, what's one more danger, give or take? Maybe it'll eat the demons." Nobody laughed. Perhaps their danger was too present and overwhelming to permit levity. His hope of the demons meeting their demise at the hands of the swamp was both too real and too farfetched to laugh at.

For four more days, the party slogged through the swamp. The sounds of life and death continued around them, including the odd, clicking speech of the lizard-kin and the deep, rumbling bellow of their mounts. But those were distant, and for the moment, the least of their worries.

Each morning, Ellessar reported on the imminent proximity of the Assassins. "Near enough to smell," he said one morning in a voice that carried no farther than a few feet, "if it wasn't for the stench of the swamp."

"Close enough to see, then." Rancid peered through the ever-present mist at the looming bulk of the trees.

"And hear," Ellessar agreed. "When it comes to tracking demons, my sense of direction is usually much more precise than my sense of distance. But now...they're close and all around us. Waiting for a moment of weakness."

"Shall we double the watches?" Otto asked.

"No." Ellessar laid his mud-coated, water-logged backpack near Spirit's saddle. "They've been nearby ever since we crossed the Divide. If our watches weren't sufficient, they'd have attacked by now."

"And doubling the watches would mean longer nights if we want to get enough sleep to keep ourselves sharp," Zen added.

"Maybe they're not waiting for a weakness," Jasmine said. "The last time we sought something, Vinra waited until we found it before he struck. These things must be working for the Master. Maybe they're waiting to see what we came here for."

"Bloody baron, she's right," Rancid said. "We should bait them. Pretend to find it."

Ellessar looked skeptical. "I don't think—"

"That may get them to attack, to reveal themselves before we become weakened by battle or disease," Jasmine agreed.

Nick let them talk, more enjoying Jasmine's renewed enthusiasm than listening to the arguments. The last time they'd baited one of the demons, it had nearly killed him. Now there were four. Prudence argued against the plan, but practicality left them few options. They couldn't just let the demons wait for a moment when the party was weak.

"Of course," Otto added, "one of them attacked us when it thought half our party was sick. If there're several of them now, they wouldn't consider our whole party beyond their capability."

"It won't work," Ellessar said.

Rancid's head snapped around. "Why?"

"Assassins have only one purpose. They'll wait to accomplish it only if they're not sure they can under the circumstances at the time, or if they think circumstances might improve. They're cunning but single-minded."

"You're saying they won't fall for it?" Nick asked.

"I'm saying they don't care about your treasure or your quest. That's not what they're waiting for."

"Well, I'm not going to let them choose their own battlefield." Rancid's hand clamped firmly around the handle of his sword. "You say they're near enough to smell. Let's find them. Force them into battle."

"Neat trick that'll be," Ellessar remarked. "If you get near one that doesn't want to fight, it'll just translocate. The only way to slay one is to wait for it to attack, then kill it before it can flee to try again later."

Rancid raised his hand as though presenting Ellessar to his friends. "Behold the demon hunter who refuses to hunt demons."

Nick hushed him. "I like the bait idea. I think it's worth a try."

They put together a whispered plan over a cold breakfast and began their daily slog.

The next day, Nick consulted the stone often. From time to time, he pulled Zen or one of the others over to examine it. They pointed this way and that. Nick held the stone at arm's length while he turned a full circle.

The stone did nothing unusual, though it now glowed brightly enough to see in the daytime gloom of the swamp. Nevertheless, he and his friends talked and gestured excitedly. For the benefit of the Assassins, they forced smiles onto their faces and a bounce into their step.

Zen hovered over the stone, chanting incantations. He produced a disembodied hand of clear, smooth ice, invisible in the mist and twilight from more than a few feet away, and used it to lift the stone from Nick's hand.

Nick glanced at him, eyes wide and hopeful, and then at the others. Their jaws dropped as the stone hovered about the area for several seconds before settling onto the ground.

Jasmine and Otto rushed forward with their shovels and turned up spadefuls of the soft dirt, digging several feet down while the others watched.

Zen fumbled a pouch from a pocket inside his robes and dropped it into one of his sleeves.

"There!" Otto tossed his shovel aside and knelt on the ground.

"Wait." Zen marched to the edge of the hole. "It might be dangerous."

Ellessar and Rancid scanned the nearby trees as though fearful someone would come to claim their treasure, though the elf did so with little conviction.

Zen waved his hands and chanted over the hole, then stared intently. "Hmmm." He knelt down, reached into the hole, and let the pouch fall from his sleeve into the pool of muck at the bottom. He rubbed it in the mud, grabbed it by the end of its drawstring, and lifted it reverently from the pit.

Nick took the bag, opened it carefully, and peered inside. "It's here."

A cheer erupted in the clearing, and Rancid broke out their last bottle of the king's wine. "Bitterroot."

"Now that's what I've been waiting for," Otto said heartily, seeming to forget the demons they were trying to bait.

The group passed around the bottle, pitched camp, passed the bottle, coaxed a small fire from damp twigs, and passed the bottle again.

By nightfall, it wasn't clear who was actually drunk and who was just acting for the benefit of the demons.

CHAPTER 30

W hisper spun away from the performance in disgust. He didn't know what Nick and his friends sought, but they obviously felt it was worth a trip through this accursed bog. Addicus had already determined that whatever the objective was, it wasn't referenced in Nick's grandfather's journal. So, as soon as they had entered the swamp, the Master had ordered Whisper to find out what it was, to wait until Nick found his prize before he and the Black Hand made their move, and then to acquire it.

Nick apparently knew he was being followed, either by the Black Hand or by Ryanna's Assassin demons, or both. And this whole charade might have succeeded in drawing out one or the other if the ice mage hadn't been so clumsy in stuffing the bag up his sleeve.

Whisper returned to the bandit's camp a few miles back. "They know we're here."

Halidreth's jaw tightened. "Did they see you?"

"No. But they tried to bait me nonetheless. When we attack, they'll be expecting us. Take that into account in your battle plan."

"Very well." Halidreth spun back to his bandits. He motioned the leaders of his fighting force—Sorowyn, Jade, and Minshara—to his side, leaving the rest to prepare camp and stand watch.

All night long, the watch was more vigilant than it appeared, with one person awake beside the fire and another, sprawled on the ground, feigning drunken slumber. Yet it seemed that the demons weren't fooled. Perhaps they remembered too well how one of them had died when it fell for a similar ruse outside Spitfire, or they didn't believe the party had found what they'd come for.

Or they didn't care.

Whatever their reasons, they withheld their attack that night. When Ellessar prayed the next morning, he still reported the demons' presence just beyond the camp.

With nothing to do but wait for the Assassins to make their move, the company continued south, hoping the day would bring them out of the swamp to pursue their quest on drier ground and with a greater range of visibility. That would force their enemies to show themselves or keep their distance. But when even the meager light of the bog failed, swampland still engulfed them.

Zen transformed himself into an eagle and made his nightly foray into the sky. The canopy of trees passed beneath him as he made his arc. To his joy and relief, he spotted the edge of the tree line, in the distant south, barely discernible in the dusk. He'd verify its presence in the morning, when the light was better. Then they'd press toward freedom from this slimy filth.

The group bedded down in the driest spot they could find, mossy ground crowded by cypress and ferns. The watch remained vigilant, or so Zen believed. But when he opened his backpack the next morning, he found a piece of rolled parchment, damp with seeped-in moisture from the swamp air.

He unrolled it carefully.

Zen,

We, the former Black Hand, hunt your party. We've no desire to do so, but Whisper, a Chosen of the Master in Mortaan's Prophecy, drives us. With the exception of Sevendeath, we bear you and your companions no ill will. We've lost so many people that we want only to rid ourselves of Whisper. Unfortunately, we don't have the power to fight it alone. If we, your party and mine, are willing to work together, we can help each other. You work with us to kill this creature, and we'll leave you alone. Our hatred of Whisper has come to surpass even our hatred of Sevendeath. We're willing to forget our grudge even against him in exchange for your help.

When the time comes, Whisper will force us to attack. I don't know when it will happen, but I believe it won't be long. I have no control over the timing, but Whisper has given me the authority to dictate our tactics.

I propose this: When the time comes, my mage, Minshara, will oppose you personally, though she won't harm you. Whisper, if it does as I ask, will come against you as well. It's invisible, and therefore difficult to combat, but as soon as it reveals itself, Minshara will change sides and attack the creature in hopes that you'll help her against it. In the meantime, my men will spread out against yours. Everyone will have to fight in earnest until Whisper is destroyed, or else it will sense the deception. As soon as the creature is dead, my men will break off the attack. We'll go our own way and let you be.

There's no safe way for you to get word to me, so when the time comes, we'll attack in the manner I've described.

Your actions will tell me whether you've accepted my proposal. The only alternative is for us to fight to the death. Then, no matter how the battle comes out, the Master will have won.

I've contacted you, rather than the others in your party, because you're the only one with the right kind of power to help us. Consider this well before you decide.

Halidreth,

Leader of the former Black Hand

"Hey, guys." Zen gathered the others around him. Under the watchful eyes of the demons, and possibly the Black Hand and their invisible creature of air, Zen spoke quietly. "We had a visitor last night." He read the text of the letter quietly, and in its entirety.

"That's goblin crap." Rancid snatched for the letter and missed. "The Black Hand would never agree to let me go."

"Oh, I don't think this is from the Black Hand as a whole." Zen continued to hold the letter out of Rancid's reach. "Just from the group that pursues us."

Rancid shook the chain of Black Hand trophies on his belt. "There aren't many left."

"You sure?" Otto asked, earning a glower from Rancid.

"A group chased us through Meuribar and Faldor to get my grandfather's journal," Nick whispered. "We wiped out most of them, yet here they are. The same creature of air, the same bandit gang. If we kill the Black Hand and not the creature, it'll find some other stooge and we'll face it again."

Rancid shook the chain of trophies again. "They won't give up on me that easily, I don't care what they have to gain from it. If that letter's from them, they're lying."

"Maybe they are." Otto stretched his hand out to Zen. "May I see it?" He took the letter and read it. "I don't know much about these Black Hand, or your history with them, but we've met them in battle. They fight well, and even if the ones we saw on the road from Dragon

Tears are all of them, they outnumber us at least two to one."

"Not for long." Rancid shook the trophies a third time.

"I'm glad you can be so confident," Otto continued. "But I have also fought this being of air, this 'Chosen of the Master in Mortaan's Prophecy,' as they call it. It can't be seen, and swords pass through it with little resistance. If it alone can drive a dozen Black Hand, we'll need help defeating it."

"Don't forget the Assassins," Ellessar said. "If the Black Hand attack, the demons will likely pick that moment to strike. In fact, I'd bet my coat that's what they're waiting for, a dozen or more strong allies."

"It really doesn't matter who wrote it. Or if the offer is genuine," Nick said.

Otto nodded. "I agree."

"Because I'm going to kill them all anyway?" Rancid said.

Nick ignored him. "The way I see it, we'll have to fight at least three things: the Assassin demons, Whisper, and the Black Hand, probably all at the same time. In the past, Whisper has always attacked me. The letter says it'll go after Zen this time."

"That's another thing," Rancid said. "If this thing is their master, how are they going to tell it what to do?"

"Easy." Zen clasped his hands before him and affected the tone of a timid servant. "Master, the ice mage is too strong. Without your help we'll die and won't be able to serve you."

"Oh, please," Rancid said.

"Either way." The firmness in Nick's tone pulled their attention back to him. "We fight what we can as it shows up."

"We should focus on the demons if they appear," Ellessar interjected. "They're probably the biggest threat."

"Screw that. I'm going for the Black Hand."

Again Nick ignored Rancid. "Truly, everything rests on who Zen targets, and when. If we can gain some advantage against Whisper by attacking it instead of the bandits' mage, we should take it. It may be our only chance to defeat it. At no time, though, do we ever let up unless the Black Hand lay down their arms."

Rancid snorted.

"If they do—" Otto handed the letter back to Zen— "we can slay two enemies with a single sword stroke, so to speak. Be rid of Whisper and the Black Hand. Then we can face the demons alone. At that point, they may back off."

"Don't forget the lizards," Zen added. In the end, it really did depend on what he decided to do. He'd make that choice based on the condition of the party and their myriad foes at the time the Black Hand broke off the attack. If Zen thought they had enough left in them to kill the Black Hand, he had no intention of letting them go.

Jade returned to the Black Hand camp just before dawn. Halidreth was waiting for her.

"It's done," she said. "Do you really think they'll help us?"

Halidreth walked her away from the others. "Who knows? Zen has worked with us before, though he may not have known we were pulling the strings."

"Were we?" Jade asked.

Halidreth sighed. "Either way, he may be willing to work with us now. After all, we've offered him a way out."

"Suppose he doesn't think he needs it. We'd have been better off taking Sevendeath's band by surprise."

He shook his head. "Whisper said they already know we're here. That's why I had you deliver the letter last night."

"I hope you're right."

Halidreth nodded. "I'll tell the others what we've done, one by one throughout the day, while Whisper's out tracking Sevendeath. In the meantime, the apparition knows I sent you to survey the enemy camp. It'll expect a report."

"Of course." Jade started to walk away, but turned back to Halidreth. "The others will never go along with this if it means Seven-death will survive."

"Don't worry," Halidreth assured her. "He won't. Sorowyn will see to that."

CHAPTER 31

ick and his friends won free of the bog just after noon that same day. Lush, green grass carpeted the plains all the way to the southern horizon.

They didn't venture far into them, however. Instead they hugged the marsh, a couple hundred yards from the tree line, close enough to hide in the darkened backdrop of the trees from anyone who might look their way from the southern plains, yet far enough that the demons and the Black Hand would have to break from the cover of the swamp to attack.

They spent the remainder of that day inspecting themselves and their horses for the leeches that had plagued them for the past week, and drying out and cleaning their gear. Ellessar prayed to Aeron for the health of the people and horses, and said a restoration prayer over their food.

Beginning the next morning, they followed the signal of the Seeking Stone westward for four days along the bends of the marsh. Zen's aerial forays allowed them to avoid any unexpected run-ins with the indigenous wolf-kin people.

According to Ellessar, the demons hovered at the edges of the swampland. The Black Hand continued to stay out of sight, and the dragon seemed to have vanished. The weather remained sunny, though cool.

For that brief time, Nick began to hope. Then the line of the swamp veered south and the Seeking Stone began to grow dim.

"What does it mean?" Otto asked.

"It means we have to go back into the swamp." Nick's stomach soured at the thought. "Somewhere in there, buried beneath layers of rot, lies the thing we seek."

"That suits me," Rancid said.

Nick glared at him. "It would."

Jasmine, ever practical, voiced Nick's own thought. "We will do what we must."

The next morning, Zen reported that the edge of the swamp turned back toward the north ahead, so they followed the line of trees for another day. By evening, the Stone was as bright as they'd ever seen it.

Before dusk, Zen went on his nightly scouting venture. This time he stayed out longer than usual, nearly an hour. When he returned, he wore a satisfied grin.

"What did you find?" Nick asked him.

"A lake."

Rancid made a dismissive gesture and went back to digging a pit for a small cooking fire.

"Perfectly round," Zen continued, "with no vegetation."

Jasmine, meditating nearby, opened her eyes. "No vegetation?"

"In there?" Nick pointed to the swamp.

"None around this lake," Zen said. "Just a few dead trees. From the air, it looks like a burn mark, as though someone dropped a lit pipe onto a fine, green rug. I perched as near to it as I could and just observed for as long as my weaving allowed." He had every-one's attention now. "There was no movement at all. No animals. No sound."

Otto let out a low whistle.

The gurgle of the fetid pools; the clicks and bellows of the liz-ard-kin and their mounts; the rustle of the ferns; and the croaks, chirps, and fluttering of the bog's indigenous wildlife had never let up during the days they'd spent in the swamp.

Nick chuckled nervously. His life had become a long string of bad omens. No. More than omens. Bad events. Everywhere that burned or stank or denied the light of day was the place he had to go. Ev-erything weird or supernatural, everything that lived in legends but hadn't been seen by the eyes of men since before the Age of Prophecy became real and pursued him. "It figures," was all he could manage.

By noon the next day, they'd gone far enough north for the Seek-ing Stone to confirm that they'd once again passed their treasure.

"That gives us a fix from two directions," Zen said. He frowned at the confused looks of the others, then picked up a stick and drew a big oval on the ground. "This is the swamp." He drew a small circle inside it. "This is the lake."

"The brightest point in our westward trek occurred here." He put an X just outside the oval, directly south of the lake. "That's as close as we got without turning north. By the time we did that, we were west of our target." He scanned the faces of the others.

"Last night, we got as close as we could heading north." He put an X just west of the swamp, marking their previous night's camp-site. Then he drew a line north from the first X and east from the second. They crossed at the lake.

With no doubt left, the group wasted little time getting there. The best speed they could manage through the bog got them to the lake near sunset.

As Zen had said, the lake was perfectly round. The water inside wasn't the oily, gray-green sludge that ran through the rest of the swamp, but a plain, opaque brown, like the watering ponds back in

Meuribar after the cows had wandered through them and stirred up dirt from the bottom.

"What do you make of this?" Rancid kicked at the five-foot-high berm of dirt that formed a ring around the lake's edge.

It reminded Nick a little too much of the antling hills that dotted the floor of the catacombs beneath the capital city of Trondor, though in this case, the berm was less pronounced and the hole filled with water. "Looks like the ring around an animal's burrow."

"No." Jasmine picked up a small pebble from the berm and walked to a patch of mud-softened ground near the ring's base. "Suppose this is the chunk of metal we seek." She held it over her head, between her thumb and one of her talon-like fingers. "If Xanth is right, it fell from the sky."

She threw the rock at the ground. Mud splattered away from it, leaving a small hole surrounded by a tiny berm of mud. Slowly, water seeped in to fill the hole.

Otto whistled again. "I guess we've found it."

"Watch your backs," Nick said a moment later, when he realized they were all staring into the middle of the lake. He scanned the darkening ring of trees just beyond the lake's perimeter.

"Watch your front." Otto nudged Nick's shoulder and drew his attention back to the water.

Bubbles pierced the surface near the center of the lake, and then a rush of air burst forth from somewhere below.

As one, Rancid, Nick, and Ellessar drew their swords. Otto snatched the ax from his belt.

The surface erupted in a cascade of brown, running off the head of some waterlogged behemoth, whose huge gray body surfaced like the ground shark had done from the plains of Faldor, and this beast was every bit as big. Its head rose ponderously at the end of its long, serpentine neck. Its eyes settled on Nick and his friends.

The behemoth's tail shot over its head at Jasmine like a whip. She dove away from its mace-like tip, which snapped up, twitching in the air as if seeking another target.

Zen chanted beside Nick. His empty hand shot out as though throwing an enchantment at the behemoth's head. The air grew cold around it.

The beast flinched and roared in pain, rage, or fear, but it didn't die the way the lizard-kin chieftain had under the same weaving.

Its tail snapped at Zen. With a crack, it sent him sprawling across the muddy ground, gasping for breath. The behemoth emerged from the water on four long, trunk-like legs, its tail whipping the air above their heads. Long streamers of matted fur, like brown seaweed, hung from its flanks.

Zen scrambled backward with one arm wrapped around his chest, his breathing labored.

Jasmine darted past the behemoth, trying to get behind it. Its tail swept her from her feet.

Nick backed to the side as the creature continued its relentless pursuit of Zen. He pointed his great sword at the ground and kept his movements slow, drawing no apparent notice from the beast as it lumbered by. As soon as its shoulder passed him, he charged forward and buried his great sword to the hilt in the creature's side before pulling it free.

The behemoth took another three steps and staggered to its front knees. It shook the ground as it toppled onto its side. Its chest heaved once and then went still.

Ellessar rushed to Zen's side with a healing prayer.

Jasmine climbed to her feet. "I'm okay." She began to walk off a limp.

Nick searched the darkening tree line for movement. The blackness beyond the lake's moonlit clearing had become complete. Not even starlight penetrated the thick canopy of trees. If there was anything out there, it made no sound. Yet the Assassins must be there somewhere. Perhaps the battle with the behemoth had been over too quickly for the demons to take advantage of it. Maybe they were waiting for the Black Hand to strike.

Zen mounted the short rise at the lake's edge, still holding his sore chest.

"How bad is it?" Nick asked.

"He'll live." Ellessar also scanned the tree line. "At least as long as the rest of us."

Nick nodded. "We'll start our search for the rock at first light. Where's Rancid?"

"Here." Rancid came around from the other side of the behemoth's body. "We'd better find it now and by the bloody baron get ourselves out of here." His face looked pale, even for being in moonlight. He waved a hand at the behemoth's body. "That thing's a baby. And based on the fresh tracks at the far side of the lake, I'd say mama's nearby."

CHAPTER 32

Zen rewove the threads of reality to form himself into the shape of a crystal clear crocodile of ice and plunged below the surface of the lake. The bottom was a soft blanket of sandy mud. He swam to the middle, the deepest point, and dug. By the time he had to resurface for air, he'd found nothing.

"Hey," Rancid yelled into the darkness from the far side of the lake. He drew his dagger and lobbed it into the canopy of branches.

Jasmine ran around the lake to join him. "What is it?"

Zen swam across and let his animal shape erode, returning to his elf-kin form.

Otto, Ellessar, and Nick remained vigilant around the party's gear, near the dead behemoth pup.

"Those infernal lizard-kin." Rancid's eyes never left the canopy. It had grown so dark beyond the moonlit opening of this dead lake that even Zen's sensitive elf-kin eyes could make out nothing beyond the first row of trees. "I saw one in that tree, but it scrambled back into the darkness. There're more. I can hear them."

"They've been following us ever since we entered the swamp." Zen had heard their voices come and go at intervals for days before they'd broken loose of the marsh into the southern plains. "Don't anger them."

The lizard-kin were speaking. "That isss no matter. The behemoth."

"Yesss. The behemoth will have them."

Jasmine placed a hand on Zen's shoulder and spoke softly into his ear. "You'd better keep looking. We'll keep an eye on things up here."

Zen nodded and began weaving. The lizards wouldn't attack—at least not until he found what they had come for. The same was true for Whisper and the Black Hand. The real concern was the behemoth mother and how soon she would return.

As soon as Zen completed his crocodile form, he slipped below the water once more.

halidreth hunched in the darkness, well back from the moonlit lake yet closer to Sevendeath's band than Whisper had previously allowed them to advance.

Whisper's approach was but a breath of wind on the ferns. "Our moment nears. Ready your people."

Halidreth nodded without knowing whether the apparition could actually see him in the utter black that pervaded the swamp like the stink of rot. He backed away to where the others waited.

"All right," he whispered. "Get ready. Stick to the plan, but wait for my signal." He could see none of them. "Sorowyn."

"Here." The elf was but a voice in the darkness.

"It's up to you now. Can you handle it?"

"Oh, yes." There seemed to be equal parts confidence and glee in his voice.

"Do it quickly." Halidreth had to listen carefully to hear the movements of his men as they took up positions around the near side of the lake. He didn't know where Whisper had gone. Or if it had gone. He could only hope the apparition would attack Zen as he'd assigned it to do. That would force the ice mage to attack it, which would play right into Halidreth's plans.

Sorowyn had perhaps the most difficult task among all of the Black Hand, even more difficult than managing the ice mage and defeating Whisper. He had to kill Sevendeath before the apparition died. If he failed to do so, the Black Hand would be unable to withdraw. There wasn't a man or woman among them willing to quit until Sevendeath lay dead.

The task fell to Sorowyn because he was the only Black Hand who'd ever bested Sevendeath in single combat. He'd given Sevendeath his scar.

He moved his team into position on the south side of the lake and waited.

The deformed female monk paced the lake's perimeter opposite Sevendeath.

The ice mage, in the form of an ice crocodile, dove repeatedly beneath the surface, searching for whatever he and his friends had come here to find.

Nick Mirrin and the elf continued to guard their party's supplies, where Zen would likely take his prize when, and if, he found it. Halidreth had deployed most of the Black Hand there.

Another thirty or forty minutes passed before Zen surfaced with an object. When he did, it looked like a mere rock, a rough stone the size of a man's head, gripped in his crocodile mouth. He dumped it onto the ground and resumed his elf-kin form.

Sevendeath and the others gathered around it. Nick pulled a polished stone, the size and shape of a goose's egg, from his backpack. Its bright glow illuminated the faces of his companions as they huddled over their prize, all grouped together now on the east side of the lake. Sorowyn, on the south side, thought to move closer, but feared he'd miss Halidreth's signal if he did. So he waited, watched, and listened.

Within minutes, Nick seemed satisfied that this stone was the thing he'd braved the Wild Lands to retrieve. Smiles shone on the faces of his companions while he used a blanket to dry the rock, and then he wrapped it with care and reverence.

Then the soft plunk of a fist-sized rock sounded from the middle of the lake. Halidreth's signal.

Sevendeath and the others spun toward the water.

Sorowyn was no mage, but Minshara had provided for him this night. He put Sevendeath firmly in his mind, tossed the rod in his hand onto the ground near the lake's edge, and spoke the elven word for *serpent*. The rod writhed, thickened, and elongated until it was over thirty feet long and as stout as an elf's torso.

The snake tested the air with a few flicks of its forked tongue and made straight for Sevendeath.

Sorowyn gave it a brief head start, long enough for it to draw Sevendeath's notice, before he and his team charged the clearing.

The trees erupted around Zen.

Nick thrust the bundle, nearly forty pounds of stone wrapped in wool, at Zen. "Put this in your pack."

As Zen grabbed it, a bandit, not large but fit, completely bald, with a stained silk tunic, raced from the trees with a sword raised to strike. He closed on Zen before he could secure the rock.

Nick strode up to challenge. The bandit hesitated, as though un-sure whether to strike Nick or Zen, a hesitancy uncharacteristic of the Black Hand and a fatal mistake in combat.

The bandit was biding his time, sparing Zen a strike that might turn him against the Black Hand before Whisper attacked.

Zen's head began to ache as though the elven band he wore had tightened. The weave tugged on his consciousness. His thoughts wa-vered, and for a moment, the bandit before him became more of a friend to him than Nick could ever hope to be. But the enchantment was fleeting, the manipulations of the bandit's mage, Minshara, try-ing to buy some magical insurance, to compel Zen to behave as she wanted.

"Get it out of here." Nick stepped between Zen and the ban-dit. "Take the stone to the best smith in the dwarven lands." Nick's sword clashed with the bald man's as he drove the bandit back. "If we survive, we'll meet you there."

Zen was his own person. More than anything else, he was that. Minshara's trick had served only to turn him against the bandits. To the Abyss with Whisper. To the Abyss with the Black Hand. Nick was right. The Master would *not* take their prize this time.

He stuffed the rock into his pack, threw it over one shoulder, and tucked his staff under his arm. In a flash of brilliance that only Zen could see, he took the form of an eagle and fled to the skies.

A cloud of sparkling lights engulfed him, the same effect his friends had used to confuse the royal guards in Gremauld's tent the night they had assassinated the king. But Zen was no soldier with a pike and sword. His own familiarity with the weave grew stronger every time he used it. He ignored the hypnotic lights and flew clear.

His heart soared as he contemplated the gift of his friends' trust. Nick had handed him an immense treasure. Zen didn't know its val-ue in coin, but if it alone could stop the Final Prophecy of Mortaan, it would fetch him anything he wanted. *Anything.*

For the first time, he no longer needed his friends or their quest. He didn't need his old mentor, or even Gwyndarren. He no longer needed anyone or anything to gain the power he sought. He had it now in his possession, or at least the means to purchase it. He no longer needed those he'd just left behind.

It was a good thing he didn't. His act of leaving had doomed them all. The moment he took flight, he'd forfeited the deal offered by the Black Hand and left the others to face all of their enemies alone, without the might of the ice mage.

He'd left them to die.

And because he was also leaving the Shield of Faith behind, he didn't even have to worry about his accursed oath to Aeron.

He made a wide circle around the clearing, counting on the thickness of the canopy and the chaos of battle to keep him safe from arrows and crossbow bolts while he took a bearing from the position of the moon and the shadowy bulk of the Great Divide.

A half-horse dragon-kin, like those Minshara had called the last time they'd met the Black Hand, appeared in mid-flight over the center of the lake. It spotted Zen and winged for him. Yes. He'd angered Minshara indeed, and the other Black Hand as well, he'd wager. At least he had drawn *her* attention from the others. He could claim that much if he ever saw Nick again.

CHAPTER 33

"No!" The bald man yelled as Zen took to the sky.

Nick pressed the advantage. He batted the bandit's shield aside and thrust his blade into the man's gut. A serious wound, but not immediately fatal.

The bandit staggered to one knee. His shield arm hung to the ground as though he'd lost his strength. When Nick raised his sword to swing at the man's unprotected head, an invisible force slammed into him and knocked him from his feet. He landed halfway up the berm that surrounded the lake. Without pausing to regain his breath, he swept his sword through the air above him.

Whisper shrieked like a storm howling past a poorly set window, and the wind receded.

Nick scrambled to his feet. "Converge on the whirlwind!" Though Nick had sent Zen away, he intended to keep the Black Hand's bargain, if the bandits would honor it without Zen. Whatever the outcome, the Master's Chosen would not steal the prize this time.

Jasmine faced the onrush of the Black Hand. *My men will spread out against yours*, Halidreth's letter had said. *Everyone will have to fight in earnest.* An orc bandit charged her and Otto as they stood with their backs to the body of the behemoth pup.

The orc barreled in with a fierce sweep of a war hammer. Jasmine ducked the hammer and jabbed him in the sternum. His grunt was more of contempt than of pain. She followed with a fist to his jaw and another to the side of his face.

He seemed to dismiss the blows.

A second bandit closed. His short sword flashed at Jasmine. Forced into a defensive posture, she divided her attention between the newcomer and the orc. The orc's hammer slammed her arm, which went instantly numb from the elbow down.

Swords clashed somewhere behind her.

"Converge on the whirlwind!" Nick yelled as though he thought they might somehow salvage the pact with the Black Hand.

Everyone will have to fight in earnest until Whisper is destroyed.

Maybe hope wasn't lost. But Jasmine had to choose between joining the assault on Whisper or helping Otto. Ultimately, it came down to this: The Assassin demons would see this as their opportunity, and once they arrived, they'd join the Chosen and its Black Hand slaves. There was only one way any of them could be saved.

Jasmine dove past the bandits' blows, over the berm, into the mud that skirted the lake, and rolled to her feet.

The Black Hand female, Jade, sped at Jasmine in the moonlight, her feet splashing in the shallow water at the lake's edge. Jasmine swung her foot up and caught the woman on the chin. The blow swept Jade from her feet to land on her back in the water. Jade's sword flew deeper into the lake.

Jasmine didn't wait to see if the woman got up. She hurried around the behemoth to stand with Nick against the Master's Chosen.

From out of the ether, an Assassin appeared beside her, claws poised and skin dripping with corrosive slime.

Rancid watched the dark bulk of the giant snake approach, more fascinated than cowed by its size. Two humanoid forms broke from the cover of the trees and rushed in behind it. Out of habit, Rancid focused his attention on the right hands of the attackers until they drew close enough for him to see the moonlight glint from their studded gloves.

Ellessar was at his side.

Another bandit rushed in from behind the demon hunter.

When the snake circled toward the trees, Rancid dismissed it and focused on the Black Hand, both elves. One was a female. The other he recognized.

Sorowyn.

The scar that split Rancid's face from eyebrow to jawbone seemed to itch of its own accord, burning for vengeance. He snatched his sword from its scabbard, leapt to the top of the berm, and waited.

Swords clashed as he and Ellessar met the onrush. The two fought together as though they'd done so for their whole lives. Sorowyn's twin swords came in first. Rancid thrust them aside with a sweep of his own, but the bandit's lightning recovery prevented a counterstrike.

Ellessar clashed with the third attacker, an elf-kin with a pair of hatchets.

The female swung her morning star in an arc at Rancid's head. He blocked it with his sword and the chain wrapped around his blade.

She yanked on the tangled weapons. Rancid released his sword suddenly and she pulled herself off balance.

In a single motion, Rancid drew his dagger and plunged it into her side. The strike left Rancid exposed to Sorowyn's sword. He dropped to his knees to duck the blade.

Ellessar's sword flashed over Rancid's head and split the female from one side of her neck to her opposite breast. A warm splatter dotted Rancid's face and arms.

He had no time to thank Ellessar.

An arrow or crossbow bolt whistled from the darkness and struck the demon hunter with a thunk. The elf grunted in pain but swung at Sorowyn.

It was too dark to see where Ellessar had been hit. All that mattered was Sorowyn, whose grin widened at Ellessar's pain.

From his knees, Rancid thrust his dagger into Sorowyn's black heart. The elf's grin twisted into a sickening mix of pain and resignation. His eyes fixed on those of Sevendeath for a moment before they lost their focus and luster.

Then the giant python struck.

Teeth the size of Rancid's thumb sank into his shoulder. Searing pain lanced through him and his good arm went numb. The weight of it carried Rancid to the ground, and the constrictor coiled around him.

Rancid jabbed awkwardly with his dagger until the snake loosened its grip, and he managed to twist away.

The constrictor's teeth sank into his thigh. The snake raised its head high enough that Rancid became a dangling piece of meat. Coils of scaly flesh encircled him and blocked the world from his view. His chest constricted. Several of his ribs snapped, and the dagger fell from his hand.

Ellessar shouted a muffled prayer to Aeron. A hand grasped Rancid's leg and a wave of pure healing power coursed through him.

The pain subsided. His strength returned.

But the python was stronger still.

Baron's blood! Rancid struggled to break the snake's hold, but the act only brought on another wave of constriction and the mercy of unconsciousness.

An Assassin demon appeared near Ellessar. It wasn't here to kill Nick, as they'd all assumed. If it was, it would have appeared closer to the big farmer. This one was here for Ellessar or Rancid. It made sense now why they'd been pursued by so many demons. There were multiple Assassins because there were multiple targets. Ellessar placed his body between it and the python. If it had come for him, let it. If it was here for Rancid, it would have to go through Ellessar.

The demon hissed. It sidestepped and tried to skirt around him toward Rancid. Then, frustrated, the demon lunged forward.

Ellessar sliced a deep wound in its gut and spun away. The demon's claws tore rents in his armor. By then, the python had pulled Rancid to the water's edge.

Ellessar's sword rusted in his hands, flakes of the blade peeling away like dead flesh. It would never withstand another strike upon the Assassin, who even now pressed toward Rancid with relentless determination. Ellessar threw the sword like a spear at the python. The blade impaled the snake's head, then snapped in two.

The python went limp and Rancid's body rolled away. The only sign that he still lived was the presence of the Assassin, who would return to the Abyss the moment its prey died.

Bleeding, wary now of Ellessar, the Assassin backed away.

Ellessar drew his demon-claw sword and lunged for the Assassin, the conviction of Aeron and a lifetime of training behind it. He or the demon would die this day.

In a blink, the demon vanished and reappeared by Rancid's side.

Too late, Ellessar realized it had lured him too far away. He couldn't get back to it in time.

The demon hissed in triumph and sank its claws into Rancid's broken body. Its task completed, the ether claimed it and returned it to its eternal prison.

As soon as Jasmine leapt from his side, Otto knew he was in trouble. Three enemies surrounded him.

One, a man with a short sword, lunged at Jasmine as she dove from the circle. Otto plunged his ax into the man's back and left the bandit dead on the ground. The others, the orc and a short man with a rippling chest and long, three-pronged pike, came at him.

Otto put his back to the body of the behemoth pup, took the handle of his ax in both hands, and dropped into a defensive stance. It was all he could do to fend off the blows of the bandits.

Suddenly, an Assassin appeared between his other adversaries.

Its arrival didn't surprise Otto. In fact, he'd been expecting it, though he'd assumed it would target Nick.

Again, Otto took advantage of the distraction. He sliced a nasty gash across the chest of the orc. Its strong ribs held. The cut was shallow, though it bled freely.

Otto shouldered the wounded orc away and placed himself opposite the muscular pikeman with the demon between them.

The ground shook as though it feared the foul Assassin. For a moment the tremor stopped. Then it shook again, a rhythmic pounding that sent tingling waves up though Otto legs.

The demon raked a row of bloody slashes across Otto's left bicep. The arm weakened and forced him to shift the ax fully into his right hand.

He slashed the demon. A vile ochre secretion smeared his blade, which rusted within seconds. When Otto tried to block a blow from the orc's hammer, his blade shattered. The hammer came through and cracked his chest.

The blow knocked the breath from him. It should have left him splayed on the ground—or worse, but the orc's strength was waning.

Another bandit, small, barely more than a boy, scrambled to the top of the behemoth pup's body and beckoned the wounded orc to him. A reprieve for Otto, momentary, but real.

He yanked his demon-claw sword from his belt and jockeyed for position against the demon and the pikeman.

Then the trees at the far end of the lake parted, with a crashing that sounded like falling timber. The behemoth mother plunged into the lake, sending a wave of water over the berm to gather at Otto's feet.

Otto stabbed the Assassin in the chest, but the demon didn't slow. Instead, it lunged.

Otto ducked, took the weight of the demon on his shoulder and back. He rocked his hips and the Assassin tumbled to the ground beyond him.

Its secretions ate their way through to his clothing. His skin burned as though he'd been dipped in liquid pain.

The boy on the pup's body glanced nervously at the mother wallowing in the lake as he prayed—Otto recognized the cadence of his chant; the boy prayed to Vexetan, not to Aeron—and laid his hands upon the shoulders of the orc, whose wounds closed.

The tail of the mother whipped over her head like a lash and smashed the boy with a sick thud. Putrid bits of flesh and shattered bone showered the nearby combatants.

The orc rejoined the battle. Surrounded now, Otto had to turn his back on the pikeman and the orc to strike the prone demon before it scrambled to its feet. He slashed the Assassin's back.

One tip of the bandit's pike pierced the back of Otto's thigh, and the man pulled him from his feet.

The behemoth mother dominated the lake. Her deadly tail struck out for her next victim, somewhere in the darkness beyond the bulk of its pup.

Otto rolled over onto his searing back to find the demon, the pikeman, and the orc looming over him.

CHAPTER 34

Z en flew inches above the treetops and tried to lose himself in the shaded textures of the swampland's canopy, but the dragon-kin beast was too fast. Zen banked to the right, tried to take advantage of his own greater maneuverability, and prayed that the thing couldn't see any better than he in the moonlight.

A giant claw raked his side. Searing pain lanced through him, and he lost strength in his right wing. The screech of triumph from the dragon-kin deafened him in one ear.

Zen dropped into the thick blanket of trees and banked painfully away from the opening. Just before he lost the light completely, he landed on a branch and shed his eagle's form. As the weave released its hold on him and his tissues strove to resume their natural shape, much of the rip in his side healed.

The dragon-kin, larger and more cumbersome, crashed through the trees nearby.

Zen's ring translated the clicks and hisses of some nearby liz-ard-kin.

"The sssacred ssstone. He takesss it."

"No. He ssstaysss."

"What about the othersss?"

"They killsss each other?"

"Then we wait and sssee."

Zen tuned out the voices. He didn't wait to see what the liz-ard-kin would do. And he wouldn't stay to battle the dragon-kin. As soon as his hands resumed their elf-kin form, he wove a portal. A smooth-walled tunnel through the pseudo-plane of ice took shape. He extended it as far as he could, hoping to stretch it all the way to Roybal Keep, to the safety and security of the Civilized Lands.

Dara, the elven girl whom he could now admit, at least to him-self, that he'd loved, came unbidden to his mind, as she had over and over again in his nightmares. The last time Zen had left his friends to face one of the Chosen, Zen had faked his own incapacitation to keep himself out of the battle, to uphold his end of a bargain he'd made with Gwyndarren, all for the sake of acquiring magic. And Dara had paid the price.

Zen had counted her as a friend. She could have been more, had he cared enough about anything but his own power to pursue her. Now she was gone from the world of men, but she was never com-pletely absent from his thoughts, no matter how hard he tried to let her go. And guilt had cost him too many nights of sleep.

As the opening formed, Zen stretched his consciousness through the plane of ice and grabbed threads of the weave that originated, not near Roybal keep, but near his friends. He had to try to save them. He was the only one who could.

This was the most dangerous weaving he'd ever attempted. He'd opened minor peepholes into the pseudo-plane of ice before, and he'd often pulled material from there into this world. He'd even cre-ated a tunnel as large as this one a few times, inspired by the translo-cation ability of the Assassin demons and by the things Ellessar had said about how it worked. But he hadn't actually gone there. He'd never left this world for another. He might not even make it back. Nevertheless, he had to try.

The portal opened. Zen stepped through and rode the funnel of ice as he used to ride the icy slopes of the Sharktooth Mountains during the bitter winters of his homeland as a child.

When he emerged from the other side, he found himself in the exact spot from which he'd left the battlefield, though he hardly recognized it now.

Nick hacked mercilessly at Whisper, but Zen could discern no damage inflicted by Nick's blade. It was too dark even to see the apparition. He knew of its presence only by the whooshing sound it made when it gathered enough strength and substance to slam its enemies.

Zen's portal snapped shut behind him with a thunderclap that might have rung only in his own mind. Swords clashed all around him. The stench of blood was thick in the fetid air. Jasmine faced an Assassin demon. Black Hand bandits surrounded them all. And the monstrous behemoth mother bellowed from the middle of the lake.

The amulet on his forehead warmed as Zen focused on the weave amid the mayhem. The sounds of battle faded beyond a wall of concentration. He plucked strands from the ether. They were short and incoherent, but he didn't have time to gather anything better.

A dragon-kin appeared in the space just above and beyond Whisper, then another.

Zen threaded the strands together. Gathering their power, he froze the air in front of Nick the way he'd frozen the brain of the lizard-kin chief.

A second demon appeared. Another Assassin. It lunged for Zen, but he was too far into the weave for the immediacy of the threat to register in his mind. His chest burned as demon claws raked into him, scoring his flesh down to his ribs.

Before he did anything else, he had to strike at Whisper. He had to keep the deal the Black Hand had offered, and hope the bandits would honor it.

He threw every bit of strength he had left into the weave and channeled the power through the catalyst of his staff.

Nick was surrounded by enemies he couldn't hope to defeat. Even the sky had begun to fill with them. Beasts hovered over the fray like specters of death. The hiss and screech of the Assassins were unmistakable. Jasmine, beside him a moment ago, had vanished in the cloud of violence.

The arrival of the behemoth mother must have shaken the Black Hand. Every one of them fell into a defensive crouch. Nick welcomed the reprieve. Blood from a score of cuts soaked his clothing and armor.

From somewhere behind him, a wave of cold blew past him with almost-tangible force to strike Whisper. It could have come from only one source: Zen.

"Fool!" Nick yelled, weak beyond endurance, dizzy from loss of blood, nauseated from the pounding of cudgels and Whisper's hammering. Zen couldn't have gotten the rock to safety that quickly. He'd hidden it somewhere in a swamp crawling with lizard-kin. Or worse, he still had it on him; he'd brought it back to the Chosen.

Nevertheless, Nick didn't waste the moment. He swung his blade at Whisper, now condensed into a frozen, lace-like body of crystallized fog.

As one, the Black Hand and the flying beasts struck the apparition. Talons, teeth, blades, and bludgeons hammered into its being.

A banshee's wail of pure hatred pierced the sky as Whisper shattered into a billion sparkling shards and then dissipated into the night.

The force threw Nick from his feet.

CHAPTER 35

Jasmine lost herself in her training. She struck at the Assassin with hands wrapped in the skins of a demon, trying to keep it at bay until the Master's Chosen was dead.

With her feet, she battered Whisper. Each time it thickened itself into a force that could slam into Nick, she struck it with a flurry of kicks.

The Black Hand didn't turn against the apparition. Without Zen, their deal was forfeit. Nevertheless, she didn't attack the bandits. Instead, she danced from point to point to avoid their strikes as well as she could.

Only her instinct for survival kept her on her feet. By the time Zen returned, her wounds were so severe that the pain alone was nearly blinding. Blood loss clouded her senses and slowed her reflexes.

The tail of the behemoth mother swept in at her from the lake, a mere blur in the moonlight. Jasmine splayed herself onto the ground to avoid the blow, which swept over her and into Jade with a sickening splat. The bandit's chest collapsed like a crushed melon, spraying gore as her body, what was left of it, flew into the darkness of the trees.

A sudden shift of the Black Hand attacks from herself to the whirlwind gave her time and space to move.

An instant later, as soon as Whisper shattered, the Black Hand began to flee into the darkness. Only the Assassin opposed her. At that point, though, the Assassin would be enough. It was fresh. Jasmine had no strength left.

"Help us," Nick yelled to the retreating bandits. "You must kill the demons. They too were sent by the Master. If they survive, they'll report what you've done to his Chosen."

Several of the Black Hand slowed. Others, mostly the severely wounded, continued to flee.

The behemoth's tail crushed one of those who hesitated at the edge of the trees.

Both of the flying beasts that had been called by the Black Hand mage swept down to engage. One sank its claws into Jasmine's demon, the other attacked Zen's. Another of the creatures appeared overhead and dove in the direction of Otto.

Minshara, at least, was doing what she could.

Zen's chest bled from the claws of the Assassin. He stumbled backwards, away from the demon as it came for him, until the bodies of Rancid and the giant constrictor blocked his way. There he could retreat no more.

He pulled some of the essence of the plane of ice into the world of men and formed a being of pure, cold fury. It was a lesser construct than Whisper had been, a blocky, clumsy thing, with a roughly human shape and bludgeon-like arms, but it was a body between himself and the demon. It gave Zen time to weave something more destructive.

The Assassin shoved the construct aside.

A dragon-kin dove at the demon's back.

From somewhere behind Zen, Ellessar's prayers rose into the night. Before the dragon-kin could strike, a blaze of pure light, the glory of Aeron himself, perhaps, burned into the demon and charred it to ash on the banks of the behemoth's lake.

Zen completed his weaving. His target gone, he launched the spear of dense ice that he'd produced into the damned heart of the Assassin that threatened Jasmine. It collapsed to the ground and lay still.

As soon as the Assassins were gone, Zen dismissed his ice creature. He had no strength left to hold it. The Black Hand receded into the swamp. Zen, Jasmine, Nick, and Ellessar stood alone in the clearing with the behemoth mother, who sought another victim upon whom she could avenge the death of her pup.

Aeron had protected his priest but not Rancid. The awkward, broken manner in which his body lay proved his death, as did the collapsed aspect of his chest.

Ellessar hoisted Rancid onto his shoulders, whistled for Spirit, and darted into the trees. Nick belly-crawled toward the wall of vegetation and the cover it offered. Jasmine scrambled past the dead behemoth pup, grabbed Otto—unconscious or dead—by the shoulders and dragged him from the clearing.

Even the dragon-kin beasts had gone.

Only Zen remained.

He raced back to where Whisper had died and picked up Nick's great sword, one of the few weapons they had remaining after battling the demons. Next to it lay a ring and a Medallion. Like that of Vinous Drakemoor, this was a Medallion of Vexetan, the enslaving device of the Dark Master, the shackles of the Chosen.

The behemoth's tail snapped in the sky, a whip drawing back to strike.

Zen didn't have time to collect Whisper's things, or even to run. The behemoth's tail, more heard than seen against the dark sky, was coming for him.

He tucked the sword under his arm, along with his staff, and began to weave a portal through the planes to a safe refuge, the threads still fragmented from the night's violence.

The tail whipped at him with blinding speed, a black streak in the moonlight, the bludgeon at its end the size of a wild boar with a dozen sharpened tusks. He was too late. He'd never complete his weaving in time.

A shriek pierced the sky and three dragon-kin soared over Zen's head from beyond the screen of trees, straight toward the behemoth.

No more than an arm's length from Zen, the tail snapped up and plucked the lead dragon-kin from the air.

Zen completed the portal. "Thank you, Minshara," he breathed as he stepped through.

When he emerged from the other end of the long ice tunnel, the night had changed. Darkness was complete. The trees around him blotted out the moonlight that had permeated the clearing of the behemoth's lake. The stink of the bog, tainted by the smell of spilled blood, and the cloying moisture in the air were gone, replaced by dry ground and the fragrance of evergreens. The bodies, the litter of discarded weapons and gear...also gone. The bellow of the grief-stricken mother had faded to a faint whisper in the distance. The rustle of the wounded, running mad into the swamp, and the ever-present chatter of the lizard-kin had been replaced by the clear call of crickets.

Zen had left his enemies, and his friends, behind. He'd fled, as Nick had bidden him, to the nearest safe place he knew: their own camp from the previous night, in the forest that skirted the western edge of the swamp.

He didn't know if he'd ever see any of them again.

If he could, he'd give them enough time to guess where he'd gone and to catch up before he moved on.

His weavings had exhausted him. His wounds required tending.

He needed rest. Yet those things could wait. He had to know if it had all been worth it.

He gathered a few dry sticks and pine needles and built a small fire in the pit that Rancid had dug the previous evening. Then he pulled the stone from his backpack.

It looked ordinary in the flickering glow. Rock. Rich in metal ore, perhaps, but rock nonetheless. Could this stone really be the salvation of the civilized races?

It warmed his hands in the chill night, a comforting, inner warmth separate from that given off by the campfire.

He carried it away from the flames to be sure. There was no mistake. It was warm to the touch. He'd pulled it from the cool waters of the lake, yet it emanated a warmth from within.

There was indeed power within it.

EPILOGUE

The mid-morning sun of the Great Sand beat down on Ryanna, L'Nordian, and the dragon's other passengers: Addicus, Ka-G'zzin, and their Master, Vornax.

L'Nordian banked toward a giant fissure that parted the desert, the only shade within a hundred miles in any direction.

Despite the heat, a chill swept up Ryanna's spine. All her adult life, she'd played with the denizens of the Abyss, called them to do her bidding, until she became arrogant and overconfident. Until she'd called Ka-G'zzin.

Never again, she'd vowed, would she call so powerful a being to her side. Never would she call a demon she couldn't control.

Today, by the order of her Master, she would break that vow.

Today, she would call the creature who ruled the Abyss itself, a creature so vile and mighty that the hordes of the damned didn't dare to challenge it.

Today, if she was lucky, she would die.

As they dropped into the fissure, walls of blazing purple and orange sandstone engulfed them. The ruins of some ancient city lay against the walls of the canyon like the filth in the alleys of Meuribar, half buried by windswept sand.

L'Nordian's head cocked as though listening to the thoughts of another. Ka-G'zzin, the demon of her nightmares, stretched out its remaining crab-like forearm and pointed ahead. Finally, the demon bade L'Nordian to land.

As soon as the dragon came to rest, Ryanna and the others climbed from its back. Ka-G'zzin began to scurry around the ruins in search of something, testing the air and clicking his pincers together in rapid agitation.

Nearby, chained to a stone pillar, the bleached bones of an elf, or maybe a teenage human girl, sprawled in death.

Ryanna turned away, choosing instead to focus on the remnants of the clay buildings around her. If the girl had been a resident of this lost city, where were the rest? What had happened to the bones of her people?

Ka-G'zzin crawled from ruin to ruin, from one canyon wall to the other, directed it seemed, by faded runes of blood inscribed all around them.

"*Alsdi.*" The demon clawed at the sand that coated the floor of the chasm.

L'Nordian cocked its head toward Vornax, listening, then lumbered forward. The dragon shouldered the demon aside and began digging with his massive foreclaws.

"You," Vornax told her, "prepare for the rite."

The right? Ryanna snorted softly. That was all the disobedience she allowed herself. *None of this is right.*

L'Nordian's head swung around to her even as he continued to dig. The dragon's look of amused curiosity warned her to guard her thoughts in its presence. To Vornax, she said, "I can't control the one you bid me to call."

"That's not your concern." Vornax watched L'Nordian's progress. A vast gridwork of metal, crafted in intricate, interlocking patterns, emerged as the dragon swept the sand away.

"Neither can you," Ryanna warned her Master, "until it places the Medallion freely around its own neck." *Assuming it has a neck.* She had no idea what the king of the Abyss might look like.

Pain exploded in Ryanna's head, and her hand burned with unholy fire. The Medallion weighed heavily on her breast. "Do not dare to question me." It was over in an instant, but the memory of the lesson would never fade.

Ryanna picked herself off the valley floor, brushed the sand from her white robes, and made her worthless preparations. She traced a circle of protection in the sand, filled it with a powder of rust and sulfur, and saturated the mixture with unholy oil, blessed by her Master. She wove protective spells about herself like a cocoon, then stripped off her robes and painted arcane symbols on her bare skin and in the air, where they hung like fruit to be devoured by the demon king.

When she'd done everything she could, she nodded to her Master. She was far from prepared for what awaited her. She could never be prepared.

"It's time," Vornax told the others. Addicus and L'Nordian turned and awaited the coming. They thought they were ready, but they had no idea what was about to find its way here through the porous walls of the Abyss.

The incantation was simple, and Ka-G'zzin had provided her with the name of the demon king. With no cause to fear even the greatest of mortals, it came at once.

The weave distended and then tore as Ri-T'rannoc strode into the Devil's Cauldron, in the Civilized Lands of men, for the first time in over three thousand years.

A hiss like water thrown on the coals of a bonfire escaped the demon king's lips as it spun toward Ryanna. It stood erect, nearly thirty feet in height. Fire filled its eyes. Smoke streamed past a mouthful of dagger-sharp teeth. A carapace covered its form like plate armor, thick and heavy. Two clublike appendages terminated in claws like the mandibles of a giant insect. Two additional limbs, more dexterous, looked like the arms of a giant three-fingered man. Horns, each the size of a wagon's yoke, jutted, defiant and menacing, from the top of its head.

Ri-T'rannoc's mouth twisted into a parody of glee until L'Nordian stepped between it and Ryanna. The dragon, though larger than the demon by half, seemed pitiful and weak against this manifestation of evil that Vexetan himself had created.

Yet the demon seemed wary.

When the Master spoke, his voice remained calm. He used the language of the demons, the unholy tongue in which he prayed to Vexetan. Ryanna could have understood his words, but she refused to wear the ring of translation the Master had provided her. She feared it would hinder the enchantment of the other ring she wore, the one that might someday offer her salvation.

The demon king hissed its reply. Ka-G'zzin, L'Nordian, and Addicus stood by to intervene on behalf of the Master—none of them could trust Ri-T'rannoc until it donned the Medallion.

The negotiation, or argument—for at intervals it seemed more one than the other—continued for interminable minutes as, one by one, Ryanna's protections expired and she stood, both naked and exposed, before the beast she'd foolishly called forth.

Only fear of Vexetan himself could persuade Ri-T'rannoc into voluntary slavery, but Vornax, the Master, the High Priest of Vexetan, wielded that fear. He also had a bargaining chip: he could offer to free all of the demons forever. And he possessed the irresistible, beguiling aura with which Vexetan had imbued him by the simple touch that had turned a small patch of Vornax's hair white when he was a young boy.

Finally, Vornax reached into his robes and held out his last remaining Medallion to the demon king, his Chosen champion.

His general.

Ri-T'rannoc took the pendant and worked the chain over its

horns and onto its thick neck. Once Vornax released the demons, Ri-T'rannoc would lead armies of them in a flood of darkness across the length and breadth of the Civilized Lands.

Nearby, the Portal of the Damned, located by Ka-G'zzin and unearthed by L'Nordian, lay as exposed as Ryanna. The twenty-yard-wide disk, the gateway to the Abyss, was all that separated this world from the demon prison.

Vornax slipped the Guardian from within his robes and tossed it casually to Addicus. He gestured to the Portal. "Open it."

The story continues in:

Host of Evil
Age of Prophecy: Book III

About the Author

Kirt Hickman, author of the award-winning science-fiction thrillers *Worlds Asunder* and *Venus Rain*, has also written *Mercury Sun*, the fantasy novel *Fabler's Legend*, and two children's books. He teaches self-editing classes through SouthWest Writers. He has been a mentor in the SWW mentoring program, has spoken at numerous conferences, and contributes a monthly column entitled "Revising Fiction" to *SouthWest Sage*. His writer's guide, *Revising Fiction—Making Sense of the Madness* won a New Mexico Book Award for Best How-To and was a finalist in the international IBPA Benjamin Franklin Awards.

www.ingramcontent.com/pod-product-compliance
Lightning Source LLC
Chambersburg PA
CBHW022207010726
47493CB00002B/457